D0974572

Praise for Patricia Rice and her previous novel, *Garden of Dreams*

"Wonderful storytelling . . . Make sure you add *Garden of Dreams* to your must read pile."

—*Romantic Times*

"Patricia Rice is a master storyteller!"

—MARY JO PUTNEY

"Ms. Rice's debut into contemporary is a huge success with this magnificent novel. Her characters are charming, and the reader will fall in love with every one of them. The plot is refreshingly delightful, and she throws in a few curves that add to the fun. A definite joy to read."

—*Rendezvous*

"Lively and fast-paced . . . Curl up with Patricia Rice's latest and hold your breath!"

—*The Literary Times*

"Engaging . . . You can always count on Patricia Rice for an entertaining story with just the right mix of romance, humor, and emotion."

—*The Romance Reader*

By Patricia Rice:

PAPER MOON
DENIM AND LACE
WAYWARD ANGEL
GARDEN OF DREAMS*
BLUE CLOUDS*

**Published by Fawcett Books*

BLUE CLOUDS

Patricia Rice

FAWCETT GOLD MEDAL • NEW YORK

A Fawcett Gold Medal Book
Published by The Ballantine Publishing Group
 Published in the United States by The Ballantine Publishing Group, a division of Random House, Inc., New York, and simultaneously in Canada by Random House of Canada Limited, Toronto.

http://www.randomhouse.com

Library of Congress Catalog Card Number: 98-92627

ISBN 0-449-15063-1

Manufactured in the United States of America

First Edition: September 1998

10 9 8 7 6 5 4 3 2 1

To Mary Jo, whose humor and common sense keep me sane.

And to Don, who, some days, probably thinks he lives with the Grim Reaper's female counterpart: I love you.

ONE

"Believe me, Phillippa, this hurts me as much as you."

Pippa heard Abigail's voice through a fog of disbelief. She recognized her supervisor's compassionate expression, but the words weren't sinking in.

"I fought against it every step of the way," Abigail continued. "You're a good worker; we have no complaints at all. We'll give you excellent references, call other hospitals in the chain if you wish to relocate, anything you ask. It's just that we're downsizing like everyone else in the business today, keeping our margins intact, and the administrative staff is the first to go. We can't cut back on essential care."

The words pounded against Pippa's skull. Any time someone said it hurt them as much as it hurt her, she knew they lied. Nothing would ever hurt as much as the blows that always followed. She just couldn't believe the blows came from this direction. She'd worked at the hospital for ten years. It had been her mainstay through her mother's illness. Her friends were here. Her family. The support network she needed for survival. How could they strip away her life and call it something so inexplicable as "downsizing"?

Especially now. They knew how her life had fallen apart this past year. How could they take away the one certainty she possessed? She had awards hanging on her office wall. She had letters of appreciation. Even those grim vultures in the administrative offices smiled at her when they passed her in the halls. She felt accepted here, wanted, needed. Her job was all she had left.

Abigail fell silent and awaited Pippa's response. What could she say? Quaking inside, Pippa stood up. To her horror, tears burned her eyes. She wouldn't go out weeping and wailing. She *wouldn't*. Her mother had taught her to keep a stiff upper lip. Chin up. Persevere. Don't let anyone get you down.

She wanted to throw up.

Scraping the chair back, she avoided Abigail's gaze as she nodded and mumbled something about finishing the Carlson case, then turned to make her escape.

"Pippa, I'm sorry." Abigail sounded as shaken as Pippa felt. "I know you've just lost your mother. If there had been any other way . . ."

Pippa waved a careless hand, keeping her face averted. "I've needed to get away anyway. I'll see you later."

Practically running, she fled the room. Despite all her efforts to contain them, tears streamed down her face, and she hurried into the closest ladies' room, the public one where the staff wouldn't go. She didn't want anyone seeing her like this, not Pollyanna Pippa. She'd always had an uplifting phrase, a word of encouragement when things looked blackest. She'd always managed a smile no matter how much the stress piled up. People relied on her when the going got tough.

She locked the stall door, yanked off a length of toilet paper, and rubbed at the tears, cursing the fact that her purse and Kleenex were back at her desk. Panic welled inside her; she wished she could think straight, but she could only wipe at her running nose. She had to get control, her mother would say. But her mother was dead.

That returned the tears in cascades. She hadn't cried like this since the doctor first diagnosed her mother's inoperable cancer.

She hadn't cried like this at the funeral. After that initial burst of tears over the shock of the diagnosis, she'd cheerfully made her mother's last years as peaceful as could be. She'd rejoiced that she'd worked at a hospital where she could learn the names of all the top physicians, knew the very best, most modern treatments. Her mother had lived comfortably for years, and Pippa had thrived on knowing she had helped.

Her brother, Mitchell, hadn't been able to contribute much. He lived too far away and had a family to support. He'd flown in occasionally for a weekend, but he really didn't have the resources to do that often, or to help financially. And her sister, Barbara, was the same. She'd called frequently, sent cards, and wished she could get away to help, but she had small children at home. They'd both married and moved away to big cities long ago, leaving Pippa, the youngest, at home. Pippa hadn't complained. She'd only felt grateful that she hadn't been otherwise attached when the doctor diagnosed the cancer. Mitchell and Barbara had been grateful to her. She'd felt needed, important, a part of everyone's lives.

Then her mother had died.

Now, she had no one who needed her, nothing to go home for. Mitchell and Barbara had their spouses and children and in-laws. They didn't need Pippa's help. She had denied the emptiness, the pain of loss, for months, and now that Abigail had ripped her open, she couldn't stop crying. She sobbed at the nothingness her life had become as much as for the loss of her mother.

She was thirty years old, with no job, no family, and no future. She was a useless piece of furniture ready for the garage sale. She didn't understand it. She'd done everything right, done everything she was supposed to do. She'd been a dutiful daughter, a hardworking employee, a good, church-going, responsible citizen. What had gone wrong?

She couldn't even think about the worst of it. She wouldn't think of Billy. She didn't need terror on top of tears. She needed to get control, march back to her desk, finish up the case she was working on, pack up her things, and go, without looking back. She couldn't handle the farewells and the tears and the pity. She wouldn't tell anyone. She would just leave. She could do that. She could lift her chin, straighten her backbone, and do what had to be done. Her mother had taught her that. She wouldn't lose a lifetime of lessons over a stupid job.

Blowing her nose, Pippa unlocked the stall door.

She could find another job. She was good. She knew she was good. She didn't have a family to support, so she could look around and be choosy. The house was paid for. The insurance was paid up. She'd never drawn unemployment, but she supposed she was entitled now. That should take care of the utilities and groceries. Her mother's illness had drained every last drop of savings, so she couldn't fall back on any nest egg, but she would survive. She had set aside part of her checks these last months since the funeral, hoping to buy a new car, but she could get along with the old one for a while longer.

She would just keep looking at the positive side of things. All clouds had silver linings.

Washing her face, she dried it with a rough paper towel and glared at the mirror. The red-rimmed eyes didn't help. Chubby cherub cheeks had given everyone the impression that she was as cheerful as her nickname, and she'd always done her best to live up to everyone's expectations. But she didn't feel like Pollyanna right now. Her mouse-brown hair escaped the clamp she'd yanked it into this morning. She really should get it cut, but Billy liked it long. It was a damned nuisance. She resolved to make a hair appointment tomorrow.

The day had no end. The phone rang incessantly, making it impossible to finish the Carlson case. Word had apparently leaked, and she endured the well-meaning consolations of people she'd thought of as family these past years. The worry on the faces of others not yet informed if their positions would get the ax hurt more than anything. So many of them were the sole support for their families. Pippa congratulated herself on not having children. In this uncertain world, how could one take care of them?

Clinging to that note of thanksgiving, she finally finished the Carlson case, closed the file, ignored the ringing phone, and grabbed her old high-school overcoat.

Icy sleet hit her face as soon as she walked out the door. It was April, dammit! Would spring never get here? Did the whole world weep with her, then? Well, it could just stop right now. She wasn't weeping anymore. She was getting angry. Furious. She'd worked her damned butt off for ten years, and for what? For a lousy note of gratitude and a polite reference?

The car door was stuck, of course. She'd run out of de-icer after that last storm and hadn't bothered to restock, foolishly thinking spring was just around the corner. Curse and drat it. This was Kentucky, for heaven's sake. Surely God knew they didn't have winter here.

She checked two of the other three doors. The back passenger door hadn't worked in years, so there was no use in trying that. The original shiny brown of the aging Escort had faded until she could no longer distinguish dirt from paint. Rust corroded both rear fenders. She had often contemplated shoving the car into the river, but it got her to the hospital and back. She hadn't needed more.

Kicking the driver-side door and adding another dent, Pippa loosened some of the ice.

The sleet slashed down heavier, obscuring much of the parking lot in the dusky grayness of late evening. She'd left early, so she didn't hear any of the cheerful chatter of staff departing for the day.

A shadow emerged from the murky veil, startling her. She yanked the door harder, this time in panic.

The voice accompanying the shadow failed to provide reassurance.

Billy.

"I've got my car here, Phillippa. I'll take you home."

Once, she had looked on that masculine reliability as reassuring. She had gratefully accepted his help all those times the car had broken down, the plumbing froze, or her mother took a turn for the worse. But the price she paid for that reassurance was way too high. Shivering, as much from fear as cold, Pippa jerked on the door again.

"Go away, Billy, I'm fine. I'll take my own car home." She knew she taunted trouble speaking to him that way. He hated it when she did that. She knew what happened when she did things he hated. But right now, the anger and frustration inside her begged for the fight that would follow. Maybe somewhere in her subconscious, she thought she deserved it. She'd taken enough psychology classes to know the complexities of the human psyche.

She wished she had a can of Mace in her purse.

"I've been waiting for you, Phillippa. You're off early. We need to talk. Let's go over to Shoney's and get something to eat."

He took her elbow, using his greater strength as a lever, forcing her away from the car. In his blue police uniform, he seemed taller and broader than most men. Wildly, Pippa imagined people thinking he was arresting her as he tugged her away like that.

"Let me go, Billy, or I'll scream." She jammed her elbow backward, striking his midsection, but there was nothing soft about Billy. He grunted but didn't loosen his grip.

"Don't, Phillippa. Don't make me mad. I want to make things up to you. I didn't mean to hurt you. You know that. I love you. I just want to take care of you and make you happy. We'll talk, and you'll see. Things will change. We can get married now. Everything will be all right."

Sometimes, Pippa wondered if he was in his right mind. Didn't policemen undergo some kind of psychological exam before acceptance? She stamped on his toe as hard as she could, but he wore steel-reinforced boots and probably didn't even notice.

"Billy, I've told you, it just won't work. I don't love you. I don't want to marry you. And I don't want to go to dinner with you. I've had a really rotten day and I want to go home. Alone. Do you understand anything I'm saying at all?"

Once, she'd believed his warm reassurances, his words of love and commitment. She'd planned their dream home, the number of children they would have, the loving partnership they would share. She'd longed for it with all her heart, given him everything he asked for and more, relying on him for everything. Stupid. Stupid, stupid. She would never let that happen again.

"I hear you, Phillippa, but you're not listening. I'm going to change. You're the woman I love, and I'm not letting you go. You're mine. We both know it. Now, come along and stop this foolishness. You can't even get in your car."

She knew this was where it would start, just as soon as he started calling her "his." Without bothering to reason any further, she screamed. She opened her mouth and let fly every frustration, every ounce of rage, every instance of self-pity, desperation, and destroyed trust she'd suffered today and every day before that. She screamed and kicked and pounded and bit until he hauled her like a howling whirlwind across the parking lot.

She aimed for his testicles when he adjusted his grip.

He let her go, then backhanded her so hard she stumbled and hit the pavement. Pain shot through Pippa's elbow as it connected with the blacktop. Her hip slammed into a concrete separator. She tried scrambling away, knowing what would follow, but his steel-toed boot caught her leg.

She kept screaming. She'd warned Billy she would report him. She'd threatened to get a court order and humiliate him in front of the entire force. He'd stayed away this past week. She'd thought herself safe.

Even as he leaned over to grab her by her hair—the long hair that he'd ordered her not to cut—a voice shouted from somewhere beyond the veil of sleet and blood and panic.

"Let her alone, you bastard! Let her alone, or I'll shoot!"

Henry. Thank God for Henry. Pippa whimpered with relief. As a night security guard, Henry looked harmless. She'd offered him plenty of cups of coffee those nights she'd stayed late. They'd exchanged pleasantries as she checked out in the evenings. He must be in his sixties, no bigger than herself, and hunched with arthritis, but he had a gun. She prayed Billy hadn't gone beyond caring. Billy carried a gun, too.

"Pippa, can you stand up? We're here. Just back away from him. Henry's got him covered."

Tears welled in her eyes once more. Quickly, Pippa backed away from Billy's dangerous feet, pushing herself up with her hands, letting other hands grab her and heave her up. She didn't know how many of them were there. She didn't care. Shaking, she kept backing away, letting the people swarming out of the building surround her, protect her, separate her from Billy and his rage. Her friends had come to her rescue. She still had friends. Weeping at the knowledge, she allowed them to lead her away.

Her scrapes and bruises neatly cleaned and bandaged, her spirits temporarily mended by hugs and reassurances, Pippa finally arrived home, only to discover the front door unlocked.

She never forgot to lock the door. Her chest tightened in the familiar sensation of fear. Mentally, she knew Billy couldn't be here. She'd called the police this time. She had witnesses. Surely he was behind bars now.

Emotionally, Pippa still felt Billy's blows. Her hand shook as she pushed open the door.

It took only one step inside before her knees crumpled under her. On the floor, she covered her mouth with her hands to hold back her cries.

He'd shredded her cozy nest into straw. Family photographs lay in tatters, ripped from the walls, glass and frames shattered. As if a tornado had swept through, the old furniture had been overturned and flung against walls, damaging plaster and delicate bric-a-brac.

Picking herself up, stumbling across the debris to the phone, Pippa nearly fell over the kitchen table before she looked down. In shock and horror, she stared at Clio Kitty lying in a pool of blood.

It was one straw too many.

Pippa threw up.

TWO

The blaring rhythm of amplified rap pounded through the doorway and into the poorly lit street. Lost in their own alien world, the shadowy figures lounging on the curb as Seth Wyatt passed by showed no evidence of hearing the beat or watching his passage.

His eyes scarcely needed the adjustment from the night outside to the gloom inside. Swaying tin lamps and blinking neon beer advertisements provided the interior's only illumination. The bar's patrons glared as he entered, but he was accustomed to hatred and let it roll off his back.

Had he been in a questioning humor, he might have asked himself why he'd chosen to meet Dirk here. They'd been over this territory before. Nothing around him seemed familiar. Nothing jarred loose the lost memory of that night. Perhaps, if he had to think about it, he hoped someone would remember *him* instead of the other way around. But he'd lost anything resembling hope five years ago.

Seth took a booth in the back with a view of the door and waited. He'd been waiting five years. He'd wait fifty more if he must. He would find the guilty party, and have his revenge.

His hired investigator didn't keep him waiting long. Dirk

wasn't a small man, but he didn't belong in this dive any more than Seth did.

A six-foot-plus hulk shoved Dirk's shoulder, and the wiry detective grabbed for his gun.

"Leave him alone, Bingo. He's with me," Seth commanded calmly, without leaving his seat.

As if by magic, the young hulk drifted back to the bar. Seth had come here often enough these last years. He knew the crowd now, even if he didn't remember them from before. They steered clear of him, as people usually did. Isolation suited Seth. Maybe that was why he'd chosen the bar. Surrounded by people, he still sat alone. He didn't bother looking up from his drink as Dirk ordered a beer.

Seth sat at the only table in the room with a lamp, not that the tiny bulb did him any favors. He knew his craggy, brooding features could frighten the sun into hiding on a good day. In here, the flickering neon lights probably cast his expression into a dangerous glower. His open-collared white shirt emphasized his darkness, so he didn't look too obvious. His hands wore no gold, but lighter lines about wrist and finger indicated where his watch and ring usually rested. He wasn't so stupid as to wear gold on this side of the city.

His expression remained impassive as Seth waited for the bartender to deliver Dirk's drink.

"Mr. Wyatt." Dirk nodded respectfully in greeting.

Seth regarded him stonily. "No names."

"I apologize. You're right." Dirk twisted in his seat, his back against the tavern wall, and one eye on the action.

"You've found nothing new," Wyatt said without prompting. He tightened his lips into icy disdain. He'd thought his new detective better than that.

"I have questioned everyone I could find who was here that night. The incident is over five years old now. Three of your witnesses are dead from drug- and gang-related incidents. Half of the rest have disappeared from sight. The others remember only what they told the cops. I'm working on it, but it will cost you a bundle if I track down all those gone missing. And you're not likely to get any more out of them than the cops did at the time. The memories of junkies are not particularly reliable."

"They're not all junkies," Wyatt responded automatically, his gaze shifting to the motley crowd at the bar.

"No, the rest are murderers and thieves. If this is where you went that night, you should have had your head examined. Have you tried hypnosis to see if you can recall why in hell you chose this place?"

"My shrink declares I'm not a good candidate for hypnosis," Wyatt answered dryly. "I think that's shrink talk for I'm too hardheaded."

Dirk bit back a smile, uncertain if Seth would appreciate a response to his humor. "It was just a suggestion." Dirk shrugged. "I've gone over the police reports, talked with the garage personnel who handled the wreckage later. The accident smashed the car like an accordion. Any evidence of sideswiping or tampering disappeared with the impact. I've corroborated every line of the police report. They did their job well, although it was a little late by the time you demanded the investigation."

"I was unconscious until then," Wyatt reminded him, again in that dry tone that gave nothing away.

Dirk shrugged. "Are you certain this is the bar you were in before the accident?"

"I'm not certain of anything. I have no memory of that night at all. The hospital didn't test my blood alcohol until well after the fact. Apparently, they spent their time trying to save my life instead. But I'm not a drinking man. I do not stop in bars without good reason. I do not drink to excess. My wife was the one who leveled the drunkenness charge, and only after witnesses reported seeing me here before the accident."

"The junkies in this place would lie for the price of an upper."

Seth turned an icy glare back to him. "They're not all junkies," he repeated with hostility. "One of the witnesses was a friend of mine, you'll recall."

Seth could practically hear his detective's thoughts. He'd heard it all before. *The drunken NFL player. Right. Like he'd stand up in court.* He hadn't, of course, which was why Seth's wife had lost the case. But even if the court hadn't believed Doug, Seth did.

"All right. So Brown saw you here. Could you have come here to meet him? Why don't you let me interview him? He's the most logical reason for your presence here."

"Doug has blackouts. His memory isn't clear on that night. I could have come here looking for him. I've dragged him out of places like this before. But he doesn't remember calling me. All he remembers is that I sat here and had a drink and that he wasn't with me. That I looked as if I were waiting for someone. And when no one arrived, I left without noticing him." Dirk grimaced his disbelief and Seth became defensive. "I know it sounds suspicious, but Doug wouldn't lie. He only mentioned the incident because he thought it would help if he told the police I had only one drink. And because I'd worried myself sick thinking I'd been as drunk as Natalie said. He swore I wasn't."

"Generous of him." Dirk's sarcasm revealed his opinion of the truthfulness of alcoholic ex-NFL players reduced to playing chauffeur for wealthy men. "I can go after the rest of those witnesses, or I can start tracking your list of people who would have benefited from your demise. Do you have a preference?"

Seth tossed back the rest of his drink and, pushing up from the booth, threw a bill on the table. "The list of my enemies is even longer and more complicated than your list of witnesses. Try the top five of both lists, then get back to me." He walked out without so much as glancing back at the crowd of thugs and thieves behind him.

Feeling a shift in the room's tension, Dirk took a final chug of his beer, then left, uncomfortable with the crowd's focus. He didn't look like a rich white boy either. Aside from his Hispanic features, Dirk wore a battered Bengals hat he'd stolen from an airport seat, a leather bomber jacket with a rip in the pocket, and no gold. He'd even dug out his oldest pair of running shoes before driving down here. But he had the distinct feeling that the crowd behind him would put a knife through his back because of his looks as easily as for his possessions.

The streetlight outside the door had been shot out and not replaced. Every store owner who valued his life had closed up at dark and gone home. Only the pounding music and flashing bar light behind him broke the silent gloom of the street. Grateful for the license allowing him to carry the shoulder holster beneath his jacket, Dirk cautiously approached his car.

He heard the first sounds of a scuffle as he reached the corner where he'd parked his Chevy. He contemplated just climbing behind the wheel and driving off, but the expensive Jag gleaming beneath a bare bulb at a nearby warehouse alerted him. With a sigh of resignation, Dirk pulled his gun and slipped along the shadows to the alley.

He didn't know why he bothered. With a grimace, Dirk shouldered the pistol, caught the man staggering backward in his direction, choked him with his arm, kidney-punched him, then let him drop as he surveyed the damage wreaked by the man felling his last opponent with a savage kick to the groin. The grace and swiftness with which Seth Wyatt moved spoke of years of combat training. Dirk grunted in sympathy for the assailant's pain but kept a careful eye on the other three men curled up and moaning in the filth of the alley pavement.

He hadn't heard gunshots. He couldn't see blood. Judging by the blow he'd seen, Wyatt had felled them all with his fists and feet. Definitely a dangerous man.

"Did they say what they wanted?" Dirk asked wryly as Seth

calmly dusted off his trousers and stepped over one of the thugs.

"I don't think they were hired to talk." Wearily, Seth walked out of the darkness, rolling his sleeves down. "Find out who hired them."

With that, he walked away.

Shaking his head, Dirk watched Seth Wyatt climb into his fancy Jag and drive off. The man either had nerves of steel or no brains at all.

Dialing his cellular, Dirk kicked the scum at his feet, and called the cops.

Wyatt hadn't gotten where he was today by having no brains.

THREE

Pippa crumpled the letter from Mary Margaret in her pocket for the thousandth time as she hurried down the plane ramp into the airport terminal. After leaving all she knew and loved behind, she needed the reassurance that someone she knew and loved waited ahead.

Reluctant as she was to lose the security of her disguise, she headed for the rest room. The uncomfortable padding around her middle had to go. As an amateur in the local theater group, she knew all about padding and makeup. She didn't think Billy would figure out that the red-haired, middle-aged, plump woman who left the hairdresser and bought a ticket for the bus to Memphis was her. She'd kept the disguise when she reached the airport and bought a plane ticket to California. Now that she was here, surely she was safe.

Her hometown police force—the same police who had let Billy out on bond—hadn't arrested Billy for the damage to her house. They'd looked at the mess and blamed vandals, advised her to buy stronger locks or move to a better neighborhood. For a while, she'd contemplated buying a gun and shooting Billy herself. Fortunately, her temper cooled quickly. The terror engendered by the viciousness of Clio's injuries did not. She'd hung around only long enough to see if Clio would live and to find her a home. She didn't linger to see what would happen once Billy came looking for her again. She knew better than to expect a restraining order to stop him. She'd seen enough abuse victims in the emergency room on a Friday night, seen some of them sent to the morgue. Half of them had restraining orders.

Locking the stall and stripping off her blouse to reach the padding, Pippa sighed in relief as her own trim figure emerged. She probably shouldn't have panicked and run, but what she'd told Abigail hadn't been entirely wrong. She needed this escape. She needed new scenery so she could put her head together again. And she needed a job.

Wryly contemplating her nearly empty savings account, Pippa left the stall, washed off the theater makeup, applied cover-up to the bruises, and examined the results in the mirror. Cosmetics barely hid the green and purple over her cheekbones, but she liked the effect of the henna on her mousy brown hair, and the way the reddish glint enhanced the green of her eyes. And she definitely approved of the sassy short cut. Running her fingers through the layered thickness, she plumped it out nicely without need of a comb. Even if she had lost everything, knowing she looked better than she ever had cheered her considerably.

To make her escape without Billy knowing where she'd gone, she'd left everything behind, all her clothes, her house, everything. She'd left keys with friends, but they didn't dare go near the house or Billy would know she'd talked to them.

She'd arranged for a friend at the clothes drive to take a box of her clothes before she'd left so no one would report to Billy that she was packing up and moving out. The box would arrive at the Greyhound station eventually. She hadn't wanted to give anyone Mary Margaret's address—not until she was sure she was safe. Surely Billy wouldn't figure it out. Until she had an address, she had only what she carried in her shoulder bag. Her wallet was severely depleted after buying the bus and plane tickets. She'd used cash, not credit cards, in hopes of curtailing any trace Billy might put on her. Right now, the only positive thought she could summon was her improved appearance.

Taking a deep breath, Pippa plunged into the heavy people traffic on the concourse. She'd told Mary Margaret to meet her at baggage claim. She had no baggage, but she needed the brief walk to become herself again. Billy wasn't that good a detective that he could trace mousy Pippa Cochran to the red-haired middle-aged woman who bought tickets at an airport three hours away. And even if by some miracle he figured that out, he couldn't find her once she walked out of the airport in California. No one would connect the plump older woman on the plane with the slim young woman walking out now. She was free.

She had thought about running to Mitchell or Barbara, but Billy would have checked with her brother and sister first thing. So she'd called and told them she was taking an extended vacation and that she would keep in touch. Then Pippa had taken out Mary Margaret's last letter and carried it like an Olympic torch to the airport, where she'd made her phone calls so Billy couldn't trace them. Despite all of Mary Margaret's problems, she'd sounded excited about Pippa's visit. The other calls left her a trifle uncertain, but she could face only one ordeal at a time.

Meg's beaming face finally appeared through the crowd, and Pippa shouted in the genuine relief of homecoming.

"Pippa Cochran! I can't believe it! I just can't believe it! Look at you! My word, you're stunning. You look like a fashion model. And look at me, a frumpy old housewife. Oh, my, it's so good to see you. Where are your bags? George has the car parked outside and they're going to run him off any minute."

Meg's maternal plumpness enveloped Pippa in a welcoming hug. Tears of joy sprang to Pippa's eyes as she returned the hug. Except for a few extra pounds, Meg hadn't changed from the exuberant, loving teenager Pippa remembered.

"When was the last time you saw a five-foot-five fashion model with chipmunk cheeks?" Pippa scoffed. "You've been reading too many romances again." Stepping back, she held Meg by the shoulders and surveyed the changes made in the last twelve years. "Having kids agrees with you. You don't look a day older than when I saw you last."

Meg blushed and grinned. "Thank you for the lie. You're going to be good for me, kid. Things have been a little dismal at home of late. We need a Pollyanna to remind us of how much we have."

Shifting her bulging shoulder bag, Pippa marched toward the door. "Then let's not keep George waiting. Is he still as handsome as ever?"

Meg hurried to catch up, glancing over her shoulder at the baggage carousel. "Your suitcase, Pippa? You are staying awhile, aren't you?"

"My bags will follow," Pippa replied airily, suddenly desperate to escape the airport and enter the real world again. She hadn't just run from Billy. She'd run toward a whole new life. She couldn't wait to get started.

Without questioning, Meg led her outside to the battered minivan.

"I figured they'd tow me off and make me leave you here stranded," George admonished as they climbed in. "Hi, Pippa, how's tricks?"

It was an old joke between them, and Pippa grinned in appreciation of the memory. "Well, your mind hasn't changed any, George, even if it does have more room to grow than before."

Starting the engine, George ruefully rubbed the bald spot at the back of his head. "All those hair roots get in the way. There's just that much less for the kids to turn gray."

They laughed and joked and caught up on old acquaintances

as George navigated L.A.'s freeways. Pippa exclaimed over the multilaned bumper-to-bumper traffic, and her hosts laughed at her Kentucky naiveté.

The space-age highways gradually reduced to four lanes along the scenic coastline. Pippa gasped at the views, at the flowers—in April, roses! She opened the windows and breathed in the sunshine, shutting out all memory of Kentucky sleet and terror.

Pippa exclaimed again as they turned from Highway 101 into the charming town of San Luis Obispo. She wanted to explore the sun-drenched mission, the art galleries, the cafes—everything.

Meg laughed. "If you stay here any length of time, you'll have your fill of tourists soon enough. You'll like Garden Grove. It's much quieter."

As they reached the narrow rural road surrounded by flat fields and framed by mountains, Pippa finally calmed down and began to talk of the present and the future.

"Meg said in her letter that they closed down the printing plant. Is there any talk of reopening?"

Both faces in the front seat turned grim. George answered first. "Wyatt tore down the plant last month."

"The town will die, and it's all Seth Wyatt's fault," Meg finished bitterly. "The plant used to employ two hundred people. Now they're moving away, looking for work elsewhere, and business has already dropped off. The people left have no money. It's the beginning of the end."

"My father and grandfather kept that pharmacy running, even through the Depression. I hate being the one who loses it," George said mournfully. "I wish the damned man would come out of hiding long enough so we could talk to him."

"Talk to the Grim Reaper?" Meg scoffed. "Since when can we reason with Death?"

Worriedly, Pippa listened to the exchange. "The Grim Reaper? Is that what they're calling this Seth Wyatt? Isn't he the man you said advertised for an assistant and a nurse's aide?"

Meg made an impolite noise. "Even starving, no one will take him up on the offer. The town has despised the Wyatts forever, but Seth has brought the name to new lows. He crippled his son with his recklessness, then sued his ex-wife with every big lawyer in the state until she finally let him have the boy. Now he's destroyed the industry that was the one good thing the Wyatts did for the town."

"They say his wife walked away with a large chunk of his fortune," George reminded her. "We don't know the whole story."

"We can see our future plowed under by bulldozers," Meg replied angrily. "What will happen to Mikey if you close the store and we move elsewhere?"

The mention of their youngest child, crippled by muscular dystrophy, brought the subject to an abrupt close. With a forced attempt at cheerfulness, Pippa inquired after all three Kelly children, diverting the conversation to happier topics.

The knowledge that her new employer held the sobriquet of Grim Reaper did nothing to reassure Pippa's sagging confidence.

"You don't really mean you took the job without an interview?" Horror written across her expressive face, Meg stared at Pippa over her cup of morning coffee.

Pippa shrugged with more nonchalance than she felt. "I have to support myself somehow. Your letter saying he couldn't hire anyone for a million dollars inspired me. I doubt if I'll make a million dollars, but just think about that little boy out there. I called Mr. Wyatt from the airport, faxed my résumé, and he faxed his acceptance. We've not discussed all the terms and so forth, but I'll not be a burden to you, Meg. I can't put Candy out of her room forever. You have enough problems without taking on mine."

"You're still afraid of that psycho boyfriend, aren't you?" Meg demanded, setting her cup down with a thump. Outside, a bird sang in the California version of lilacs.

Looking at the bright sunshine pouring in the double kitchen windows, Pippa decided Southern California weather was as predictable as Kentucky's was unpredictable. So far, she loved it. She was determined to stay here, one way or another.

"Billy is not my boyfriend," she pronounced carefully. "He's a mistake I made when Mama was ill. A mistake I'll not make again. I can take care of myself. If this job doesn't work out, I'll find another. I just want to start someplace where I have friends."

"You'll need friends if you work for Seth," Meg warned. "He's lucky he still has his father's housekeeper. She's too old to go anywhere else. I don't know where he found his secretary, but it wasn't from around here. None of them come to town. They have their groceries shipped out to that mausoleum of a house. What will you use for transportation? That gothic horror is way out in the hills."

"He's sending a car for me," Pippa admitted. "Will everyone despise you for having a friend who works for him?"

Meg grinned. "No, they'll pump me for every detail. Stand up and let me have a look at you. If you insist on doing this, then let's do it right."

Pippa stood and pirouetted in the dress she'd bought with some of her last few dollars. She didn't exactly look a fashion plate, but the soft green shirtwaist was businesslike and practical, and the wide belt made her feel feminine. She had contemplated continuing the disguise of a middle-aged woman, but the idea of wearing that stifling padding every day quenched the notion quickly enough. The only part of the disguise she kept was the hair. And the cover-up cream on the bruises.

"You look like a prim schoolteacher," Meg informed her, avoiding any mention of the bruises. "I hope when your clothes arrive, they have a little more style, or I'll make you spend your first paycheck on something a little classier."

Pippa grimaced. "Fashion critic. This is how we dress for work in Kentucky. What do you wear out here, halter tops?"

They launched into the old argument with zeal and laughter, until a car horn blew outside. The time had come and the insistent horn was an inauspicious beginning.

"Chad, I know you're not happy about this, but we have to allow Miss MacGregor out of the house once in a while. Unless you like sitting here by yourself or listening to Nana complain, you'll need someone else with you. I'm certain Miss Cochran will be fine. She'll just be here in case you need her. The rest of the time, she'll help me with my work."

Chad Wyatt made a sour face and swung his wheelchair away from his father so he could look out the window. This room had one of the best views in the house, offering an untouched vista of towering evergreens and craggy rocks overlooking the valley below. From the other wall, a glimpse of distant purple mountains looked like a picture postcard. Chad scarcely acknowledged it. "She's just coming so she can smile at you and hope she'll get lucky," he replied scornfully. "That's what Nana says. Why couldn't you hire a man?"

Seth looked at his son and bit back a growl. He'd spoiled the boy, but what other choice did he have? Chad could never lead a normal life—because of him. Cooped up inside all day with only a grouchy old woman for companion as the boy was, what else could Seth do but offer him all the time and attention he could provide?

"I would have hired a man if one had applied," Seth soothed him. "But Miss Cochran is the only person who wants the job. Miss MacGregor wants to visit her family. Her father's ill. I need someone here to help. We'll try her out, and if you don't like her, we'll find someone else. How's that?"

The boy nodded curtly. "I won't like her," he warned. "Especially if she's pretty."

That was definitely too adult for a six-year-old. Making a mental note to have a good talk with his querulous housekeeper, Seth spun around and stalked toward his office. He already had a dozen phone calls to return, and the day had scarcely begun. He wondered why he'd ever thought he could balance two careers at once.

Older than Seth's mother and a fixture in the house since his childhood, Nana stopped him in the hall. Seth halted and waited impatiently for the housekeeper to speak. Sometimes, that took a little while. Right now, she was busy glaring at him from beneath an incongruous wig of blue curls. Idly, he wondered what her hair really looked like these days. Once, it had been thick and blond, not the only trait of her German ancestry. She would have nearly matched him in height had age not stooped her shoulders and worn away her flesh. But her eyes were as sharp and blue as ever.

"I sent Dumbwood for the woman," she informed him.

Seth considered howling his fury at her for sending the demented gardener but decided she would play deaf if he tried. He'd taught himself how to deal with the rude and obnoxious, including his employees. Unfortunately, Nana thought of herself as family.

"*Durwood* is the gardener," he reminded her curtly. "Why didn't you send Doug?"

"Because he's sleeping it off in the garage, as usual." She glared at Seth as if it were his fault. "You fired him again yesterday."

His generally thin patience stretched to the breaking point at the thought of the mentally challenged gardener driving the BMW into town to pick up a new employee, Seth gritted his teeth, spun on his heel, and headed for his office again. Whatever Nana had really wanted would wait. He couldn't handle one more domestic crisis today.

He could deal with Hong Kong and New York. He could deal with publishers, printers, the IRS, and any of a dozen recalcitrant agencies, all at the same time. Why the devil couldn't he deal with his own damned household?

The private line rang as he entered. Staring out the bank of floor-to-ceiling windows overlooking the peaceful hills and valley in the distance, Seth grabbed the receiver. "Yes?" he demanded curtly.

"Is that any way to talk to your own mother?" the voice over the wire whined.

Collapsing into his desk chair, Seth propped his head on his hand and held the receiver from his ear as his mother droned on without waiting for a reply. At times, he felt sorry for her. She'd lived a miserable life with his father. The old man had treated her like so much trash cluttering the floors. More than once the old goat had claimed he'd married beneath him, though *she'd* been the one with money. Maxim Wyatt had taken the money and created an empire, then scorned the source. Lillian had retaliated by turning her life into one giant shopping spree.

But now that his mother was free from the old man's thumb, Seth couldn't help but feel a certain amount of sympathy for his late father. The woman had raised complaining to an art form. She probably complained in her sleep, too, but fortunately, Seth didn't have to listen to that. When he'd bought her the outrageously expensive condo in the senior citizen's community in L.A., she'd declared herself happy. No one there had ever heard of Maxim Wyatt. No one there cared if her husband had systematically demolished anyone crossing his path and turned an entire town into a feudal fiefdom.

"Mother, I can't visit you this week. Miss MacGregor is leaving for an extended absence and I'm trying to find someone to take her place. And I've got a deadline on this latest manuscript, which I can't meet unless I get off the phone."

He heard the expensive whine of the BMW racing up the drive at a speed too fast for that last turn. Confound Nana, anyway. She should have told him Doug was sleeping off another binge. If Durwood ran that car into the oak . . .

The unmistakable crash of speeding metal striking an immovable object shattered the peaceful cry of a mourning dove on the lawn.

As soon as Seth slammed down the receiver, the phone rang again.

FOUR

Pippa grabbed the door handle as the car swerved around another oak-lined hairpin turn at a death-defying speed. The Grim Reaper had sent her a maniac for a driver.

In a moment of carelessness, she opened her eyes and glanced out the windshield, praying for some sight of their destination. Ahead, stone towers rose from the serenity of an evergreen forest, and she gawked at the fantasy. Unfortunately, the breakneck pace crystallized details much too quickly—the Disney image warped into a gawdawful gothic castle lacking only a moat and a woman screaming from the turret.

In the front seat, the crazed driver muttered an ominous "Uh-oh," and the car swerved with a squeal of brakes.

The crash jerked her head backward into the headrest as the car ground to a halt. Thinking motionlessness a good thing, Pippa closed her eyes and assessed the internal damage. Whiplash, possibly. No broken bones. No flying glass. Her legs appeared capable of moving. And moving them immediately seemed the wisest thing under the circumstances.

Without further internal consultation, she popped open the rear door and dove for safety.

"Durwood!" a voice thundered from somewhere beyond

her. "You're fired! If I've told you once, I've told you ten thousand times, you can't drive the car! So help me, I'll put both you and Nana in a box and shove you over the cliff! What in hell did you think you were doing?"

Pleasant chap, Pippa decided, examining her scraped knees where she'd hit the pavement in her haste to escape the car. Other than a dirty hem, her dress seemed in good shape. She couldn't say the same for her panty hose. Luckily, she carried a spare pair. Now, if she only dared go back in the car for her shoulder bag . . .

Scrambling to her feet, she warily glanced around. Firmly wedged against the oak, the car appeared in no immediate danger of tumbling off the cliff. If there was any danger at all, it was from the furious man descending the mansion's pretentious front steps two at a time. Had he worn a black cloak and carried a scythe, she wouldn't have raised an eyebrow.

Pippa expected steam to pour from his ears. Not that she could see his ears amid the thick, curly black hair, uncut and uncombed by any self-respecting hairdresser. It waved and curled in layers that would have made her faint with joy had they been on her own head. Instead, they framed a distinctly masculine, long-boned face that made "harsh" seem a mild word.

Scarcely heeding the furious tornado headed his way, the gnarled driver examined the car's steaming engine with detached interest. He appeared only mildly surprised when the dark man jerked him from the roadway by his shirt collar.

"You're fired, Durwood! Do you hear me? Now get back to the garden, where you belong."

Feeling like Alice tumbling through the looking glass, Pippa backed away from the rising fracas. The man in the long-sleeved black turtleneck was twice the driver's size, and in her present state of mind, looked like some dangerous combination of Frankenstein's monster and Heathcliff. His biceps bulged beneath tight shirtsleeves as he lifted Durwood off his feet. She preferred not to look at the nearly triangular shape of his back. The broad shoulders she'd seen from the front had scared her enough, thank you very much. As reaction set in, she edged away from the stone castle with its towering turrets and moved toward the driveway.

This cyclone couldn't be Mr. Wyatt. She didn't think wealthy eccentrics dressed like athletic thugs. A man with Seth Wyatt's reputation would have cold eyes, a sharp weasely face, and wear double-breasted Italian suits. She'd never actually seen a man wearing an Italian suit, but she imagined she could spot one easily enough. Perhaps Frankenstein was Wyatt's bodyguard.

An ear-piercing shriek cut the air, followed by the crash of breaking glass. The thug cursed loudly. Pippa swung instinctively toward the house. There was supposed to be a crippled boy in this household, and that had sounded like a child's scream.

The still cursing long-haired man hurtled past her with unprecedented rudeness.

Pippa hurried up the stairs after him, nearly stumbling as she fell through the rabbit hole into the most incredible house she'd ever seen. Impressions of stone and timber walls and soaring cathedral ceilings blurred as she raced in the direction of the screams. She followed the man across a mahogany foyer, up flagstone stairs, and down an immense, winding corridor, toward the back of the house.

Abruptly, her leader halted in the doorway of what appeared to be a solarium. Pippa skidded, nearly crashing into his broad back. He propped his hands on his hips, blocking any view except the one between the crooks of his arms. From that angle, she could see the spectacular view from the windows but no sign of an occupant.

"Chad!" the man bellowed. "That's enough!"

The man did indeed have odd reactions to trauma. Tired of her apparent invisibility, Pippa shoved her way past him, trying to locate the boy. She finally discovered him in a wheelchair.

If the smashed glass door was any evidence, he'd attempted to wheel his chair onto the balcony beyond. But remembering the scream preceding the breaking glass, Pippa accepted the possibility that an escalating temper tantrum could be the culprit. She saw no signs of blood or physical trauma. The behavior of the man behind her corroborated her instincts.

As the youngest of three children, she didn't have a lot of experience in caring for siblings. She had, however, spent a good deal of time in the hospital's pediatric ward. She'd seen anger and frustration before, but never a tantrum like this one. The boy's pale face had nearly turned purple with rage. Something in the similarity of the dark curls and long face warned of the relation to the man behind her, but she'd about had enough of the screaming and didn't heed the warning.

Not one for vacillating, Pippa took the first workable solution available. Screaming at the boy obviously presented no solution. If she could get the man out of the doorway, she might try closing the door and letting the kid exhaust himself, but she couldn't move nearly two hundred pounds of solid muscle. Now that he had the attention he wanted, the boy wouldn't stop soon, and not knowing the particulars of his condition, she feared for his health. With tight-lipped decision, she grabbed the wheelchair handles and steered him through the doorway, over the broken glass, onto the balcony.

The boy applied his brakes, but she kicked them loose with an expertise that surprised him—for about two seconds. Then he screamed louder, twisting and turning and attempting to fling himself from the chair.

Pippa reached for a nearby watering can. Apologizing to the colorful plants decorating the railing, she dumped the can's contents over the boy's curly head.

Howls instantly turned to sputters and pitiful wails. The man behind her roared and stormed into the room.

Calmly, Pippa held up the half-full can as if it were a shotgun and threatened him with it.

"He's unharmed and doesn't have a scratch on him," she informed him patiently. "Which is more than I can say for myself," she added, finally feeling the ache in her neck and the scrapes on her knees.

The long-haired monster pushed her aside, strode across the stone balcony, and jerked his sobbing son from the chair. Hugging the soaked boy, wetting his shirt in the process, the Grim Reaper glared at her. "You're fired."

That seemed reasonable. She didn't want to work in a madhouse anyway, particularly now that she realized this was her employer and he was as lethal as promised. His stony glare would have put Medusa to shame. But Pippa's protective nature couldn't help pointing out the obvious. "Pardon me if I'm in error, but I believe you've just given him exactly what he wanted. Who's running this household, him or you?"

Cuddling his shivering, sobbing son against his chest, Seth couldn't fling the irritating female over the railing as he would like. He doubted if she reached his shoulder or possessed half his weight, but she stood there calmly defying him. He didn't know how else to get rid of her if he couldn't throw her off the balcony. As usual when forced to words instead of action, he cursed. Chad imitated him, and the language spilling from the boy's tongue turned his attention away from his new employee.

Seth stared down at his son in disbelief. "What did you say?"

The boy glared back at him with the same ferocious expression Seth had seen in his own mirror. "Make the silly bitch go away."

Seth could hear himself in those precise words. In horror, he glanced at the interfering female, daring her to comment.

Instead of looking properly outraged, she grinned like a damned Cheshire cat. Only then did Seth notice she appeared more female leprechaun than qualified nurse. That absurd cap of obviously tinted red hair bounced with her suppressed laughter. Green eyes danced in a ridiculously cherubic face. She needed only a green stocking cap and leotards to complete the image. The totally out-of-fashion shirtdress didn't suit her at all. She appeared everything but tailored, in his opinion. Flighty, uncontrollable . . . He would need a thesaurus.

"He will be a joy as a teenager," the cheerful leprechaun observed. "I don't suppose you have another car and driver to take me back to town? I'd rather walk than ride with that maniac again."

"It's twelve miles," he said gruffly, ignoring her predicament. Wiping his son's tears, he looked past the woman to Nana, who had quietly watched the entire scene without offering a word or hand. Efficient as usual when called upon, she stepped forward to take the boy from Seth's arms.

At Chad's vehement protests, Nana dropped him into his wheelchair and lifted the watering can over his head.

The annoying female snickered. Frustrated, irritated beyond all redemption at his inability to control any portion of his household, Seth caught the woman's elbow and steered her toward the door. "We'll discuss this in my office."

To his surprise, she jerked her arm from his grasp and stalked out the door ahead of him. "We will discuss this on the front steps while we wait for my ride, which you will summon now," she informed him coldly.

He didn't deal with women much anymore. Natalie had effectively killed any illusions he'd once possessed about the female gender. But he'd never lacked confidence in the effect his looks and wealth had on women. He didn't expect this female to fawn all over him immediately, but a respectful "Yes, sir; no, sir," accompanied by a lingering smile would have sufficed. That's why he endured the battle-ax, MacGregor. Sixty and carved from granite, she couldn't flirt if she tried. But this leprechaun . . .

It didn't matter. She wouldn't suit. He couldn't have an appealing female prancing around the house day and night. Even if Chad wouldn't throw a tantrum every time she crossed the threshold, he didn't have the patience for withstanding temptation of this sort. He definitely didn't need one more uncontrollable force in his life.

Sometimes, Seth believed this monstrous fortress of his childhood was built to keep the inmates in, instead of keeping the world out.

He followed her past the hall leading to his office and out the front door before pulling his thoughts up short. This particular female didn't *want* to stay. She'd laughed in his face and walked out the door without a single backward look. And she'd shut Chad up within minutes, instead of the usual hours. Furthermore, he had absolutely *nobody* to fill MacGregor's shoes.

The possibility of enduring the anarchy he'd just suffered for weeks, maybe months, drove Seth to run after her.

"We got off on the wrong foot," Seth apologized as he nearly fell over her in his haste. He grabbed the post and regained his balance while searching for the best means of intimidating her.

Scanning the magnificent view from the porch, Pippa paid her host little heed. The isolation out here appealed strongly to her need for escape. The locked gate at the bottom of the drive offered badly needed security. This fortress would be protection beyond her wildest dreams. She liked this place. The towering cliff she had seen beyond the balcony appealed to her sense of the dramatic. She could push Billy off it if she liked.

"I'm certain we can come to terms, Miss Cochran," the terrifying man beside her said. "I'll send my regular driver in for you every day. If you can give me eight hours a day, I might survive. I'm prepared to pay you well."

He certainly would if her job entailed taming that spoiled wildcat inside. The kid would have been a stubborn handful if healthy. Caged by his useless legs, the child had become a volcano of raw energy ready to explode at any excuse. She didn't relish finding an outlet for that energy. And she didn't relish working for a man who bullied his employees.

"We discussed a thousand a week," she replied absently, still debating the wisdom of this move. Actually, they'd discussed nothing of the sort. His original offer had been considerably lower. That had been before the maniac driver and volcanic kid.

"Of course, but I'll need you seven days a week," he countered.

"Even God took a day off." Shocked by his easy acceptance of her outrageous proposal, Pippa turned to him with a wry look. The expression on those dark, brooding features should terrify her. She couldn't find an ounce of kindness in the grim set of his mouth, or compassion in the forbidding stance of muscular arms crossed over powerful chest. He'd grabbed her arm and tried physically hauling her around. Experience screamed for her to run like crazy.

That he still stood there discussing her ridiculous demands showed his desperation. She could understand his point. Trapped in that madhouse all day, she'd want some form of comic relief, too.

"Fine, Sundays off, then." He waved his hand impatiently. "How soon can you start?"

She liked the feeling of having a bully under her thumb for a change. The man truly was desperate. No matter how he tried hiding it, she could see it in the way he avoided her gaze.

With a sudden sense of mischief, she stared over his immaculately landscaped lawn and replied in her best Kentucky accent. "Way-el-l-l, Ah guess Ah could start oncet I get muh trailer up here. Cain't see makin' that drive ever' day."

Shock glazed his eyes, and Pippa noted that they were

shades of gray and not shards of stone. He recovered rapidly, and frost froze his features and coated his words. "A trailer is completely out of the question. It's against building codes."

Liar, she murmured spitefully to herself. According to everything she'd heard, *he* determined the building code around here. If he wanted an entire trailer park on this mountain, not a soul would object. Aloud.

"Way-el-l-l, that's a pity. Don't cotton to sharin' a room with a kid lahk Ah'm doin' now. Don't much cotton to ridin' with none of yer crazy drivers either. Looks like we reached an impasse, Mr. Wyatt."

A hint of something resembling humor momentarily warmed his expression before he schooled his harsh features into coldness again. "I don't much cotton to my son talking like a hick either, Miss Cochran. If this is your strategy to get out of an unpalatable job, you didn't reckon on my determination."

Unpalatable. She liked a man who could throw words like that around. She grinned at his bad mimicry. "I don't suppose you cotton to teaching your son manners either, Mr. Wyatt. Not that you have many to teach him. Let me introduce myself." She held out her hand. "I'm Phillippa Cochran. Nice place you have here."

He glanced suspiciously at her hand, back to her cheerful grin, and very, very reluctantly unbent sufficiently to shake her fingers. "Miss Cochran, I'm Seth Wyatt. I apologize for your rude reception."

"Very good, Mr. Wyatt. Your mother did teach you a thing or two, then." She waited patiently, still smiling.

He hesitated. Gradually, his gaze drifted from her implacable smile to the smashed auto in the drive, then back to the sprawling house behind them.

"If it would not be an imposition, you might take one of the rooms in the guest wing," he suggested stiffly.

"One at least a mile away from you and your son," she agreed. Meg would kill her. Pippa thought she had possibly breathed in too much California air and lost her mind. She had the distinct feeling she was selling her soul to the devil.

Still, this hell of his was damned attractive from her perspective, considering what she'd left behind.

FIVE

"You know, it's always those men who live alone, the ones neighbors describe as loners, who end up blowing away their families or bombing buildings. Look at the Unabomber, and the guy who blew up the federal building in Oklahoma."

Sitting at a table in the local cafe after a shopping expedition that had probably maxed out Meg's credit cards, Pippa listened as the local banker speculated about Garden Grove's favorite subject—the Wyatt family. She supposed that if Seth Wyatt closed the town's main industry, the bank would be left with any number of uncollectible loans.

"I think it's only *poor* loners who blow up buildings," Pippa offered magnanimously in her new employer's defense. "Rich ones buy armies and blow up countries."

Taylor Morgan shifted his California-bronzed, golden-haired head in her direction. Until now, he'd concentrated on Meg and his wife, who were apparently good country club buddies. His glance wasn't particularly friendly, and Pippa gave him her best Pollyanna smile. She might not much like men right now, but she knew how to charm them. The man seemed to defrost slightly.

"I don't think you fully understand the relationship between the Wyatts and this town, Miss Cochran. Maxim Wyatt came here during the Depression, bought up every acre of land he could lay hands on, and successfully prevented any meaningful economic development for decades."

"He wouldn't use Taylor's bank," Meg whispered in explanation from behind her fingers.

The banker continued. "After Maxim Wyatt bankrupted the remainder of the valley's inhabitants, he used them as slave labor to build that monstrosity of a house out there. People had to put food in the mouths of their children somehow. They took whatever he offered. Wyatts have controlled this town ever since, kept us in poverty and repression simply by their ownership of every valuable piece of land in the county."

"We could put in an industrial park where he tore down the printing plant," Lisa, Taylor's wife, added, "but Seth won't sell the land. There's good farm acreage out there, but he just rents it to sharecroppers. He has an absolute stranglehold on the economy. I think he enjoys holding an ax over our heads."

"A scythe," Pippa muttered to herself, but the others were so engrossed in their topic that they didn't hear.

"He's dangerous," Taylor said. "You really should reconsider your decision, Miss Cochran. They say he keeps his only son a prisoner, and his few employees are all slightly deranged. That black driver of his terrifies the shopkeepers. They only accept Mrs. Jones because she's been around forever. She once broke a chair over a man's head. Seth has had the grounds wired and runs the current so strong that some of the kids have received severe shocks. They kept the court session quiet, but his wife countersued in the divorce for abuse. I've friends down in Orange County, where they used to live. They say she's a broken woman."

Pippa stirred her Coke with a straw. "Mrs. Jones?" she asked casually, wondering if he could possibly mean the stooped old lady she'd met yesterday.

"The housekeeper." Impatiently, Taylor scraped his chair back from the table. "I've got to get back to the office. It was good meeting you, Miss Cochran. I wish you well on your search for employment here, but I recommend that you don't accept Wyatt's offer."

Fat chance. As if she could turn down an offer of a thousand a week with free room and board. Pippa bit into her hamburger. The driver she'd seen looked like a nutcase, but he wasn't black in any coloring book she knew. Maybe Seth Wyatt was the kind of man around whom legends grew. Admittedly, she found him physically terrifying, but in her present frame of mind, she didn't like Taylor Morgan all that much either.

"I understand Mr. Wyatt is an attractive man," Lisa Morgan said conversationally after her husband's departure. If Pippa was any judge of character at all, the light in the other woman's eyes was almost predatory as she opened this topic. Wearing a chic fawn silk tunic top to complement her blond good looks, she dangled more gold jewelry than Pippa had seen in the Gold Nugget back home.

"If you like Grim Reapers, I suppose," Pippa replied offhandedly. She was used to gossip. She was just uncomfortable discussing a man she'd barely met, a man who looked dangerous but defended his son with all the ferocity of a wild wolf.

"Pippa doesn't notice men," Meg offered in explanation for her friend's reticence. "I swear, in high school, she had half the football team breathing down her neck, and you know what she did with them? Set them to decorating the gym for the prom. And she went to the dance with the class nerd."

"He owns his own software company now," Pippa offered with a shrug. "And except for the receding hairline, he's quite handsome. He started working out in college while the football team filled up on beer and got paunchy. I'm not entirely stupid when it comes to men."

"If you're not stupid, why didn't you marry him?" Meg demanded, pursuing one of her favorite topics.

Pippa grinned and wiped the ketchup off her fingers with a paper napkin. "He didn't ask me. He wasn't stupid either."

Meg laughed but Lisa merely looked bored.

"Well, I'll leave you two to catch up on old times. If you do decide to accept Mr. Wyatt's offer, Phillippa, I hope you'll do everything in your power to make him see reason. If he'd only come into town and talk with us, we might make some progress around here."

Pippa smiled automatically and waved farewell. Like, sure, an ant could move a mountain. She'd do well to avoid being crushed by runaway boulders.

As soon as Lisa departed, Meg's expression changed to a worried frown. "I don't like this, Pippa. If you must take the job, at least stay in town. With that much money, you could buy a car and rent an apartment."

Pippa couldn't explain why she felt safer in a madman's fortress than in the openness of her friend's community. Billy had stolen something from her she couldn't get back so readily—security.

"I like it out there," she answered carelessly, scraping up the last French fry. Both Meg and Lisa, in their California health-consciousness, had been appalled by her choice of meal. She hadn't explained she'd needed the familiarity of comfort foods right now. Once she adapted to this odd new world, she'd learn their ways.

Meg nodded slowly. "It's hilly and reminds you of home, maybe. That's why I was so glad I could see the mountains in the distance. But that's not sufficient reason for risking your life."

Pippa grinned and considered the ice cream selection. "I doubt if I'm risking my life. If he hasn't killed his insane driver by now, I'll survive."

"Doug? Doug's not insane. Frightening, maybe, but not insane. I think he was in the National Football League until his drinking interfered with his career. Don't let Lisa scare you about Doug. He's the most harmless person out there. If the shopkeepers are intimidated by him, it's because he's big and black. We grow bigots out here as well as anywhere."

Pippa instructed the waitress on the amount of fudge syrup and nuts she wanted on her mocha sundae, then returned her attention to Meg. "Black? Football player? That's not the driver I met. Maybe Wyatt has killed someone, after all. The driver I met was a grinning dwarf maniac."

Meg sat back in her chair and relaxed, lifting her mineral water in salute. "Durwood lives, then. I'd wondered. He used to be our gardener, but he wouldn't take a word of instruction. George would tell him to plant roses in the left corner of the backyard, and Durwood would line the driveway with them. I'd ask him to remove those horrible yuccas, and he'd stick them in between the roses and plant peppers in their place. Peppers! We could have supplied half the valley with them. I'm not certain he even speaks English."

A drunken football player, a maniac gardener, and a Nazi nanny. Quite a household, Pippa mused as she dug into her sundae. Could it be any worse than working with the administrative vultures at home? She'd certainly get paid more here, and have fewer bosses to work around. She could handle Seth Wyatt.

She felt less sure of that later that day when Miss MacGregor arrived to pick her up.

Wyatt's current assistant stood nearly six feet tall and wore a business suit like a suit of armor. Pippa had the urge to pinch the shiny gray material and see if it squished or clanked. How could she compare with a monster of efficiency like this?

"If you'll drive me to the airport in the morning, Miss Cochran, I'll leave you the use of my car while I'm gone. You'll need one living out there. Doug isn't reliable, and Mr. Wyatt won't let anyone else drive his vehicles."

Considering what Durwood had done to the BMW, Pippa could understand his reluctance. He had trouble hiring qualified employees, it seemed. She wondered how he'd kept Miss MacGregor.

As if hearing her unspoken question, MacGregor supplied the answer. "I would have left the place long ago if he hadn't bought me this car and offered a pension plan. I'm near retirement age, and it's quite a temptation, believe me. I could have worked for any major corporation in the country. I've had them inquire often enough. But I'm accustomed to doing things my own way now and don't think I could change."

Oh, swell, another neo-Nazi with no loyalty whatsoever. Wyatt certainly knew how to pick them. Or maybe his employees just reflected his own character. She didn't have any difficulty believing that.

"I'll show you my filing system this evening. I hope you're familiar with Microsoft. It's the only software Mr. Wyatt uses. I understand you'll have some charge over the child also. I wish you well. He's completely uncontrollable. I hope Mr. Wyatt is paying you well for the extra duty while I'm gone. I'm certain the boy will be your main duty when I return."

Pippa was beginning to suspect she wasn't paid half so well as Miss MacGregor, or even half as much as she deserved if she survived. No wonder the cad had agreed to her terms so easily.

"I dislike leaving Mr. Wyatt when he's so close to deadline, but the circumstances can't be changed. Supply him with plenty of coffee and don't let anyone disturb him until he's done for the day. He's quite irrational when disturbed. You won't need a strong grasp of grammar and spelling for your editing duties. The software is quite good and Mr. Wyatt knows his business well. You'll learn his few idiosyncrasies after a chapter or two. You can learn from the work I've already completed."

A chapter or two? Pippa stared at the lantern-jawed woman expertly guiding her candy-red Mazda coupe up the road. "A chapter or two of what?" she inquired politely, hoping the question wasn't too stupid.

It was. Miss MacGregor turned and gave her a disbelieving stare. "Of his book, of course. Why do you think he hired you? We're halfway through it now. He writes one a year, but he always waits until the last minute. It's due the first of June, but he's hit his usual midbook slump. It would help if he could bounce ideas off you. Once he gets back in stride, you won't hear anything out of him for days at a time. You'll just find the pages on your desk in the morning."

"I thought he was in the publishing business," Pippa answered weakly. Actually, now that she thought about it, they had never discussed precisely what business he was in. Meg's letter about the printing plant had led her astray.

"Oh, he is," Miss MacGregor replied airily, navigating the last hairpin turn with surprising speed. "He owns an independent publishing house for small-press books and magazines here in California, another in Tokyo, and he's negotiating for one in Boston. He has printing plants and warehouses across the country. He's in a position to compete with the big houses, but he spends so much time on his writing career that he neglects his father's business."

Writing career? She didn't have a lot of time for reading, but she belonged to the Book of the Month Club and knew the current best-sellers. She couldn't remember ever hearing the name of Seth Wyatt in that context.

"Does he write under his own name?" she asked tentatively.

This time, Miss MacGregor's look contained scorn and a certain amount of pity. "Of course not. He likes his privacy. He writes as Tarant Mott, Miss Cochran. His horror novels make the *New York Times* list regularly."

Tarant Mott. Pippa couldn't believe it. Mitchell had collected all Tarant Mott's books for years. She saw them everywhere: on the library's new release shelf, in the front of bookstores, in the Book-of-the-Month Club catalog. She'd never read one. She saw enough horror and gore at the hospital. But Tarant Mott . . . !

Miss MacGregor may as well have said she worked for God. No one knew anything about Tarant Mott. He didn't make personal appearances. He didn't include his bio or photo in his books. He just sold humongous numbers of novels to impatient buyers waiting in line for his latest release.

Rumors abounded, of course. Rumors always did, especially around Seth Wyatt, Pippa decided wryly. She'd seen a magazine article calling Tarant Mott a hermit after a tragic accident that had left him half blind and disfigured and had cost him his wife. Another squib had speculated that his son was dying of an undiagnosed wasting disease. If she thought hard enough, she supposed she could remember more, but she could see the basis of the rumors had very little relation to fact.

Miss MacGregor pulled up to the mansion and handed Pippa over to the housekeeper. As Mrs. Jones threw open the door to her new bedroom, Pippa decided the public could have all the rumors it wanted. She'd come home.

Apparently every room in the house had a spectacular view. Whoever had designed the gothic exterior hadn't had a hand in the interior beyond the strange public entrance with wood where stone should be and vice versa. The room opened into an entire suite of rooms, she realized as Mrs. Jones walked through, opening doors. Sparsely decorated in simple Mission style, the suite contained all the basic necessities and nothing more, which suited Pippa just fine. She smoothed her hand over the fine old wood of the long dresser, admired the crocheted duvet cover on the bed, and stared in awe at the climactic landscape of tumbling rock and cliff outside the patio window. Patio window. She had her own deck overlooking the canyon.

She must have died and gone to heaven. Not noticing when the housekeeper left, Pippa strolled through a closet large enough to hold an entire bedroom, admired the Jacuzzi in the bath, and breathed a sigh of pleasure over the spacious sitting room. A simple wooden sofa held cushions of natural woven linen. A hemp rug served as carpet. Spare bookshelves lined either side of a small hearth. The shelves held an assortment of natural ornaments: seashells, dried grasses, items seemingly plucked from the land and left here to be admired. The few books had titles like *Moby Dick* or *Scarlet Letter*, but she could excuse the designer that faux pas in a house owned by a horror writer. A classic would put her asleep faster than a nightmare story.

Just in case she developed any strange ideas that she had walked into a free California vacation, the phone on the streamlined desk in the corner rang.

Well, no one could live on fantasy forever.

Picking up the receiver, she listened to the voice on the other end.

"Dinner is at seven. Don't wear perfume. Chad has a cold. Check his temperature and see if he needs a doctor."

The click on the other end didn't allow any reply.

SIX

Wondering if she should drop bread crumbs so she could find her way back, Pippa wandered through the guest wing, across the central block overlooking the two-story foyer, and down the long hall she hoped led to Chad's room. She supposed if her mind weren't already so thoroughly occupied by thoughts of her employer and this new job, she might enjoy a leisurely stroll through mahogany and marble, priceless Oriental carpets, and stunning artwork. But she couldn't concentrate on objects right now.

No matter how casually she had treated Wyatt's offer, she needed this job as desperately as he needed her services. Until she'd lost it, she hadn't realized how much she had depended on her job as a reason for living. Without the constant daily demands of people she knew, she felt like a kite without a tail. Grimly, she faced the fact that she was one of those stupid women who needed to be needed. She didn't like believing that at the grand old age of thirty, she could be washed up, worthless, unneeded by anyone.

Pippa couldn't even excuse her desperation as an escape from Billy. She figured she'd pretty well escaped all on her own. She hadn't reached total incompetence yet. But the horror stories of abusive men who chased their wives and girlfriends until they killed them haunted her. This fortress Seth Wyatt called home could protect her. She liked the solidity of these stone and mahogany walls.

So when Pippa entered the boy's room to the splat of a water gun drenching her hair and new dress, she managed a smile quite effortlessly.

"Good shot, cowboy, but didn't anyone ever tell you that it's against the Code of the West to shoot unarmed, defenseless women?" Briskly swiping the bright orange machine gun from his hands, she turned the barrel on him and pulled the trigger.

Chad yowled. He screamed bloody murder. He pounded his fists against his wheelchair, then charged forward in Pippa's direction. She dodged it expertly, grabbed the handles, and swung it in an arc toward the open balcony doors.

"We can play water games out here. I don't think the floor in your room can handle a flood. Do you have another water pistol or do I get to use the watering can?"

When Chad didn't immediately stop screaming, Pippa shoved the gun back in his hands and picked up the watering can. "Count to three or shoot anytime?"

He shut up. Eyeing her warily, he aimed the pistol. Pippa smiled and dodged the squirt of water. Whistling, she anointed him with a spray from the can. Truly furious now, Chad swung his chair and shot again, following her steadily everywhere she jumped. Within minutes, they were both drenched head to foot and Chad had started sneezing.

"Okay, cowboy, that did it. The first one who sneezes, dies. Let's get you into your coffin." With the assurance learned from years of dealing with temperamental doctors, Pippa removed the water gun from the boy's hands, dropped it on the balcony, and spun him back into his room.

"I'm not dead," he complained, sneezing again.

"Are too. I'm burying you on Boot Hill." Expertly, she lifted him from the chair, dropped him on the massive playground she assumed was his bed, and began stripping off his wet clothes.

He couldn't kick his legs, but he twisted and turned and fought her every step of the way. Still, a forty-pound six-year-old didn't have the strength or stamina of a two-hundred-pound man, and she'd fought patients bigger than that before. She had him out of his wet clothes, dried off, and into a pair of cowboy pajamas before his screams alerted the entire household.

"What in hell is going on?" Seth demanded, stomping through the doorway with murder in his eyes.

"I'm burying Cowboy Bob on Boot Hill," Pippa replied calmly, applying a towel for one final drying to Chad's hair. "If you've got some decongestant medicine, he could probably use a spoonful before we tuck him in. Corpses shouldn't sneeze all night."

Seth eyed her drenched dress and cheerful expression with the same wariness his son had earlier. "I see. I take it Chad lost the gunfight at the OK Corral?"

"I did not! She cheated," Chad protested from his throne among the pillows and stuffed animals. "Dead men don't sneeze."

Pippa thought she detected the hint of a curve on Wyatt's chiseled lips, just enough to send something wickedly delicious plummeting fast and furious through her middle. Startled by her primal reaction to his proximity, she turned her attention back to the boy. For all she knew, Seth Wyatt was a dangerous psychopath. She should be afraid of him, not attracted. She had sick hormones and lousy taste in men.

"Okay, so I lied," she said breezily, dismissing her unpleasant thoughts. "Dead men don't sneeze. We'll fight it out again tomorrow, and you can make the rules. But I want the machine gun next time."

"The machine gun's mine," Chad grumbled, snuggling back

into the pillows and making a face as his father spooned the medicine down his throat.

"Then I'm going to look for a hose," she warned.

Chad gave her an evil look that would have done his father proud.

"Good night, cowboy. I've got to go change, before I join you on Boot Hill." Pippa hoped that was a small snicker she heard as she swept out. If her new charge didn't have a sense of humor, she would have her job cut out for her. Surely he hadn't lost all his humor by the age of six, even in this grim prison.

Seth caught up with her as she reached the open library overlooking the foyer below. "Miss Cochran, wait a minute. I must apologize for my son."

She halted and gave him a quizzical look, grateful for the dim lighting. She still felt as if a catfish bellyflopped in her stomach when she looked at Seth Wyatt. Perhaps it was the penetrating arctic eyes beneath those craggy brows that had her feeling as if she'd just been hooked and reeled in. She needed to be afraid of him for more than one reason.

"Your son has nothing to apologize for except an excess of pent-up energy. Does he have access to a gym or pool?"

Seth stopped short and glared down at her. "What in hell would he do with a gym?"

Pippa stared at him in disbelief, her concern instantly diverted to the child and away from the father. "Hasn't his doctor recommended a competent physical therapist? She would put together an exercise plan that would strengthen his muscles as well as work off some of that energy. You can't keep a growing boy confined to his room."

She couldn't read Wyatt's expression. She suspected that even if the room contained more light than the dusk currently glimmering through stained glass, she wouldn't discern a hint of emotion behind that stony mask.

"The doctor says his lungs are too weak for vigorous exercise and that encouraging him beyond his physical capabilities would only traumatize him further."

"Then get another doctor. That one's a quack." Not having patience for a man who gave up so easily, and not having patience for her own jangling nerve endings, Pippa left her new boss leaning on the library railing, staring after her.

She really should quit arguing with her employers, she told herself. Look at where it had led last time. Instead of firing the incompetent hacks who sat quietly drinking coffee at their desks, doing as they were told, the hospital had fired the troublemaker first. Would she never learn?

Still, she couldn't leave that child cooped up in his miniature palace for the rest of his life. She couldn't live with herself if she did. Of course, if she insisted on arguing with Wyatt, she'd find herself bounced out on her nose. What good could she do the boy then?

The age-old question. Sighing, Pippa struggled out of her wet dress as soon as she hit her room. Was there any point in going down to dinner now?

But if she didn't, she would not only starve, she would lose her last chance to have Miss MacGregor show her the ropes before the woman left in the morning. Pippa seriously suspected it would be much easier getting a clear idea of her duties from the efficient secretary than her taciturn employer.

Wishing for a map like the ones convention hotels handed out, Pippa eventually wended her way through the maze of rooms to the dining chamber. She could only call it a chamber. The antique crystal chandelier danced over a table long enough to host a state dinner. Idly, she wondered if the servants wore roller blades. Pedometers maybe. Then they could be paid by the mile.

Deciding the businesslike red suit Meg had insisted looked spectacular with her complexion was definitely not the choice for a formal evening in the Reaper's mansion, Pippa hesitated on the threshold.

Crystal and china place settings for two glittered in the light of the chandelier. An acre of starched linen covered the table, an enormous floral arrangement occupied the center, but the settings had been placed only at one end. Perhaps they expected her in the kitchen.

"Debating which silver to use, Miss Cochran?"

Pippa nearly jumped out of her shoes at the sound of the voice behind her. Swinging around, she glared at the man standing with arms crossed over his chest. He'd at least changed from the turtleneck to a fitted white dress shirt, although the contrast with his dark coloring created dancing images in her head that were far from businesslike. Pippa detected a mocking smirk on his glacial features. "Debating which *table* to use, Mr. Wyatt. I think I prefer the kitchen."

Damn. She had just done it again—flapped her tongue before putting her brain in gear. There was just something about this man that rubbed her in all the wrong ways.

"Miss MacGregor prefers eating in her room. Since I have no business to go over with her this evening, I didn't object. You, however, will need to take notes."

When she didn't immediately leave the doorway, he gave her a pointed glare rather than ask her to move.

Pippa hurriedly got out of Wyatt's way. She held her tongue also, although the question of whether pen and paper came as part of the cutlery scorched the roof of her mouth.

Sure enough, he snapped open a leather notebook and handed her a Mont Blanc pen as soon as she took her place.

"Miss MacGregor wants you to drive her to the airport at eight tomorrow morning. Allowing for traffic, you should be back by two. Miss MacGregor hasn't had time to edit the last two chapters. They're still sitting on her desk. You'll start with those. I'll have another before you're through."

The first course arrived. Ignoring the pen and notebook,

Pippa sipped the delicious onion soup and wondered if the omnipotent Mrs. Jones managed the kitchen, as well as the house and nursery.

"Your responsibilities include sorting and answering the mail, taking all phone calls, and directing to me only those from people on the list on your desk. I'm on deadline and haven't time for trivial questions. You will handle all other calls."

Pippa tasted the wine and tried not to grimace. She had never developed a taste for alcohol. The sparkling water suited her better. Blind obedience came hard, and swallowing all the questions and protests burning her tongue made her thirsty.

"You haven't written a word of this down," he accused as grilled swordfish and sautéed asparagus replaced the soup.

Pippa didn't think she'd ever eaten swordfish or asparagus. She wouldn't have known what they were without the neatly printed menu card in front of her. She wondered if one of her responsibilities was printing these little cards every day. After tasting the vegetable, she decided she would make a point of going into town and filling up on French fries the nights asparagus appeared on the list.

The icy silence from beyond her left elbow warned Tyrant Tarant had finished another lecture. Giving him a brief smile, she answered, "I have a tape-deck memory. It records everything I hear."

"A tape-deck memory?" The question dripped sarcasm.

Pippa shrugged. "Other people have photographic memories. What would you call it?"

"A tape-deck memory." He shook his head in disbelief. "Do you want to reel everything I've said back by me?"

"Not particularly. It was spectacularly boring. Where in the schedule does Chad fit in? I promised him a return bout."

"Chad amuses himself. Nana is available if he needs anything. You might check on his cold before you begin work on the chapters, I suppose. And it probably wouldn't hurt to drop in on him before dinner as you did tonight. Your duties with Chad will be quite light."

Rebellion raised its ugly head, and Pippa finally focused her attention on her employer's forbidding features. "Your damned book is more important than your son?"

Wyatt's face shuttered more than before, if that was possible. "I am available to my son every moment of the day, which is more than most parents can say. I did not hire you to question my parenting, Miss Cochran."

"He's six years old. He should be in school making friends all day." Pippa had heard the ominous tone in his voice, but she couldn't help herself. Getting fired the first day on the job wasn't part of her game plan, but her conscience wouldn't let her leave the subject alone.

"He has a tutor. His intellectual skills are well beyond those of most six-year-olds, Miss Cochran. I ask you to refrain from any further interference with my son."

She bit her tongue until it hurt. She beamed a smile at him and nibbled at the sugar biscuit accompanying the raspberry sorbet that had just arrived.

"Aye, aye, Captain. I won't be around when he turns thirteen and burns this place to the ground. He's all yours."

The look he gave her was definitely suspicious and on the fair side of venomous. She should be terrified of living in a lunatic asylum with a potential murderer in charge. Apparently the beauty of the countryside had given her a false sense of security. She simply couldn't fear a man as desperate as she was.

Pippa had ten dozen questions she could have asked, but like Scheherazade, she thought she'd drag them out for a thousand nights or so and avoid beheading. Some of the answers she could find out for herself. As her brusque host finally took his towering frame off to whatever cave he inhabited, Pippa went in search of her new office. Thoughtless of him not to show it to her, but she had already begun to suspect "thoughtless" was just the tip of the descriptive iceberg for Mr. Seth Wyatt.

In his office, Seth glared at his computer screen. The words swimming before him could have been little white lines for all he noticed. Instead of focusing on the gore and havoc wreaked by a deadly gopher run amuck, his inner eye produced visions of a redhead with a blinding smile.

He'd have to write angel books if this continued. Grunting in dissatisfaction, Seth rocked his chair back and took another sip of coffee. He wasn't even certain he could bed a woman with a smile like that. Did she smile when she was on her back and between the sheets?

Contemplating Phillippa Cochran naked wasn't conducive to concentration either.

Dammit! He knew this would happen. His libido always churned into overdrive when he'd gone without sex for a while. He'd have to arrange to go into L.A. for a few days.

But he didn't like leaving Chad that long, especially with a new member of the household. And he really didn't fancy getting within reach of Tracey's claws again. She'd accommodated him more than once since his divorce, but she was developing dangerously territorial habits. The last time, he'd practically had to lock her in the house to stop her from following him. He definitely did not want another predatory female in his life.

Seth glared at the computer screen a minute more, then popped open the lid of hard-coated English toffees and helped himself to one. He'd given up cigarettes when the doctor had told him Chad had weak lungs and would suffer from the secondhand smoke. But the damned candies were every bit as addictive.

A sound from the outer office roused him.

Pippa! Ridiculous name. He shoved away from the desk. He

didn't need her rattling around and disturbing his concentration again.

He found her examining the framed book covers Miss MacGregor had arranged around the room. He hated the things, but Mac regarded them as some sort of trophies. He suspected she considered herself two-thirds responsible for his success. Miss Cochran, on the other hand, seemed to regard the gruesome artwork with revulsion.

Even though he'd slipped quietly behind her, she sensed his presence. Without turning around, she pointed at a particularly striking black cover with a mummy's head eerily lit from the inside. "That's physically impossible, of course," she informed him coolly. "The skull would disintegrate if unwrapped and the wrappings would catch fire. They're highly flammable, you know."

Seth had never given it any thought. "That book wasn't even about mummies. The blamed cover artist just had a thing for them."

He'd told her not to wear perfume, but he caught a whiff of some elusive scent. He knew all the expensive fragrances, had learned to recognize the exorbitant French designer perfumes Tracey and his ex-wife favored. But he couldn't identify the light, herbal scent wafting around him now. The fragrance was provocative, especially as she turned and gazed up at him with those devastatingly long-lashed eyes. He felt as if he stood on the edge of an unfathomable pool, teetering on the rim.

"I won't read them," she announced firmly. "I'll have nightmares. I can type without reading and run spelling and grammar checks with the software, but I don't think I can edit them, as Miss MacGregor does. You didn't mention anything about editing when you hired me."

That was because he preferred dissociating Tarant Mott from Seth Wyatt. Still, her declaration irritated him. He'd hired an executive assistant. Assistants did editing. "If you can work in the real-life nightmare of a hospital, Miss Cochran, surely you can manage my books. They're only words, after all. They won't hurt you." It had taken him years, but he'd learned to be brutal with people. They would walk all over him otherwise. Still, he winced in regret as she stiffened at his words.

"I quit working the emergency room for good reason, Mr. Wyatt. I'm incapable of developing the hard shell necessary for coping with that amount of human tragedy. It's probably one of the reasons I ended up in administration instead of on the wards. If I have nightmares, I want combat pay."

The little gold digger meant to screw as much money out of him as she could. He hadn't thought those big innocent eyes could hide that much greed, but she'd succeeded in driving her price up to exorbitant heights just by blinking her long lashes.

Considering what else he might get for his money, Seth let his gaze drop from her face to the rest of her luscious little body. She wasn't the willowy model type like Tracey. She stood barely higher than his shoulder. But the atrocious polyester suit curved in all the right places. Heated blood surged to his loins at the thought of peeling back that red jacket and finding what lay beneath. He hadn't meant to approach her, but she offered major temptation to a starving man. And obviously, greed ran high on her list of priorities. He had lots of experience with scheming women. He could handle it.

"What other services must I pay extra for, Miss Cochran?" he asked cynically, expecting her to name a price.

Her eyes narrowed. "I think I have more than enough duties on my roster already, Mr. Wyatt. Continue looking at me like that, and I'll remember everything I ever heard about the law against sexual harassment."

To Seth's astonishment, she swung around and brushed right past him, walking out the door without another word.

Damn, but he'd just been rejected by a hick from Nowheresville.

That was just the inspiration he needed to create murder and mayhem.

SEVEN

"She's filing another custody suit, Seth," the voice over the telephone warned. "I just received the papers this morning."

Seth buried his hand in his hair and pulled. "She hasn't taken advantage of the weekends the judge granted her," he said through clenched teeth. "What pretext can she use?"

"We'll find that out in court, but it sounds as if she must have new evidence against you to try this stunt again. Have you taken to drinking in public, picked up a gay lover, something I need to know?"

Seth knew Morris meant to be funny. Someone should have told him lawyers shouldn't tell jokes. Swinging around, he stared out the window at the front lawn. He'd seen the red Mazda spin up the drive half an hour earlier. He'd heard Chad's howls of rage halt shortly thereafter. He hadn't seen any sign of his new assistant arriving at her desk, but his gratitude for the silence had put him in a lenient frame of mind. He bit down on his pencil now as giggles floated through the hall outside.

"I don't even leave Chad with a baby-sitter, for pity's sake. Listen to me! I don't even swear anymore. I gave up smoking. I don't drink. I'm with my son more than any other parent in the entire country. She can't say I'm an unsuitable father.

There's not one blamed thing she can pin on me. She must have someone willing to falsify evidence. Get a mole in her lawyer's office, Morris. Find out what's going on."

Seth tried to control the red rage throbbing through him as the lawyer continued the conversation. He turned back to his computer screen and scanned his e-mail. He clenched and unclenched his fist around the pencil. He reached for a toffee and crunched it in two as soon as it hit his tongue. He still wanted to punch something.

She couldn't have Chad. No lying, scheming, two-timing bitch would get her hands on his son. She had no proof that he'd had more than one drink that night. She had no proof that his recklessness had driven that car over the cliff. But he had proof enough that she and her layabout new husband needed his money, that they had lied and schemed to get Chad before, just as they lied and schemed to do it now. Natalie wanted revenge, but that bastard of a husband of hers wanted money. Seth wondered if Natalie knew how much of her funds her lover-boy had gone through since the divorce. He'd kept close watch on them over the years. One thing his father had taught him, never take your eyes off the enemy.

As he hung up the phone, Seth heard screeches from the front lawn, and he swiveled in his desk chair to look outside again.

A bathing-suit-clad nymph cavorted on the lawn with an equally scantily attired Chad. Seth dropped the pencil in his hand as his son swung his wheelchair on the paved drive, aimed his water gun, and sent a shrieking Miss Cochran running after him with a similar gadget. She must have stopped and bought a water gun of her own.

For a few seconds, Seth sat there in blank incomprehension. He'd never seen Chad racing his wheelchair across concrete before. He'd never seen him in just shorts, his skinny arms wielding a toy gun like a professional while he punched the electronic buttons of the chair with a dancer's skill. Seth blinked in pure disbelief before his temper got a stranglehold on him, and he jumped from his chair, roaring.

Pippa saw the Grim Reaper flying through the front doors first. Wearing his usual daytime attire of black shirt and chinos, he didn't look quite so dangerous this morning. With a grin, she yelled to Chad, "Here comes Bad Bart! Bust him, Buster!"

Shrieking with manic glee, Chad swung his chair and sprayed a tidal wave across his father's broad chest while Pippa charged up from the side and aimed for her employer's head. Within seconds, the Reaper looked more like a drowned rat than a dangerous monster. A mad drowned rat.

"What the devil do you think you're doing?" he roared, more at Pippa than his son.

Unstoppable, Chad squirted him again, smack in the belly this time. Pippa tried not to admire the result of soaked cotton clinging to a taut abdomen.

"The hose, Bart!" she yelled. "Secure the hose!"

Not too slow for a man obviously clinging to his last shred of temper, Wyatt dashed for the hose they'd used to refill their guns and shot it full blast at Pippa. To Chad's shrieks of delight, Pippa dodged and fled behind the wheelchair. Heaven only knew what the water would do to the electronics, but exhilarated, she didn't care. She'd accomplished what she'd set out to do—make Chad laugh.

Chad shrieked and tried swinging the chair in circles so he could chase Pippa off, but she danced around behind him, using him as a shield.

"Don't let Bad Bart get me, cowboy! I'm just a helpless female, remember? You're obliged to protect me."

A burly black man appeared from the rear of the house, and the maniac gardener materialized, cackling, from the shrubbery. To their amusement, Chad got off a head shot, hitting his father squarely between the eyes.

"We win! He's deader than a doornail. Bury him on Boot Hill, pardners!" Pippa called to their audience. She thought she might need their protection shortly. Obviously, plain ordinary old water didn't cool her employer's hot head.

"Haven't you ever heard of water shortages, Miss Cochran?" Seth asked ominously as he dropped the hose and stalked closer.

"We're pumping it from the pool," she replied indignantly. "Just ask Mr. Brown. He set it up for us. If we can't swim in the blamed thing, we might as well use it somehow."

"I want to go swimming, Dad." Chad chose that moment to throw his challenge into the ring. "Pippa says she can teach me."

"Her name's Miss Cochran, and she's supposed to be sitting at her desk right now, working." Seth swung around to confront their audience. "Just like the lot of you. I'm not paying you to stand there gawking."

The big man crossed his arms over his massive chest and glared back. "You fired me, remember?"

"So, you're rehired. Go unplug this blasted hose. Then you can take Miss Cochran back to town when she's finished packing."

Uh-oh. Pippa crossed her arms over her chest in imitation of the chauffeur. Chad instantly set up a howl that should have alerted half the valley of an approaching storm. She knuckled him on the head to shut him up, and he shot her a resentful glare over his shoulder.

"It's only a little after one, Mr. Wyatt," she informed him coldly. "I made good time getting back from the airport. If I choose to use my lunch hour playing with Chad, you have no reason for complaint. Besides, I finished your chapters this morning."

She had a moment of triumph while the mighty Seth Wyatt regrouped. Then his menacing eyes narrowed and his cutting voice ended her brief victory. "Chad is highly susceptible to pneumonia. Overexertion, overexcitement, and cold water on top of a chest cold will have him in the hospital. You're a nurse, Miss Cochran. You should know better."

"If he exercised more, his lungs wouldn't be so weak," she retorted. Knowing she was right in this didn't quite ease her guilt. Yes, Chad should exercise. But she probably hadn't chosen the best time or place. She did know better. She was just too wrapped up in making the child like her.

Chad prevented any further reasonable confrontation. "I want to swim!" he screeched. "I want to swim! I want to swim!"

His face contorted into the red rage of an infant, and his hands bunched into fists as he pounded the controls and sent his chair flying toward his father. Hitting the edge of the pavement, the chair tipped, propelling Chad outward. Seth leaped to his rescue, catching him just before he hit the ground. Oblivious to his near disaster, Chad pounded at his father's shoulders, screaming at the top of his lungs. Deep-set eyes glared their rage at Pippa as Seth lifted his son and endured the pounding without a flinch.

"You have half an hour to pack and get out of here, Miss Cochran."

"You and Chad have the rest of your lives to suffer, Mr. Wyatt," she retorted. She had nothing to lose now. She might as well say everything that needed saying. "I'm a licensed professional. I've had ten years' experience in nursing. I have seen children in wheelchairs. I have seen grown men in wheelchairs. They are not cripples. They do not need to be wrapped in cotton batting. They can swim, play basketball, enter races, do almost anything anyone else can do. Your treatment of him is the next best thing to child abuse."

She spun on her heel and stalked up the drive before he could lambaste her with any further tirades. If she had to surrender, she would do it with all flags flying.

* * *

Chad's high-pitched shrieks of outrage reached renewed heights.

Seth hung on to his twisting, squirming, screaming son while he watched Miss Cochran's bewitchingly curved rear end clothed in spandex parade up his front stairs and into the house. She probably dripped a trail of water across Nana's neatly polished floors, but his mind wasn't focused on that any more than it was on his son's screams or Pippa's bathing suit. Only her last words had registered fully, and his thoughts gnawed on them furiously now. Child abuse. She had accused him of child abuse.

"Anything else you need in town when I go in?" Doug asked dryly from behind him. "Or am I packing my bags, too?"

The child in Seth's arms wept openly now, clinging to his neck and sobbing as if his heart would break. She'd accused him of child abuse. He'd watched over Chad every single day of his life, hired the best tutors, bought the most educational toys, provided Chad with everything a child's heart could desire. How could she possibly accuse him of child abuse?

Seth wanted to wring someone's neck. He didn't know how else to react to the emotions raging through him. He needed to punch something, kick something, fire someone. Anything to release the frustration threatening to explode through his skin.

He turned and glared at Doug. Doug had been his friend since college. As much of a friend as he'd ever had, anyway. He didn't have real friends. They'd shared drinks together. Seth had helped Doug cheat so he could pass a course and stay on the team. Doug had given him free passes to the games. Seth had pulled Doug out of the gutter, cleaned him up, and given him a job after he'd lost his NFL position. Doug quit once a week. Seth fired him every day in between. They never talked about their problems. They didn't need to.

Seth dropped Chad into Doug's arms. "Dunk him in the pool, then take him back upstairs."

Giving Seth a doubtful look, Doug took the sobbing boy,

threw him over his shoulder, and jogged down the path around the house. Seth could trust Doug with the boy. He wasn't so certain he could trust Miss High-and-Mighty Cochran.

Stalking toward the house, belatedly realizing he was soaked from head to foot, Seth headed for a showdown.

Pippa jumped a foot as the door behind her slammed open. Still furious, she had only gone so far as to locate her suitcase and throw a drawer of newly purchased underwear into it. Too blind-mad to think, she hadn't bothered dressing, hadn't even thought about it. Until the door snapped open and Seth Wyatt stood there.

That was all it took to make her realize she stood in his stylish mansion, in his impressive suite of rooms, wearing nothing but a dripping bathing suit. Unaccustomed to that kind of awareness of herself, Pippa debated turning around. Maybe if she ignored him, he would go away.

Not bloody likely. Grabbing her polyester nightshirt, the one that imitated silk, she jerked it over her head, blessing Meg for making her buy it. Setting her jaw, she swung around.

She could see rage in the way Seth's black brows pulled together in a straight line and his jaw clenched so tightly that the muscle jerked over strong cheekbones. She couldn't imagine why he was here unless he meant to dismember her personally and ship her back to town inside her suitcase. But he clung to the doorknob as if it were a life raft and remained where he was.

"What do you mean, child abuse?" he roared.

Pippa blinked. She couldn't remember throwing that particular insult, but she supposed she might have. She'd been too angry to think clearly. As he was now. Warily, she threw open another drawer and removed her new collection of shorts. She'd sent for her old clothes. She wondered what would happen if they showed up on Seth's doorstep long after she was gone.

"People who tie their children to beds and don't let them out of the house are child abusers. They're arrested in any state that I know of," she informed him coolly.

"That's ridiculous!" His roar should have rattled the windows, but they had obviously been built for men like Wyatt. Not a single pane shivered. "He has a chair. He isn't tied to the bed. I had the house remodeled for the chair. Where in hell else would he go that he can't get there with the chair?"

Pippa stopped and stared at him. "Is that really what you think? That he has everything he needs right here in this house? Where did you grow up, Mr. Wyatt? Inside a computer?"

"I grew up here! It's a perfectly normal home. If it was good enough for me . . ."

She shook her head. ". . . it's good enough for your son. And here I thought California had progressive thinkers. You make me feel right at home. Go away, Mr. Wyatt. I've got to get dressed if I'm leaving here in half an hour."

"If Natalie is paying you to spy on me and tell the court that I'm abusing Chad, so help me, I swear I'll see you never work again in any state in this country!"

This was well beyond her patience or ability to understand. Pinching her eyebrows together in an effort to quell the headache that threatened, Pippa said politely, "I have no idea what you're talking about, and right about now, I don't care. I just want out of this madhouse before I make a bigger fool of myself. Leave me alone so I can go in peace."

"The devil if I let you go so you can take my son away from me! Whatever she's paying you, I'll pay you more. Just tell me what the hell you mean about child abuse. I've given Chad everything I know how to give. What else can I possibly do?"

Somewhere behind the roars of rage Pippa thought she actually heard a note of pain. Surprised, she glanced at the man in the doorway again. He still looked like the Grim Reaper, like an iron man untouched by any human emotion except anger. She must have imagined the plea in his voice because she wanted to hear it. He was just seeking some means of controlling her or his son or the person called Natalie. She knew better than to fall for those tactics. Still, if there were any chance . . .

"If you won't listen to me, then take your son to doctors familiar with wheelchair-bound patients. They'll tell you he needs interaction with other kids his age, that he needs physical activity suiting his age group. He is no longer an infant, much as it would be convenient for you to think of him that way. He's a growing boy, and he needs stimulation you cannot provide in this mausoleum. You are doing him no favor by sheltering him from the slings and arrows of real life. He must learn to deal with reality on his own, not from behind the shelter of your wealth and protection. Would you like to yell at me some more so you don't have to listen to what I'm saying?"

She could see his tension as he squeezed the door frame. She hadn't been as polite as she could have been. She had thought him impervious to pain. But some emotion wrinkled his forehead, and anguish flickered briefly in his eyes. She turned away so she wouldn't see it again.

"Chad's doctor says he is too frail for crowds. Exposure to a variety of germs would almost certainly make him ill, and he hasn't the strength for fighting it. Are you telling me you know more than his doctor?"

"I'm telling you that doctors come in a variety of capabilities and the one you're using is living in the Dark Ages. The medical profession isn't perfect. Doctors are not gods. If you'd like, I can call a few of the doctors I know in Kentucky and ask for recommendations out here. Always get second opinions." Still unable to look at him, Pippa folded her clothing more neatly and straightened the contents of the suitcase. She remembered having this struggle when her mother first became ill. Had her mother gone to a competent physician in the first place, the cancer might not have advanced as far as it had. But her mother insisted on going to the doctor she'd gone to most of her life. Loyalty had its place, but not when it came to a person's health. Pippa would like to scream that at the stubborn man behind her, but it wasn't her business.

"Chad's doctor saved his life. If I can't trust him, I couldn't trust any other."

"How old was Chad when this doctor saved his life?" she asked wearily. She didn't want this to hurt so much, but that frail boy needed a guardian angel right now. It shouldn't be any of her concern, but she'd never learned to keep her nose where it belonged.

"Barely nine months."

She heard the pain this time, the agony just below the surface, and it ground into her, as it always did. She'd gone into hospital administration for just this reason. Tightening her lips, she searched for a suitable reply.

"An infant of nine months is very different from a child of six. A physician who has the capacity for life-giving surgery is not necessarily a physician who understands a patient's needs outside the operating room." She didn't want to lecture, but she figured she only had this one chance to make him see. "Wellness is affected by emotional health as well as physical health. You may be protecting Chad from physical illness but not emotional illness. He shouldn't be getting colds sitting around here where he's scarcely exposed to any germs at all, but he does. This isn't necessarily because his health is delicate but because his mental and emotional health is depressed. Don't rely on my advice. Find a new physician and ask him."

Seth's silence forced her to look at him. The fury had finally seeped from his face. Briefly, he looked like a heartbroken father, until he saw her glance. Then he stiffened and went cold again. "Get me those recommendations. Then get dressed and down to the office. The blasted phone has been ringing off the hook all day."

He swung around and walked away.

Pippa stared at the place where Seth had stood not seconds before. Had she imagined that last command? And if she hadn't, did she want to obey it? Who in their right mind would continue working in a madhouse like this?

Someone as insane as the inmates. Giving her suitcase a look of resignation, Pippa opened the nearly empty closet in search of a suitable working dress.

EIGHT

Still making notes, Pippa set the receiver back on the hook, underlined a name on the list beneath her hand, and sat back to take a breath. The phone rang again.

She eyed the jangling machine with disfavor. Sleek, black, and sporting half a dozen buttons, it epitomized the efficient monstrosity of Seth Wyatt's operations. One line related to his printing businesses, another to the publishing houses, still another seemed designated for the editors, agents, and whatnot for his writing career. She'd become quite proficient with the hold button while manipulating those three lines. The last two buttons hadn't blinked once since she'd sat down. One of them was blinking now.

Shoving a strand of hair back, Pippa answered, "Wyatt Enterprises." She had no instructions for this line, and Wyatt had expressly told her he didn't want to be disturbed for anything short of a spurting jugular.

"Seth? Where is Seth?" a woman's irritable voice demanded. "Is this Miss MacGregor? Let me talk with my son."

Son. Uh-oh. Family line, Pippa concluded.

Her next thought was one of amazement. The Grim Reaper had a mother. Unbelievable. Actually, if she thought about it, this one sounded every bit as impossible and annoying as

Wyatt. And years of experience had taught her a great deal about voices.

"This is Phillippa Cochran. Mrs. Wyatt?" She ended on a questioning note. In this day and age of multiple divorce and marriage, one could never be certain.

"Where is Miss MacGregor? I want to speak with my son, Miss Cochran. Put him on now." A hacking cough followed this command.

Double uh-oh. The maniac gardener's words as he rammed the BMW into the oak were strangely comforting, if not prophetic. "Uh-oh" covered it all. The lady already sounded furious. What did she do now?

Remembering an uncle who had only called when angry, upsetting her mother often during her illness, Pippa chose the tactic that worked best on him. "I'm sorry, Mrs. Wyatt, he isn't available at the moment. Could I have him call you back?"

"I know perfectly well he's sitting right there working on one of his wretched books, Miss Cochran. If you don't put me through to him right now, I'll have you fired. My son *always* takes my calls."

Well, the lady wasn't dumb, at least. Pippa was beginning to understand where her employer had garnered some of his bad habits. Double checking her list of callers Wyatt would accept and finding his mother nowhere among the honored, Pippa clucked her tongue against her teeth and grinned. In for a penny, in for a pound.

"I've already been fired three times since my arrival, Mrs. Wyatt. I suspect I'll withstand another firing. I'll be happy to pass on your message when he becomes available. Or is there anything I can help you with in the meantime?"

"Miss MacGregor always puts me through." The imperious voice developed a distinct whine. "What has this world come to if a mother can't talk with her own son?"

Pippa tipped her chair back, stared at the elegantly carved wooden ceiling, and wondered if her job description included counseling lonely mothers. "Well, Mrs. Wyatt, you know," she drawled, stalling for an effective reply, "my mother never called me at work unless it was an emergency. She respected my need to do the best job possible while I worked, God bless her soul."

Silence.

Pippa chewed the eraser tip of her pencil and listened to the rapid clacking of computer keys from behind Seth's closed office door. He wrote his manuscripts in longhand. She wondered what he was doing if not writing. As she sat patiently waiting for the next bombshell to explode, she knew better than to think he would appreciate this little conversation she was having with his mother. She ought to get combat pay for working in his household.

"Your mother is dead, Miss Cochran?"

Her smoker's sandpaper voice wasn't much better than her whining one. Sighing, Pippa returned her feet to the floor. "Yes, she died this past year. She taught me a great deal about life, and I try to follow her maxims every day. 'Smile and keep your chin up, Pippa,' she used to say. 'Stand on your own two feet and you'll never have to beg,' she told me. My mother was a very wise woman. Is there anything I can help you with, Mrs. Wyatt?"

"Just exactly who are you, Miss Cochran?"

Ha, at least imperiousness had replaced whimpering and whining. Pippa smiled at this progress. "I'm Mr. Wyatt's temporary assistant while Miss MacGregor is on leave of absence."

The silence following her declaration was shorter than the earlier one. "Have Wyatt send a car for me. I think I'm overdue for a visit."

Pippa wrinkled her nose in dismay. She had the distinct notion Wyatt would not be pleased with this development. "Of course, Mrs. Wyatt," she purred, thinking rapidly. "Chad will be delighted to see you, I'm certain. He has a cold and he's quite bored while confined to his room. Mr. Wyatt is on deadline and doesn't have much time—"

"Forget the car." Abruptly, she changed her tune. "Simply tell my son that Natalie is on the warpath again. *That* should have him calling me."

The phone slammed in her ear. Charming family, Pippa observed, hanging up the receiver. From the way her employer had said the name "Natalie" earlier, she could assume his mother was quite correct. The invisible Natalie invoked violent emotion in Pippa's already volatile employer. She wondered if Seth Wyatt ever experienced emotions of a pleasant nature.

Even his sexual innuendoes—if that was what they were—had contained more insult and anger than pleasure or anticipation. She would have slapped any other man silly for his offer of money, but for some reason, Seth's insult had seemed aimed at himself as much as at her. She hadn't encountered that kind of self-loathing before.

Deciding her job didn't include psychoanalysis of her rigid employer, Pippa picked up the list of names and numbers she had compiled before Mrs. Wyatt interfered. She nibbled on the pencil, glanced at the closed door, and decisively picked up the receiver and punched out the first number. For the kind of money Wyatt paid her, she would be the best damned self-directed administrative assistant in the country.

Half an hour later, with the information she needed and a faxed parental consent form in hand, Pippa penciled in the appointment on her calendar, underlined the doctor's name, and smiled with satisfaction at a job well done.

The closed door to Wyatt's office slammed open, and the Grim Reaper stalked through. Thick dark hair standing on end, a day's beard shadowing the harsh lines of his jaw, he appeared ready to behead the first unfortunate crossing his path.

As he turned his bleary glare on Pippa, she cheerfully passed him the fax.

He scribbled his consent without reading it. "Have you read the manuscript yet?"

"I told you I would type it but I won't read it." Pippa sat back in her chair—a wonderfully supple leather with lumbar support and heated massage—picked up the stack of paper on her right, and dropped it on top of his messages. "Here's yesterday's work for your approval."

"Yesterday's work was crap." He viciously plowed his hand through his hair, stalked up and down the narrow office floor, then slammed his fist into the wall, until the framed covers jumped. He swung his furious gaze back to Pippa. "How in hell am I supposed to talk plot with you if you haven't read the damned book?"

"I'm a nurse, Mr. Wyatt, not an editor. You knew that when you hired me. I am a very efficient administrator. I have typed up your scribblings, edited and formatted them, I've answered your phones, opened your mail, paid your bills, filed your invoices, and dealt with your irate mother."

She twined her fingers together and rested her elbows on the chair's broad arms. "I'm perfectly prepared to sit here and let you throw slings and arrows at me if that will help. Why don't you tell me what the problem is, rather than make me read the gore?"

"It's not gore." He gave her a disgruntled look, paced up and down some more, then decided to explain. "I write horror, not gore. The world is full of horrifying things, and people want the thrill of experiencing them as well as the triumph of controlling them. I can give them in the pages of a book what they cannot have in real life."

"Mad gophers?" Pippa asked, raising a satirical eyebrow.

"Ha! So you did read it." He swung around and glared at her, bristling with male rage and pride. "I've dug myself into a hole . . ."

". . . a gopher hole," Pippa murmured unrepentantly.

Seth ignored that. "A hero, by definition, must act heroically. He can't run, he can't cry, he can't wait for someone else to solve his problems. But in yesterday's pages I dug my hero in so deep he cannot possibly get himself out. What do I have him do, carry explosives in his back pocket? That's patently ridiculous."

She really hadn't read the pages. The reference to a gopher had briefly caught her fancy, but the material was far from whimsy, and shuddering, she had shut off her brain as she typed after that. But Seth's talk about heroes rescuing themselves struck another chord.

"Must heroes stand alone?" she asked diffidently, not at all certain of her thoughts. "Aren't heroes more heroic for having friends they can call on? Like Jimmy Stewart in *It's a Wonderful Life*. Alone, he was helpless, but with his friends—"

Seth flung the telephone book against the wall, quite a feat given the size of the tome, Pippa noted with admiration.

"I don't write sentimental claptrap, Miss Cochran. I write about the dark forces that inhabit this earth. About the only thing that could save my hero at this point is if an equally dark force . . ." Clenching his fists, he stopped in midpace and stared blankly at the wall. "That's it. An equally dark force. I can do that."

Distracted, he swung back to the desk, riffled through the newly typed manuscript pages, and idly picked up his phone messages. "Where's Chad?"

He was reading the messages and Pippa didn't think he was listening, but she answered anyway. "He's resting. Mr. Brown is reading him a story."

She was mistaken. Wyatt's shaggy head jerked up and his cold glare fixed on her at once. "Doug is reading him a story?"

Pippa shrugged. "It's better for him than moping around in his apartment feeling sorry for himself. Everyone needs to feel useful. And Chad's quite thrilled."

"Doug reading storybooks," Seth muttered, wandering toward his office. "The NFL's best linebacker reading bunny books. I swear . . ." The door slammed after him, cutting off any further commentary.

"And thank you so much, Miss Cochran," Pippa mocked, glancing at the closed door. "Job well done, keep up the good work."

The phone rang. Swearing, she picked up the other unmarked line, and heard Mary Margaret on the other end.

"Wow, Pippa! I found the number in the book but didn't think I'd actually get you. Why haven't you called? I've been worried sick."

"Did you think he ate me for dinner?" she asked wryly. "No one's tried to push me in the oven yet."

Mary Margaret laughed. "I'd think it far more likely if you pushed Wyatt in the oven. Have you?"

Pippa grinned. "You've always known me too well. It's been entertaining, to say the least. I'll tell you Sunday when I come to town. How are the kids?"

"They're fine, full of questions, but fine." She hesitated, then asked cautiously, "I don't suppose you've heard if he has any plans for rebuilding the printing plant, do you?"

Understanding the importance of the question from Mary Margaret's hesitation, Pippa sought some reassuring reply, but there wasn't any. "He's working on something else right now. I don't think he's given thought to anything beyond that." Uncertain as to whether the town knew of Seth's alter ego, Pippa refrained from mentioning book deadlines.

"Oh, well, it was only a thought. The plant was archaic and probably needed tearing down before someone got seriously hurt. We just hoped he might . . ."

"I don't think he's given to altruism," Pippa offered dryly. "If he tore down the old plant, he had a reason; it's just not uppermost in his mind right now. I'll let you know if I hear anything else."

After making plans for Sunday and hanging up, Pippa decided her duties included checking on Chad at regular intervals. Hearing only silence from behind the closed door and concluding Wyatt was writing, she turned on the elaborate voice mail system and hurried up the flagstone stairs. Why in the world anyone would make a foyer of wood and stairs of stone was beyond her comprehension, but she wasn't an architect.

She reached Chad's room just as Doug Brown tiptoed out, closing the door. The sight of a six-foot, two-hundred-something-pound man tiptoeing should have boggled her senses, but he did it with a certain degree of grace. She grinned as he looked up and caught her watching. "Did you tie him up and gag him?"

Doug eyed her uncertainly. "Nah, the cold medicine knocked him out pretty much. And he insisted on hearing one of his dad's books. That had him snoring quick enough."

Pippa raised her eyebrows in surprise. "I should have thought one of those would have had him up with nightmares for the rest of his life."

Doug shrugged. "They ain't exactly kids' literature. He didn't understand half the words." Shifting from foot to foot, obviously uncomfortable in her presence, he blurted out another topic on his mind. "Did you do something about calling them other doctors you talked about? That kid needs to get out of here."

Pippa beamed. "I surely did. I've even made an appointment for the day after tomorrow. Do I take him in Miss MacGregor's car or will you drive?"

"The Beamer's still in the shop, and the Jag's too small for Chad's chair. I can clean up that old Rolls, if you like. Kinda been wantin' to take it out for a spin."

"A Rolls? He has a Rolls?" Pippa rolled her eyes in delight, then grinned mischievously. "I don't suppose he'd let me drive, would he?"

"No, sirree, ma'am," Doug answered emphatically. "Ain't no way. That old car belonged to his daddy and ain't nobody touches it. I figger I'll have to get down on my knees and crawl before he'll let me get it out. And he'll probably give me a sobriety test before he hands over the keys."

Pippa wrinkled her nose. "One *hint* of alcohol on your breath, Mr. Brown, and you'll not even get close to Mr. Wyatt. I've got a nose for liquor better than any test mankind can develop. And much as I disliked it, I worked enough emergency room shifts to recognize drugs when I see them, so don't bother with those either. This is a family outing, and if you need sedation for a family outing, we don't need you."

Brown drew himself up in an intimidating stance that should have sent her screaming down the hall, given that he could have bench-pressed her just as easily as weights.

"I don't do drugs, Miss Know-It-All, and I ain't about to hurt that kid none neither, and just you remember it."

Well, perhaps she had been just a little hasty in calling this one, Pippa reflected as she took a step backward. Nah, she decided a moment later in Brown's own inimitable words as she watched him rumble down the hallway, book in hand—in a household of egotists, maniacs, and admitted alcoholics, she had to give as good as she got.

She had learned something about survival in these past months.

NINE

"Why don't you just die, Seth?"

The voice whispered sibilantly through sluggish brain cells. The steady drip-drip that had filled untold nights and days registered more clearly than the whisperer. The drip had provided constant companionship in the absence of human voices. Sweat broke out on his brow as he struggled to understand the whispered words.

"If you died, it would make life easier for all of us, Seth—for me, for your son, for your employees, for everyone. Even your mother would be happier."

Some word or inflection in this string of sounds connected. Urgency gripped his breathing. He struggled to grasp the voice, but pain shot like an arrow bolt through his head, driving conscious thought into hiding again.

"I wonder what would happen if I pulled out this little needle in your arm?" the voice asked wonderingly.

The sheer shock of that innocent tone shot another warning rocketing through his brain. Again, sluggish brain cells fought for coherence. The drip-drip echoed louder. A siren in the distance screamed closer. Only sound registered. Blackness wrapped the void of his consciousness.

"Or what if I just loosened it a little? I don't suppose you would be so obliging as to knock it free, would you? You were never obliging in your whole life. I'm not sure you even know the rest of us exist."

Bitterness roiled up inside of him, an ancient bitterness accompanied by a deep despair.

"The only thing that ever interested you was your damned work. Do you see any of your books sitting at your bedside now? If I didn't have to pretend concern in case you die, I wouldn't be here either. If you dare live, I swear I'll take your son away."

Fury sprang full blown through his entire core, parting the bitterness and despair like storm clouds flung by the wind. His son! What had they done to his son? Where was Chad? He couldn't think, couldn't open his eyes, couldn't move, but he fought for consciousness. The urge to grab the whisperer by the throat surged through him.

"I could loosen that for you," the voice said thoughtfully. "I could tell them it bothered you and I just meant to help. Do you know what you've done to your son, you bastard? Do you have any idea?"

Icy fingers gripped his arm. He could feel his arm. He stretched his fingers, then balled them into a fist as unseen hands worked the strap until it loosened. Pain shot straight through every muscle. The word "Chad!" screamed in his throat. He couldn't get the sound past his tongue. The woolly haze of drugs seeped through his brain again, but the terrifying emotions wouldn't die. He fought against the drugs and the pain.

"You've turned Chad into a vegetable," the voice continued pleasantly, relentlessly. "He'll never walk again. Maybe never talk. It would have been better if you had killed him outright. It would have been even better if you had just killed yourself!"

Agony! He writhed in semiconscious pain, fighting off this nightmare. If he could just scream, maybe it would go away. But he couldn't. He had to get up, had to run to Chad's room, check that he breathed, as he had a dozen times a night since his son was born. He had to touch that cherished little face with its serious expression, the dark brows all drawn down in deep baby thoughts. He would tuck the covers over the rounded posterior hunched up with knees drawn under. He'd never understood how the child could sleep like that, but Chad had since he'd learned the trick of rolling over. The doctors had said babies should sleep on their backs, and he'd turned him over countless times during the night. But Chad determinedly returned to his favorite position until Seth couldn't bear disturbing him again. He would go to Chad's room, see that he slept soundly, that his favorite teddy awaited his waking, that he didn't get cold from the drafts in that spacious, elegantly decorated emptiness his wife called a nursery.

"Damn you, Seth, I hate you. I despise you, do you hear me? You've destroyed my life, destroyed your son, destroyed everything you've ever touched. You deserve to die. I'm taking everything, do you understand? I'll take everything. No judge in the world will deny me. Do everyone a favor, including yourself; give up and die."

The black clouds swept back again, obscuring little more than the sound of heels tap-tapping to the door. He could move his arm now. He could feel the pain of the needle piercing it. He wanted to jerk the needle out, get rid of this one irritating source of pain. Yet the pinprick in his arm scarcely compared to the agony in his heart.

The voice lied. Surely it lied. His son slept soundly in his crib, where he belonged. He'd checked on him carefully, watched over him every minute. Nothing could happen to Chad. He wouldn't let it.

Despair choked a cry from him when he couldn't move his feet out of the bed so he could look one more time. He must see Chad. His son had just taken his first baby steps . . . when? Yesterday . . .

The piercing agony shot through him so surely, Seth woke.

Sitting up, he wiped sweat from his dripping brow. His head pounded and his arm throbbed just as it had that night over five years ago.

The nightmare wouldn't go away. He couldn't remember it now any more than any of the other times he'd woken in pain, straining at invisible bonds. But the bleakness and despair lingered for days.

He turned and checked the infant monitor beside the bed to make certain it worked. Turning up the volume, he could hear Chad's labored breathing. He didn't have to go in there and bother his son. The boy was fine. He just had a cold.

But Seth couldn't rest easy until he made sure.

Steadying his shaking nerves, Seth grabbed a robe and padded barefoot through the darkness in the direction of his son's room.

Snarling at the morning light streaming through the foyer windows as it hit his sleep-deprived eyes, Seth halted in midstride at the tableau in the foyer below him.

"Where the hell do you think you're going?" From the loft, he noted his capricious assistant in jeans and what vaguely resembled a pirate's billowing white shirt, and Chad and Doug waiting on the drive. "I didn't give you permission to go anywhere."

"You signed a parental permission form for a new doctor just the other day," she reminded him. "I wangled an immediate appointment with one in L.A. We'll be late if we don't go now."

Stunned, Seth glanced from Pippa to his son sitting in the sunshine outside. Chad had never gone anywhere without him. Never. This beastly little elf was beyond presumptuous. He could strangle her. He needed to finish this blasted chapter, he was waiting on an important call from the printing plant in New Jersey, and now he'd have to drop everything and spend the day driving to L.A. and back.

"I don't have time," he growled. "Check my schedule and make a new appointment. I can't go today."

"You don't need to go." Impatience edged her voice. "Chad's perfectly safe with us. I've turned on the voice mail, Nana will screen the calls at noon and pass any important messages to you with your lunch. I'll type your chapter when we get back this afternoon. Let it go, Wyatt." Looking up at him, she tapped her foot with undisguised annoyance.

He narrowed his eyes as he contemplated his recalcitrant employee. He could throw her over his shoulder and heave her into the pool, he supposed, but she didn't appear in the least concerned about her fate. Damned defiant little autocrat.

Seth gritted his teeth and tried to summon all the caustic words he knew, but he stopped short.

Amazed, he realized he was actually *relieved* that he didn't have to go. He hadn't had an entire day to himself since Chad's birth, and certainly not since the accident.

"Chad hates doctors," he called as guilt made him pause.

"Understandably," she agreed. "But I told him we're going to Universal Studios afterward. He'll get up and walk there if I don't hurry."

Deflated, unable to argue with her logic, but fighting this separation from his son every step of the way, Seth shoved his hands into his pockets and glowered at the gleaming Rolls in the drive. "That car will break down before it gets halfway there."

"I'll call your mother and have her send her driver," she promised maliciously.

"You've even got *her* eating out of your hand," he muttered disagreeably. "If *I* asked for her driver, she'd insist she had to go shopping first."

Pippa smiled, and this time Seth was convinced the look in her eye was malicious.

"She has to get through me to reach you. I'll have her

sending me Godivas before the week's out. I *told* you I was good."

Too damned good for his own good, Seth agreed silently, looking anywhere but at Pippa's cheerful countenance. He understood women who whined and complained and flirted easier than he understood this willful leprechaun. What the hell was her agenda anyway? Everyone had one.

But he couldn't find hers. He'd had Dirk check to make certain she wasn't one of Natalie's minions, but Dirk hadn't been able to verify that she'd flown here from Kentucky as she'd said. Natalie could possibly have hired her as a spy. He needed to be wary. Still, the personnel officer for the previous employer had waxed enthusiastic over her former employee, and he'd found no connection to Natalie anywhere.

"I want a report before you leave the doctor's office," he informed her. "Call my private line."

"Aye, aye, Captain." Before he could halt her with further admonitions, she dashed out the door and down the steps.

The silence of the house echoed in his ears as the car rolled away.

For the first time in six years, he was totally alone.

The eerie silence gave him an idea.

Feeling sinfully free, Seth hurried down to his office and his favorite Mont Blanc pen.

"And there was this monster tyrannosaurus! With blood dripping from its teeth. And we rode . . ."

Seth tuned out his son's excited chatter. The boy was wound so tight, Seth was amazed he didn't spring right out of his chair.

"Did the doctor give you anything to sedate him?" he asked wryly, directing his question toward his "assistant," who was transcribing messages from his voice mail.

"Physical exercise," she murmured absently.

Chad growled, emulating a dinosaur and rattling his chair in accompaniment.

Physical exercise, right, Seth grumbled to himself. Since admiring his assistant's competence had led to admiring the tilt of her head and the way her shiny hair bounced against her bare arm, he figured he could use a little physical exercise, too. Maybe he should take the boy out and teach him a few martial arts lessons. That ought to work well when Chad tried kicks.

He shouldn't be so grumpy. He'd written two chapters in the oasis of peace he'd had today. But he still resented Pippa's experiencing Chad's first visit to Universal. Torn by conflicting emotions, he took his resentment out on the only target available.

"You have a call from your lawyer," his target said from her seat at the desk. "He wants you to call him immediately."

His lawyer. Damn. How had he forgotten Natalie and her threats? His mind deteriorated to ashes when he reached this point of a book.

"Have you called that gym yet, Pippa, have you?" Chad asked eagerly, interrupting Seth's thoughts.

"Not yet, love, give me time." Still immersed in her note taking, Pippa didn't even look up at the question.

Seth shook his head in amazement at her ability to concentrate on one thing and still hear a child's chatter. He'd be losing his freaking mind by now. He *was* losing his freaking mind.

He shot Pippa a suspicious look. "What gym?"

Chad started chattering about all the things he could do in a gym, but Seth focused his glare on Pippa. No one had mentioned a gym to him. The house had a perfectly adequate exercise room beside the pool. His son didn't have to go to any gym filled with muscle-bound rednecks where he'd be laughed out of the room.

Pippa set down her notepad and looked up. "With physical therapy, Chad can strengthen his arms and upper body so he can accomplish a great many things on his own. A gym with a good therapist would have sessions for kids like Chad."

Damn, but she had laser eyes that seared right through him

as if he were made of paper. Seth instantly threw up the shield he'd wielded so well for years. "I'll hire a therapist, then. Find the best."

"He needs the company of others in similar circumstances," she replied adamantly, not dropping her gaze from his.

Even Mac couldn't stand up to him when he laid down the law. What the hell did it take to bring Miss Pippa Cochran into line?

"Chad, go see what Nana has baked for you," Seth snapped.

"I wanna go to a gym!" Chad whined, instantly aware of the tension in the room.

"I said—" Seth began.

"Don't worry, kid, I'll take care of this," Pippa reassured Chad, breaking eye contact with Seth to smile at the boy. "Bring me back some of the goodies."

Chad grinned and cheerfully wheeled away without even a semblance of a tantrum. Seth would have to figure out how she did that, but he was too preoccupied with the impending argument. No one ever argued with him.

As Chad left, Pippa stood to confront him where he leaned against the wall, arms crossed, in one of his very best intimidating stances.

"You can't keep him cooped up behind stone walls all his life." She threw the first grenade in a calm voice reeking of defiance.

He could almost visualize the vibrations emanating from her, but the signals he was picking up had little to do with anger. "I won't have him laughed at and picked on by ape mentalities," he replied as frostily as he could, hoping to chill some of the heat.

"He has to learn sometime." Pippa knitted her fingers into fists and lowered her voice to a less belligerent tone. "I'll arrange private sessions with only similarly challenged children at first. He has to develop social skills as well as mental ones."

Seth had the distinct feeling she'd pulled back her guns with reluctance, that given equality, she would have shot him down in cold blood. He toyed with the idea of egging her on, but he could see the argument deteriorating into name-calling. The "social skills" crack had been a direct hit. Chad had none. And neither did his father.

"Where are you going to find a gym, therapist, and a class of physically challenged kids out here in the middle of nowhere?" he scoffed. Even as he asked, he discovered he was almost hoping she had an answer. Her accusations of child abuse and Natalie's threats still scorched his conscience.

"We could use your exercise room if you really don't want Chad going into town." She backed away now that she apparently thought she had the upper hand. "I already have a list of therapists in the area. And I know of at least one child in town who will benefit from training."

Amazed that she had advanced so far in her planning, amazed that he even listened, Seth could only stare at her. "What child?" he finally asked, for lack of any better argument.

"A friend of mine, Mary Margaret, has a son with muscular dystrophy. He's about a year older than Chad. Meg will know about others. She's despaired over the lack of facilities around here. You'll be doing everyone a favor."

"I don't want to do everyone a favor," he replied irritably, aware that he sounded like a recalcitrant child. The idea of a passel of screaming youngsters and their scheming mothers invading his privacy stirred a nest of hornets he didn't need.

"Why? What would it hurt?" she demanded. "You have everything money can buy and you would deprive a few less fortunate children of the opportunity to improve their lives?"

Damn, but he hadn't meant to sound like a miser. He gave a fortune to charity every year, anonymously. He disliked attention. He simply didn't know how to explain that to her.

"Find a gym in town," he finally offered, magnanimously, he thought. "I'll pay for the equipment."

She wrinkled her nose, and Seth realized she had freckles across the bridge. He didn't want to recognize any such thing.

"All right," she condescended. "I'll find a gym."

Then she turned her back on him and switched on the computer.

She'd turned her back on him. *She* had dismissed *him*. Worse, he had the distinct feeling that he'd just been manipulated into giving her exactly what she wanted. Obnoxious twerp.

Beyond irritated, Seth slammed out of the office in search of Chad and Nana's baking.

Behind him, Pippa sighed in relief and nearly collapsed over the keyboard. Round two, score two. Now all she had to do was find a gym, a competent therapist, and a class of physically challenged kids. So, even God had taken six days.

"Meg, don't you go stubborn on me. It's been like plowing a mountain with an obstinate mule around here. I don't need you planting rocks in my field."

Exasperated, Pippa ran her hand through her hair and glared at the telephone. She should have gone into town and looked her friend in the face, but she was too far behind in her work already. The dratted man had scribbled forty pages in her absence today. It would take her all night to translate his chicken scratching and type it into some semblance of readability.

"I'll not turn Mikey into a specimen for some kind of crazy experiment just for the benefit of Seth Wyatt." Meg's voice penetrated loud and clear through the wires. "He's never done one damned thing for this town and we return the favor."

"He's *trying* to do something for the town," Pippa pleaded. "If there isn't an adequate facility, I'll twist his arm until he builds one. But the kids would get the benefit much sooner if the school will provide the use of their gym."

"Why is he doing this?" Meg demanded suspiciously.

"For his son. Chad needs therapy and he needs friends. Don't you see? This is the break you and the town have been waiting for. If we get Seth involved in community activities . . ." At the sound of feet in the corridor outside, Pippa halted. "Listen, think about it. I'll call you later."

She hung up just as Seth walked in.

He plopped a plate of chocolate chip cookies still warm from the oven on the desk. "Tell me exactly what the doctor said," he demanded.

He never asked, never offered a "please" or "thank you," he just commanded his troops and expected them to snap into line. Pippa wondered what kind of childhood had created such a man.

"The doctor is sending a full report," she reminded him. "I doubt there's anything new about his physical condition. Children are remarkably resilient. There's been some definite growth and improvement in the nerve damage, but nothing to give hope that he'll ever walk again. With proper therapy, he might eventually develop his upper body so that he can get around with crutches for brief amounts of time."

Did she imagine it, or was that uncertainty flickering in the Grim Reaper's eyes? For just a moment, he appeared almost human, a father who wanted what was best for his son but didn't know what it was. That expression tugged at her always vulnerable heartstrings and stirred something deep inside her. She resisted the tug easily as his face froze up again.

"I don't want him laughed at," he said coldly. "He's only known encouragement, and I don't want that changed. A child's mind is just as important as his body."

"One affects the other," Pippa answered quietly. "'Build strong minds with strong bodies' is not just a hackneyed cliché. You cannot protect him forever. What would happen to him if you were hit by a truck tomorrow?"

His icy features turned glacial. "That's a fear I live with

every day of my life. Set up your gym, Miss Cochran. I want approval of every step."

He stalked back to his office and closed the connecting door after him.

Maybe it was time she found out a little bit more about Seth Wyatt, a.k.a. Tarant Mott, Pippa mused as she glared at the closed door. She'd met controlling men before, but this one seemed bent on twisting the world to suit his own obsessions.

For her own peace of mind, she should understand his obsessions.

A rifle shot shattered the cool dusk as Pippa pushed Chad over a rough cobblestone on the terrace. She recognized rifle shots when she heard them. She'd grown up in a part of the country where hunting was practically a religion. She just couldn't imagine what hunting season would be open this time of year.

Glancing up to where Chad's father had been sliding down a slope in search of a particular oak leaf for Chad's science project, she saw Seth duck behind a ridge as another shot rang out, splintering a tree limb not far from their heads.

Stunned, Pippa sought the spot where she'd last seen Seth. Not until she realized she couldn't see him did she shove Chad toward the open French doors.

"Hunters again," Chad announced calmly. "Dad will get rid of them."

She'd seen what misguided rifle shots could do to innocent bystanders. She shoved Chad safely into the house, ordered him out of the room, and reached for the phone. Did California have sheriffs?

Holding the phone, watching through the open doors, she saw Doug burst from his garage apartment, shouting obscenities as he loped down the hill where Seth had disappeared. Just as she wondered if she should call an ambulance, she watched

Seth emerge near the stand of trees at the lawn's edge. Damn, that man could move fast.

Pippa nearly swallowed her tongue as Seth dived into the trees, tackled a red-capped hunter, and rolled onto the lawn with him. The telephone in her hand beeped frantically at the incompleted connection.

In fascinated horror, she watched the hunter clip Seth with his rifle and make a break for the trees. Seth kicked his long legs, twisted, and hurled the other man to the ground again.

How had she thought herself safe in a household with a man who lost his temper and used his legs for weapons?

As Doug slid down the hill to join them, Pippa slowly lowered the receiver back to its hook. Maybe it was better if she didn't call the sheriff just yet. Seth certainly appeared to have taken matters in hand. She winced as she watched him smash a fist into the hunter's abdomen while Doug emptied the rifle and broke it against a tree.

Turning away from the sight and hurrying after Chad, she wondered if the warnings of Garden Grove's inhabitants didn't have a little more truth to them than she'd wanted to believe.

Seth Wyatt was definitely a dangerous man. And living with dangerous men could be hazardous to the health.

TEN

"What if they don't like me?" Chad whispered as Pippa rolled him up the ramp to the old high school gym Meg had recommended.

"They probably won't if you throw a tantrum to get your way." Pippa shrugged as she tipped the chair back over a broken piece of pavement. The incident with the hunter had faded with the break of day and under the importance of Chad's introduction to town. "Whether they like you or not is entirely up to you. Scary, ain't it?"

"Dad said you ain't supposed to say 'ain't,'" Chad muttered, avoiding a reply.

"Just think about how you'd like to be treated, and treat other people the same way," Pippa suggested, as if she'd been asked.

"They'll be dorks," he scoffed, watching the gray double doors with apprehension.

Pippa cuffed him affectionately. "You're a dork."

"Am not."

"Am too."

"You can't say 'am too'!"

Son of a writer, all right. She could push all his buttons. Grinning, Pippa halted before the nonautomatic steel doors.

"Well, if we decide on this place, your father will have to do something about those doors. They must have been built in the prehistoric age."

"By the dinosaurs!" Chad exclaimed happily, still entranced by his expedition to Jurassic Park at Universal.

Lord, but the boy could run the full scale of emotion in two minutes flat. He exhausted and exhilarated her at the same time. If it weren't for her stubborn, irritable employer, she'd love this job.

Someone jerked the doors open from inside.

"There you are!" Meg jammed a door peg under one of the doors and helped pry the chair over the doorstep. "We thought you got lost." Her eyes danced with curiosity as they quickly took in Chad's militant expression and Pippa's grin. "Did Durwood run you into another tree?"

"Doug brought us." Determined to hold the center of attention, Chad jumped in unrepentantly. "The Rolls had a flat. Dad says the Mercedes won't be delivered until Friday."

Pippa knuckled his head. "Don't speak until spoken to, and wait to be introduced." She frowned at Mary Margaret's raised eyebrows. "Mrs. Kelly, this is Chad Wyatt. Chad, this is Mrs. Kelly. Say 'how do you do,' scamp."

"Why?" Chad demanded, turning to look at her over his shoulder, his thin face puckered in a studious frown. "It's a silly question. How do you do what?"

Meg laughed, grabbed the wheelchair from Pippa, and shoved it across the gym floor in the direction of a similarly chair-bound child.

"Tell Miss Cochran she needs to brush up on her training in dealing with six-year-olds," Meg said gaily. "Just try to remember my name and I'll be happy."

"Mrs. Kelly," Chad parroted agreeably, but his gaze had fixed on the other child.

"Right you are. And this is my son, Mikey."

The two boys stared at each other.

Mikey finally broke the silence. "My mom says you're filthy rich."

Meg groaned, and Pippa laughed.

Chad took it in stride. "I've got the new Nintendo."

"Cool. Could I play with it sometime?"

Meg shook her head and, grabbing Pippa's elbow, steered her away. "Boys and toys. It never ends. Quit watching him as if he's dancing on a cliff's edge. He won't fall off. Come look at what this place has. After all, that's why we're here, isn't it?"

Frowning, Pippa glanced over her shoulder. Chad was showing Mikey the buttons that spun his chair around. Maybe it would work. Maybe. If it didn't, Seth would probably not only fire her, but kick her into the next county, and sue her for what little she possessed. She shivered and tried to remember if her liability insurance was paid up.

She hid her gloomy thoughts with more rational ones. "Okay, let's see the place. It must be falling down if the school built a new one."

"This was the original high school gym. It's been here since 1940. The board replaced it last year and they want to tear it down and build a new middle school, but with the plant closing and everything, they've put it off. The middle school we have was built about the same time as this place."

"Then they should have replaced it first," Pippa said scornfully. "Typical, the athletes get first priority."

"It's more than that, so get your nose out of the air, Miss Priss." Meg opened the doors to the locker room. "The high school gym is our community center. We get together for games, meetings, dances, graduations, everything and anything. Just like home."

Pippa heard the warning in her friend's voice. This might be California, a whole new world for her, but it was still a small town. She'd better watch what she did and said.

She hadn't thought about it when she'd fled Billy and Kentucky, but she'd run smack-dab into a whole new life. She didn't have to be Pollyanna Pippa, but somehow, she doubted she would be different. Now that she was away from the security of familiar people and surroundings, uncertainty gnawed at her underpinnings. She needed the "cheer up and smile" attitude to keep functioning.

"Do you have any idea what a physical therapy room needs?" Pippa asked as she surveyed the grim interior of peeling metal lockers and cement floors.

"Nope. I thought you did. You're the RN."

"Physical therapy is a whole 'nother degree." Pippa stared glumly at a door sagging on one hinge, then carefully checked around the corner at the shower stalls. She grimaced. "Maybe six-year-olds don't need to shower," she offered hopefully.

"If we fix this place up, then it's got to be for everyone," Meg reminded her. "The school board can't provide the entire facility for private use."

"I suppose," Pippa sighed. "How many others in this age group can we expect?"

Meg ticked the list off on her fingers. "Beth's daughter lost her leg in a car accident last year. She's eight. And if we count all disabilities, Toby has severe diabetes and needs a restricted exercise program. Anna's arm is deformed by a birth defect. They're all in the five-to-nine age group."

"That's a good start," Pippa murmured as she inspected the remainder of the locker room. "We really need a swimming pool."

"That'll be the day." Meg glanced out the door to see what the boys were doing. "The swim team uses the pool at the hotel."

"That figures. Some things never change." Remembering her own dream of being the next Olympic swim star when she was a kid, Pippa stalked back to the gym where the boys were racing their chairs across the warped floor. The rural high school she'd attended didn't have a pool either. And there hadn't been any friendly hotel pool available. "Seth has one going to waste. He never uses it. But he doesn't want anyone up there."

"It's too far for most of the kids anyway. Their parents don't have chauffeurs and Rollses to drive them around in. I figure I'll end up picking most of them up in the van."

"I doubt if a Mercedes or even a Rolls can hold many wheelchairs, but Doug can pick up the ones who don't need chairs," Pippa offered idly, without thinking about it.

"I'll believe it when I see it," Meg muttered. "The whole town is falling apart, and the Grim Reaper decides to build a gym. It will never happen."

"Pessimist," Pippa hissed.

"Optimist," Meg hissed back.

They laughed at the old epithets.

Watching the boys cavorting like any two six-year-olds, Pippa vowed to make it happen. She'd almost swear Chad was losing the race on purpose. His state-of-the-art electronic chair could run circles around Mikey's ancient one. This was precisely what Chad needed, even without the therapist.

"I'm interviewing three therapists tomorrow. Got any input?"

With determination, Pippa started taking notes. The Grim Reaper would just have to start acknowledging that a world existed outside his fortress—not that that world was a very friendly one, she realized. That hunter had to have known whose land he was on.

Pippa contemplated screening the therapists from the relative sanity of Meg's kitchen, but Seth had insisted on sitting in on the interviews. Since she didn't think her reclusive employer would appreciate the eyes of the town on him in the fishbowl of Meg's home, she reluctantly arranged for the interviewees to visit the mansion.

The mentally challenged gardener accidentally anointed the first candidate with a hose, soaking her carefully hair-sprayed coiffeur. As Doug hastened to her rescue, the tiny blonde took one look at the hulking black ex–football player racing in her direction, screamed, and leapt back into her car. Pippa watched her screech her Civic down the drive and shook her head.

"No stamina," she said as Doug stopped on the porch stairs and watched the car speed off.

Doug grunted. "If that means no brains, you're right."

Pippa grinned. "That's what it means, all right. Let's sic Chad on the next one."

Doug threw her a suspicious look. "You ain't supposed to be enjoyin' this so damned much."

"If I'm not, who is?" Lifting an eyebrow, Pippa returned his look with aplomb. This bachelor household didn't need cute blondes swinging their hips around anyway.

The next candidate agilely dodged sprinklers, Doug's menacing arm-crossed stance, Nana armed with blue wig and vacuum, and Chad's mutinous "She's butch" insult. Pippa gave the woman credit for keeping a cool head. But the newcomer's reaction to Seth showed how little six-year-olds knew about sexual preferences.

Tall, blond, and stacked, the therapist stopped cold in her tracks as Seth stood to greet her.

"Why, Mr. Wyatt, I had no idea you were so young," she purred.

As if a six-foot Amazon could purr, Pippa added to herself. And since the Amazon was clearly just out of college, and Seth was pushing his late thirties if she knew anything at all, the Amazon was lying through her gleaming, milk-fed white teeth. Thirty-somethings were ancient to twenty-two-year-olds.

Get a grip, Pippa, she muttered to herself as she gestured Miss Amazon toward a chair. Seth was a big boy. If he wanted to play with children's toys, that was his business. She pulled out her clipboard of prepared questions.

Seth glowered silently, staring out the window as Pippa

worked her way through the basics of education and experience. Other than having very little experience with children, Miss Amazon qualified on all counts. Pippa still didn't like the woman any better. She wished Seth would lend a hand here. He was the one who had insisted on sitting in on the interview. He was supposed to have corporate business experience. He ought to know how to ask those tricky questions that caught out the irresponsible types.

Diving into treacherous waters, Pippa threw away the prepared list and plunged into her own concerns. "You'll be dealing primarily with a five-to-nine age group, both boys and girls. Your experience has been mostly with adults. Are you prepared to handle their hyperactive energy? How would you deal with a child who doesn't cooperate?"

Miss Amazon smiled confidently. "I have two younger siblings and I baby-sat the neighbor's children for years. When they got out of hand, I just bopped them on the rear or whacked their hands and they straightened out. Children need discipline."

Pippa's mouth dropped open. Too astonished to form a reply, she merely stared.

Seth reared up from his cave and towered over them. "The interview is over. You may go now." He stalked out without further explanation.

Well, she'd have to give him credit for terminating an interview without wasted breath. Standing up, Pippa gestured toward the doorway.

The bewildered therapist looked from the doorway to Pippa and back again. Shaking her head, she stood up. "What did I say?"

"You just suggested physical abuse to the father of a child who is already physically damaged. I'd suggest you acquire a little experience dealing with children before seeking employment in this field. Corporal punishment might have its place; that's not an issue I'm prepared to argue. I just know that it has no place with these kids. They've already suffered enough. Good day."

Pippa watched her second candidate depart. If these were the best the area offered, what the hell was she going to do? Take physical therapy classes and teach them herself?

She found Seth stalking up and down her office, wearing a path in the Persian carpet. She liked that carpet. The browns and golds had faded and blended into a pattern that intrigued her imagination. It would be nothing but bare threads if he didn't halt soon.

"Cretins!" he shouted, as if she couldn't hear.

Well, at least he knew she was in the room. She took a seat at her desk. "Just very young," she modified. "I dumped water on Chad and he survived. You would have had a conniption if I'd told you beforehand that's how I'd shut him up."

Seth spun around and glared at her. "And I fired you. Why the hell didn't you just leave then?"

Good question. She should have. She really should have. But they both needed her so much. . . .

Dumb, Pippa. Seth Wyatt didn't need anyone or anything. But Chad did. The old need-to-be-needed urge raised its ugly head. Pippa stuck out her chin. "I needed a job and Chad needed a friend. I couldn't leave."

Seth's glare didn't waver. "I'm not buying that tripe. With your credentials, you could get a job anywhere. So help me, if I find out Natalie is paying you, I'll have your reputation cut into mincemeat. I can do it with just a phone call."

"You're such a pleasant person when riled, I do love talking to you. Will you just fire me and get it over with so I can get back to work?" Pippa didn't flinch as Seth's temper visibly flared. The mule-headed grouch had had his own way entirely too long, but she'd seen the fear in his eyes the day she'd arrived. Maybe he could deal with illegal hunters, but he couldn't deal with the chaos around him alone. She had him over a barrel.

And he knew it. She could see it in his eyes and the way he snapped his mouth shut on his first impulsive reply. He shoved elegantly long fingers through his thick mop of curls and tugged with frustration. "This isn't working," he snarled, not specifying to which "this" he referred.

"It's working very well; you just don't like it," she suggested, supplying her own definition. "We'll find a therapist who has experience with children. Sometimes credentials aren't everything."

"I won't leave Chad with strangers," he stated obdurately, returning his hand to his side and clenching it into a fist.

"I'll stay with him and keep watch," she reassured him. "You can't protect him from the world. It's out there. He has to learn to deal with it."

"Children are too young. They're not prepared to deal with it by themselves."

He said it with such emphasis, Pippa realized there was more to it than that. She'd been raised in a small town and had seldom known a stranger as a child. Seth's experience had apparently been different.

"Okay, tell me where you're coming from." She set her pencil down and waited for his explanation.

He paced. He shoved his hand through his hair again. He glared out the window. Then he swung around and glared at her some more. But he didn't scare her. She saw the pain in his clenched jaw, the uncertainty hidden behind the intimidating scowl. She wanted to stroke his face and tell him everything would be all right. The man was a menace to society and probably to himself. Why couldn't she remember that?

"Look, just take my word for it, all right?" Some of his scowl faded as she did no more than watch him patiently. "Kids need the protection of the adults they know. You can't just heave them out into the cold world and let them fend for themselves."

He was speaking from experience. It was in every ounce of

pain he held back. Thoughtfully, she nodded agreement. "We don't have an argument there. They need to be certain of the adults around them so they can proceed with confidence on their own, knowing they have a fall-back position. Chad has you. He'll learn soon enough that he has me. And once he gets to know the therapist, he'll have still another person. The whole point is for him to gradually explore the world outside and learn which people he can trust and how to deal with others he doesn't know about. Where's the problem?"

"I can't trust you or any therapist," he stated coldly. "I can't trust anyone."

Pippa quirked her eyebrows. "Not even yourself?"

For a moment, his glare blackened, and then it disintegrated entirely as he shook his head in sadness. "Not even myself."

With that, he stalked into his own office and slammed the door.

Well, dammit, then, Pippa muttered to herself. She'd just have to place her trust in God or that poor kid wouldn't have anyone.

But she'd always believed God helped those who helped themselves, and it looked like Seth Wyatt and his son needed one whale of a lot of helping.

ELEVEN

"Look," the voice answered over the phone, "I've got a couple of live leads, which is a hell of a lot more than I've had up till now. I've tracked the owner of the house on the hill where you went off, and the tow-truck driver who pulled the car out of the ravine. The thugs you laid out cold aren't talking, but they're out on bond and I've got tails on them."

Seth grimaced and clenched his pen so hard it should have broken. He dropped the pen and tapped his fingers against the desk. The phone in the other room rang and he heard Pippa answer. The clatter of her computer keyboard barely halted long enough for her to pick up the receiver. He'd like to know how she did that. That unfathomable mind of hers apparently had different compartments for different tasks. He wished he could say the same.

He was postponing making the decision Dirk was demanding he make. The horror of that night five years ago never stopped haunting his sleep. He had to solve it. He'd like to know who the bastard was who'd hired those thugs, too, but Natalie and her lawyers were in his face now. He had to strengthen his current position before he could indulge his fantasy of finding out what really happened that night. Chad's present was more important than his past.

Or was he rationalizing, avoiding what Dirk might uncover? That thought brought him up with a jerk. If Dirk could prove he wasn't drunk that night, it would pave the way to unquestioned custody of Chad. But if Dirk proved the opposite? He could lose Chad forever.

Choosing Chad's future over his own need for justice, he reluctantly gave Dirk his orders. "If you've got someone you trust, put them on those leads. I want you on Natalie's case right now. They've set a court date for the custody hearing, dammit. There's no way in hell I'm letting her have Chad. Have you made any headway in that direction?"

"Not much. Her husband got sacked from that last consulting position. Far as I can tell, they're living on future earnings and they're up to the year 2006 by now. I'm not real sure she understands the debt outstanding. Their maid said she overheard her asking him how come the restaurant wouldn't take her charge card, and he told her he'd canceled it because the interest rate was too high. Is she that dumb?"

Seth gritted his teeth and swiveled his chair to absorb the view of mountains in the distance, but they were obscured by morning fog. "She's not dumb, just oblivious. And single-minded. She's always had money, thinks it pours from faucets like water. I doubt if it has ever occurred to her that it can run out. And he's deliberately keeping her in the dark. She's focusing on getting Chad back, slandering me across half the state. If I walked into the country club down there, they'd probably draw and quarter me on her behalf."

Seth leaned his head back against the leather headrest and waited out Dirk's silence. Dirk was damned good at what he did, but he was a detective, a man with a cop mentality and blue-collar middle-class values. He could practically hear Dirk's brain ticking as he sought a polite means of telling Seth what he should do.

"I don't suppose it ever occurred to you to talk to her," Dirk finally said.

If he were capable of humor, Seth would have grinned at the predictability of Dirk's reply. "Is it self-defense if I throttle her?" he asked facetiously.

"Look, man," Dirk replied with exasperation, "I don't want to tell you how to live, but the woman ought to know she's got bigger problems than that kid right now. If you don't tell her, who will? You must have had something in common when you married her."

"My mother. We had my mother in common. She wanted me to get married, Natalie wanted to get married, so we did. It shut them both up."

Dirk snorted. "You're a wimp. Big tough guy like you, and you're a wimp with women. Get over it. Give the woman a clue. She'll back off. She might even appreciate the favor."

Seth didn't even think about chuckling over that one. With a sigh, he reached for his pen again. "Natalie won't back off until I'm dead. She loathes me, she despises what I've done to Chad, and she thinks the world would be better if I fell off of it. If I told her that butthead husband of hers has blown her fortune, she'd accuse me of stealing it. I told you, the woman is single-minded. Just do what I told you to do and cut the pop psychology. You're lousy at it."

Seth hung up the phone and tried to return to the business projections for the printing plants, but the conversation had shot his concentration to hell. On days like this, he wished he'd never heard of printing plants. If his father had run the presses instead of owning the plants, his life might have been a good deal more sane. But no, his damned ambitious father had married the plant owner's daughter, expanded the company to international proportions, then died and left it all to him.

Chad's voice chattering in the outer office diverted Seth's perverse thoughts. Chad had never ventured into that office while Miss MacGregor ruled it, but Pippa turned everyone into pets. Pippa, ridiculous name. She'd even turned his recalcitrant son into a trained lapdog. Seth didn't like the idea, but it certainly made things a hell of a lot more peaceful.

He couldn't hear the words, but he recognized the pleading whine in his son's voice as Pippa admonished him about something. All right, so maybe she hadn't made the boy into a lapdog yet. He was just projecting his vivid imagination on her, creating the illusion of a fairy godmother who would turn this haunted castle into a home and the toads back into princes. On the other hand, maybe it was witches who did those things.

Rising from the desk, Seth strolled into the outer office. He couldn't think anyway. He might as well see what entertainment was to be had in the rest of his small world.

"Dad!"

Chad visibly brightened at his approach, and that one tiny soft spot left in Seth's heart melted. He couldn't afford any more soft spots than this one, but he indulged it—and his son—with regularity. "I thought you were studying." He quirked his eyebrow, not wholly giving in to his urges to pamper the boy.

Chad grimaced. "It's spring. Other kids get spring breaks." He threw a hasty glance at Pippa, who was busily making notes while talking on the phone, then lowered his voice. "I wanna go swimming. Pippa says I can learn."

Seth's temper shot upward until he noted the frown between his assistant's eyes and the accusing pencil she pointed at his son while still managing the phone conversation. Chad's guilty look forced Seth to wait for further explanation. He wasn't much good at waiting. He wasn't much good at letting other people interfere in his life. He liked running things himself so he knew what to expect and when to expect it. He couldn't rely on other people to think like him, and Pippa Cochran was no exception. Still, he owed her a chance to explain.

She hung up the phone and punched the voice mail button.

Before she could speak, Chad interrupted. "I wanna learn to swim. I'm old enough. You said I could." He glared at Pippa.

Seth raised his eyebrows and waited for her reply. To his surprise, she leaned back in her chair and grinned at him. That mop of red hair swung down in her face and her cheeks bunched into pink apples and her wide lips opened invitingly over neat rows of pearly teeth. The urge to take a bite out of her covered up a baser urge. Growling at the unwelcome stirring below his belt buckle as his thoughts took a wayward path, Seth crossed his arms and continued waiting.

"He is old enough," Pippa agreed with Chad cheerfully. "You want to teach him?"

"He's supposed to be studying. He has homework to do before his tutor arrives. And I'm damned well not a swim coach." He stepped around the real problem. How in hell did she think she could teach a kid to swim without the use of his legs? That everyday reality ground into Seth's soul like fine glass beneath a boot heel.

Pippa shrugged. "Neither am I. And he's right. He's six years old and other kids his age get spring breaks. I'll admit, I think school should be year-round, but on a modified basis. Study in the mornings, learn other things in the afternoon, maybe."

She didn't look at Chad for his reaction. Seth shifted his shoulders uneasily beneath her steady gaze. Out of the corner of his eye, he saw his son hunching up for a tantrum. He didn't need a tantrum right now. He needed to get some work done. He really wanted to finish the damned book, but that was too much to ask.

Before Seth could respond to either his assistant's challenge or his son's frustration, Pippa swung her chair around and pointed her pencil at Chad again. "One word, and I'll dunk you in the pool headfirst. Let me handle this, okay?"

Chad's pointed little face glowered back at her. He crossed his skinny arms in unconscious imitation of Seth's stance. But he shut up.

Amazed, Seth almost smiled at the standoff. If he couldn't

see the pencil in her hand, he'd think she held a gun on the kid. Maybe she *was* a witch. Aware that her attention had switched to him, Seth crossed his arms tighter until the muscles of his shoulders strained at his shirt seams. He knew his effect on women. With satisfaction, he watched her gulp and glance away. So, witches weren't totally immune to human nature. She was as aware of him as he was of her. That soothed his temper appreciably.

"You were saying?" he asked pleasantly.

She shot him a glare that said she not only knew what he was doing, but she didn't intimidate easily. "I'm saying it wouldn't hurt to take him out to the pool and teach him to float. You've got all that expensive concrete out there for some reason. You might as well put it to use."

"Are you offering?" The argument wiped all thought of Dirk and Natalie from Seth's mind. His uncontrollable imagination flashed images of his assistant cavorting about the swimming pool in a bikini. Without a bikini. He was a damned sight more human than she gave him credit for. Maybe she could turn her libido off upon command, but he couldn't. Since Pippa's arrival, his baser urges had edged out his concentration to the extent that he'd even included a sex scene in his book. He'd never done that before.

She shrugged. "I can keep him from drowning, in any event. I can't promise more than that. The next candidate for therapist is coming tomorrow. We can ask her if she teaches swimming."

Seth frowned as he imagined the blond Amazon from the other day cavorting about his pool in a bikini. The image had a strange tendency to wear leather and carry whips and chains.

"Can I, Dad, please? Please?"

Chad's eager plea dispelled any further evocative fantasies. Seth rolled his eyes upward, then had a stroke of genius. Just to prevent Pippa from realizing he was enjoying this, he nailed her first. "How do you plan to answer the phones while cavorting about the pool?" Damn, he hadn't intended to let that part about "cavorting" slip.

It didn't arouse her suspicions. She pointed at the voice mail button. "Your calls can survive an hour without me. We'll need to wait until the fog burns off anyway. No one calls at lunch. I can take the cordless out if you want to yell at me for anything."

"You don't think I'll trust you with my son in a swimming pool without my supervision, do you? I don't remember life-guard training on your résumé."

Ha! Score one for him. She glared at him as if she wished he'd drop through the floor and straight to hell. Seth had perfected his implacable facade decades ago. Her glare bounced right off it. Inside, he smiled in satisfaction. He'd get away from the phones, from the confounded business plan, and take his writing pad and sit in the sun for a while. And drive his assistant as crazy as she was driving him.

All things considered, the day had taken a promising turn.

Pippa refused to let her employer's glowering presence annoy her. In fact, with a little manipulation, perhaps she could turn him to her own purposes.

It would be much simpler if she could just sit here in the warm California sun, basking in the heat off the lovely cobalt-blue tiles, soaking up rays like a sponge, but she was well paid to work a million hours a week. So, work she would. Sort of. She could still enjoy the sun and sparkling water and Chad's delighted laughter.

Beneath the concealment of the rippling water, she adjusted the position of her hide-all one-piece bathing suit. She'd never had exhibitionist tendencies. She'd always had more male attention than she needed, and deflecting it was second nature to her. But Seth's masculine interest aroused a self-consciousness she'd never experienced before. She'd seen his frown when she'd appeared in her knee-length cover-up. She wasn't certain if her unfashionable attire or her less than twiggy build had inspired that scowl, or if it was just his usual ill humor. She just knew that frown awakened an awareness of the size of her breasts and hips that she didn't like to acknowledge.

So she stayed in the pool at Chad's side, where Seth couldn't see her. As she showed Chad how to hold his breath and put his face in the water, she caught a glimpse of her employer scribbling furiously in his notebook. She would breathe a sigh of relief except she knew she had to have his attention to accomplish her goal.

Talk about your conflicting emotions. Pippa grimaced, held her nose, and floated facedown so Chad could see what she wanted him to learn.

Chad yelped, and she shot back to her feet again.

"Idiot!" she scolded, grabbing him by his armpits and pulling him back up again. "Wait until I'm looking before you try that." She held him over her arm and pounded his back until the water he'd swallowed spurted back up.

Chad squealed and lashed his arms in protest until a shadow blotted the sun. He hastily shut up and Pippa sighed. The Grim Reaper had a bad habit of dampening high spirits.

Squinting, she glanced up at the figure towering over the pool, then realized she really shouldn't have done that. Now that she had her head craned upward, she couldn't look away. Gad, in that brief swimsuit, Seth Wyatt looked like something off a movie screen. Wide, bronzed shoulders, lean torso, taut abs—mentally, she skipped the part encased in spandex and admired muscled legs that went on forever. With legs like that he could have been an Olympic skier or runner. . . .

Exasperated by her train of thought, Pippa returned her attention to Chad, wrapping his fingers around the pool's edge again.

"Hi, Dad," Chad piped nervously.

"Are you listening to Miss Cochran?" Seth asked flatly.

"He's doing just fine," Pippa reassured him. "It's only three feet of water here. He won't drown." She'd say anything to get the man back in his chair and away from the edge of the pool.

"He can't stand," Seth reminded her calmly. "He can drown in a bathtub."

"He has arms and a brain," she snapped, frustration and a modicum of fear getting the better of her usual common sense. "And I'm not likely to stand here and watch him drown."

Possibly to prove her point, Chad released his grip on the edge and promptly sank to the bottom.

Pippa dropped below the water's surface, grabbed the boy again, and hauled him upward, swearing mentally at the child's perversity. Like father, like son. The two of them made a great pair. She really ought to have her head examined. Maybe she was a closet masochist.

Flinging hair from her eyes as she stood up with Chad pressed tightly in her arms, Pippa nearly hit her head against Seth's square jaw.

Standing midwaist in the water, he hauled the boy from her arms and glared at her from so close that Pippa thought he might pierce holes in her skull with just the power of his eyes.

"You're fired," he gritted from between clenched teeth.

The anger radiating off all that bronzed, wet skin should have produced steam. Thick black hair molded his skull and dripped down his neck. He needed a haircut, Pippa thought irrelevantly. She crossed her arms to glare back at him but regretted the gesture instantly as Seth's gaze dropped to her chest. She could almost feel his hands where his gaze rested, and a tingling she hadn't felt in a long time took residence in her lower belly, irritating her even more.

"Don't be ridiculous," she snapped in an effort to distract him. "He's fine. Didn't you ever sit on the bottom of the pool when you were a kid?" Defiantly, Pippa reached for Chad.

The boy hugged his arms around her neck and wriggled to escape his father's hold.

Seth's expression darkened. "No, I never sat on the bottom

of the pool when I was a kid. I never learned to swim when I was a kid. And I don't see any particularly good reason why Chad should try now. I think it's time we went in."

She couldn't believe her ears. He had this grand mansion and enormous pool, and he'd never learned to swim? He had all the dreams she'd never had, and he'd never taken advantage of them? Was the man mad? Or was there something here he wasn't telling her?

She'd minored in psychology. She would figure it out sooner or later. Kissing Chad's cheek, she set him in neutral territory on the pool's rim.

Then she confronted her nemesis. "Do you know how to swim now?" she asked.

He blinked at the change of direction but recovered rapidly. "I taught myself the basics," he admitted, watching her warily.

"Fine, then I'll teach you the rest. I had swim classes at the public pool, and the teachers said I was half eel. But I've not had the advantage of physical therapy classes, so I can't do more than teach Chad the basics. Once we find a therapist, she can teach Chad and I can teach you. Agreed?"

She knew she had a tendency to take bigger bites than she could chew. It came from never having enough while growing up. She got greedy sometimes. This time, she'd even managed to scare herself. But she wouldn't let him know that. She put her hands on her hips and dared him to back down.

He stood a head taller than she and probably weighed sixty pounds more. He could throw her over his shoulder and into the deep end of the pool without straining one of those well-defined biceps. For a moment, Pippa detected a gleam behind his relentlessly glaring eyes, but then his gaze dropped to the rise of her breasts above the swimsuit, and she remembered why she was really afraid of him. And it had nothing to do with his greater strength. The tingling sensation intensified, and she nearly turned tail and ran.

"*You* will teach *me* to swim?" he asked as if he hadn't heard right.

"Breaststroke, crawl, whatever." She tried to shrug offhandedly but she didn't think she pulled it off very well.

"Breaststroke," he repeated, the amusement not quite lightening his tone. "In exchange for—what?" The inquiry was obvious in his voice.

"A therapist who can teach Chad." She couldn't remember a man ever looking at her in quite that way before, as if she were a morsel he could gobble up in one bite. She'd never been a morsel in any man's eyes. She was a handful in more ways than one. Maybe it was time she reminded him of that.

Recovering some of her equanimity, she slam-dunked the goal she'd had in mind from the first. "One who can teach all the kids. Here, if necessary."

That socked him between the eyes. He backed off immediately.

"We'll see," he replied noncommittally, pulling himself up on the side of the pool and reaching for a towel.

Chad grinned at Pippa. "Does that mean Mikey can come out here and learn with me?"

"Yeah, kid, that's what that means." Triumphantly, Pippa met her employer's threatening glare. Just let him deprive his son of this privilege. She dared him.

"The breaststroke," Seth replied evenly. "That's what I want to learn."

He walked off, leaving Pippa to wonder who had won this particular battle.

She had the awful suspicion it wasn't her.

"I wish to speak with my son, Miss Cochran," the voice from the phone spoke haughtily. "And I will not be put off another minute."

Pippa glanced at the clock on the desk. After nine. Well, at least the woman wasn't spewing steam. She sounded all too together, actually, as if she could casually whip Pippa's head off through the wires. But Seth was working.

Throwing a glance at the closed office door, Pippa hesitated. Considering the impassioned quality of the work that appeared on her desk every morning, she knew Seth needed this time to himself to create the brilliant nightmares that had made him famous. She didn't want to disturb him.

But she didn't want to alienate his mother, either. She wished she knew the woman better. Chad needed a female in his life. A grandmother would do nicely. But the relationship between mother and son was obviously a rocky one. Of course, any relationship with a hermit like Seth would be rocky.

"He's writing, Mrs. Wyatt," Pippa whispered into the phone. "I can't disturb him."

"Nonsense. I only wish a minute of his time. I'll not be put off again. My son will hear about it if you keep me from him any longer."

Pippa thought rapidly. She shouldn't do this. She shouldn't interfere. But "shoulds" and "shouldn'ts" had never stopped her before. "I really shouldn't say this, Mrs. Wyatt," she said confidentially, "but he's scarcely had time to write lately, what with this business over the school board and physical therapists and all. That's why he doesn't have time to visit."

"Physical therapists?" The voice rang with disbelief.

"The one he interviewed was extremely attractive," she murmured mischievously.

"Attractive." Flat statement, followed by dry tones. "Perhaps I underestimated you, Miss Cochran."

"Everybody does," Pippa replied cheerfully. "Shall I tell him you called?"

"You do that." Seth's mother hung up.

Wondering what dynamite charge she'd lit now, Pippa switched on the voice mail and answering machine, switched off the computer, and wandered off in search of a snack. Playing with dragons made her hungry.

"Hi, Nana, got any milk and cookies?" she asked, discovering the housekeeper still puttering around the kitchen, her blue wig slightly askew. The formidable old woman intimidated her more than Seth ever had, but she tried not to show it.

The cook snorted and cast her a knowing look. "Seems to me, someone already ate the cream."

All right, so Seth didn't have the corner on enigmatic in this household. Innocently, Pippa opened the refrigerator and removed the milk carton. "Cream is fattening. Low-fat milk will suffice."

"He does not like meddling," Nana warned.

"He doesn't like meddling, he doesn't like people, and he resents the hell out of me. So what else is new?" Well, at least the woman hadn't bitten her head off yet. Pippa reached for the cookie jar.

Nana slapped a slab of chocolate cake on the table. "You need more flesh on your bones. Men like their women to look like women," she said with a slight German accent.

Pippa stared incredulously at the thickly frosted cake. No one had ever told her she needed more flesh on her bones. Far from it. But the cake oozed temptation. "I'll eat carrot sticks the rest of the week," she promised herself fervently, reaching for a fork.

She expected a rebuttal from Nana, but when she looked up, the old woman was gone. Damn, but this house was full of spooks.

And the spookiest of them all joined her shortly after Nana's disappearance.

He'd crumpled his hair into a nest of curls, shoved his shirtsleeves above his elbows, revealing the powerful muscles of his forearms, and looked as if he'd just awakened from a bad dream. At the sight of Pippa, he glared. At the sight of her cake, his eyes widened.

"Where'd you get that?"

"Nana." She licked the fork contentedly. She tried not to

notice as his gaze focused on her mouth, but her stomach did a back flip and plummeted to her shoes. The man was definitely good for her libido, if not for her psyche. "I thought you were working."

"I'm out of coffee." He glared at her as if it were her fault, then began searching cabinets for the cake.

"Try the refrigerator. This stuff's rich as sin."

"I've always considered poverty a sin, not riches." Locating the cake in the refrigerator, he placed it on the counter and carved out a slice. Not bothering with a plate, he held it in one hand and bit into it. With the other hand, he produced the makings for coffee.

"Interesting concept. 'The meek shall inherit the earth' doesn't apply? Or 'It's more difficult for a camel to pierce the eye of a needle than for a rich man to enter the gates of heaven'?"

"That's not what I meant, and you know it." He poured water into the coffeemaker.

"My, cranky, are we? Maybe you've had enough coffee for the evening." Pippa rose to put her plate in the dishwasher.

Without any warning at all, Seth grabbed her wrist and hauled her toward him. Electricity arced between them. Seth's eyes smoldered with the same heat pulsing through her, but fear simmered equally between them.

"Don't push me, Pippa. I don't respond well to force."

"Neither do I." Shaken, she snapped her wrist free. She'd been pushed around once before, and didn't like it. Despite the electricity, she refused to believe this was any different. "Shall I leave?"

Panic instantly replaced fire and Seth retreated a step. Awkwardly, he brushed his knuckles against her bare arm. "My mind's still on that scene I'm writing. I apologize if I've offended you." With what could have been embarrassment, he turned away and concentrated on the coffeepot.

With surprise, Pippa tipped her empty glass into the

dishwasher. He'd been writing a scene, not seeing her. She should feel relief, not this odd sense of disappointment. "That must be some scene," she murmured, easing toward the door.

"It is now," Seth muttered under his breath. "One hell of a scene."

TWELVE

"Handle it. That's what I pay you an exorbitant salary to do," Seth replied dismissively, not raising his gaze from the computer screen. As graphics formed on the screen, he jotted notes with one hand and hit a keyboard command with the other. The graphics reformed into a different pie chart.

"I'm just an employee," Pippa asserted, but she could see he wasn't listening. If she were two feet taller, she might be able to reach over his enormous desk and grab him by the throat, but without that physical advantage, she could only throw her voice. She understood why Chad resorted to temper tantrums. After the incident last night, she was more inclined toward tantrum than physical confrontation, too. Her skin still tingled. "What the hell are you afraid of, anyway?" she demanded. "That the school board is made of three-headed gorgons who'll eat you alive if you show up?""

Seth snorted and hit the keyboard with a few more strokes. "Close enough. I haven't got time to deal with this, Miss Cochran. It's your problem, you handle it."

She had already learned that when he called her "Miss Cochran," she might as well talk to a steel door. His vulnerability where his son was concerned had given her the impression that he might possibly be human and amenable to reason.

But the man who sat behind the desk manipulating industries around the world had no such humanity. He was a walking, talking machine. She didn't even want to consider his dark side, the one that created man-eating gophers on paper. The man was certifiable. If she considered the sexual aura he'd exuded last night, *she'd* be certifiable. Better to stick to business.

"All right, if I'm to act in your place, you'll have to give me power of attorney." He hadn't invited her to take a chair, but Pippa took one anyway. She knew she should be wary of him, that she shouldn't keep pushing his limits. For all she knew, he really was a psychopath, but if she had to play the part of psychiatrist, she'd do it from a comfortable position. "The school board won't take my word that you're willing to spend a small fortune on a crumbling gym just so the physically challenged kids in the community can have therapy classes. They might buy it if I told them you simply didn't want to be bothered with strangers out here, but I thought maybe I should get in a little PR and keep that side of you hidden."

Seth glanced up long enough to give her his cyclops stare. "Power of attorney? What the hell do you know about powers of attorney?" He went back to the computer before she could reply.

Gee, it was a pleasure talking to the side of his head. Pippa considered throwing the tin of toffees at him to get his attention but decided irritating him wouldn't accomplish her purpose. "I am a thirty-year-old hospital administrator. What do you think I know of powers of attorney?"

That jerked his head back around again. She thought she almost caught a gleam of interest in his eyes.

"Thirty, hmm? Old age creeping up fast, isn't it? And if you're such a damned good administrator, what are you doing hiding out here in the back of beyond?"

That cut a little too close to the bone for comfort. Pippa ignored the sharpness of his perception. "I'm administrating.

There's a legal-forms program on the outer computer. I can check and see if there's a form that would work. It's just a matter of specifying how far my powers extend. Give me numbers. That's all the board wants."

Seth crossed his arms on the desk and leaned forward. "Just wave my magic wand and produce money?"

"This wasn't my idea!" Irate at the sarcasm she recognized in his expression, Pippa lost her usual cool, again. She had definitely abandoned her Pollyanna persona working for this man. "You're the one who won't go in and talk to them. I don't know what it would hurt for you to show your face at one meeting, shake a few hands, assure them that this is all legal and aboveboard, whatever. But if you won't do it, you've got to give me power to do it. Or send your damned lawyer. He ought to have something more productive to do than hassle your ex-wife."

Uh-oh. She might have stepped a little far out of bounds with that one. Seth looked as if steam might emerge from his ears at any minute. Of course, with Seth, it would more likely come out of his mouth.

"I can see why you lost your last job," he said dryly.

Well, that wasn't precisely steam. Warily, Pippa sat back in her chair.

He didn't say anything else. He bounced his pen on his desk, apparently lost in thought. Or maybe it took time for Jekyll to replace Hyde.

"No, I don't see any reason I should have to deal with them," he finally said. "They've never done anything but stand in my way or throw sticks and stones in my direction whenever they had a chance. I don't see why I should have to put up with their narrow-minded intolerance now. I'll have Morris draw up a legal power of attorney. You handle it." He swung around and returned to his pie charts.

Pippa knew she'd been dismissed. She knew she should be content with what little he'd given her. It just wasn't in her nature to settle for less. Sometimes, she almost understood why Billy beat up on her. Sometimes, she could kick herself. But she couldn't just leave the topic where he'd dropped it.

"I think there may be a failure to communicate here," she offered tentatively.

He ignored her.

"The people in town think *you're* standing in *their* way."

He didn't raise an eyebrow.

This wasn't productive. Considering her alternatives, Pippa stood up and walked out of Seth's office. He didn't seem to notice her retreat.

Sitting down at her computer, Pippa grinned. She'd never particularly liked computers. She was a people person. But she'd learned to manipulate machines to make them do what she wanted. She typed a few paragraphs, hit the send key, and waited.

The fax in Seth's office started chattering.

Maybe now was the time to take a lunch break. Crossing her fingers, Pippa casually strolled from her desk into the corridor.

Doug leaned against the wall in the foyer, his massive arms crossed over his chest as he idled away his time waiting for Chad's tutor. He looked up and blinked twice at her expression. "What you been up to now and do I need to get out of the way before he steamrolls over both of us?"

"You're seriously underemployed, my friend. You ought to be the one in that office dealing with him." Pippa jerked her head in the direction of the doorway she expected Seth to emerge from any minute now. "I'll just go sit in the kitchen and admire the view. You can be the wall between us."

Doug grinned in appreciation but caught her shirt collar before she could escape. "Uh-uh, baby. You started this, you finish it. I ain't up to bein' fired today."

Pippa stomped on his sneaker-clad toe. "Brute force will get you nowhere," she admonished as he howled and released her. "But sweet talk will take you far." She backed away and grinned just as Seth slammed from the office, waving the fax at them.

"It's been nice knowin' ya." Doug retreated to his position against the far wall and watched implacably as Seth advanced toward them.

Pippa made a face at Doug, pasted on a smile, and did her best sashay in the direction of the corridor to the kitchen, ignoring Seth.

"What the devil does this little essay mean?" he yelled after her. "Damn you, get back here!"

"It's lunchtime. Even slaves deserve a meal a day," she called over her shoulder. "Care to join me? And by the way, I think you underestimate Doug. I bet if you sent him to the school board, he'd have them convinced he was you in no time."

Leave 'em laughing, that's what she always said. She didn't dare turn around to see how Doug took that retort, but she figured Seth wouldn't laugh, no matter how humorous the joke, and that one was certainly well below par.

To her amazement, he didn't follow. Swallowing her disappointment, Pippa slapped together a sandwich under Nana's disapproving gaze and wandered upstairs.

The place was a mausoleum. She would swear those were burial urns occupying the niches in the hallway. The person who had decorated the guest wing hadn't been given a free hand in the public areas. Or maybe someone had come along later and imposed their own morbid tastes. No wonder Seth had grown into a writer of macabre stories if he'd had to live here all his life. Someone really needed to drag him out of this funeral home and into the light of day.

If that fax hadn't angered Seth enough to drag him out, she didn't know what would. Maybe Doug could hit him over the head, and they could roll him out the door.

Grinning at that image, she popped into Chad's bedroom for some cheerful conversation. The school board meeting was tomorrow night. She needed to remember why she was sticking her neck out like this. If she wasn't careful, the hunters of Garden Grove would be using *her* for target practice.

Pippa nervously shuffled the papers in her hand and shifted from foot to foot as she stood in the hallway outside the boardroom. She could hear the rumbling of male voices as they discussed personnel issues. Just her luck, she'd run into a school board comprised only of men. And she'd thought Kentucky backward.

"I don't see what you're so nervous about," Mary Margaret whispered. "You've got the authority to spend money without them having to raise a dollar. It's a shoo-in."

Pippa shook her head. "Nothing is a shoo-in where Seth Wyatt is concerned. They'll ask questions I can't answer and then ask why Seth isn't here to speak for himself. Sometimes, I could strangle the man."

Meg grimaced. "Want me to say 'I told you so'?"

George hugged his wife's shoulders. "Don't make Pippa any more nervous than she is, sweetheart. That gym means too much to too many kids."

Meg shot him a look of irritation. "You don't know Pippa, then. The angrier she is, the better she gets. She confronted her first school board at the age of fifteen when they wanted to move the junior-senior prom to the school cafeteria. Had some of them in tears before she left. She missed her calling."

Pippa shrugged her shoulders nervously beneath her conservative shirtdress. She'd lost some of that fifteen-year-old confidence in the years since then. Life had a way of sapping strength and confidence, rounding off sharp edges, and carving at ideals. She really didn't want to fight other people's battles anymore. How had she gotten herself into this?

Someone opened the boardroom door and the public shuffled in to take chairs. Pippa glanced at the evening's agenda.

Her petition was last on the list. She still had time to cut and run.

But the image of Chad's and Mikey's expectant faces glued her to the chair. So, if she couldn't have kids of her own, she'd be everybody's old maid aunt. Bearding a school board in its den was a far sight easier than marrying and spending eternity with a male of the species. She was good at many things, but picking men wasn't one of them.

Sitting in the front of the room, straightening her shoulders, she waited while the discussion of new desks and new buses droned on around her. The audience coughed and twitched restlessly as one topic after another passed with little argument. Pippa began wondering why the dickens all these people were here. Not one of them had so much as chirped a protest about anything.

She understood the moment the board president announced her name and everyone in the audience turned and stared at her. They were here because of her.

That didn't ease her nervousness. Not knowing whether they were here out of curiosity or opposition, Pippa stood up and read aloud her petition for renovating the old gym.

Someone coughed into the silence following her reading. She waited expectantly, scanning the group of men sitting at the table in front of her. The last time she'd stood in front of a school board, she'd known everyone in the room. This time, she recognized only the banker to whom Meg had introduced her. He was frowning.

"You say Seth Wyatt is willing to pay for the renovation of the gym to turn it into a facility for the disabled in the community?" The balding, paunchy board president looked at her with suspicion, as if she had just asked to hire a terrorist as teacher.

Pippa took a deep breath before replying. "The building is empty. A contractor would have to be hired to make certain it's structurally sound, but if it is, the renovation shouldn't be lengthy or too costly. And it would be a benefit to the entire community."

"Miss Cochran, what Ronald is trying to say is: Why would Seth Wyatt bother doing anything for Garden Grove at this late date? He never has before."

That was Meg's smooth-talking banker friend, Taylor Morgan, speaking. Pippa had already decided she didn't like him. "Mr. Morgan, did no one ever teach you not to look a gift horse in the mouth? Why question Mr. Wyatt's generosity? His son will benefit just as much as everyone else in the area."

She heard the clucking of tongues around her but ignored them to the best of her ability. She really shouldn't have answered with irritation, but she was nervous. The last time she'd done this, she'd had a crowd of supporters around her. This time, she had only Meg and George. She didn't know how the rest of the crowd felt, but she could sense their agitation from the way they shifted in their seats and whispered behind their hands.

"So, in essence, Mr. Wyatt is willing to convert our gym for the benefit of his son?" Taylor asked with malice aforethought.

"In essence, Mr. Wyatt is generously giving the community a gift they can use for generations to come." She really, really didn't like Taylor Morgan, she decided. He had an ax to grind, and if he had to grind it on her before reaching Seth, it wouldn't cause him any grief. She despised people like that. She turned and faced the people sitting in the front row with her. "Can any of you see the harm in turning a worthless building into a community asset without any cost to you?"

A man at the end of the row shook his head thoughtfully. "It costs money to keep up a place like that. Heat, air, maintenance, whatever. Who's paying for all that?"

Oh, shoot. She hadn't gone that far in her planning. She had Seth's power of attorney for the renovations. She couldn't promise he would pay upkeep without asking his permission first. Well, in for a penny . . . "I should think we would need an estimate of those costs first before any decision can be made. And I think it's up to the community to decide how to finance operations. Perhaps we could set a small entry charge or a monthly maintenance fee for those using it. That's a matter for the board to decide."

The whispers became an instant uproar. The board president pounded his gavel until quiet fell again. He glared at Pippa. "I can't see how we can decide on a matter such as this without Mr. Wyatt's presence. We'll set the matter aside until . . ."

"Ronald, you're still avoiding decisions. You'd think after all these years, you'd have learned to make the simple ones," a bored voice spoke from the back of the room.

The rustling and whispering erupted again, and Pippa swung around, realizing too late that the noise hadn't been because of her or the topic, but because of the man standing at the back of the room. He lifted a heavy eyebrow in irony now as he met her stare.

Seth. In public.

Heart dancing to a faster pace, Pippa returned a glare of her own, then swung back to face the disconcerted board. "I don't think there's any point in delaying the matter indefinitely. If the board has no other use for the gym, it can approve a recommendation for a contractor's survey, or it can vote to tear the building down. One will cost the board money. The other won't. The decision is yours, gentlemen. Use it wisely."

She sat down. A smattering of applause followed. She didn't dare look to see what Seth was doing. For all she knew, he'd disappeared in a puff of smoke, just as he must have appeared. Taylor had slid down in his seat without a word. The board president frowned, but that seemed a perpetual expression for him.

She breathed a sigh of relief as one of the board motioned for the contractor survey and another quickly seconded it. A few members of the audience rose to protest any use of their taxes for a "haven for the wealthy." George stood up and politely reminded them about Mikey and the other children who would have the use of it. Someone else recommended the building be torn down and the land sold. Taylor looked interested. The board president announced the sale of the land would scarcely cover the cost of the building's demolition.

Taylor rose to his feet and glared over the audience. "If you're interested in helping our community, Mr. Wyatt, why didn't you spend your money on renovating the printing plant and retaining a few jobs around here instead of sinking good money into an old gym?"

"Because the cost of maintaining that old plant was a constant drain on resources while renovating the gym is a onetime cost. Even a banker should understand that, Morgan. If you wanted to keep the plant open, why didn't the bank buy it when I offered?"

A gasp of expectation raced around the room, and all eyes turned to Seth. He stood in his favorite position, with arms crossed, leaning against the doorjamb. Pippa thought he looked a lot like Rambo waiting for the next blow, but she could see that others might not catch that implication. They'd see the long, dark hair, the defiant stance, the bunched muscles, and read distaste and rebellion into his posture. Stupid man. She could see why he ran his businesses over the telephone. Body language was definitely not his forte.

Shooting him a warning look, she stood up and addressed the board. "Perhaps you could vote on the matter at hand and save the other discussion for later, gentlemen?"

"I take it Miss Cochran has your full permission to act in your behalf on this matter, Mr. Wyatt?" the board president asked, glancing over Pippa's head to Seth.

"That's why she has my power of attorney," he agreed, without inflection.

Pounding his gavel, Ronald called for a vote. Only Taylor Morgan voted against it.

Beside Pippa, Meg yelled in joy. The audience clapped and talked excitedly. Almost everyone in the room moved to have a word with Seth.

Pippa didn't have to turn to know he was already gone.

THIRTEEN

"I trust you're content with the results of the evening," Seth said frostily, dropping a stack of handwritten pages on the desk beside Pippa.

She didn't look up at him. Couldn't. He was throwing off vibrations so powerful that she could barely fasten her gaze on the computer screen. She couldn't actually determine if they were angry vibrations, but she'd rather not investigate the workings of this enigmatic man's mind. He was her employer. She needed to hold that thought.

"We made progress," she replied evasively. She wouldn't ask why he'd left so suddenly. She wouldn't ask why the town thought of him as some sort of reclusive monster. She wouldn't even ask if hunters regularly took potshots at him. Her business was typing these pages.

"They're narrow-minded bigots."

Obviously not prepared to let the subject drop, Seth paced restlessly behind her chair.

Pippa pursed her lips but refused to rise to the bait. Chad was asleep and she wanted this time to catch up on some of the work she'd neglected while playing with him.

"If they choose the contractor, Morgan will see that it's one who will recommend the building be torn down," he stated flatly.

That cinched it. Giving up on the computer screen, Pippa swung her chair around and glared at Seth Wyatt. "Then *you* hire the contractor. You're the one paying for it. Just call someone up and send him out there. There isn't a blamed thing they can do about it."

He'd actually worn a shirt instead of a turtleneck to the board meeting. Even though the shirt was black silk and worn with jeans, he created an impressive, if not precisely businesslike, figure. He had long arms that he swung restlessly, when he didn't have them crossed over his chest, intimidating someone. Pippa had to admit that shoulders as wide as his, combined with biceps that bulged when tensed, were as intimidating as all get-out. But unlike Billy, Seth didn't use his strength to push her around. He didn't have to. He could look at her and scare her half to death.

And still she hadn't learned to keep her mouth shut. She wondered if stupidity ran in the family or if she was the only one blessed with it.

Seth's fingers formed fists, and Pippa eyed them askance, pushing her chair back as far as it could go before he finally stopped pacing. As he halted in front of her but said nothing, she got a grip and glanced upward.

The expression in Seth's eyes was curious, and wary. "Why do you keep watching my hands that way?"

Startled, Pippa blushed and almost turned away. Taking a deep breath, she forced herself to face him. He was entirely too observant. "I don't like it when people bigger than I am make fists. If you're really in the mood for talking, sit."

He hesitated, towering over her as he did so. To her relief, he finally sprawled in an upholstered wing-back chair beside the desk. "Call a contractor in the morning. There should be a list in the Rolodex." He glanced at his hands, then laced his fingers and rested them on his chest, sprawling his legs in a more relaxed position as he watched her. "You're afraid of me."

"I am not," she lied. Of course she was. She was afraid of everything right now. That was why she was here, behind the safety of his locked gates, where she was safe from Billy. The question here was, was she safe from Seth?

"Are too." He challenged her with his look. "I don't hit women."

Okay, she could do this. Billy had robbed her of something precious, but she wasn't entirely a cringing ninny yet. Her employer had the social graces of an overgrown boy. She could handle that. "Fine, you only hit men," she agreed with a shrug. "I'll remember that."

"I don't hit men unless they hit me first."

This was an idiotic conversation. Pippa tapped her pencil on the desktop. "Do men frequently hit you first?"

"Not frequently, no. I mashed Taylor Morgan's pretty nose once, though. I don't think he's ever forgiven me."

Ahh, now they were getting somewhere. Wondering why he'd pursued the topic, Pippa left the path wide open. "Did you go to school together?"

Seth looked vaguely startled, then shrugged. The motion threatened the top button of his shirt, widening the V there. He didn't seem aware of it. "I had tutors. My mother didn't believe in public schools."

That explained more than Pippa cared to examine. "Then why did you hit Taylor?"

"Because he hit me first. I told you that. At the time, I wasn't very good at it, but I made a lucky punch. Broke it. I think he's had plastic surgery since. His family blackballed me from the country club for years." He grinned, a wolfish grin entirely alien to his usual demeanor.

He was leading her on, right down the old garden path. She'd had some infantile idea that he was opening up to her, trying to explain what was between him and the town. Instead, he was giving her the runaround. She sighed in exasperation. "All right, I'll bite. What did you do, buy the country club?"

"You're no fun at all, you know that?" He got up and started pacing the floor again. "You'd have to live in this town all your life before you'd understand the relationship between me and them. It's just much simpler if I leave them alone and vice versa. We don't mix. There's no point in trying."

"I'm not asking you to mix. Rot here in your ivory tower if you like, I don't care. I just want that gym for Chad and the others, and I'll do whatever it takes to get it. But the whole thing is childish, if you ask me."

"I don't remember asking you," he growled, swinging around. "Just keep me out of any more of those performances. I don't want anything to do with them."

"Fine, see if I care. I didn't ask you to come tonight. That was your own doing."

"Right. And sending me a fax telling me I set a poor example of a father for Chad by playing the part of coward was supposed to keep me out of this."

He hovered belligerently over her now, but oddly enough, Pippa had lost her fear. She stood up nearly toe-to-toe with him. His proximity set her back, but not from fear. The physical electricity emanating from him jolted her as if she'd stuck a finger in a socket. She rested her hand on the desk, hoping to ground herself.

"Everything you do sets an example for Chad. Try remembering that the next time you get the urge to bop Taylor Morgan in the nose." Easing between Seth and the chair, Pippa edged toward the door. She wasn't equipped for these games right now. Seth Wyatt made her damned nervous, and she didn't intend to examine why.

"And now you're a child psychologist?" he taunted as she reached for the knob.

She swung her head so hard, her hair bounced in her face.

"And just exactly who are you emulating when you bray like a pompous jackass like you're doing now?"

"As," he muttered as she stalked out the door, "as you're doing now." But she was gone and didn't hear him.

Deflated and depressed, Seth paced the floor a few more times. He hadn't realized until tonight that Pippa was afraid of him. He glanced guiltily at the hands that had already curved into fists again. He cursed and unclenched his fingers. She had every right to be afraid of him. Sometimes, he was a monster, just as Natalie claimed. He had no business around normal people. He just hadn't thought it mattered to his defiant, courageous pest of an assistant. He'd thought they'd reached some understanding: He'd growl and she'd bark. He could live with that. He couldn't live with the nagging guilt of her fear, or the darker desire flowing hotly beneath it.

The office had gone empty and silent with Pippa's departure. As long as she'd been here, he could block out the banshees of doubt, but their howls haunted the chambers of his mind now. Alcohol would blot them out, but he'd given up that solution years ago.

He should never have gone to the town meeting. He should never have exposed his uncertainties to Pippa. A man in his position was supposed to be self-assured, competent, in control—not a freaking adolescent.

Damn.

Slamming into his own office, he grabbed pen and paper and cranked his chair back. At least the freaking adolescent could shatter his demons on paper.

Sitting on the pool's edge, kicking her feet in the cool water, watching Chad with the grandmotherly therapist Seth had finally hired, Pippa tried to let her mind float. She'd read about people who could achieve a Zen state beyond the conscious mind. She wished she could do it. Instead of a state of peace, she merely achieved a headache blocking out thoughts of Seth and the town and the gym and the always hovering fear of what Billy might be doing now.

She'd talked to a friend back home. Billy had taken a leave of absence from the police force.

Maybe he'd checked into a psychiatric hospital for counseling.

Fat chance.

So she sunned herself on the tiles, listened to Chad's irate screams of protest, admired the therapist's patient admonitions, and considered means of bringing Seth and the town together. If she had to concentrate on something, it might as well be a worthwhile project. There was nothing productive about conjuring images of Seth's fists and anger. The potential might be there in his simmering anger and greater strength, but she had no right confusing Seth with Billy.

She knew the moment Seth walked through the open French doors. There was definitely no comparison with Billy. In her mind's eye, she could see the gleaming bronze of his chest, the curl of dark hairs there and on his arms. . . .

She stopped herself. She could admit that her employer was a handsome man. Sort of handsome, she amended. His features were more striking than pretty—sharp, angular, with planed surfaces instead of curved. But he had the personality of a poisonous serpent. She didn't need any more psychotic men in her life, thank you very much.

"I believe you owe me a swimming lesson, Miss Cochran."

She admired the long elegant bones of his tanned feet as they stopped beside her. "Shouldn't we wait until Chad is through with his lesson?" she inquired, with what she hoped was composure.

"He's in the shallow end. We can use the other side. I want to keep an eye on Chad, and it will be a more efficient use of time if we work on my lessons now."

Right. And it would be damned smarter to do this with an audience. Taking a deep breath, Pippa swung her legs from the water. A tanned, long-fingered hand reached down to help her up.

She didn't want to take it. It would be akin to wrapping her fingers around a live wire. She was perfectly aware that libido and brains had nothing to do with each other, and hers were working at opposite purposes. But she couldn't refuse him. She just didn't have it in her to be rude.

Gingerly, she lay her too-white fingers across his palm. His hand closed around hers and he drew her up in one powerful surge. She tried not to focus on long legs or broad chest or any of the other things practically sliding under her nose as she reached her feet. But she couldn't ignore the knowledge that whatever she thought of her employer's rotten disposition, she was drawn to his body entirely too much.

"Cat got your tongue, Miss Cochran?" he taunted.

He knew what he was doing to her, the cursed man. Reaching deep down inside herself for the confident teenager she once had been, Pippa boldly straightened the shoulder strap of her swimsuit, drawing Seth's attention to her breasts, then strolled toward the other side of the pool, fully aware that she now had his complete attention. It was childish. Everything about this—relationship—was purely adolescent. She hadn't felt anything like this since she was sixteen and enamored of the college lifeguard at the public pool. She was thirty years old and fifteen pounds heavier now, yet her toes curled and her heart raced faster knowing she held the attention of Seth Wyatt. And she deliberately rolled her hips in response.

"Very impressive performance, Miss Cochran," Seth murmured as he strolled up beside her.

"One more crack like that, Mr. Wyatt, and I'll hit you with a sexual harassment suit," she replied with equanimity. For years she'd defended herself against randy interns and doctors who should have known better. She knew how to post "Hands Off!" signs. She was just doing a damned poor job of it around Seth.

"Charming. I apologize. I should have known better." His tone turned as frosty as his usual glare.

Insanely, she wanted to take it back, to comfort him, to tell him—what? That it was perfectly all right to admire her as much as he wanted? That she liked knowing she wasn't completely over the hill? That she liked it even better that he thought her attractive? She had the brains and morals of a rabbit.

The shrill ring of a phone intruded upon the pleasant lap of water and music of birdsong.

Seth cursed.

Returned to the mundane business world, Pippa dared to look at him again. "You turned on the voice mail, didn't you?"

"That's the house phone. Doug's calling me."

He looked truly put-upon as he strode off toward the other end of the pool. Maybe there were disadvantages to wealth and fame. Even a simple thing like a swim in a pool or a mild flirtation had time limits. That's all it was, Pippa reasoned. A mild flirtation. They were stranded out here all alone with no one else to distract them. It was normal male/female behavior. She'd have to see about finding a boyfriend in town.

She didn't want a boyfriend.

Sighing at her perverse nature, she wandered back toward Chad and his teacher. Chad had his father's charming personality. The boy cursed and thrashed and fought every minute of the way, but he persevered. She suspected she might see tears of frustration streaming down his cheeks if water hadn't already streamed from his hair. But he refused to give up. He wouldn't even get out of the pool when his instructor called for a rest.

Seth's loud curse as he flung the cordless phone back to the lounge drew Pippa's attention away from the pool. The pure frustration written across his screwed-up features warmed her heart. She wanted to pat that broad, bronzed back and say, "There, there, it can't be that bad." Why had God cursed her with this nurturing nature? It was a wonder she didn't take up the care and feeding of vipers while she was at it.

"Someone bombed the Japanese printing plant?" she asked pleasantly. "Your latest book didn't make the *Times* list?" Teasing him added some distance, but not enough. His look of fury only tickled her toes.

"My mother's at the gate." Glancing up, he focused his fury on her. "You wouldn't happen to know anything about that, would you?"

Smiling inside, Pippa lifted her hands in a helpless gesture. "I only told her you were too busy with the school board and Chad's therapist right now to come visit her."

She could almost see the venom in his eyes. Odd, she'd thought vipers had venom in their teeth.

"I'll get even with you for this."

He stalked off, pulling on a shirt as he did so. Well, that took care of the swimming lessons for the day.

Now, what else could she do to turn Tyrant Tarant into a human being again?

FOURTEEN

"Seth, dear, fetch my cosmetic case, will you? I know I brought it. It must still be downstairs somewhere."

Lillian Wyatt's strident voice carried from the upper loft to the open foyer where Pippa waited. She glanced at Doug, who shrugged his massive shoulders, looked around at the baggageless entrance, and sidled toward the door.

"Check her car again," Pippa whispered before he could escape. "And take real good care of her driver or you'll be the one driving her around."

"I'll quit first," he grumbled, reaching for the door. "Somebody shoulda put her out of her misery long ago."

The phone rang in the office behind her and, distracted, Pippa let Doug escape. She could hear Seth's low, rumbling voice reply to his mother's querulous tones, and was amazed at his patience. She'd expected him to throw her over the balcony.

Even as she answered the phone and directed the call, she listened for voices in the hall. Chad would be coming in soon. How would Mrs. Wyatt treat her only grandchild? Chad needed a female influence in his life, if only to soften the hard edges so similar to his father's.

What was she thinking? Lillian Wyatt had raised Seth without any noticeable softening. She must be getting desperate trying to avoid the sticky trap of all these needy people. She really ought to learn the trick of minding her own business and looking out for herself.

But she couldn't. Looking after others was so ingrained that she'd postponed her own life as a result. She couldn't—wouldn't—go looking for still another case to nurse at the expense of her own future. Let Lillian Wyatt look after Chad.

Even as she thought that, the plump, pleasant, pepper-and-salt-haired therapist appeared in the doorway.

"Excuse me, Miss Cochran, but our lesson is over for the day. Do you think someone could show me the gym that is being remodeled? Mr. Wyatt asked for my suggestions."

Outside the office, Lillian Wyatt's whining tones had escalated to anger. Seth's patient reply sounded a little frayed around the edges.

As the idea struck her, Pippa flinched. She just couldn't keep from getting involved. With a bright smile, she punched the voice mail button and gestured for the therapist to precede her out of the room. Tomorrow, or the next day, she would practice noninvolvement in the dysfunctional family.

"If you'll wait a few minutes, Mrs. Turner, I'll speak with Mr. Wyatt. I believe he wants to inspect the premises also."

Wondering if she'd truly lost her mind, Pippa hurried up the stairs and into the rampaging storm.

"Excuse me, Mr. Wyatt." She halted in the open doorway of the spacious master suite Lillian Wyatt had sailed into as if it were her own. As it had been at one time, Pippa surmised.

The look of relief on Seth's face was so obvious, Pippa almost laughed aloud. The rueful apology in his eyes as he edged toward her made her day. Seth Wyatt might be big and strong, more worldly, talented, and wealthy than she'd ever be, but he had a definite zero IQ in personal relationships.

"Mrs. Turner is ready to inspect the facilities now. I'll have Doug bring around the car. Did you want Chad to go with you?"

With proper arrogance, Seth nodded curtly. "Of course, Miss Cochran. Have him meet me outside." He turned to Lillian, who followed the tableau with suspicion. "Mother, I have an appointment. Nana will look for your missing luggage. If you'll excuse me?"

He hurried after Pippa, closing the door on his mother's rising protests. "You sounded just like Miss MacGregor," he whispered approvingly. "What facilities are we inspecting and can it take a week?"

"We're inspecting the gym and unless you're moving it to Alaska, no, I don't think it can take a week." Pippa turned down the wing leading to Chad's room but glanced back at her crestfallen employer. "You do have an appointment with your lawyer in L.A. this evening, so you can be absent for dinner with good excuse."

"Thank God," Seth whispered reverently, shoving open the door to his room. A sudden recollection turned his expression suspicious. "What appointment with my lawyer?"

"The one I just made." Grinning cheekily, Pippa hurried off to find Chad.

A quarter of an hour and a few phone calls later, Pippa had the expedition arranged to her satisfaction. Nana had scolded Lillian Wyatt into submission and quiet reigned in that part of the house. Chad chattered happily as Pippa steered him out the front door and down the ramp installed just for him.

"I floated, didn't I? You saw me float," Chad announced to the world as Doug hurried to help him into the new Mercedes.

"We saw you float, cowboy, now let's hear you quiet. My ears are still ringing." Pippa ruffled his hair affectionately, then stepped away from the car as Seth approached.

"Get in the back with Chad, Miss Cochran. I'll ride up front with Doug." Seth held the car door, impatiently waiting for her obedience.

"I'll ride with Mrs. Turner."

He'd changed into a casual black golf shirt, open at the

collar, and he'd shaved with something light and refreshing that smelled like lemon and lime. The impact hit Pippa in her lower abdomen, and she inched away carefully.

"Nonsense. Get in. I want to talk about those chapters you typed last night."

Okay, so that's what an assistant did. She could deal with it. Gesturing to Mrs. Turner in the car behind them, Pippa climbed into the backseat with Chad. The scent of new leather engulfed her, alleviating the impact of Seth's subtle aftershave as he climbed in and closed the door.

Seth discussed alternative gruesome deaths for his deadly gopher as the Mercedes glided down the drive and through the gates, but Pippa sensed his thoughts were elsewhere. She suspected that, if they were alone, he would have a good deal more to say to her, and none of it pleasant. But he let Chad add his enthusiastic suggestions without complaint, and the ride continued in an amicable fashion.

Knowing what waited at the other end, Pippa was certain his good humor wouldn't last. She shouldn't harass the poor man so, but someone had to do it, and she already knew hers was a temporary position. Being the most expendable, she could stick her neck out farther.

She just refused to consider what she would do should she lose the security of Seth's ironclad fortress.

The battered van waiting outside the gym lifted her spirits. Meg hadn't been a cheerleader for nothing. She rallied round the home team at any call.

Ignoring Seth's ominous silence, Pippa helped with Chad's chair, greeted Mrs. Turner as she parked her Escort, and chattered aimlessly as they approached the gym.

Seth scowled at the rusting metal doors, remained stonily silent as he held one open, and crossed his arms and leaned against the gym wall after they entered.

Pippa contemplated kicking him, but decided that wasn't

conducive to a pleasant atmosphere. Instead, she greeted Meg and Mikey, leaving Seth sulking in the shadows of the entrance.

Meg had brought several of the other children she'd mentioned. Pippa kept a reassuring hand on Chad's shoulder as he eyed the strangers warily. Tension vibrated from the boy. There was nothing laid-back and easygoing about these Wyatt men. Their intensity could fuel rockets.

"When Mikey introduces you, find something nice to say to each of them, or smile real big when you say hello, and you'll be halfway there," she whispered into his ear as Mikey wheeled his chair forward.

Chad nodded stiffly, and pulling away from her steadying hand, entered the arena alone. The kid had courage, Pippa thought proudly.

Meg emitted a soft whistle beside her. "All you can do is pray, Pippa. I've got my rosary in my pocket." She glanced furtively over her shoulder at the doorway. "That wouldn't be Seth himself back there, would it? How'd you pull that off?"

"I'll tell you another time," Pippa murmured. "Mrs. Turner, shall we show you around?" she asked aloud.

As Meg and the therapist consulted over Mikey's condition, Pippa stepped back. The children were circling each other, one doing somersaults to show off, while another stood shyly, holding a malformed arm. Chad didn't look any more or less uncertain than the others. Nodding in satisfaction, she turned to see if Seth had disappeared yet.

He'd wandered from the doorway to examine an old rope hanging from the deteriorating ceiling. Giving it a hard tug, he brought it down in a shower of rotten plaster.

The kids cheered, and at Chad's instigation, ran, wheeled, and skipped over to examine the gaping hole.

"Good work, cowboy," Pippa said wryly, strolling over to join them. "Gonna lasso a dogie now?"

"A doe-gie?" he asked, imitating her accent. "Let me guess, you grew up on old Westerns."

"Hey, Dad, can we have that rope?"

"Depends on what you're going to do with it." Seth gazed absently at the hole in the ceiling, dangling the rope in his hand.

"Play tug-of-war," Mikey replied excitedly. "I seen 'em do it on TV."

"Saw them," Seth and Chad chimed together.

Pippa laughed and pinged her finger on Chad's head. "It's impolite to correct others. And if you play tug-of-war, you're likely to jerk each other out of your chairs."

"That's okay, Pippa, I can get back in mine by myself," Mikey declared proudly.

"All right, but you've all got to share. Divide up by ages, the youngest with the oldest to balance out."

"I can only hold with one hand," the girl with the unformed arm said hesitantly.

"That's okay, you've got two legs," Chad chided. "Come on. Let's do it over there, away from this mess."

As the children raced excitedly across the warped floor, Pippa dared a swift glance at Seth.

He stood as if stunned, staring after the children. Apparently sensing her gaze, he blinked, and shut down his expression.

He lifted an imperious eyebrow. "You have a question?"

"No, just an observation. Your son has the makings of a true leader."

Seth's frozen features almost softened. "Or a bully, depending on circumstances," he agreed.

"I hadn't thought about that. There's a fine line, isn't there?" Pippa watched all traces of shyness between the children disappear as an animated discussion over ages and teams ensued.

"And now you're going to tell me it's adult guidance that will determine which path he follows." Seth shoved his hands into his pockets and glared at the noisy group as if he could force the right decision with the power of his vision. "And if you tell me I haven't got what it takes, I'll fire you."

Pippa chuckled. "I'm stupid, but not that stupid. Anyway, I was going to say that a lot of it *isn't* in your hands. Peer pressure, the child's own nature, anything can mold a character. Maybe Meg has the right idea—pray a lot."

"Right, and throw coins in a fountain. I—"

"Mr. Wyatt, could we speak with you a minute? We've had an idea for the shower room."

Seth threw a disgruntled look toward the two women across the room. "You had to drag me into this, didn't you?" he said in an aside to Pippa.

"You could have stayed home with your mother," Pippa replied cheerfully, leading the way since it was obvious Seth would drag his feet otherwise.

"I suppose you invited her just to drive me out of the house," he grumbled. "Next time, I'll specify a male assistant."

"Next time, you'll be lucky to find anyone at all. They won't bite, I promise."

"They'll chatter. They'll whine. They'll expect me to agree with everything they say and cry if I don't. I don't get along well with women, Miss Cochran."

"You don't get along well with anyone, Mr. Wyatt. And none of that has stopped you from disagreeing with me at every corner."

"That's because I can fire you." Straightening his shoulders, Seth stalked up to join Meg and the therapist.

They ignored his glower and launched into a description of whirlpool baths and safety ramps.

"Kids don't need whirlpools," he interrupted coldly.

"This is a *community* gym," Meg reminded him. "There are veterans here who have to travel all the way to L.A. for treatment. How much more could one whirlpool cost?"

"Find out," Seth ordered, "but let the damned state pay for it. There ought to be federal funds for vets."

"Excellent idea!" Mrs. Turner's eyes lit with enthusiasm. "I'll look into it. We might be able to get grants for those ramps, too."

Pippa had begun to recognize the stunned look at the corners of Seth's eyes. He'd expected to terrify, not excite them. It made one wonder what kind of women he'd dealt with all his life.

Remembering the whining, querulous old woman at the house, she had some idea. Which gave rise to the question: What had his ex-wife been like?

An ominous cracking noise and an outcry from the direction of the children immediately turned their attentions elsewhere.

"Shit," Seth muttered under his breath before loping across the floor to the place where Mikey's wheelchair tilted dangerously into a hole created by a rotten floorboard.

Racing after him, Pippa picked up speed at the pop of still another cracking board. Mikey's chair tilted even farther, and the children screamed at the top of their lungs.

"It's all right," Seth shouted at the children. "Just back off so you don't fall through, too."

"Mikey's hurt," Chad cried in response. His knuckles were white as he grasped the arms of his own chair. "Look, his foot's caught!"

"It's all right," Seth answered soothingly, stopping behind the tilted chair. "There are big supports under the floor, so it can't go through. Can you hang on, Mike?"

With amazement, Pippa watched Seth quiet the children, survey the problem, decide on a solution, and put it into action, all without requesting help from anyone. The man behaved as if there weren't another adult in the room. She wouldn't argue with the result, but her curiosity inched another notch higher. Had he grown up in such total isolation that he relied only on himself?

As Seth eased the chair out of the hole and backed Mikey to

safety, Meg cried out in relief and raced to examine the damage to Mikey's foot.

"Do we need to get him to a doctor?" Seth asked.

Startled, Pippa realized Seth stood beside her. She had been so focused on Mikey that she had lost track of everyone else. Watching as Meg gingerly moved her son's foot, she shook her head. "Just for safety's sake, maybe, but I don't think there's any harm done. He'll be bruised, no doubt. We'd better get the other kids out of here before someone else gets hurt. Looks like this place may not be as sound as we'd hoped."

Seth looked vaguely perplexed as he contemplated the problem. "If your friend needs to get her kid to the doctor, she can't take all these others home."

Pippa bit back a smile and nodded solemnly. "Maybe you can drive her to the doctor in the car, and Doug and I can take the van."

The expression of alarm on his face was priceless. Pippa would give anything for a camera. The man very definitely was not accustomed to dealing with people.

"You drive her to the doctor. I'll go with Doug in the van," he decided, not looking particularly happy about this solution either. Then another thought occurred to him as Meg tried to wheel the bent chair toward the door. "That kid's chair isn't worth the metal it's made of. Why the hell didn't they get him something stronger?"

"Because they don't have any money," Pippa said softly. "Because his father is self-employed with limited insurance, and his customers are moving out of the valley as fast as they can find jobs elsewhere."

Seth shot her a malevolent look. "And you probably planned this whole incident. I'll carry him out to the car. You round up the kids." With that, he stalked away.

A good swift kick to the rear wasn't sufficient. Maybe a shotgun blast to the head might succeed.

Seth Wyatt very definitely needed his priorities rearranged. And she was just the woman to do it.

Hell, she'd done dumber things in her life, and for less reason. As long as he was blaming her anyway, why not?

FIFTEEN

"We can call in Social Services to observe Chad's home life. It will sound much better to the court if a state employee gives a positive report than if we paid someone. And they could recommend a child psychologist who will verify that your son is well adjusted and well cared for."

Seth gave a mental groan and covered his eyes. He could just imagine a state employee observing Doug staggering down the drive in one of his drunken sprees or getting hit with a blast of water from the demented gardener. Better yet, they could observe the dynamics of his household with his mother in full sail. That should give them a unique observation or two. He wouldn't even consider what a child psychologist would report about a six-year-old who read Stephen King.

He shook his head. "It won't do, Morris. I'll not have smarmy clerks crawling all over the place. Chad can speak for himself. I have an assistant who's also an RN. She can testify, if necessary. Natalie is just drumming up excuses. She has no case. I'll not dignify her charges with my protests."

His lawyer sat back in his leather chair, twirling a pen between his fingers. Seth didn't like the considering look Morris gave him, but he didn't flinch before it. He'd dealt with lawyers all his life. They were a different species from women and kids—lawyers understood authority.

"Your assistant isn't exactly a disinterested third party."

"You haven't met my assistant," Seth replied, attempting to keep the wryness out of his voice. "If she saw anything so much as resembling abuse, she'd be down my throat and calling for the authorities faster than a speeding bullet. I'm not entirely certain she wouldn't be on Natalie's side if presented in court."

Morris raised his eyebrows. "I'd like to meet her sometime. I don't want to present a witness who'll do more harm than good."

Seth let his imagination roam to a meeting between Pippa and the stiff-necked Morris. She'd probably pinch his cheeks, pat his head, and offer him a cup of herbal tea, then sit down and take dictation of the exact testimony he wanted presented. Morris would swallow his teeth. It should be a good show.

Realizing he was thinking of that pestilent nuisance almost with affection, Seth ground his teeth and sat straighter. "You're welcome out to the house anytime, Morris, you know that. I'll warn you, my mother's visiting."

Morris coughed into his fist, flushed red under his dark skin, and nodded. "Well, we'll see about that. I just want you to understand the seriousness of the situation. The courts traditionally favor the mother. The public thinks you bought off the judge the first time. A new judge will have to be harsher just to keep his image clean. You really ought to reconsider my advice about the social workers."

Seth stood. "Visit sometime, Morris. You'll reconsider your own advice."

He left his lawyer's high-rise L.A. office with a twisted, sinking feeling in his stomach. He *had*, essentially, bought the original judge, not with money, but with influence. The Wyatt name carried wealth and power. Natalie had neither. Her family had left her enough to be comfortable on, but not enough to build an empire. It took empires to wield influence, and Seth owned one. Not that he particularly cared about owning one, and not that he arbitrarily used the influence that was at his fingertips, but he'd inherited the whole ball of wax from his father and was stuck with it. The judge had known that and been impressed with his power.

He supposed he could do it again. In general, people couldn't resist a man who could command the best that money could buy. He could trot out the high-priced physicians and psychiatrists again, prove that a boy needed a father, that Chad's condition required facilities and treatment Natalie couldn't afford, that Natalie's high-society life didn't leave her with the time or inclination to give her son the attention he needed. Heaven only knew, the doctors had been right about that one. Despite all her screams of protest, Natalie seldom took advantage of the visitation rights she'd been granted. He could use that against her, too, along with his detective's proof that Natalie was bankrupt and married to a financial idiot and professional snake-in-the-grass. It would serve her right for telling everyone that her first husband was a drunk who had wrecked the car and destroyed Chad's life.

If only he could prove that he hadn't been drunk and hadn't done just that.

Not liking the direction of his thoughts, Seth slammed his Jag into gear and steered toward Tracey's house.

Tracey had arrived to hold his hand shortly after Natalie had filed for divorce. A so-called friend of Natalie's, she'd just gone through a nasty divorce herself. Seth suspected she'd marked him for Husband Number Three, but she'd offered sex with no strings attached and he'd been too shell-shocked to refuse. Once he'd won Chad and returned to the isolation of Garden Grove, he hadn't been offered any similar opportunities for physical gratification, and the pattern had been set.

He needed sex right now. Mindless, selfish, greedy sex with any available female body. He needed oblivion, and without alcohol, sex filled the duty. Maybe then he could quit looking at his annoying mosquito of an assistant as if she were the last cookie crumb on the face of the earth.

Although Pippa Cochran was more like the whole cookie.

Fantasizing about round curves and plump cheeks, he missed the turn to Tracey's condo.

Cursing, he jerked the car around in a driveway and screeched back to the road. A line of cars backed up on the cross street prevented his driving through the green light.

Left with engine humming and libido steaming, Seth summoned the image of his assistant in her oh-so-proper one-piece bathing suit. No Hollywood bikini for Miss Kentucky. What did she think she was hiding anyway? No amount of spandex could disguise curves like those. Administrative assistants ought to be skinny and flat as a board. Like Miss MacGregor.

Following that line of thought, assistants ought to be efficient, obedient, self-effacing, and invisible.

So how had he hired a cheerful, disobedient, overconfident busybody instead?

She was efficient. But definitely not invisible. Far from invisible. She flaunted herself when she wasn't even in the same room with him. He could hear her soothing Chad's tantrums and wanted that honey-coated voice pouring over him. He'd watched out the window as she exchanged bouquets with Durwood and wanted her to bring one in to him. And damn it, he'd watched her with Chad and the others at the gym and wished he could be a similar beneficiary to her quiet guidance. She knew how to handle people. He'd never had the knack.

By the time he'd recovered from his reverie, he was on the road back home. Without a second thought, Seth hit the gas and continued in that direction. Tracey might offer sex, but she had never stimulated his imagination or convinced him that life could improve, given the proper care. Miss Pippa Cochran had opened a window and let in more sunlight than he'd seen in a lifetime.

So, he was nuts. He'd hire a psychiatrist and sue himself.

"Did you and my mother have an enjoyable dinner together?" Seth asked maliciously as he picked up his phone messages on the way past Pippa's desk the next day.

"After I convinced her that she had to smoke outside, we did fine." She jotted another note on her steno pad, stuck a pencil in her thick, bobbed hair, and swung her chair to face the computer instead of him. "I think she's lonely."

"I paid several million dollars for a condo in a neighborhood of suitable people so she could have all the friends she wanted." Seth dismissed his mother's complaint and sifted through his messages.

Pippa pushed a box across the desk. "Doug opened these. They didn't have a return address."

Seth glanced at the colorfully wrapped box of toffees and shrugged. "They're not my brand. I didn't order them. Heave them out."

She raised her eyebrows in apparent condemnation of his wastefulness and didn't do as told. As usual.

The dress she wore today had a green top resembling a high-collared halter, revealing rounded white shoulders and little else. Had it been Natalie or any other woman of his set, the collar would dip down to reveal the curves of her breasts. Not Miss Proper. Oh, no. Hers buttoned right up to the neck. She just didn't realize he could tell as much from the tailored fit of the dress as if she wore nothing at all. Imagination was a wonderful quality.

Miss Proper hit a few keys and the computer screen swirled, but Seth could see the wheels in her head whizzing faster than the computer. Instead of proceeding to his office to return phone calls, he lingered, waiting to hear the result of her thought processes.

"Family is more important than neighbors," she announced, apparently following their earlier conversation about his mother and the condo. "There's a bond there that doesn't exist anywhere else."

All right, so he'd asked for that. Imagination was always better than the real thing. Seth wandered toward the escape of his office. "Dream on." He dismissed her lecture.

"My mother died last year."

Damn. He'd almost gotten away. Leaning against the doorjamb, Seth watched her through narrowed eyes. She still wasn't looking at him. "I'm sorry. You were close?" What else could he say?

"I was the youngest. I guess so. I still want to pick up the phone and call her, ask for her advice, or her sympathy, or just an understanding word. She's still here with me, somehow. How about your father? Do you miss him?"

Now that she had him by the throat, she swung around and nailed him to the wall with those wide, green eyes. Double damnation.

Seth shrugged. "Not particularly. We didn't see each other much. He was always away on business trips, and then I went off to school and didn't come home often."

"I thought you were privately tutored."

He didn't want to go into all this. It wasn't any of her damned business. Nobody ever questioned him. No one else had the impertinence. Irked at his inability to slam the door in her face, he shoved his hands in his pockets and contemplated the space above her head.

"Through most of grade school. Then they sent me to boarding schools." After his mother started gambling, after he'd caught his father with one of his bimbos, after he'd nearly burnt down his parents' wing of the house, and other similar disasters. He had no desire whatsoever to reminisce over those years.

"That must have been hard," she said nonchalantly, her fingers flying over the keyboard as if she weren't listening at all. "Home-schooled kids always have a hard time adjusting to public schools. They don't know how to cope with other kids. And middle-school age is one of the roughest for boys."

Tell me about it, Seth snorted mentally. He hadn't been too successful at setting fire to the first school they sent him to, but the experiment had been enough to get him kicked out. After that, he'd discovered it was just as easy to insult the class bully and get pounded to a pulp, resulting in his mother's jerking him out of school. He'd been something of a wimp at that age, to put it mildly. He'd overcome that handicap with an adolescent growth spurt and an education his parents had known nothing about, but the wimpy kid still cowered inside him. He supposed that feeling never went away.

"I survived," he replied grumpily. "Have you finished those chapters yet?"

"I've almost finished the typing. I have to format them and run spell check. Must you write such gore? You know teenage boys drool over this stuff."

"And if they go around killing gophers, that's a bad thing?" he asked dryly, turning toward his office and away from his too perceptive assistant.

"Some teenage boys understand analogies," she sang out.

He shut the door between them.

Standing at the pool later that day, watching Seth Wyatt emerge from the cabana in his swimsuit, Pippa wondered how much California psychiatrists charged. She really ought to have her head examined for suggesting the swimming lessons. She'd dated a lot of men, but she couldn't think of a single one who matched Seth's physique. Billy had been big, but beefy. Seth was . . . Heck, Seth was everything a woman could wish for, and then some. He crossed the blue-and-earthen-colored tiles with the athletic grace of an Olympic swimmer. He must work out regularly.

Glancing down at her own less than svelte figure, Pippa considered doing the same, then forgot about it as Chad shouted in triumph from the shallow side of the pool.

"You've got it, cowboy!" she yelled back as he clung to the edge of the pool and shook water out of his eyes after traversing the width on his back under his therapist's watchful eye.

"That's still not swimming," Seth murmured as he reached her side.

"Knowing how to float can save his life, and it uses muscles he wouldn't otherwise be using. Besides, it gives him confidence. All children need to know they can accomplish what they set out to do." Pippa focused on the child in the water and not on the man beside her.

"And how do we teach him to withstand the blow to his self-esteem when he realizes most children can do a great deal more than he can ever hope to do?"

The bitterness in Seth's voice surprised her into looking up at him. She had thought to see pleasure at his son's accomplishment. Instead, his mouth had a grim set, and his eyes wore a tortured look she longed to erase. She didn't know why he was beating himself up like this, and she had no business asking.

She was an employee, and she'd better start behaving like one. If she could just treat Seth Wyatt like one of the doctors she'd scorned in her prior life, she'd be all right. But somehow, in her flight to California, she seemed to have lost that protective shield.

"Breaststroke?" she asked in her best clipped nurse's voice.

"Good a place as any to start. Did you ever discover who sent those toffees?"

With a clean, swift motion, he dived into the sparkling waters with every apparent expectation that she would follow him to continue their conversation.

With his dark hair plastered to his sculpted skull and long

neck, he resembled Errol Flynn in an old pirate movie. Maybe she should suggest he grow a mustache. Unable to dismiss the smile that image wrought, Pippa dived in after him, then stroked slowly in circles around him where he stood.

"UPS only has the address of the package pickup in L.A. Who knows you eat the nasty things?"

Seth shrugged and broke into a strong, if less then elegant, crawl across the pool. "Almost anyone who knows me. Lawyers, accountants, CEOs. I would have thought any of them would have had the presence of mind to include a note with their name on it. What's the point of buttering up the boss if he doesn't know who's doing it?"

"Someone probably has an inefficient secretary. And obviously insufficient knowledge of your habits if they sent the wrong brand. You need to find out who it is just so you can fire them." Pippa grinned as her thoughts jumped one step ahead of his. She had begun to understand the demented man. Scary thought. As he caught up with her in the section of the pool where she could stand, she demonstrated the breaststroke.

He repeated the motion carefully. "They'd have to have access to the place in England where I order them. Only my English associates recognize the brand."

"Ooo, so snooty you can't eat the American kind," she mocked, before striking out across the pool again, showing him the pattern of the kick and stroke.

His natural coordination lent his awkward first strokes a certain grace as he followed her. Damn, but he was good, Pippa observed as the tight little knot inside her spiraled tighter. Muscles rippled beneath bronzed skin glistening with water diamonds, but it was the wary look in Seth's eyes as he sought her approval that floored her completely.

"You catch on quickly," she admitted as he halted beside her. "I don't know why you wanted me to teach you. You could probably swim an ocean without need of any fancy strokes."

For just a moment, his eyes lit from within, and then that

wicked smile danced across his lips. "If you have to ask why I wanted you to teach me, you don't deserve an answer."

That couldn't be a come-on, not from Seth Wyatt. He didn't know she existed as anything beyond one of his office machines. She stared at him incredulously until a shout from beyond the hedge jerked her back to reality.

"Miss Cochran! You out here? Durwood's come up real sick. Maybe you'd better take a look at him."

Bursting through a break in the greenery, Doug halted, sweating, at the pool's edge. Finding Pippa, he gave her a hand and half hauled her from the water.

"It's those damned toffees you gave him," he spurted. "The damned fool must have eaten half the box. He's spewing his guts all over the place."

Frowning at the idea of a grown man getting sick on candy, Pippa followed Doug, and Seth loped after them.

SIXTEEN

"Toffee poisoning! That's a new one," the doctor scoffed as he scribbled a prescription. "He's probably just allergic to something in the candy coating. Some people are. Give him this to settle his stomach. Don't let him eat anything for a few hours. He really ought to be in an institution, I hope someone realizes. He's dangerous to himself, if nothing else."

Pippa scanned the prescription the doctor handed her, grimaced, and shoved it into her purse. "If one looks at it the right way, he *is* in an institution. At least this way, he's gainfully employed and a useful part of society. We just can't watch over him twenty-four hours a day."

"Neither can an institution," the doctor agreed. He switched his focus from Pippa to the man beside her. "Good to meet you, Mr. Wyatt. Heard a lot about you."

"Don't doubt that. How much do I owe you?" Seth replied without inflection, reaching for his wallet.

"Heard about your proposal for the gym. You wouldn't happen to have time for lunch some day this week, would you? I have a few ideas you might not have considered. . . ."

"I'm booked, but submit a proposal to my assistant, if you like. She's handling the matter." Brusquely, Seth laid out the required bills and strode out.

Pippa shrugged at the doctor's amazed expression. "If they're suggestions for making money, forget it. He won't be interested. If they're suggestions for helping the kids, he'll consider them. But I make no promises. He has a warped view of the world."

And she had some glimmer of why Seth's view was so warped as the doctor nodded and wandered back to his next patient. Everyone wanted something from him. No matter where he went or what he did, someone had their hand out. Half the town wanted the printing plant back. Meg and George wanted the gym for Mikey. The first few therapists she'd found had wanted money, power, or sex, or some combination of them all. Even Doug and poor Durwood wanted the haven Seth's estate offered. So did she, for that matter. When was the last time anyone had offered to give Seth something in return?

She pondered that realization all the way back to the house, with Durwood groaning in the front seat beside Doug, and Seth beside her in the backseat, glowering beneath his black cloud. She'd never had much acquaintance with rich people, not of Seth's standards, anyway. The doctors at the hospital had been wealthy far beyond her means, but even in their arrogance, they didn't wield the kind of financial power Seth had. Doctors might dangle gewgaws in front of the nurses, but Seth could dangle clinics and printing plants and security for untold hundreds. Maybe more. She didn't fully comprehend the extent of his wealth. But she was beginning to understand its limitations.

"I'll take Durwood to his room and see he takes his medicine," she offered softly as the car stopped in front of the garage. Not that she would have called it a garage. It was bigger than the house she grew up in. She'd like to get her hands on that candy. Maybe George knew a chemist who could analyze it. "You go look in on Chad."

Seth merely shook his head, and opening the front car door, hauled the still groaning Durwood from the seat. "No, I want to make certain the rest of that candy gets thrown out somewhere he won't find it, or he's likely to eat it again. I can get the medicine down him."

"I still think someone ought to look at that candy. . . ." she called after him. He didn't turn around.

He'd assumed his tough, arrogant pose again. He hadn't had time to brush his hair as it dried, and a dark curl cascaded across his forehead as he practically carried his small gardener toward the stairs to the garage apartment. Had he lived on the streets as a kid, he would have been a gang leader. She'd have to get her hands on the candy some other way.

The whining cries of Lillian Wyatt as Pippa entered the house reminded her of the other man behind Seth's tough exterior, the one who couldn't handle his own household. She could fix that. She could do something for him, even if he wouldn't acknowledge it.

Hearing his mother's voice in his outer office, Seth almost swiveled on his heels and escaped out the front door. But the incident with Durwood and the clinic had put him well behind schedule. He needed to get back to work.

He'd successfully avoided any interaction with his mother for years. He could manage a stroll past her now. As Pippa said: Chad needed a grandmother. He couldn't exactly remember her arguments as to why, but he could accept that kids needed grandmothers. He barely remembered his, but they were one of his more stable childhood memories. Maybe kids didn't see things in quite the same manner as adults.

Shoving open the office door, he thought to just nod and hurry back to his private sanctum. Instead, he halted in the doorway and stared at the amazing scene within. Had he encountered circus dogs and clowns, he could not have been more surprised.

Pippa had set up a card table in the reception area. He didn't doubt it had been Pippa who had done it. It would certainly never have occurred to his mother. On one side of the table Chad had parked his wheelchair. He sat there now, industriously sliding envelope closures over a damp sponge to seal them.

The more amazing sight was his mother on the other side of the table. Garbed in flowing turquoise silk, her artfully tinted white hair neatly coiffed, her ears and throat shimmering with heavy silver, Lillian Wyatt carefully applied self-sticking stamps to the envelopes Chad handed her. She then handed the envelope to Pippa beside her, who applied address labels.

Neither Chad nor Lillian looked up as he entered, but Pippa did. Flashing him one of those Pollyanna smiles of hers, she gestured at her assembly line. "I thought it made more sense to do it ourselves than to send them out."

Nothing made more sense. He didn't even know what they were doing. Didn't care. He had never—not ever—seen his mother sitting complacently at a table doing something besides playing cards and smoking. In the early days it might have been coffee instead of cards in her hands, but never had it been work of any type, manner, or form.

He didn't know how to react. He had an odd urge to take the remaining side of the table and join in the family fun. Once upon a time he'd glued himself to the television and watched old reruns of sixties programs where families sat around the supper table together and talked of the day's activities. At the time, he'd thought that was how families were supposed to work and resented the hell out of his for not meeting the norm. Since then, he'd learned differently, but that old ache remained. He wanted to be part of a real family.

Stupid, utterly irrational thought. His meddling assistant was simply playing another of her hocus-pocus tricks. Shortly, Lillian would grow bored and wander off in search of a cigarette. Chad would grow impatient with something that wouldn't go right, and he'd have a tantrum and fling the table across the room. Seth didn't want to be there when it all fell apart. He'd just store this idyllic image and run like hell before it exploded.

"Whatever makes you happy," he muttered, striding for his office as fast as his legs could carry him.

"Coward!" Pippa called cheerfully from behind him.

Exactly. Seth closed the door and leaned against it. She was taking his entire universe and turning it upside down. He had to put a stop to this. Maybe Mac's father had died quickly instead of lingering. Maybe he could bribe her into returning immediately. Things had to get back to normal or he'd start believing he belonged down this rabbit hole.

He snickered at the image of his mother as the March Hare and Chad as the Mad Hatter. He wished he could paint. What a scene that would make!

But he had business to conduct: a crisis in the Japanese plant, a pending merger in New York, and dozens of routine calls needing his attention. He didn't have time to imagine March Hares and Mad Hatters. If Lewis Carroll had spent more time tending business instead of rowing boats, smoking dope, and admiring little girls, he'd not have had time to create impossible worlds either.

Seth sank into his desk chair and attacked the mountain of paperwork waiting. Tonight, when all the phones stopped ringing and everyone went home, he could lose himself in the world of his imagination. That time was his and no Pollyannas could steal it from him.

Laughter rippled from the outer room. His attention half on the voice on the other end of the line and half on Chad's giggles, Seth forgot who he was calling. Shaking his head to clear it, he tried to focus on the conversation. Finally giving up on the details of the merger his CEO in New York was spelling out, he spat out a few curt commands and assigned the matter to his legal firm out there. He didn't give a damn who got what stock option.

His father should never have left him the business. He had no head for it, no desire for it, no ambition for it. He had the brains for it, maybe, but that was about it.

Picking up the phone to return the next call, he heard another round of laughter in the outer room. He still couldn't believe it. She was definitely a sorceress of some sort. Or maybe they were keeping a pitcher of martinis under that card table. Firmly, he pounded in the proper numbers.

As soon as he hung up, his door opened and Pippa's head popped from behind it.

"Did you get those toffees away from Durwood?" she whispered over the chatter from behind her.

"I did." Seth threw open his desk drawer and held up the box. "They even smell nasty. Why in the devil would he put the things in his mouth?" Relieved for this excuse not to think about the Japanese crisis, he opened the lid and offered her a sniff.

She shook her head and refused to enter his inner sanctum. "I'll take your word for it. But you'd better not leave them in your desk. Chad might take a fancy to them, or you might forget and pick one up. I think they're tainted. I've never heard of allergic reactions to toffee that resulted in intense vomiting."

"Well, the syrup of ipecac you forced down him didn't help," he reminded her. "The poor guy will have to eat for a week to make up for it."

"He behaved more like a victim of poisoning than someone with an allergic reaction. It seemed like the sensible thing to do at the time. He was in *pain*. The doctor didn't see that because Durwood was feeling better after getting all that stuff out of his stomach. I just think it's awfully odd that you receive a box of candy with no return address and it makes your gardener sick. Let me take it in to George. Maybe he knows someone who can do a chemical analysis on it."

Seth grinned. "And I thought I was the one with the imagination around here. Who would want to poison me? My competition wanting to eliminate me from the bestseller list?" Even as he said it, he remembered the muggers at the bar, but he dismissed them summarily and continued, "My voracious instincts for business have annoyed one too many printing companies? My publisher thinks I'll start my own company and put them out of business?"

"In case you haven't noticed, this world is full of nuts. Humor me. Give me the box." She stuck out her hand. "Then come have tea with us. We're having a party."

Seth laughed out loud. He couldn't help it. The Dormouse had just invited him to tea. It felt good to laugh, as if someone had just filled him up with helium and let him drift. He couldn't remember the last time he'd really laughed. Maybe never.

Pippa wore a peeved expression and seemed prepared to slam the door on his rude reaction. Seth waved his hand to prevent it until he calmed down.

"It's a private joke," he sputtered finally as a tentative smile returned to her face. "I'm still trying to decide whether you're Pollyanna or the Dormouse."

She grinned. "Dormouse? I've heard the Pollyanna bit, and I promise you, I am very definitely not Pollyanna. I've seen the bloody side of life too often to believe everything will always come up roses. But Dormouse?"

He assumed his best stoic executive expression. "Or Pippi Longstocking. Quite possibly Pippi Longstocking. She had a definite mischievous bent to her actions."

"Larcenous is more like it, so I don't thank you for the comparison. Will you have tea with us or not? Nana has made chocolate chip cookies."

"Those are the only kind of cookies Nana knows how to bake." Unfolding from the chair, Seth followed the path of least resistance. Tea and cookies—even with his mother—seemed much more appealing than a paper crisis in a Japanese printing plant.

Of course, some niggling voice at the back of his mind said tea and cookies with Pippi Longstocking was an even stronger attraction.

Sometime, when he had the time, he would have to see if Pippa was seducible.

The possibility added an extra edge to the day, a certain anticipation he hadn't felt in a long time. He knew better than to seduce an employee, of course. He would never really do it. But just the *thought* of it would keep him occupied for hours. He had lots of experience in imagining what he would like to have. He had limited experience in obtaining it, since very little of what he wanted could be bought for coins.

As he sat down at a shabby card table littered with envelopes and sipped at weak tea, nibbling cookies with his son while his mother looked on approvingly, Seth wondered if he'd just reached one of his imagined goals: sitting down at the table with his family.

Glancing askance at his impish assistant and finding her contentedly licking chocolate off her finger, he felt the impact of an unexpected blow to the gut.

It had taken Pippa Cochran to open a door he'd thought long since sealed shut. It had taken his nuisance of an assistant to make one of his dreams come true.

SEVENTEEN

"I think we need a committee, Pippa." Meg sipped her coffee with an unusually serious expression. "We don't want Seth pulling the strings and then cutting them."

"He's not like that," Pippa insisted with irritation, fanning herself with a magazine. Meg's air-conditioning had quit and the dry breeze through the window scarcely stirred the air. Already, she longed for the cooler air of the evergreens and hills of Seth's mansion. When she left this job, she would have to make certain she took another one in the hills. She definitely did not like the valley.

Nor did she like thinking about finding another job.

"Seth has so many things to do at once. He just can't keep up with them all. That's why he needs me. I won't let the strings drop. But maybe community input would help. I don't like the word 'committee.' In my experience, they hinder more than help."

Meg pondered that for a minute. Then wiping her brow with a paper napkin, she shrugged. "I don't know how you can get community input without a committee. Let me get together a few people. Some of the parents, maybe Taylor Morgan, and the mayor—if he's interested—people like that. Taylor and the mayor will know about grants and stuff. And we'll need a representative from the school board since they own the building."

Pippa grimaced. "Taylor will give you a hard time. Seth broke his nose once."

For the first time that morning, Meg perked up. "Really? How? Why? Tell all."

"Accidentally, I suspect. Seth's not very communicative. But I think the bad blood goes both ways. You didn't grow up here any more than I did, so you probably don't know the half of it. Maybe it's up to outsiders to bring the town and Seth together again."

Meg brushed a wisp of frizzy hair from her face and stared at the ceiling as if listening for some sound from the children above. Shaking herself from her reverie, she sipped at her coffee again, but her smile had disappeared. "It may be too late, Pippa. George is applying for positions all around the state. It's breaking his heart to leave his daddy's store, but we've got expenses we can't meet, and the kids come first. It's always been his dream to come back here and take over that store. Those visits with his father every summer were what he lived for as a kid. I hate seeing him like this."

Pippa's heart sank. Meg was her best friend. She loved George and the kids like family. She'd been driven from the one home she'd ever known and now her adopted one was about to crumble under her. She couldn't let it happen, not if there was any way of preventing it. There had to be a way.

"Don't give up, Meg," she urged. "Better things will come along if we work at it. Let me loan you some of this ridiculous salary Seth is paying me. I don't need it. I just pried it out of him out of spite for what he's done to you. So, in a way, it belongs to you."

Meg almost smiled. "There's Pollyanna speaking. Thanks, Pippa, but you've earned every bit of that money putting up with him. And you might need it someday. He's likely to turn you out with a bad reference."

"He's not like that." Really cross now, Pippa stood up and paced the tiny kitchen. "He puts on this ugly face to drive people away, but underneath, he's this scared little boy. I don't think he was ever allowed to interact with other children when he was a kid. And I suspect he had some pretty unpleasant experiences once he was thrust into the real world."

She swung around and glared at Meg. "We may have grown up poor, but by golly, we grew up happy, with loving families and friends. Money can't buy that, you know."

Meg stared at her in astonishment. "You aren't falling for that man, are you? Phillippa Cochran, you have the worst taste in men I have ever seen. Positively self-destructive. You need a psychiatrist."

"Yeah, I know that." Filling a glass with water from the sink, Pippa took a long pull. "But not because I'm 'falling' for Seth Wyatt. I need to have my head examined for trying to save the world when most of the time, the world doesn't want to be saved. Let me start some kind of fund for the kids. Isn't that what a godmother is for?"

Meg shook her head, but she was smiling again. "You're a case, Pippa, and that's a fact. Okay, we'll leave Taylor off the committee. Anyone else I should blackball?"

Pippa swirled the water in her glass and watched it slosh to the edge. "Did George do anything about that candy?"

Meg raised her eyebrows. "You were serious about that? I thought it was some kind of joke. Durwood's quite capable of eating poppy seeds until he hallucinates. It doesn't take poison to do him in."

"The candy was intended for Seth," Pippa reminded her. "I may be overreacting, but if so many people hate Seth, wouldn't it be possible someone would wish him ill?"

"Possible, maybe. Probable, no. Besides, if it took half a box to make Durwood ill, what could a few pieces do for a man as big as Seth?"

"Eat his stomach out," Pippa answered matter-of-factly.

She'd had time to think about it and hadn't liked her thoughts at all. "Durwood was saved precisely because he ate too many and spewed it all back up. Seth would have eaten just enough to keep them down and let them go to work."

"You're certifiable, I swear you are." Meg got up and rinsed out her cup. "But because I love you, I'll humor you. Let me call George and see what he did with the stuff. And *then*," she added firmly, "we'll form a committee."

"The candy was probably an early birthday present. I wish you would drop the subject and tell me what you think of the last chapter."

Slapping on suntan lotion, Seth watched Chad and Mikey with the therapist at the other end of the pool. Pippa hadn't even asked his permission to bring the kid out here. She'd just appeared with him after her trip into town. Seth clung to his irritation, but Chad was having such a good time, he couldn't remember why he was irritated. Maybe it was that cough Chad had developed overnight. But Pippa had told him it could be an allergy.

Pippa's reply brought Seth's wandering attention back to the subject of his last chapter.

"I don't like books where the hero walks into the sunset and leaves the heroine behind."

Seth could almost swear she sounded disgruntled. Amazed that she'd even read the material, he tried to maintain his attitude of uninterest. "I don't write Harlequins," he answered with what he hoped was the proper disdain.

"You couldn't," she scoffed. "It takes a heart and soul to write romance, and you haven't got them. You just need a sick mind."

"Listen to the brilliant literary critic!" Refusing to listen to any more of this nonsense, Seth dived into the water to hide his scowl. Miss MacGregor had always given his writing her complete and enthusiastic support. He was a bestseller, damn it. Who did Pippa think she was to criticize him?

But unease at her words tugged at his thoughts. Why shouldn't the hero "walk off into the sunset," as she put it? That's what heroes did. They didn't hang around waiting for some female to slobber over them. Females would more likely stab them in the back.

Even as his mind conjured that vicious thought, Seth recognized its origins. Cursing to himself, he dove down and skimmed the bottom of the pool. Emerging from the water between the two boys, he grabbed one in each arm, shoved off from the side of the pool with his feet, and swept them to the other side of the shallow depths with a few quick kicks.

The kids squealed and hollered, excited by the new game. Rather pleased that he'd found a way of playing with his son that didn't involve books, Seth tried to ignore his redheaded assistant lapping leisurely in the other end of the pool. "Tried" being the operative word. He knew the instant she pulled herself from the pool to answer the cordless.

She already knew he wouldn't accept calls during the hour he spent monitoring Chad's lessons. The business could crumble and fall, for all he cared. His father had lived and breathed those damned printing plants. Seth didn't need reminding of how neglect felt. If he did nothing else in his worthless life, he wouldn't do that to his son.

Pippa hung up the phone and wandered over to sit on the edge of the pool. Brave in their new abilities, the boys shouted and paddled the few strokes to her side, ducking their heads under the water as Seth had done and pulling themselves up by grabbing her legs.

Pippa obligingly squealed and played the hapless female caught by monster squid. The corner of Seth's mouth crooked at the sight. Maybe she had it halfway right. Giant gophers weren't the real dangers in this world. Giant gophers and squid were the stuff of fantasy. People were the really scary forces of the universe. Maybe his damned hero rode off into the sunset because he was scared to death of the heroine.

His fingers suddenly itched for his pen. He didn't write wimpy heroes. Maybe they had more brains than brawn, but they didn't lack courage. Pippa was right. His hero needed to face his inner demons and stand up to the heroine.

He didn't know what the hell would happen after that, but that was half the fun of writing. He hadn't been this excited by a scene in years. He could see sparks literally flying off the page.

He pulled himself out of the water without thinking, aiming for his office and a pen. Pippa's cheerful call stopped him in his tracks.

"We're having a committee meeting this evening to discuss plans for the gym. Want to go?"

Now he knew what the hero would do when he confronted the heroine. He would kill her. She probably crossbred the man-eating gopher in the first place.

"No, I don't want to go to a committee meeting," Seth enunciated carefully. "I would be quite content to never see another person in that town." He should have amended with "except Mikey," but he didn't.

"It's your loss," she replied with the same cheer. "Your mother says she'll go."

His mother. Oh, God, in one of her moods she was quite capable of promising Mikey's family the Taj Mahal and bashing a vase over the banker's head.

Not that bashing a vase over Taylor Morgan's head wasn't a good idea, but the police and the lawsuit that would follow were more hassle than he could tolerate right now.

"I don't think that's such a smart move." He actually clenched his teeth as he said that. How did she manage to drive him so far off the tracks all the time? A disabled roller coaster couldn't be worse.

"No?" she asked with such wide-eyed innocence, he could

see right through her ploy. Damn, but the little witch was trying to manipulate him!

Seth scowled and lowered his voice as the boys climbed out of the pool at the end of their lesson. Was he imagining it, or was Chad's cough a little worse? Trying not to be the overprotective father, he responded to Pippa's taunt. "And if you think I'll go with her to keep her out of trouble, you thought wrong. This is *your* idea. *You* deal with it."

He grabbed his towel and stalked off toward the cabana.

Grinning, Pippa watched him stride away. She loved pushing his buttons. He was just so damned *easy*, not at all like those polished sorts who would stab a person in the back while smiling and shaking hands. Now, if she could just make Seth Wyatt smile and laugh as easily as she made him scowl and mutter, she'd have accomplished something.

"Surely Seth keeps cigarettes around here somewhere," Lillian complained. "I need something to relax my nerves before that terrible drive down the mountain."

"We'll stop in town before we come back," Pippa promised absently, searching through her stack of papers to make certain she had everything. "Do you have your checkbook? There's nothing like a flash of money to keep a committee in line."

Sighing with resignation, Lillian checked the foyer mirror, patted her hair, and nodded confidently. "I know how to wield a checkbook. That's what I do best."

"I thought you might. Let's go, then." Picking up her keys, Pippa headed out the door.

"Surely we're taking the Mercedes," Lillian called in dismay. "We're not going down that road in that horrible little car of yours?"

"Miss MacGregor's, actually," Pippa said cheerfully. "My car is back home in Kentucky." What was left of it. Reports from her neighbors had said the poor Escort had been smashed into junk metal the night before Billy left town. They'd called the police but didn't think anything had come of it. Maybe he'd worked it all out of his system and would leave her alone now.

Fat chance. She was staying right here until someone nailed Billy to a wall. She had no intention of becoming another domestic violence statistic.

Outside, she discovered Doug leaning against the Mercedes, massive arms crossed as he waited for them. Pippa raised her eyebrows in question and Doug shrugged.

"His Lord and Master says I'm to keep an eye on you." His gaze traveled skeptically to Lillian, indicating the real source of Seth's concern.

"Did His Lord and Master ever consider you might have a life of your own?" Pippa asked dryly as she contemplated rebelling.

"He knows I ain't got one." Doug opened the door. "Get in and don't give me no lip. I'm no pushover like some I could name."

"You lack respect, sir," Lillian protested, catching this last as she reached the car. "I shall report you to my son."

"Yes, ma'am." Keeping a stoic expression, he gestured for her to enter. After she did, he winked at Pippa. "If I'm lucky, he'll fire me," he murmured as he handed her in.

"I'll hire you," Pippa declared as he climbed into the driver's seat. "Do you think he'll let me keep you in the garage?"

Doug chuckled as he turned on the ignition, but respectful of his employer's mother, he didn't offer the reply her facetiousness deserved. Sitting back in the luxurious leather seats, Pippa smiled to herself. Whether he liked it or not, Seth had one friend. How could she give him others? If she meddled enough, maybe she wouldn't ever have to leave this haven.

Of course she would have to leave this haven. Hiding out here with no friends or family or social life to speak of was not only unhealthy, but temporary. She had known that when she had taken the job. Miss MacGregor would return and handle the assistant's position quite efficiently. By that time, Chad would have his therapist and the gym and maybe even his grandmother to rely on. She would have done her duty. She would have to move on.

She usually liked challenges. She didn't know why the thought of leaving depressed her. Maybe it was some psychological quirk left over from the episode with Billy. She'd heal. A positive mental attitude always helped, her mother had taught her.

Diverting her thoughts, Pippa chattered about the night's meeting, relaxing Lillian's tense posture as she related the exploits of Meg and George and a few of their friends. Apparently Lillian didn't have a much better handle on people than her son did, but she did seem to have an unerring grasp of money when they reached that topic. She knew as much about getting her hands on it as she did about spending it.

As Lillian chatted, Pippa listened with half an ear as her mind drifted to Chad. He hadn't been running a fever, but his cough was getting worse. Kept inside as much as he was, he could quite possibly have just developed an allergy to some pollen outside. She wondered if she should call off the swimming lessons for a day or two. Chad would have a fit. She'd have to check his breathing when she returned. Maybe she could find something else to entertain him if the congestion continued.

As Pippa entered Meg's well-worn living room with Doug and Lillian in tow, the small group gathered there gaped in surprise. Doug had wanted to stay in the car, but Pippa had refused to let him wait in the heat. At least George had stuck a window air conditioner in the front room so they wouldn't swelter.

After the introductions were made, Doug tried to shrink his massive frame into a corner while Lillian sat her relatively diminutive one on center stage. Pippa simply sat back and enjoyed the circus, memorizing particularly choice moments for Seth's delectation in the morning.

Mikey sneaked in to sit in Doug's lap as the discussion whirled around grant applications. He fell asleep before Lillian whipped out her checkbook and offered to finance the automatic doors herself if the grant committee couldn't pay for it.

The parents of the little girl with the disabled arm wanted to know why so much of the money should go toward the wheelchair-bound. The mother of a blind child wanted to know how the facilities would aid her son. Lillian asked for a cigarette. Pippa brought her water.

By the time they reached a tentative agreement on improvements, contractor estimates, and financing, Pippa was ready for one of Lillian's martinis.

Amazingly enough, Lillian seemed energized by the hours-long argument. She rattled on about the personalities of the various committee members, the disabilities of the children involved, and a hundred other subjects as the Mercedes glided through the night. And her comments showed a remarkable perception, Pippa realized through her weariness.

Sleepily, she wondered what Doug thought of his assigned role as exercise leader for a bunch of physically challenged children, but she didn't want to intrude on Lillian's excitement. If he didn't like the assignment, he should have kept his mouth shut when they debated salaries for professional personnel. Who would know about physical exercise better than a former NFL linebacker? So, maybe he would meet a single mother and get a life.

Happily tabulating the evening's accomplishments, Pippa scarcely noticed the lights at the top of the hill as the car drove the winding path. Not until Doug muttered a curse and hit the accelerator did she realize there was trouble.

As the car screeched to a halt at the front steps, Pippa scrambled out and raced for the door, all the adrenaline of her emergency room stint pumping through her veins. A strange car parked by the curb did nothing to alleviate her fears.

A bolt of light shot down the steps as the door opened, and Seth stood silhouetted in the doorway.

"Thank God you're here. Chad's been vomiting all evening. The doctor's with him now. I want to take him to the hospital."

He sounded terrified and furious at the same time. Pippa wanted to believe she imagined the cry for help behind his curt commands, but she couldn't. She heard his tears instead of his anger.

EIGHTEEN

"It's the flu. There's no purpose in hospitalizing the boy," the doctor insisted stubbornly.

"I want him under the best possible medical attention," Seth growled, stalking back and forth at the foot of Chad's immense bed.

"And that's saying I'm not the best?" the doctor replied with indignation.

Foreseeing a clash of the Titan Egos, Pippa hastily intruded. "Seth, Chad's much better off here than in a hospital. I'm a nurse. You can afford to have medical equipment sent in. And Dr. Macintosh can consult with Chad's regular physician over any concerns about his condition. He's far less likely to be exposed to dangerous infections at home."

She hoped to divert Seth from his hysteria with that last statement. Instead, it drove Seth over the edge into other, murkier waters.

He swung toward her. "If he hadn't been exposed to other children, he wouldn't have caught the damned flu in the first place."

She refused to flinch under the blow of guilt directed at her. "You want to keep him in a plastic bubble? Casting blame never solves problems. Go beat up a gopher and let me do my job."

The doctor appeared taken aback by the reference to a gopher, but once he realized Seth had backed off on his demands, he rattled off a list of instructions. Pippa jotted them down in a shorthand she had taught herself long ago. It took every ounce of her training and experience to concentrate on medical procedures and not the boy lying fevered and tossing beneath the covers. His cough had worsened. With Chad's weak lungs, that wasn't a good sign.

"I'll have the oxygen and IV sent out as a precaution, so they're available should you need them. Have you got all that, Miss Cochran? Any questions?"

Pippa finished her last note and stabbed the pen behind her ear. "I've got it. Did you leave your pager number? And will you call his regular doctor or shall I have him call you?"

Chad cried out. She gritted her teeth and concentrated on the doctor's reply while Seth rushed to his son's side. She was a nurse, dammit. She would behave like one.

"I'll call his physician. Mr. Wyatt has my number, but here's an extra card, just in case." He jotted a number across the bottom of the card before he handed it to her. "I'll call in the prescriptions, too. Do you want them delivered?"

"I'll get 'em. They'll likely leave 'em waiting otherwise."

The doctor jerked his head up in surprise at Doug's booming voice from the doorway, but he nodded agreement once he recognized Seth's bulky chauffeur. "All right, then. Miss Cochran, do you have anyone to share shifts with you? I can have someone sent out tomorrow if you like, so you can get some rest."

"I'm not likely to sleep anytime soon, Doctor, and he's only one little boy, not an entire ward. I'll let you know if we need reinforcements." She said it automatically, knowing the chances of her sleeping while Chad lay ill were little to none, not at this stage of the game.

After Doug and the doctor departed and she'd sent Lillian off to fetch ice water, Pippa finally gave herself permission to stand beside Chad's bed and touch him, if only to check his pulse.

"You should have told him to line up several nurses. You can't stay awake twenty-four hours a day."

Seth's words caught her by surprise. Finishing her count without reply, Pippa lifted Chad's head and slipped another pillow beneath him. Heat emanated from his pale forehead, and she stroked his moist brow with cool fingers.

"Have him call someone else if you don't trust me," she finally replied as coolly as she could. "Any reputable nurse can monitor his pulse and breathing and administer medication. There really isn't much else we can do, except pray. If we've caught it soon enough, it may not affect his lungs. He could be up and around in a few days."

Pippa didn't mention any of her other concerns. Chad hadn't vomited since her arrival. Generally, pulmonary flu didn't involve vomiting. Maybe it wasn't in his lungs. Or maybe he'd coughed so hard, it had induced vomiting.

Or had Chad somehow gotten one of those toffees?

Sitting on the edge of the bed, his face haggard with worry, Seth brushed a lock of hair from his son's face, apparently just for the sake of touching him. "I'll trust your prayers over a stranger's, but you don't owe us that kind of duty. If you want help, I'll hire all you need."

Another bout of coughing prevented immediate reply, but Seth's thoughtful response reinforced Pippa's badly eroded self-confidence. The hospital firing and Billy's beating her up in a single day had damaged parts of her she hadn't known existed. Seth's reassurances repaired some of that damage. A nagging voice at the back of her mind wondered if any man's reassurances would do, or just Seth's.

Lillian appeared with a silver coffee urn filled with ice water on a silver tray adorned with white linen and crystal water glasses. Nervously, she adjusted and readjusted the tray on the side table.

"I couldn't find the Waterford pitcher," she complained querulously. "You don't take care of things, Seth. That pitcher belonged to my grandmother. Nana's getting too old—"

"This is wonderful, Mrs. Wyatt," Pippa interrupted the litany of criticism. "Chad will feel like a celebrity when he wakes up. Thank you."

Only slightly mollified, Lillian backed away, twisting her hands and glancing anxiously at her grandson. "What else can I do? I want to help."

Seth looked incredulous, but Pippa discreetly pinched his arm before he could speak.

"Why don't you get some sleep now so you can spell me for a while in the morning?" she suggested, crossing her fingers behind her back where Seth could see them.

Lillian looked uncertain, but casting a glance at her son's implacable expression, she nodded hesitantly. "All right, but you'll call me if you need anything, won't you? He's going to be all right, isn't he? It's just the flu. All kids get it. I remember when Seth . . ."

Gently, Pippa eased her from the room. "He'll be just fine. We'll have a devil of a time keeping him in bed shortly. Did you make notes of all the things we discussed at the meeting this evening . . . ?"

With Lillian otherwise occupied and out of the way, Pippa closed the bedroom door and returned to the bed. She ignored Seth's openly questioning look as she took Chad's temperature. The shot had lowered it a degree or two, but not enough.

"He won't be fine in the morning, and my mother isn't a nurse by any stretch of the imagination," Seth said bluntly.

Maybe those charming, smiling chaps had their advantages, Pippa thought sourly as she took the chair beside Chad's bed. Sweet-talking men could lie to themselves as easily as to everyone else. Blunt men like Seth expected honesty.

"He *could* be fine in the morning," she hedged. "Children have remarkable recuperative qualities. Do you have any plastic cups?"

Seth stood and opened a cabinet in the bookshelves, removing several McDonald's jumbo plastic drink cups, filling one with ice water and removing the crystal to safety. "He's coughing."

So, he'd figured out that danger by himself. "Flu affects the lungs. It can't be avoided. But we can hope it won't go into pneumonia or bronchitis or anything more severe. Did he get his flu shots last year?"

Now it was Seth's turn to flinch with guilt. He winced and stroked his son's brow. "He got sick last time he had the vaccine."

Pippa nodded wearily. "It may not even be the same strain. It's kind of late in the year. We make choices based on the facts we're given and that's all any of us can do."

When Chad stirred and opened his eyes, she smiled at him, lifted his head, and helped him sip some water.

"Ugh," he grunted. "It's not Coke."

"Drink this, and you can have Coke," she promised.

"My stomach hurts."

He turned away and buried his face in the pillow.

"A straw?" Seth suggested, hope lighting his eyes.

Pippa shook her head. "Maybe later. Right now, he needs rest more. He aches all over." Gathering her courage, she added, "Why don't you get some sleep? He may need entertaining come morning."

Seth snorted and paced to the floor-length uncurtained windows overlooking the night sky and the dark silhouette of the hills. "I've watched his every breath from the day he was born. Do you know what it's like to get out of bed in the middle of the night to watch an infant sleeping, just to make certain nothing's happened to him in the few hours since he woke you last?"

Pippa shook her head, wishing she could say she understood, that she'd experienced the miracle of childbirth, but she couldn't. The children she'd watched over had always been someone else's.

She didn't know if he could see her reflection in the glass, but he continued without waiting for a reply.

"I was there when Chad took his first step. He wasn't even nine months old at the time, but he saw his favorite toy on the table and he was determined to have it. He pulled himself up and marched right over as if he'd been walking all his life. He hit the seat of his pants as soon as he got what he wanted, but he didn't cry."

She didn't know why he was telling her this. She doubted if Seth Wyatt ever talked to anyone—really talked. Chad seemed to sleep more peacefully within the sound of his father's voice, so for both their sakes, she let him ramble.

"The car accident severed his spinal cord the next day."

Shock flooded her eyes with tears. She'd read Chad's medical history but never asked for details on the actual accident. Hadn't wanted to know. It was always easier that way, she had learned. Now, the horror of the boy's devastating accident shot through her.

Her gasp must have given her away for Seth turned toward her.

"What's the matter, Miss Cochran? No uplifting comments for the occasion? No cheerful insight? Want to hear the really juicy details? Everyone does, you know."

She shook her head vehemently. "I don't need to know anything but what is now and how it affects the future. He's a healthy, brilliant little boy with all the years of his life ahead of him. Be glad of that. Some have much less."

Seth knotted his hands into fists and looked away. "Don't you ever wonder about all those calls from my lawyer? Or why my ex-wife is challenging my parenting abilities when it's obvious I can do more for Chad than most?"

"I wondered why you wouldn't share Chad with his mother. Children need to know their mothers." Cautiously, Pippa walked on what she thought was firmer ground.

The noise Seth made in response caused Pippa to wince.

Facing a bookshelf littered with children's classics, Seth clenched his fingers around the upright posts and bowed his head against the wood. His voice rang out as if hauled from the utmost depths of his soul.

"My ex-wife claims I was drunk the night I picked Chad up from my mother's house. My mother wasn't there to deny it. She'd left Chad with a maid who was apparently asleep when I arrived."

Stunned by what she thought he was saying, Pippa replied carefully. "I've never seen you drink to excess."

"Tell that to the tree I smashed into at sixty-five miles per hour."

Silence smothered the darkened room, broken only by Chad's strangled breathing. Pippa could imagine the whining tires, crashing metal, and breaking glass of the accident. She had seen so many limp and broken bodies carried into the emergency room—tiny creatures too helpless to protect themselves, thrown away like bits of trash in the wind by the forces of human cruelty or stupidity. A boy with the intelligence, courage, and background Chad possessed could have been an Olympic champion one day. And one moment's carelessness had severed him in two.

She'd never seen Seth drink more than wine at dinner, never seen evidence of a liquor cabinet or wet bar. If there was a wine cellar, she'd only seen samples of it at dinner. But he must have imbibed at one time for his wife to throw such charges at him.

"Was your wife right? Were you drunk?"

Seth's shoulders slumped as he twisted back to face her. "I don't know. I can't remember a damned thing of that night. I can remember every single detail of the day before, but absolutely nothing of that night."

"Shock, trauma, and denial could cause memory loss, I suppose." She tried to remain logical, removing herself from her patient's emotions as she'd been taught. It didn't do to get involved. But she *was* involved, and Seth wasn't her patient. Her heart wept for this bitter man lost in his lonely world, who so obviously loved his son. She didn't want to believe a man who so lovingly and proudly remembered his son's first footsteps would be callous enough to drink and drive with that child in the car. But people did strange things, and she'd already proved she was a poor judge of men.

Taking a deep breath, she went on. "I don't remember hearing that alcohol in general impairs memory in accident cases. Alcoholics have occasional blackouts. Are you an alcoholic?"

Seth stepped into the ring of light thrown by Chad's Mickey Mouse night-light. Even through the shadows, Pippa recognized the twisted upturn of his lips. Just watching his mouth, recognizing the emotion there, tightened something deep inside her. It was the intimacy of the situation, she supposed. He couldn't be feeling this tension, too.

But his voice held a note of warmth that hadn't been there earlier. "No, I'm not an alcoholic. I have an occasional glass of wine or beer, but I avoid hard liquor. I wasn't drunk that night. I would swear it."

"I believe you," she stated with the conviction of her heart. "You would never drink and put Chad in the car with you." Still, no matter what her heart said, doubt lingered in the back of her mind. Seth was a dangerous man. What did she know about men like that? She hadn't even understood the workings of Billy's mind.

The shadows accented the harsh planes of Seth's face. "I pay you well enough to believe that," he said cynically.

This time, Pippa snorted. "No, you don't. If I thought you were that kind of careless idiot, I'd be out of here and visiting your wife's lawyer so fast your head would spin."

"Now, *that* I believe." With a heavy sigh, Seth slumped into an armchair on the other side of the bed. "There's no point in both of us wearing ourselves out watching him breathe. Why don't you get some sleep?"

"For the same reason you won't," she answered placidly. "I'm comfortable here. I'll doze off while he's quiet. I'd advise you to do the same. I suspect he'll make a miserable patient come daylight."

"You're a hard woman to argue with," Seth grunted from the depths of his chair.

"Then don't."

Silence descended again. Rain began to patter against the window. The Big Ben toy clock with the revolving figures whirred a silent midnight, its clamor turned off at some earlier hour.

"Don't let him suffer, Pippa," she heard Seth say through her light doze. "I can't bear to see him suffer."

Startled awake, she opened her eyes to discover Seth leaning over her, his hands propped on the arms of her chair. Instinctively, she reached out and brushed a comforting hand against his stubbled jaw.

He grabbed her wrist and held her hand to his face for a blinding second, closing his eyes as if in prayer. Then, with a reluctant sigh, he turned into her small caress, brushed his lips against her palm, and pulled away.

Pippa watched in shock as he strode from the room.

NINETEEN

On the third day of Chad's confinement to the sickroom, Meg reported two children in town with flu, though milder than Chad's. Chad simply didn't have the resistance the other children had developed.

Pippa stubbornly refused to feel guilt. Checking the oxygen monitor, listening to Chad's ragged breathing, she prayed as hard as she could, and wished things were different, but she wouldn't lay the blame on herself any more than she would put it on Seth. Laying blame wouldn't bring Chad back to health. She damned well wished she knew what would. She so desperately wanted Chad to wake and throw a temper tantrum again.

She could hear the fluid building in his lungs without need of stethoscopes, knew the sound well. Fighting the tears that constantly welled in her eyes, she checked the IV medication, jotted notes on her chart, performed as efficiently as she had been taught. But this time, the habits of years couldn't erect the wall that blocked emotion. She'd become much too attached to this obstinate little boy. Her tears washed away the mortar and dissolved the brick of her carefully constructed defenses. The little boy who only days ago had turned his bed into a Martian cave now lay so still and silent, he could have been a stuffed doll among the toys.

He'd never ridden a bike or a roller coaster, never gone on a picnic, never cavorted through the green grass, laughing at the clouds and screaming for the sheer exuberance of it. Every child should know those pleasures at least once in their lives. Or the challenges: the first day of school with shiny new pencil gripped firmly in hand, boy scout camp-outs and rubbing sticks together to make a fire, kissing a childhood sweetheart. He hadn't yet begun to live. She wouldn't let him die.

Like a wraith, Seth appeared silently on the other side of the bed. He didn't bother sending her questioning looks anymore. He simply picked up the chart she'd finished, scanned the notes showing no improvement, and turned away.

He looked like hell. He hadn't shaved or changed his clothes since that first night. She'd threatened him with an IV if he didn't eat, so he munched whatever anyone put in front of him as he sat by his son's side. Sometimes, when Chad seemed restless, he read aloud. Most of the time, he said nothing.

Since that first night, when there'd still been a little hope that the illness wouldn't turn serious, he'd not come within arm's length of her. She rejected any memory of that brief touch. It opened too many questions, too many hopes and fears she hadn't the fortitude to address right now.

Pippa knew Seth must be choking on misery, but he sat stoically beside the bed, day in, day out, monitoring everything she did, holding Chad's hand, occasionally falling asleep in the chair, a thick lock of hair falling over his eyes. In another day or two, she'd have him for a patient also, if he kept this up.

But she couldn't fault his bad habits when hers weren't much better. Occasionally, Pippa let Lillian sit beside the bed while she went to her quarters to shower and change, but she ate and slept beside Chad. Could she find anything humorous in the situation, she might have teased Seth about their living together and never exchanging a word like an old married couple. She didn't think he'd appreciate the humor.

She set up a temporary office at Chad's small desk, answering the more important phone messages Lillian or Nana brought up. Lillian had turned out to be surprisingly helpful in handling the filing and answering letters. Seth wouldn't even look at his correspondence. Pippa approved Lillian's replies for him. Some things she couldn't handle, but once apprised of the situation, most of Seth's staff figured out how to deal with their problems on their own.

Every so often, she would mention a phone call to Seth that would drag him briefly from his torpor. Usually the questions pertained to one of his books. He even raised himself to the point of cursing at an error on the cover for a paperback, but he told Pippa to call his editor about it rather than doing it himself.

Pippa knew what he was doing. She'd done the same thing when her mother lay dying. He was telling himself if he never left Chad's side, everything would be all right, that if he hung in there, feeding Chad his prayers and promises in the same way the IV fed him medication, maybe Chad would recover through sheer willpower alone. For all she knew, it might work. Maybe his willpower was stronger than hers. But Seth was killing himself in the process.

Had Seth ever learned to roll in the grass and laugh for the sheer joy of hearing himself laugh?

She didn't think so. The more she saw of him and this mausoleum he'd incarcerated himself in, the more she understood the bleakness of his life. She doubted if he'd ever been a child. He'd probably been one of those little automatons, stiffly trying to please the conflicting desires of both parents, until one day, he blew apart trying. And no one had bothered putting him back together again.

She shouldn't waste her time psychoanalyzing a man who could afford the best shrinks in the country, but she had time aplenty on her hands and had never found a more fascinating subject. She could only check pulse and temperature so often. If she didn't occupy her mind somehow, she would go insane listening to Chad's raspy breaths and praying she'd heard improvement. That way lay madness, she'd learned during her mother's illness. Keeping her mind occupied helped.

Pippa threw open the French doors and let the fresh evergreen scent filter through the room. She rearranged Chad's books, repaired his stuffed toys. She actually sat down and read through Seth's entire manuscript, making notes in the margins. The written word couldn't be as horrifying as the sight of a six-year-old child laboring for each breath.

She dropped the chapters in Seth's lap. He threw her one of his murderous looks, though his lined face was too haggard to carry it off well. After a while, his curiosity drove him to glance at her notes. His fury took over from there.

He didn't like criticism, but she'd take the furious Grim Reaper over a hollow-eyed zombie any day. She watched him jerk a red pencil over one of her notes and almost smiled for the first time in days. With a little practice, she could get as good at making people angry as she was at uttering pleasantries.

Chad gasped for breath and Pippa dropped everything. Beside the bed in seconds, she checked the oxygen gauge, raised his pillow, listened for any liquid in his lungs. Unconscious, he grumbled and twisted his head from side to side. His temperature had shot up again.

Trying not to panic, and praying hard, Pippa hit the memory button on the cordless she'd programmed with the doctor's pager number. Fists clenched, Seth stood at her side, watching her every move.

"The medicine isn't working," she replied to his unspoken question. "There is no known effective treatment for viral infections. The body has to get rid of it on its own."

"He's not strong enough," Seth stated flatly. "If his temperature rises any higher, he'll go into convulsions. Do something."

She could. A cool bath would bring a decline in temperature.

Instinct screamed against logic, however. And the instinct flowing through her veins now told her bringing down Chad's temperature would only worsen the problem.

How could she explain that feeling to Chad's father? She knew she walked a fine line. He was entirely right. If Chad's temperature shifted another degree, convulsions were quite likely. Brain damage could occur in that lively mind. Chad didn't need another strike against him. She played with fire if she went against all accepted rules and practices.

She bit her lip and choked on the confidence she had lost. Not so long ago she would have said to hell with the doctors, she knew what she was doing. Maybe it was just the maturity that came with age instead of the recklessness of youth, but she didn't have that confidence any longer.

Pippa glanced out the window at the setting sun. Already, the breeze through the open doors was cooler. For some reason, the crisis in cases like these often came at dawn or sunset.

Despairingly, she raised her eyes to Seth's. "I can give him a cool bath to bring the fever down."

"Then do it," he demanded.

She expected him to explode at her hesitation. Instead, the demanding glare faded, replaced by cautious curiosity. "What is it? Why are you waiting?"

He was listening. He wasn't bullying her around, flaying his arms in futile fury. He'd heard what she hadn't said and respected her enough to listen.

With a lump in her throat, Pippa tried to explain in a manner that might make sense to him. "People run fevers for a reason. High temperatures kill infection." She saw the objection in his eyes and nodded reluctantly. "High temperatures also affect the brain, I know. It's a fine line. But think about it—he has pneumonia. He has fluid in his lungs. Which treatment sounds more logical: high temperatures or cool bath?"

The doctor hadn't responded to her page. The room

remained eerily silent as Seth contemplated the problem she posed. Chad lay still again. Pippa could almost feel his temperature soaring. The flu would have worked its way out of his system by now, leaving him weak and drained. Pneumonia thrived on weakness.

They hadn't turned on the lights. As the sun slipped behind the hills, shadows spilled across the room, casting corners into darkness, hiding the bright colors of the toys on the shelves behind layers of gray. As shadowed as the room, Seth's face mirrored uncertainty.

"I can't do it," he finally whispered. "I can't make that decision. If I killed him, I'll have killed myself. Why doesn't the damned doctor call?"

"It's Saturday night. He may not be near a phone. I have to decide now, before Chad's fever climbs higher." Pippa pressed her hand to Chad's flushed forehead. "He's holding steady," she half whispered. "I can't do it."

"Can't do what?" Seth asked instantly, sharply.

"Can't put him in the bath. Let's wait."

Returning to the bed, Seth watched his only child lying still beneath the plastic tent, his small face even smaller against the stack of pillows. If he could somehow lay his hands on hot, dry skin and pour his own life into the boy, he would, without even thinking about it. He'd never known love until Chad was born. Unconditional, irrefutable love was a damned painful condition, but he couldn't live without it. He'd meant what he'd said to Pippa. Chad's death would kill him, even if the shell of his body continued to live and breathe. His own lungs ached with the pressure in Chad's, and tears welled in his eyes.

Surreptitiously wiping at them, Seth watched as Pippa used the ear thermometer to check Chad's temperature. For the last three days she'd remained calm, cool, and efficient, always looking crisp and fresh in her tailored dresses and pantsuits, as if she were on the way to an office. The vomiting and diarrhea of the first day hadn't fazed her. She could make a bed in the flick of a sheet. She'd monitored phone calls, medicines, his nervous mother, and a worried Doug. And him. She'd been managing him since she arrived.

But right now, as she literally held Chad's life in her hands, those hands were shaking. A fat tear rolled down her cheek and splashed against the bright blue sheet.

That tear terrified Seth more than anything else. He'd never seen Pippa Cochran cry, and he didn't want to now, not while he was so close to breaking down himself. He wanted her cheery smile and one of her asinine aphorisms. He wanted her to say everything would be just fine, because if Pippa said it, he could believe it.

That showed his obsession had gone over the edge. In another minute, he'd imagine her in a fairy godmother outfit, waving a wand.

Chad began to shiver. He whimpered in his sleep, and his teeth chattered as he brushed restlessly at his sheet.

"Get a light blanket," Pippa ordered.

Orders, he could handle. Just not tears. Orders meant hope. He brought a stack of blankets of different thicknesses.

Pippa chose a light one to throw over the lush midnight blue coverlet. Chad's head still tossed and turned against the pillow beneath the plastic tent. Pippa sat on the edge of the bed, offering him Pedialyte from the ridiculous plastic cup. Chad sipped, then settled sleepily against the pillow again, but soon he was shaking all over.

Nana appeared, followed by Doug and Lillian, their anxious glances saying more than words.

Pippa offered what hope she could and chased them out again, although she did it far more politely than Seth would have done. He didn't want anyone interfering, coming between him and Chad at a crucial point like this. He couldn't handle the distraction. Pippa wasn't a distraction. She was the only reason he was still sane. She knew what to do and did it without being told. He'd entrusted her with his life.

She cursed and Seth jerked his head up, frantically searching her face. She wasn't crying any longer. She looked mad enough to chew nails. She dismantled the oxygen tent and began wrapping Chad in a cocoon of blankets.

"Hold him as close as you can, and talk to him. He's not convulsing yet, but his body thinks it's cold. His temperature isn't rising more, but it's still like a fire inside him."

Seth didn't have to be told twice to climb on the bed and hold his son in his arms. He'd been wanting to do just that for days.

Chad was six years old, old enough to go to school on his own, but to Seth, he was still the infant he'd cuddled, the helpless toddler, the little boy with nightmares. He cradled him carefully, wrapping him tighter until the shivering stopped and a weary dark head rested on his shoulder. He could feel Chad's chest heaving. He still breathed.

Just that knowledge was enough for Seth to look up to Pippa for reassurance and approval.

The tears had returned to her eyes. One trailed down her cheek, leaving a wet stain behind. He sensed these weren't tears of terror though. They didn't shake him as badly as the earlier ones. The way she looked at him and Chad, he'd say they were just a woman's tears. Women cried at everything. One had never cried over him before. The thought tore at his already shredded heart.

"He's sleeping," Seth whispered, wanting to console her.

She nodded. "The fever isn't down yet," she warned, testing Chad's forehead, leaning so close Seth could smell her lemon-scented shampoo.

"I know." *I know,* Seth repeated to himself, leaning back against the headboard, resisting the need for her touch. He'd been in this lonely place before, all those horrible nights in the hospital after the accident, wheeling himself to Chad's infant bed, watching him sleep, looking so tiny and frail attached to respirators and monitors. He hadn't been able to hold his son then, had barely been able to hold himself up, but his arms had ached for that tiny burden. He didn't think he would ever let the boy go again.

He'd had so many long hours to think over the years. He'd quit asking why God had punished a tiny child so cruelly when he started asking why he couldn't remember what happened that night. The nightmares had begun when Natalie served divorce papers on him. He would wake up sweating in the middle of the night, then go to his lawyer the next day, eager for blood. He couldn't fight God, but he sure as hell had fought Natalie, and won.

But here he was, fighting God again.

"Is there never any end?" he whispered, out of habit forgetting anyone else was in the room. He seldom had anyone to hear his midnight railing.

Pippa had been so silent, he'd accepted her as a part of him, a third arm that knew what to do without his speaking. But she answered him now.

"There's always an end. Sometimes, it comes sooner than others."

He sought her face in the dim glow of the night-light. For the first time, he noticed how tired she looked. Black circles shadowed the frail skin beneath her eyes, and her mouth drooped. He'd never seen her without a smile, or at worst, a tight-lipped determination—the red-haired tigress. But now she was just a tired woman, saying things she wouldn't normally say.

"I want him to live," he insisted, trying to explain his earlier sentiments. "I just want the suffering to stop."

The look she gave him was so inexpressibly sad that Seth wanted to hold her in his arms, as he held Chad.

"Sometimes, I think that's what life is, a kind of purgatory we must suffer until we learn to handle it right."

He couldn't argue with that logic. He hugged Chad tighter. "That's all right for adults, but what kind of God would make children suffer?"

"Who said God is responsible for what we do to ourselves? Meg's brother had muscular dystrophy. She knew the women in her family carried the gene for that particular form of it. She's Catholic. She thought about becoming a nun so she wouldn't pass it on. But then she met George."

She shrugged, and Seth watched her struggle with the rest of the story. Sometimes, his isolation left him thinking he was the only person in the world who suffered. He needed to be reminded there were others far worse off than he.

"Their older children didn't inherit the disease," he reminded her.

"And they should have stopped while they were ahead. But they love each other very much, and they love their kids, and they were still young. . . ." She sighed and ran her fingers through the thick bob of her hair. "Meg had three kids by the time she was twenty-four. Meg and George brought their suffering and Mikey's on themselves. God had nothing to do with it."

"Muscular dystrophy isn't fatal, is it? And Mikey's strong. He still has a lot of use of his legs, I noticed. He could probably walk with the proper aids and therapy."

"Most children with this form of dystrophy are still walking at his age. His disease has progressed more rapidly than normal."

Seth heard the death knell in her voice but wouldn't believe it. She was just tired and depressed. He knew the feeling. But Mikey looked ten times healthier than Chad. He was a big child, strong, cheerful, outgoing, a delight for anyone to know. He might be wheelchair-bound for life, but that wasn't a death sentence. Seth could see Mikey and Chad growing old together, attending the same college, joining the same law firm, maybe. He'd been harboring all kinds of secret hopes these last weeks, hopes for the kind of life he'd never had.

"Therapy will help," he assured her. "I'll have the contractor speed up the gym renovation. Mikey can come out to the pool more often. He'll be fine."

"Boys with Mikey's form of dystrophy seldom live past the age of eighteen."

Silence fell between them. Then Chad cried out and began to shake violently.

TWENTY

"The bath," Pippa said at the same time as Seth swung his legs over the edge of the bed and aimed in that direction, stripping off Chad's blankets in the process.

"Daddy!" Chad cried out, flinging his arms frantically as the blankets fell to the floor. "Daddy!"

"I'm here, son. I'm here. I won't let you go," Seth soothed him, his deep voice as calm as his eyes were terrified.

Pippa's heart twisted at the expression on his face and the tone of his voice. He was scared out of his wits but doing everything within his power to lend strength to his child. That's why God gave men strength and courage, she decided. Not for war, but for protecting their children.

"I'm hot." Chad pulled irritably at his pajama top. "I want a drink."

Incredulous, Seth halted his progress to glance at Pippa. She hurried to test Chad's temperature. Was it just her wishful thinking, or did he feel slightly cooler? The shaking had almost stopped.

Big dark eyes opened and blinked at her. "I want Coke," Chad demanded, "not that nasty stuff."

"That nasty stuff is called Pedialyte," she told him, but she grinned inside and out as she said it. Trembling with hope, she kissed Chad's dry cheek and made him grimace. "I don't have Coke. Drink the other now, and I'll have Doug get you some."

She nodded her head toward the bed. Chad coughed with great hacking whoops and Seth hesitated, but finally returned his son to the bed. Chad refused to lie down.

"Coke," he commanded again.

"Water," Pippa replied firmly, offering him an alternative.

"I'll get the Coke. You drink what Pippa tells you." Seth hurried toward the door.

"Coward," Pippa called after him.

Chad grimaced at the taste of the water, but he gulped it thirstily, then pushed the cup away. "Coke."

It was going to be a damned long convalescence, but Pippa couldn't wipe the smile from her face.

The doctor finally arrived, checked the new statistics showing a falling temperature, tested Chad's lungs, gave him another shot, and left with a much stronger prognosis. Pippa nearly wept with relief and exhaustion as Chad returned to a healing slumber.

Lillian, who had appeared at Seth's frantic yell for Coke, patted her on the back. "You need to get some rest, Phillippa. The doctor said Chad will sleep. Why don't you let me and Nana sit up with him tonight? You and Seth will need your strength tomorrow when he wakes. Both of you, go on now. Everything will look much brighter in the morning."

Pippa almost choked on that cheery sentiment, one she had expressed herself so many times. She didn't know whether to laugh or cry, and a glance at the wry twist of Seth's lips said he felt the same. Biting back what could only be hysteria, she nodded. She definitely needed rest.

Seth looked dubious at the thought of leaving his mother in charge, but rubbing his hand through his tumbled hair, he followed Pippa into the hallway.

"Maybe I should stay in there a few hours more, just in

case," he muttered as he closed the door to the sickroom so his mother couldn't hear him.

Pippa shook her head. "The doctor gave him a sedative. He'll sleep for hours. Your mother will call me if his temperature goes up again. I'll come and get you if there's any problem. You've got to get some sleep. He'll be a handful in the morning."

She didn't feel sleepy any longer. Standing in the shadowed hallway beside the man she'd come to know better than any man in her life, she felt buoyant, energy racing through her veins as if there were more to do and the night was young. The night *was* young, actually, but she had no right to feel this way.

Seth hesitated, as if the same mood had struck him. He offered a tentative smile. "It's over, isn't it? That was the crisis? He'll definitely get better now?"

She grinned back. "For the moment. He might break his leg bouncing off the bed in the morning, but for right now, for right this minute, everything is just fine. He's breathing normally. His temperature is falling. It's over. I told you, kids recuperate quickly."

Seth closed his eyes briefly and a wide smile of joy and relief spread across his narrow face. "Thank God." His eyes sprung open again, and he beamed down at her. "Do we dare share a drink?"

And for that moment in time, it seemed the perfect thing to do. A celebration of life, an acknowledgment of a job well done, a breaking of bread and sharing of wine in thanksgiving.

She nodded, and he led the way down the hall.

"I keep wine in here, a kind of test, I guess," he said diffidently, throwing open the door to his bedroom. "I've never felt tempted before, but tonight . . ."

She should have thought twice about crossing the threshold, but he had a suite of rooms larger than her own. Inside, there was nothing more than an innocuous sofa and a few chairs in front of a stone fireplace, and the usual bank of windows overlooking still another view of the mountains and valley. No etchings, no artwork, no framed pictures. He may as well not have lived there.

Seth crossed the room to an oak cabinet, unlocked the door, and removed a bottle and some glasses. Maybe he kept all his secrets locked behind closed doors.

"I don't celebrate very often," he apologized, wiping out the glasses with a paper napkin. "I'm always afraid of celebrating too soon."

"And then the moment passes and it's too late for celebrating. Or there's no one to celebrate with." Pippa could empathize. She'd never thought herself lonely until she'd met this man, and the vacuum of his life resonated with an emptiness in hers.

She drifted toward the windows and the magnificent landscape. The house might be a mausoleum, but the views were spectacular. She could never get enough of them. She wished she had a periscope to see the ocean and the waves on the other side of those purple hills. "One celebrates the moment, not the past or the future. Celebrate right now, and let tomorrow take care of itself."

"I like that philosophy." He stood beside her, looking out the windows, too, as he handed her a glass. "I used to pretend that was a foreign country out there, the Himalayas sometimes. I dreamed of roaming those hills and never coming back."

She heard the sadness in those words. She heard so many things when he spoke, things she didn't necessarily want to hear. She heard the man he was, the boy he had been, the person he could be. And she wanted them all.

Shivering at that thought, she sipped the wine. She wasn't much of a wine drinker, but this slid down so smooth and soft, she gasped with the pleasure of it.

He glanced at her with a smile. "Improved with age, has it? I can't remember the last time I opened a bottle." He sipped his own and nodded approvingly. "You're right. Celebrations are for the moment." He clinked his glass against hers. "To the best damned nurse in the world."

Pippa grimaced. "I can't drink to that. I know a hundred better ones. Let's drink to Chad and a long and happy life."

They both sipped, and he chuckled. "We can't even agree on a toast. How about this one: to life and health."

"Amen."

They struck crystal chimes again, grinned foolishly at each other, and sipped some more.

Pippa couldn't blame the wine, although it bubbled like champagne through her veins. She couldn't remember when she'd eaten last and she'd never had a head for alcohol, but it wasn't wine that kept her standing here, exchanging increasingly sillier toasts. It was the man. She'd never known a man like this one, probably never would again—probably shouldn't want to. But she couldn't resist him any more than if he had been Pierce Brosnan, Sean Connery, and Richard Burton all rolled into one. Seth was every fantasy she'd ever had, and even knowing the complex depths of his character, the narrow corridors of his mind that he hid in darkness, she couldn't run away. Despite the craggy face gray and lined with worry and lack of sleep, she couldn't resist him.

"I can't thank you enough," he whispered with a catch in his voice.

Before she could stop herself, she said, "Yeah, you can. Rebuild the printing plant in town. I think that should be payment enough." She nodded solemnly, as if passing judgment.

He shot her a sharp gaze, then relaxed as he read the mischief in her eyes. "You're having me on, as the Brits say. I'm not good at jokes."

She snorted, unladylike. "Cutting wit, maybe, but jokes, probably not. You need to lighten up, get a life, see a circus. But I wasn't kidding about the printing plant. They're desperate for it down there."

"See a circus?" Ignoring the remainder of her comment, he

emptied the bottle between their glasses. "I've never seen one, actually. Neither has Chad. Where would we find one?"

Okay, so he wasn't ready to listen. Pippa savored the wine and tried to watch the moonlight on the hills rather than the reflection of the man beside her. The window glass made her look more slender than she thought herself, and she admired the way they looked together, his wide-shouldered leanness next to her more feminine curves, like images on a movie screen. She really was drunk.

Noting the sudden silence, she glanced up guiltily. She'd not answered him. And he hadn't repeated the question. He wasn't looking at the window any longer either. He was watching her.

"I'm going to regret this," he murmured, taking her glass and setting it on the table with his.

"This is a mistake," Pippa agreed, not removing her gaze from the fascinating conflict of emotions struggling behind Seth's expression.

"Mistakes were meant to be made," he replied solemnly, wrapping his arms around her waist and bending his head toward hers.

"You made a joke," she whispered, just before his lips touched hers.

"I'd rather make you." The words brushed across her mouth before he captured it with his.

She opened her arms to hold him as naturally as she hugged the wind on a brilliant spring day. It was the same wild, exuberant experience, the imaginary capturing of a force of nature, the windswept tossing of all her cares and woes in pursuit of madness. He lifted her from her feet as the wind never did, swept her up so lightly and twirled her around, she forgot where and who she was or how she got there. She only knew they were celebrating life in the one manner, and in the one moment, that made sense.

The heated pressure of Seth's mouth against hers deepened the excitement into something much darker, more powerful and explosive. Pippa clung to his shoulders, her fingers digging into solid muscle as his grip around her waist tightened, becoming at once both tentative and demanding. He asked the question without words, and she answered in the same manner. Her hand dived into his hair, and opening her mouth, she pulled him closer, savoring the wine, the man, the moment.

Life and joy surged through them like fine wine, and they celebrated the occasion with heated kisses and touches that became ever more daring, more exciting, more impossible to resist.

On the thick carpet, before the magnificent expanse of night sky, they shed their clothes in bits and pieces. Pippa arched into Seth's exploring hand as he slid it down her side, surveying the curve of waist and hip before rising to stroke higher. She kissed the salty texture of his throat as he tried to restrain himself, but the desire tugging at her middle wouldn't put up with his holding back. She stroked his wide chest, admired the ripple of muscles beneath her fingers, and slid her hands lower, pulling him closer. Seth moaned and opened his mouth over her bare breast. Overwhelmed by a primitive longing she couldn't deny, Pippa responded out of instinct rather than thought, drawing Seth into her, reaching up for him.

Their affirmation of life took its most elemental form. She needed this reassurance that she was still an attractive woman and not an object to be beaten or cast aside, needed it as much for his sake as for hers. She sensed Seth's desperation, his struggle for control, and reveled in it, encouraging rather than fearing the strength of his need. Here, at last, in this, he could be himself and let go, and she could have the man he hid from others.

The force with which Seth finally surrendered and drove into her cast Pippa sailing over the edge, into the moonlight like the Owl and the Pussycat, floating on gossamer wings. She wept and clung and shuddered again as he did, not wanting it to end, knowing it couldn't last and could never be again, grasping as one does for that last bit of dream escaping with the morning light.

They slept briefly, curled upon the carpet and into each other, waking in a tangle of arms and legs and stumbling to the bed. They christened the bed, sinking into its softness with the power of their joining, collapsing in complete and utter exhaustion afterward, reaching out to touch and hold, even as sleep again overcame them.

The intercom buzzed. Through the infant monitor, Chad's irritable complaining broadcast loud and clear, along with Lillian's and Nana's anxious replies.

She cast a glance toward the uncurtained expanse of window, recognizing the gold on the hills as dawn, and rubbed her eyes sleepily.

Seth stirred beside her. She wouldn't think about how long it had been since she'd had a naked man stretched out in bed beside her, his bare leg entwined with hers in an erotic embrace she hadn't known she desired. In any case, she'd never had a naked man as beautiful as this one. He was all lean grace and sinewy muscle, even when he did no more than reach for her.

It was time for the fantasy to end. With a sigh, Pippa turned off the monitor and intercom. Let him sleep. He needed it. Exhaustion still shadowed his eyes. He hadn't shaved in days; she had bristle burns from his beard over half her body. Let him wake gradually.

She slipped from the bed and hastily donned what clothes she could find. Lillian could hold down one little boy while she ran back to her room, showered, and changed.

Stepping from the warm cocoon of soft bed and hot man into the coolness of the morning-chilled room almost drove Pippa's good intentions out the window. All her life she'd dreamed of the time she'd marry and spend her nights with a man, wake up in the morning to a beloved face, chat cheerfully with the one person in the world who understood her. She wasn't a feminist in the extreme form of the word. She enjoyed working, loved nursing, but more than anything, she wanted marriage and family. But as Meg had said often enough, she had terrible taste in men.

Sighing with the realization that once again she'd fallen for what could never be, Pippa forced herself away from temptation. With the intercom and voice monitor off, Seth fell sound asleep again, wrapping his arms around the pillow instead of her. She cursed herself vividly and fluently as she hurried out the door. What remained of her tattered self-esteem couldn't withstand the emotional battering a man like Seth would subject her to, wittingly or not. For her own good, she couldn't stay here any longer than it would take to nurse Chad back to health.

She showered and, after catching a glimpse in the mirror, donned a dress with a high neck. She didn't need everyone in the household knowing how she'd spent the night. She blushed even to think about it. All those years of self-righteously avoiding the doctors she worked with, and she had to fall into bed with the man who hired her. Boy, if that wasn't dumb, she didn't know what was.

Her mother had taught her better. Her mother had taught her to respect herself, and she did. She knew precisely what she'd done and why she'd done it, and she would probably do it again. She couldn't regret it. But she sure as hell could regret the results.

Too late now. She hurried toward Chad's wing of the house and prayed Seth continued sleeping. She couldn't face him on an empty stomach with alcohol still fogging her brain. She needed normality to clear her head.

Lillian sighed with relief as Pippa hurried in.

"Thank goodness! I can't wake Seth. Chad wants Coke for breakfast. I told him he couldn't have it, but he won't listen to me."

"You promised Coke," Chad rasped from the bed. "I don't want water."

"Coke it is," Pippa agreed, testing his forehead and finding it slightly warm but nowhere near what it had been the night before. "How about some orange juice first, though? And what would you like for breakfast?"

Mollified that she'd agreed with him, Chad considered the question. "Strawberry pancakes. And a hamburger."

Lillian made a noise of disgust and shook her head. "I think I'll turn over the nursing duties to you now, Phillippa. I'm much too old for this. Nana has gone to start breakfast, but I don't imagine it includes hamburgers."

"Seth really appreciates everything you've done," Pippa said sincerely, halting the other woman before she escaped. "I don't know what we would have done without you."

Pippa could see the resemblance to Seth as Lillian's gaze sharpened knowingly.

"Wyatts seldom appreciate anything or anyone. You'd best remember that." She swept from the room before Pippa could think of a reply.

Chad didn't give her time to consider the implications of the older woman's words.

"Am I going to get hamburgers?"

"Probably not," she answered cheerfully. "But that's okay. You wouldn't be able to eat them if you had them. Cowboy Bob will be lucky to keep his pancakes down. Let me get you some clean pajamas."

For Chad's sake, she had to stay cheerful. He wasn't out of the woods yet. He could have a setback anytime. She had a few days to think about what she would do next.

But then, for the protection of her own mental health and emotional well-being, she would definitely have to leave.

TWENTY-ONE

Doug was showing Chad how to play cat's cradle and Pippa was on the telephone with one of Seth's CEOs when Seth finally sauntered into Chad's room, freshly shaved and looking better than he had in days. Her stomach did a couple of knee jerks at the sight, but she managed her best professional nod as his gaze immediately swept in her direction. She ignored the accusation in his eyes. He couldn't say a damned thing while Doug was here.

Chad shouted for his father to see what he could do, then instantly launched into a bout of coughing. Pippa hung up the phone and calmly handed him a bowl to spit into. When he had the cough under control, she pushed him back into the pillows. "Time to rest, young man. Just close your eyes and breathe deeply for a little while."

"Don't want to," he protested, although he didn't sit up again.

"You want to go swimming again?" she reminded him.

"Yeah." Scowling, he closed his eyes and took a deep breath, his narrow pajama shirt moving up and down with the effort.

Beside Doug's massive hands, Chad looked tiny and too frail, and Pippa watched the big man shake his head in dismay.

She touched his arm and shook her head. "He's strong. He'll be fine. Make sure we've got plenty of Coke."

She could swear the ex–football player was blinking back tears. He nodded carefully before looking at her with a surprisingly shrewd gaze. "You're a witchy woman, girl. You watch it, okay?"

Pippa bit back a smile and didn't look at Seth until his chauffeur left the room. Then she sent him a warning look. "Chad's not asleep."

Seth glanced down at the boy, the look of love so blatant in his eyes that Pippa thought her heart would burst. What had happened last night was simply an extension of Seth's love for his son. She understood that, just as she understood that patients frequently thought themselves in love with their nurses. He was grateful, and he'd needed someone to reach out to as much as she had. It had been a mistake. They'd both known it. Now it was over.

When Seth looked up again, he'd retreated behind the mask of remoteness he'd cultivated until it had become a part of him. He nodded toward the corner of the room.

She didn't want to go. She didn't want to hear what he had to say, whether it was words of regret or apology or demand. She wanted everything to go back to the way it had been before. But she'd blown that last night.

Okay, so she had to face the music. Straightening her spine, keeping a stiff upper lip, she marched to the far corner of the room where they could speak with some semblance of privacy.

"You should have woken me up."

Those weren't exactly the words she'd been prepared for. Pippa dared a quizzical glance at Seth's expression. She could read nothing into it.

"You needed your sleep."

"I'm not your patient. Let me be the judge of that. I'll take care of myself, thank you."

They'd had some weird conversations before, but Pippa

thought this might top them all. Seth's view of the world definitely had some strange twists to it. She eyed him carefully. "Okay, I won't take care of you. You take care of yourself. Is there some point to this conversation? Shall I go back to work or leave?"

"Leave?" He blinked in confusion, then responded in anger. "Don't you dare leave! Chad needs you. I haven't finished this damned book yet and Miss MacGregor hasn't returned. If you leave, I'll come after you and strangle you with my bare hands."

That figured. He'd completely wiped out what had happened last night. Maybe alcohol did affect his memory. Or his mind simply operated on the here and now, without regard to past or future. She could buy that—for the moment. She couldn't live with it forever, however.

Maybe she should jog his memory just a little. "All right, but only on the condition that what happened last night doesn't happen again. That was a mistake, remember. I don't repeat mistakes."

Something danced in his eyes, but she didn't know him well enough to trust it. For a moment, she thought she saw a flicker of regret around the corner of his mouth, but he nodded agreement.

"If that's the way you want it. I'll do whatever it takes to keep you with Chad." Again, something danced behind his opaque eyes. "But mistakes happen."

"Yeah, they get made. Don't even think about it," she warned, edging away as he raised his hand to touch her.

He dropped his hand and grunted in disbelief. "How can I damned well not think about it?" he muttered, but obediently, he stayed put as she retreated behind her makeshift desk.

Seth supposed he respected Pippa's position. She had a professional reputation to maintain, and she was nothing if not a consummate professional. He watched as she bent over her work, jotting notes until her hair bobbed. All she needed was one of those jaunty little nurse's caps to complete the image, although he really couldn't see her wearing one. No matter how Pippa Cochran might dress, she couldn't disguise the life and cheer brimming over in her eyes. It was that life and cheer he craved, like an addict craves crack. He was almost that desperate.

But he wasn't a weak man. He could resist temptation. She'd given him more than physical release last night. She'd given him back some measure of himself and an insight into how things could be, if he wanted to reach out and grab them. And he did. He wanted that circus she offered. He wanted laughter and jokes. And he wanted his son to share it, to live as he never had. Somehow, he would have it all.

He wanted it all. That realization hit him by surprise, and Seth groped around the edges of it. Of course he wanted it all. Everyone deserved a little happiness and laughter. Nothing strange about that. He just hadn't realized his life had been so bereft of them, that was all. And if it took Pippa to provide them, so be it. If he and Pippa hadn't killed each other by now, they weren't likely to later. Maybe he needed her constant needling to remind him of what he was missing. He could accept that. He wasn't so narrow-minded as to reject all change.

It was just a matter of planning, Seth decided. He could do anything if he applied his mind to it. Checking Chad and discovering he'd actually drifted into sleep, he smiled. The "witchy woman" had cast a spell over his son as well as over him. "I'm going down to the office for a while. Call me when he wakes."

Pippa nodded with evident relief. So much for his effect on the opposite sex. At least this one didn't fawn all over him in a pretense of love just to get at his money.

Not that Natalie had ever fawned over him, Seth thought with a mental snort as he took the stairs two at a time. She'd always complained he messed up her hair or her makeup, but then, she'd already captured him and hadn't had to work at it.

Wondering why his bewildering assistant didn't play her advantages for all they were worth took Seth the final steps to the office. Any other woman of his acquaintance would have him wrapped and trussed in the tentacles of marriage after what had happened last night. He hadn't even offered her protection. He'd never done that in his entire life.

Alarmed at that thought, wondering if Pippa had been prepared and unable to believe she was the kind of woman who would have been, Seth stared at the tower of mail and packages on his desk. He couldn't click his mind back to the work to be done. His thoughts spun like a gerbil in a wheel. She was a nurse. Surely she knew what she was doing. Hell, he knew what he was doing most of the time, but not last night. They must have both been drunk on wine, exhaustion, and relief. Or she was a scheming witch out to nail him with a paternity suit. . . .

He groaned and sank into his desk chair. He couldn't think that of her. Yeah, he could, but he didn't want to. There was no point in borrowing trouble, as Pippa would say. He groaned again. He was even beginning to think like her.

Hell, if she threatened him with a paternity suit, he'd insist she marry him. That would serve her right. She could be trapped in this insane institution with him for the rest of her life.

Satisfied with that solution, he reached for the first box. He liked opening boxes. The kid in him enjoyed seeing the first copies of his books off the press, or the cover flats or press kits or publicity gimmicks his publishers sent him. He'd start with the fun stuff before he started on the real work.

Slicing through the top tape, Seth jumped at a resounding crash from the lawn outside. Reminded of the day Pippa arrived, he spun around and pushed his chair toward the window.

The universe exploded around him.

Screams. He heard screams. Unable to focus, Seth shook his

head, trying to clear his oddly blurry mind. The screams paralyzed him. Needing to seek the source of those screams, he struggled to stand, only to discover he was lying flat on the floor.

How in hell had he gotten on the floor?

The office door burst open just as it dawned on him that he was lying beneath the debris of his desk. Pens still rolled across the floor. A shard of something that could only be his computer lay on top of his chest. A sharp pain on his forehead warned he hadn't escaped unscathed. He just couldn't figure out what he'd escaped. Or if he had.

The explicit curses roaring over his head told him Doug had arrived. Doug had an extremely colorful vocabulary when aroused, Seth thought idly as he brushed the computer shard off his chest. He ought to write some of those phrases down. Never knew when they would come in useful.

"You stay right there. I'm callin' the medics." Doug stepped on Seth's hand and held him pinned to the floor.

Seth chuckled at Doug's idea of aiding the injured. Twisting his wrist to grasp Doug's ankle, he jerked.

The big man stumbled and almost fell, but he caught himself and glared downward. "I'll get you for that."

"Get Pippa instead," Seth ordered. "I haven't decided how many pieces I'm in. What the hell happened?"

"How the hell should I know?" Doug grumbled, righting himself. "You're the one covered in 'puter dust. Did the damned thing finally explode in your face?"

Seth thought about it. He couldn't remember turning any of his machines on.

The women burst through the door then. He remembered the screams and struggled to sit up again. This time, Pippa came along and practically sat on his chest. Seth eminently preferred her round rear end to Doug's fat foot. He stayed put.

"Get me a towel or cloth to stanch this bleeding," she commanded, without any preliminary questioning.

"Businesslike as always," Seth muttered.

"Shut up or I'll think you're delirious."

But he could see her quick grin as she applied the clean kitchen towel Nana handed her. He couldn't be dying if Pippa was grinning. Her cheeks bunched up like a little cherub's when she looked at him like that. He probably was delirious, but he kind of liked it. He didn't have to think, if he was delirious. He could just lie here and enjoy her cool fingers against his head. Maybe there was something more to this male/female business than an exhausting tumble in bed.

Then those cool fingers ran over the rest of him, and Seth had an entirely different response. He nearly jumped from the floor in a mighty leap. One part of him made it.

Pippa blushed and tapped his chest warningly. "I'm just checking to make certain you haven't broken anything else. You'll survive the broken head. You don't use it anyway."

Oh, God, it hurt to laugh. He'd bruised every damned rib in his body. He'd done it before, so he knew how it felt. He took a deep breath but didn't discover anything broken. Pippa's skilled fingers did a definite number on his libido however. He was rapidly shedding his conviction that what they'd done last night had been a mistake. Hands like that could drive a man to ecstasy and back. Maybe pretending it had never happened was the mistake.

"Can you move your toes?" she asked.

"If you haven't noticed how much of me is moving already, then you're no damned nurse," he answered gruffly, pushing himself up on his elbows. He had to escape this exquisite torture somehow.

She held up her hand in front of him. "How many fingers am I holding up?"

"Two too many. Stick with the middle one next time. I'm all right. Will someone just tell me what the hell happened?"

He groaned and grabbed his ribs as he finally sat up. Maybe one was a little more than bruised. Glancing around at the destruction of his office, Seth fought a moment's panic. The manuscript. He pulled himself to his feet to check the damage beyond his desk as he remembered Pippa had a copy on her computer.

"Doug, tie him to a chair or I'm calling an ambulance."

Discovering the damage appeared to be only in his office, Seth willingly accepted Doug's offer of aid. The leather recliner in the corner remained intact, and he sank into it with gratitude. He noted his mother's worried face hovering in the doorway, Nana right behind her. He wasn't used to being the recipient of so much concern. It embarrassed the hell out of him.

Seth sought Pippa and almost caught the scowl of worry on her brow before she donned her professional mask of pleasantness. "Where's Chad?" he demanded.

"He slept through it all." Pippa turned to the women in the doorway. "Somebody had better check if he's still sleeping. And if there's a first-aid kit in the house, I need it."

Once she scattered the onlookers, she turned back to him, and Seth saw her troubled look reappear.

"Do you want me to call a doctor?" she asked carefully. "That rib might be broken."

"First, tell me what happened." He didn't like doctors hovering over him. He didn't like this constant invasion of his privacy. Doug knew that. It looked like Pippa might understand it, too. He breathed a little easier.

Pippa glanced to Doug for explanation. Doug shrugged his massive shoulders. "Durwood cracked the lawn tractor into the redwood. Then all hell broke loose."

Maybe he'd hit his head harder than he'd thought. Rubbing it where it ached, Seth glanced around his office again. The window behind his desk had shattered. His chair lay on its side, broken in two. His desk had a hole the size of a meteor crater in the center of it. His computer lay in shattered pieces all over the room, along with everything else that had been on his desk. The place looked like a blizzard of paper had struck overnight.

"Lawn tractor?"

Pippa glanced out the broken window. "The tractor is pretty much part of the tree right now, but the tree's still standing. Where's Durwood?"

"He ran for the gate when the place started showering glass. We'll probably have to send the police after him. He gets lost in the woods every time he goes through that gate." Doug glanced uncertainly to where the phone should have been. "Maybe we ought to call the police anyway."

They all stared at the crater in the desk.

Damn, Seth groaned to himself as he leaned his head back against the chair. The box. Cautiously, he opened his eyes and glanced around, trying not to move his aching head too much. He saw no sign of the box, unless that tattered piece of cardboard hanging from the overhead light was it. He saw no sign of books or bookmarks or anything else that might have been the contents either.

The box. If he wasn't mistaken, he'd just been mail-bombed.

TWENTY-TWO

"You didn't happen to notice the address label before you opened it, did you, Mr. Wyatt?"

The police officer asking didn't wear the traditional blue uniform, but khakis and a denim shirt. Grimacing under the ice pack Pippa had insisted on applying, Seth shook his head. "Cut the 'Mr. Wyatt' crap, Bert. You used to whale the devil out of me and call me 'sissy.' "

Bert moved his shoulders uncomfortably beneath his shirt and jotted a note on his pad. "Yeah, well, I can be a lot more imaginative these days, so be thankful for what you get. Just answer the question."

"No, I don't remember the address label. I assumed it was from my publisher. Pippa doesn't open any packages from them. She just stacks them on my desk."

"She opens your other packages?"

"Doug does. I do exercise a certain degree of caution. He's taken some bodyguard classes." Seth wished his head didn't hurt so much. He couldn't think clearly. Why hadn't he noticed the label?

"I'm going to call Doug in here. You haven't had any disagreements with him recently, have you?"

Seth gave a morbid chuckle. "If you mean have I fired him lately, probably not. I've been otherwise occupied."

"You fire him regularly?" Bert jotted another note across his pad.

"I fire everybody regularly. They just don't take the hint. You'll probably find the lot of them outside the door, hovering like vultures." Like guardian angels, more like it, but that was too embarrassing to admit. He liked it better when he could snap and growl without compunction, but lately, a certain administrative assistant had changed his outlook. Even his mother was beginning to look human. If it weren't for Chad, he'd toss the lot of them out. Life was much simpler when lived alone.

Before he realized Bert had opened the door, Pippa was hovering over him again, and Doug was barking surly replies. Just for the hell of it, Seth looked up and winked at her. She pinched his arm.

He could rely on Pippa to keep him in his place. Grinning inwardly and feeling more grounded now, Seth tuned in on Bert's questioning. He didn't like the direction in the least.

"Lay off him, Bert. If Doug wanted to cream me, he wouldn't have to build a bomb to do it. Have you got men searching for Durwood? I don't want him out there at nightfall. He hasn't the sense of a six-year-old. He'll fall off a cliff."

Bert punched his radio and after an exchange of static, nodded and turned it off. "They found him down in a corner of the property. He couldn't locate the gate, apparently."

Doug snickered, but at Bert's glance, quickly stiffened. He'd been in trouble with the law one too many times to be comfortable with cops, Seth knew. He didn't like seeing his friend intimidated by a small-town bully. "Doug, there were several boxes on the desk when I came in. Were they all from publishers?"

Doug frowned. "I only brought in one I didn't open. But things been kinda crazy 'round here these last few days. Durwood brought some up the other day. I looked through them before he brought 'em in here. There's that FedEx from Japan, the one from your publisher I didn't open, a package from Kentucky for Pippa, and a couple of junky things from people trying to sell you something. I reckon Pippa left most of 'em on the desk since I told her they ain't nothin' to worry about."

Behind him, Seth felt Pippa stiffen at the mention of the package to her. Her fingers tightened on his shoulder. He wanted to reach up and grasp them, to ease whatever had bothered her, but he knew how the minds of men worked. He wouldn't let Bert think those kinds of things about her. Carefully, he asked, "Did you get your box, Pippa?"

"I forgot about it," she whispered. "Doug told me it was down here, but you know how things have been. I just forgot about it."

Odd, he heard terror in her voice. Why should she be terrified that she hadn't opened a box addressed to her? Surely there weren't maniacs out there threatening nurses? Or had she been threatened because of him?

Feeling a sudden rush of anger at that thought, Seth worked even harder not to betray his thoughts. "Where did you put Pippa's box?" he asked, ignoring Bert's frown.

Doug shrugged. "I didn't. That was one of them Durwood carried in. I was on the way to get more Coke for the kid."

Bert interrupted. "Let me get this straight. The only people with access to the mail are Mr. Brown, Miss Cochran, and the gardener?"

"And Lillian," Pippa mentioned quietly. "She's been helping while Chad was sick."

"So any of the four of you could have put that box in here?" Bert asked in a voice spilling suspicion.

"No member of my household would deliberately plant a bomb in my office," Seth declared adamantly. He refused to think it. Couldn't. Not now, anyway. Without turning, he asked Pippa, "The box from Kentucky isn't in your office?"

"No," she whispered. "Durwood must have brought it in here. I doubt he can read."

"Is there any reason to believe someone might address a mail bomb to your assistant in hopes of harming you?" Bert asked sternly.

It didn't make sense. Seth waited for Pippa to say something, but she remained ominously quiet. Pinching the bridge of his nose, Seth admitted he didn't want to think about it any longer. That was what he had Dirk for. He'd better call Dirk as soon as he got Goody Two-shoes out of here.

"I can't think of any good reason for this. Maybe it was a harmless prank that went bad. I still can't believe it was actually a bomb. Can't other things explode if they get too hot or are left too long or something?"

"I'm no bomb expert. That's why we called in the state police. They'll tell us more in a few days. But it would help tremendously if we had the return addresses of all the packages that arrived here." Bert glared at Doug again. "I don't suppose you remember whether these were mail or UPS or whatever, do you?"

Doug glowered back. "I told you, the one from Japan was FedEx. The junk was post office. Pippa's and the publisher's came UPS. Can't you trace those UPS things?"

"We'll do that." Bert flipped a page of his notepad and turned to Pippa. "Now, Miss Cochran, were you expecting anything from Kentucky?"

"That's my home," she murmured. "A friend picks up my mail. She forwards anything important. And . . ."

Bert leapt in with the question that Seth wanted to ask. "Why didn't you have the post office forward your mail?"

Again, her fingers tightened on Seth's shoulder. Her voice shook slightly as she replied. "I didn't know how long I'd be out here. I didn't think about it before I left and didn't think I could do it from here. Besides, I didn't want to clutter up Seth's mail with my personal correspondence. It just seemed easier."

Seth heard the gaping holes in her story, but Bert didn't. Impatiently, Seth threw aside the ice pack and stood, however shakily. "I've got to look in on my son, Bert. He's been ill, and I don't want him worrying. I'll be cautious with any further packages. Get back to me if you hear anything useful."

Bert knew a tone of dismissal when he heard one. The look he threw Seth wasn't a pleasant one, but he jerked on his baseball cap and headed for the door. "Maybe you ought to start thinking about why anyone would want to kill you, Mr. Wyatt," he said sarcastically as he grabbed the doorknob. "Make a list of suspects. It should keep the police department employed for several years."

The door fell off its hinges as he tried to slam it. Glancing down at the shambles, Bert had the grace to look ashamed before he nodded in Pippa's direction, then stalked off.

"Doug, out of here," Seth ordered, not turning around to look at Pippa yet.

Doug raised an eyebrow but did as told. Seth didn't miss the concerned look he threw Pippa. Everybody in the whole damned house kept looking at her as if she were the one harmed when he was the one swaying on his feet. What did they think he was going to do, bite her head off?

When they were finally alone, Seth turned cautiously so as not to unbalance himself and eyed his currently unbouncy assistant. The smile had disappeared from her eyes, the color from her cheeks. She looked haunted. No wonder all the men around here wanted to wrap her in cotton batting.

"Sit," he ordered.

She glanced around and a wry quirk returned to her lips. Clearing a place on the floor with her toe, she sat on the scorched remains of his hideously expensive Oriental carpet. She looked up at him like a frog on a lily pad.

"Oh, hell, now I see why men take up drinking." Too exhausted and battered to seek another solution, Seth leaned over, grabbed her by the armpits, lifted her from the floor, and dropped her into his undamaged recliner.

She gasped in surprise, her eyes widening into circles that inexplicably pleased him, but she said nothing. Cautiously, Seth tested the corner of his desk. It had once been solid mahogany, an immense acre of wood that had provided a barrier against the world. Even with a hole in its middle, it stood firm. He leaned back against it and crossed his arms. He knew the body language of intimidation well enough. He applied it now.

"Who do you think sent the package, Pippa? And don't give me that runaround about the mail. You left home so hurriedly that you didn't leave a forwarding address. And you were afraid someone might follow you if you sent one in once you had a permanent place to stay. I might even venture to say you blackmailed me into letting you stay here because you liked the isolation. You're not a person who likes isolation, Pippa Cochran. So spill it. I'll not have some maniac endangering Chad because of you."

She paled even more. She had the translucent skin of a redhead, even if he suspected the red was enhanced. That enhancement was the only color she sported right now. He should be ashamed of himself, but he was too frightened of the consequences to think beyond them. If he hadn't leaned over to look out the window, he could have had his head blown off. If Pippa had opened the box, she'd be in as many pieces as his computer. The image of her torn and bloody body scattered across his office ripped at his soul.

"Billy," she whispered. "I can't see how it's possible. It doesn't make sense. But if it was the package addressed to me . . ." She looked up at him again. "Do you think, could that package possibly have been blown to bits when yours blew up? Maybe it wasn't mine that exploded."

"It's possible," he grudgingly admitted. "Someone could have stolen a label from my publisher. They'd have to know

Doug didn't open those packages though. That's not very likely."

But there was the candy. That had been addressed to him. What if it had been poisoned, as Pippa thought? This Billy person wouldn't have tried to poison *him*, would he? If he were the jealous type, he might, Seth conceded. He didn't mention that to Pippa. She was frightened enough as it was.

"You and Miss MacGregor and Doug and I are the only people who know I don't open my packages," he said, continuing his earlier train of thought.

She nodded and covered her eyes with her hand. "And stealing a label is pretty elaborate planning, unless your publisher decided to blow you up. I don't suppose you could have ticked off someone over there?"

Seth snorted. "I've ticked them all off at one time or another, but people don't generally go around blowing up the goose who lays the golden eggs. That would take a really sick mind."

"It would take a really sick mind to send a bomb," she murmured.

He had the ridiculous urge to gather her in his arms as he would Chad, to hold her in his lap and comfort her. But he couldn't get involved. She was the cuckoo in his nest, and he had to protect his family. "Who's Billy?"

She shook her head, keeping her eyes covered. Then with sudden decision, she dropped her hand and stared at him. Her eyes were enormous, unfathomable green lakes against her pinched skin, but he resisted their pull.

"My ex-fiancé. He beat me to a pulp the day before I left town."

Seth tried not to let the sickness flood over him at her blunt admission, but it was there anyway, all those years of helplessness, of getting his teeth kicked in, his ribs bruised, his head pounded. Applying those images to this soft woman in front of him . . . Horror gripped him as he remembered the makeup she'd worn so thickly when she'd first arrived. He realized now that she seldom wore any cosmetics but lipstick. How many bruises had she carried that day?

He could deal with this. He'd learned how to deal with violence. It had taken years of training, mental and physical, but he could do it. Steeling himself, Seth questioned her coldly, pulling out all the details of her brutalized kitten, her decimated home, and her vandalized car. If the sickness gnawed at his guts, he didn't let it show. He would have to verify what she told him. People lied for strange reasons. He never trusted anyone.

But if Pippa told the truth . . . He would have this Billy the Cop crucified.

Seth argued with his conscience, but he couldn't hold himself back any longer. Pippa had nursed his son as tenderly as if she'd been Chad's mother. Better. She had loved him last night and given herself without strings or regret. He couldn't believe her guilty of anything but loving the wrong man.

Feeling a pang of regret at the realization, Seth reached over and pulled Pippa from the chair. Wrapping her in his arms, he held her until she stopped shaking. She didn't weep, oddly enough, just rested her head against his shoulder and let him hold her. He supposed that was weakness enough for a woman like Pippa. All these weeks, she'd been smiling and tending his tempers and loving his son, and she'd been hiding this black devastation from them all. He'd never learned to smile on the outside while cringing on the inside. She might be stronger than any of them. But right now, she felt frail and vulnerable in his arms.

"All right, I'll put someone on looking for this jerk," Seth heard himself telling her. He didn't want any freaking maniacs sneaking around the place. "I don't want you leaving the grounds unless you've got me or Doug with you. You're not to open any of the mail. Doug knows how to handle that. Have you ever thought of taking self-defense courses? I can teach you some basics."

Her fingers dug into his shirt. He could almost feel her gathering the strength to push away from him. He didn't want her to move. He kind of liked pretending he was the big strong male who would protect the helpless little female. He didn't get that chance very often. Most of the time, he felt like fishbait with women. But she would hate the feeling of helplessness. He understood that much. He'd been there too often himself.

She took a deep breath and stepped back. Boldly, she met his eyes. "I'd better leave. I can't take the chance that Billy might hurt Chad."

The blow hurt worse than Seth had thought possible.

"You're not going anywhere. Chad needs you here, and I won't let you hurt him by deserting him now. I'll decide what's best for my son. I'll expect you in the exercise room after lunch, when he takes his nap. If there's any chance of that chickenshit coming near you, I'll show you how to kick his nuts into orbit. I promise you, he won't ever hurt you again."

Amazingly, Pippa seemed agreeable. He'd expected rebellion. He'd expected her to tell him to go to hell. Instead, color returned to her cheeks, a sparkle appeared in her eyes, and she nodded with a grin of relief on her delectable lips. He could almost see her imagination grinding out the image of kicking Billy the Cop where it hurt.

What she didn't know was that he'd do it first. And a damned sight harder than a hundred-pound weakling could manage.

TWENTY-THREE

"Hell, Wyatt, I'll have to hire three more agents if you put me on any more cases. You want to list your priorities, here?"

Dirk scuffled through the debris beyond the yellow police tape, knocking aside larger chunks to examine smaller pieces. He leaned over to snag a shard of paper, examined it, and shoved it into his pocket.

"They're all top priority. Don't think I don't know you've probably got half a dozen divorce cases and who knows what else you're playing with on the side. Drop them. Get on these. Who's to say there isn't some connection?" Seth clenched his fists as he watched his private investigator shuffling through the remains of his office. His privacy had been invaded to hell and back. What did it matter that one more stranger poked through the shattered pieces of the only haven he'd known? "If I wasn't drunk the night of the accident, then it could very well have been caused by someone trying to kill me."

Dirk's sharp blade of a nose came up, but the more piercing gaze of his dark eyes held Seth pinned. It was that look in Dirk's eyes that had caused Seth to hire him in the first place. He could look right through a man and see the crawling worms in his innards.

"Seems like they waited a mighty long time to finish the job," Dirk drawled. "Got any thoughts on why?"

Actually, he'd had very few coherent thoughts lately. When he wasn't worrying over Chad, cursing his deadline, and imagining a certain red-haired witch sprawled across his bed, his mind checked out. A self-defense mechanism of some sort, Seth figured. He didn't want to imagine who would want to kill him. The memory of Pippa's wild idea about poisoned candy suddenly replayed across his mind's eye.

Dirk caught whatever tic gave the thought away. "Spill it, Wyatt. If you want me to do my job, I've got to know it all."

Seth explained about Durwood's reaction to the gift box of candy. Dirk nodded but didn't take notes. As Seth finished, Dirk leaned back against the desk. "Looks to me like the same people keep popping up here. The same ones who put the bomb on the desk could have put the candy there. Let me talk to your assistant."

"No." Seth paced the outer office, beyond the fallen door where he wouldn't kick debris and dust. "Leave her out of this. Just find her renegade boyfriend and nail him to the wall."

"He could be out fishing somewhere and know nothing about nothing." Dirk watched him. "I already pegged you as a wimp with women. She bats her pretty lashes, and you defend her until death. Send her down here and let me at her. For all you know, she planted the bomb."

Dirk was right. Pippa was the cuckoo in his nest, as he'd admitted earlier. But he wouldn't believe her guilty of anything but faulty judgment. Hell, he knew all about that himself. At least Natalie didn't go around cutting the throats of cats and wrecking his cars.

Wrecking his cars. Surely not Natalie? No, that wouldn't make sense. She would have known Chad was in the car the day of the accident. She wouldn't have hurt Chad. Natalie might be a bitch, but she'd never been a bad mother, not in an evil sense, anyway. She'd just always been wrapped too tight around herself.

"After that crack, I ought to let you at her," Seth muttered. "But I want to be there for the performance."

Dirk scowled, which made the beak of his nose more distinctive. "She's not likely to talk while waving her fanny in your face."

Raising a wicked eyebrow, Seth leaned over and punched the intercom on Pippa's desk. She would be working in her makeshift office in Chad's room. When she answered, he ordered her down to his office.

"I've almost beat Chad's score on Monster House. Can't it wait?" Her impatience rang loud and clear through the machinery.

Leaning against the desk, Seth watched his private investigator's expression with sardonic amusement. He hit the intercom again. "Now, Pippa," he commanded in his most authoritative tone, the one that had his CEOs leaping through hoops.

"You're mad because I've beaten your score," the feminine voice taunted before the intercom clicked off.

Seth crossed his arms and lifted his eyebrows. "Any more wisecracks before she gets down here?"

"Run like hell," Dirk remarked as he sorted through the varying pieces of debris he'd picked up from Seth's floor.

"Wimp," Seth returned as the impatient *click-clack* of Pippa's shoes hit the stairs.

She burst into the room, her thick bob bouncing against the pink of her cheeks as her inquisitive gaze darted from him to Dirk. She didn't have an extensive wardrobe, Seth had already noted, and today she wore the green dress with that annoying halter top she insisted on buttoning to the neck. Seth admired the pale curve of her shoulders and tried to recall how she looked without the protective covering of her clothes. The memory was hazy. He needed to do something about that.

"You called?" she asked with a slightly wry tone that should have annoyed the devil out of him. Instead, he welcomed the acid as he glanced in Dirk's direction.

His P.I. was still piecing together scraps of paper on the console and had scarcely noticed Pippa's entrance. Stupid man. Maybe he ought to look into hiring someone else. Anyone who didn't notice Pippa Cochran had to be blind.

"Mr. Ridgewood has a few questions for you," Seth replied without inflection.

Pippa's eyes widened, but she entered the room without hesitation. Seth noticed with interest that she chose to lean against the desk, next to him. One glance at the situation and she'd already sided with him. He didn't have the arrogance to think she sought his protection. Not Pippa. She'd just chosen an adversarial stance against Dirk.

"Is he from the police?" she asked.

"Dirk's my hired investigator. You can tell him anything."

"Hired investigator?" Interest danced in her eyes as she inspected Dirk. "Does he hire you often?"

"Often enough," Dirk replied bleakly, looking up from his puzzle. His eyebrows lifted with the first indication of surprise he'd expressed since entering.

Obviously, Pippa wasn't precisely what Dirk had expected. Had he thought she would be another long-legged, tanned, blond California beauty like Tracey?

"Do you think you're more likely to find the bomber than the police?" Pippa continued her interrogation.

"I'm privy to more information than the police," Dirk answered stiffly. "Now, if you would just answer a few questions for me . . ."

"Oh, well, if you really want to hear answers, we'd better find someplace more comfortable. Would you like some tea? I've taught Nana how to make a mean pot of iced tea, just the way my mama made it."

Seth watched in fascination as Pippa led his hard-nosed

detective by that selfsame nose. She had Dirk ensconced in a rattan chair by the swimming pool, sipping iced tea, before either of them knew what hit them.

"Wimp," Seth murmured contentedly as he lounged in his chair, sipping tea and watching Pippa rearrange the sun umbrella to her satisfaction.

Dirk grunted and glared at his gently clinking glass. "I don't even like this stuff. How do you stand it?"

"The tea or the manipulation?" Seth asked with amusement. "Want to ask her if she planted that bomb?"

"Hell, from what I can tell, she's more capable of it than all those other losers you've got me investigating. Maybe you ought to hire *her* for this job."

Pippa slipped into the chair on the opposite side of the round glass table. "Did Seth tell you about the candy? George couldn't analyze it, so he sent it to a lab. We haven't received the results yet."

Seth laughed aloud. Dirk glowered.

"Are you gonna let me do my job, or you want to do it for me?" Dirk demanded.

"I don't have time," Pippa replied blithely. "I've got to get back to Chad. Shall I call George and tell him you're stopping by to pick up the rest of the candy? I assume you know someone who can get faster results. Do you have any idea why anyone would want to kill Seth?"

Seth watched as Dirk eventually reclaimed control of the conversation. Pippa's replies to his questions were succinct, intelligent, and blunt. At Dirk's insinuation that she might be involved, she didn't pout, cry, or throw things. She cut him off at the knees, turned the question around, and shoved it down Dirk's throat. Seth admired the performance. He still wanted to hold her and kiss away those red spots of anger on her cheeks, as if she might need the reassurance.

"I think you've said enough, Dirk," Seth finally intruded. "We have every reason to believe Pippa is in as much danger as I am, if not more. Fortunately, we know precisely who would want to harm her. Pippa isn't as inclined toward making enemies as I am."

Dirk unfolded his lean form from the patio chair. He nodded his acknowledgment in Pippa's direction. "If you'll call your pharmacist friend, Miss Cochran, I'll stop by and pick up that candy."

"You'll let us know what you find out," Pippa responded, reaching for the cordless phone.

Seth noticed she didn't ask but ordered Dirk, as if he were her employee. To hell with administrative assistant. The hospital should have made her CEO. She'd have slapped the place back into line soon enough. Maybe he ought to put her in charge of running his printing companies.

She wouldn't take the position, Seth realized. Her heart was in nursing. Pippa would rather run herself ragged over a little boy than hop on a plane in a power suit and negotiate billion-dollar deals. He'd never met anyone like that before. The country would fall apart if everyone thought like Pippa Cochran.

Of course, considering the state of the country, that might not be such a bad thing.

Seth sipped his tea and waited as Pippa showed Dirk out. He had the ominous notion that she would return shortly with a thundercloud over her head.

Idly, he wondered why—with all his wealth—he couldn't hire meekly obedient yes-men.

"*That* was a particularly nasty specimen," Pippa announced as soon as she returned and sagged into the lounge chair.

Not completely a thundercloud but close, Seth reflected as he sipped his tea and ignored her opening volley. He might actually be coming close to understanding one woman in this world. Of course, this one woman had a nature as open as the valley beyond his window. He'd have to be pretty simple-minded not to notice the storm brewing.

"I've been thinking about what you told me about Mikey," he replied irrelevantly.

That brought her up straight.

"Have your friends taken him to the best specialists? Perhaps there's some new treatment. . . ."

Her eyes narrowed and Seth could see the lightning flicker.

"Did you think I'd let them go anywhere but the best? I've been researching this disease and—"

Seth waved his hand and cut off the coming diatribe. "All right, I had to ask. You yelled at me for not taking Chad to specialists. Now, play the part of psychologist. How difficult will it be for Chad if he grows up to be friends with Mikey and has to watch him slowly die before he ever has a chance to live?"

Seth waited out Pippa's silence. He could see the torn loyalties evolving. She wanted the best of everything for Mikey, things she knew Seth and Chad could provide, but she didn't want Chad hurt. That she wanted to protect his son as much as she wanted to protect Mikey reassured him.

"Chad needs a friend," she replied slowly. "So does Mikey. Right now, they're good for each other. They may grow apart as years go by. If they don't . . ." She sighed, swirled her tea, and stared over the pool. "I have no easy answers."

"All right, we'll take it one step at a time. Do you have access to Mikey's specialists? Can you find out what he needs most to help him lead an active, normal life for as long as possible?"

"Money," she replied dryly. "Money for experimental medicines, money for doctors and hospitals, money for equipment. The list is endless. That's why George has to sell the pharmacy and find a job with good insurance. You may not have to worry about Chad and Mikey. George is considering a position in 'Frisco."

"And if I rebuild the printing plant?"

Pippa swung around and stared at this stranger she thought she'd known these last few weeks. Seth wore dark glasses to shield his eyes. He wasn't even looking in her direction as he sipped his tea. She thanked the heavens he was fully dressed in one of his long-sleeved turtlenecks. If he'd been in his swim trunks, looking accessible, she'd probably have leaned over and kissed him, and she knew where that would lead. As it was, the distance he carefully preserved through his mode of dress and body language served her well. She kept her response as low-key as his.

"I know very little about printing plants except that they apparently employ large numbers of people. Any industry employing large numbers of people in the valley will turn the economy around. George could stay here and pay his own insurance."

"The people in town despise me. I've never seen any particularly good reason to help them out."

Land Mine Number One. Pippa edged around it carefully. "I don't know the group dynamics here. Is it possible they think you despise them, and so return the favor?"

He didn't answer. He swirled the ice in his glass, frowned at the pool, then stood up. "I do despise them," he answered calmly, before striding into the house.

"Oh, hell," Pippa muttered, draining her glass. Maybe she should learn to drink beer.

"I hope you don't mind, but I've filed these invoices in different order. Now you can see the last billing instantly and can compare it to the last payment on the computer."

Lillian slid the manila folder into the file cabinet and patted the drawer almost affectionately. "I set up this system when I was a teenager. It's nice knowing it still works, even in this age of computers."

Pippa stared morosely at the stacks of bills and invoices that had grown this past week of Chad's illness and convalescence. "Whoever said computers would eliminate paperwork had turpentine for brains. Computers generate more gunk than a prize cow."

"Gunk?" Lillian asked delicately.

Pippa shrugged. "My mama told me not to use those other words."

"Gunk." Lillian's cosmetically polished facade almost cracked a grin. "Cow gunk, that's all it is." She swept a beringed hand over the stacks of mail. "We could shove it all in the basket and tell everyone the bomb blew it away."

"After that newspaper story hit the press today, I'm sure they'll all believe you. The phone's been ringing off the hook. If we had one of those telephones with TV monitors so I could watch their expressions, I'd tell Seth's editors the book got blown away. They're about to have cows as it is."

"You didn't by any chance grow up on a dairy farm, did you, dear?" Lillian asked wryly. "Your language is quite bucolic this morning."

"I'm just trying to avoid the part that involves bulls." Sighing, Pippa grabbed a handful of envelopes, scanned the return addresses, and dropped them in the wastebasket. "I could almost wish it was my desk they blew up. Seth doesn't keep anything in his. . . ."

Her gaze met Lillian's, and in unison, they scanned the contents of Pippa's desk.

"Besides the book, is there anything else of importance in here?" Lillian asked tightly. "Something someone might want destroyed?"

Pippa ran a mental checklist as she recited: "Current bills, correspondence, checkbooks, Rolodex, reports from various companies—nothing important."

"Reports," Lillian repeated, pleating her perfectly made-up brow in a frown. "List all the reports."

Pippa stared at the older, white-haired woman she'd once considered a pampered layabout, but obediently, she searched her memory. "There's always financial statements. I just file them. Seth hates looking at them."

Lillian clucked her disapproval but signaled Pippa to continue.

"In the last week he's received a report on the new plant merger, the paper crisis in Japan." She shuffled through the stack in her in-box. "And a lot of stuff I haven't opened yet. Here's one addressed 'confidential.' The address belongs to that man who was here yesterday."

They looked at each other again.

"That wouldn't make sense," Pippa murmured in protest. "He could always write another report. It's probably on his secretary's computer."

"Call his secretary," Lillian ordered. "And give that envelope to Seth right now."

Pippa picked up the lightweight envelope and shook her head. Even maniacs didn't blow people up over a report that could just as easily be transmitted by phone or fax and was probably copied in triplicate and buried in file cabinets in three different locations. Seth probably knew everything in the report already.

Maybe someone wanted to destroy his book. That made much more sense. Blow up the computer and the backup disks, and it would take months to reconstruct from the scribbled-over hard copies kicking around the office. But why would anyone want to destroy a book?

She didn't have time to consider the idea. Before she could carry the report to Seth, the intercom buzzed. Hitting the button, she heard Doug's exasperated voice.

"Tell Seth he's got a visitor and there ain't no way in hell I'm trying to keep his ex-wife waiting at the gate. She looks like she's gonna run over me right now."

TWENTY-FOUR

"He's been ill, he's under a nurse's care, he slept right through the explosion, and if he were in any danger, I'd have him out of here faster than your tongue can flap." Disgruntled, Seth stalked up and down the acre-wide living room.

Pippa had never been in this room before. Seth never used it, but she surmised it served his purpose in keeping his distance from Natalie now. Instinct urged her to get the hell out of this domestic dispute, but Seth's glare every time she edged for the door as well as her own curiosity held her back.

"He's in danger just being in your vicinity," Natalie snapped back. "Time has proven that well enough. You haven't seen me drive my car off a cliff into a tree or receive packages that explode."

Low blow. Pippa watched Seth flinch but she was in no position to protect him from his ex-wife's venom. She focused her concentration on the tiny woman revolving around the room like a dervish ready to implode at any minute. Natalie was definitely not the elegant socialite Pippa had expected. Instead of the tall, blond Miss America type, she was short, dark, and workout hard. Pippa could envision her taking Seth down in a physical confrontation. She had that kind of energy and pent-up hostility.

"That has nothing to do with anything," Seth replied wearily, amazing Pippa with his lack of anger. "You don't have the time, facilities, or money to provide Chad with everything I can. Hell, someone could kidnap him from that country club you call home and you probably wouldn't notice for three days. Just let it be, Natalie. Don't dredge up more excuses for your lack of maternal instinct."

Oh, wow, talk about hitting a sore toe. Pippa waited for the fireworks.

"Lack of maternal instinct!" Natalie screamed. "What do you mean, lack of maternal instinct? I—"

". . . would rather play golf than take Chad to doctors," a voice completed the sentence from the doorway.

Breathing a sigh of relief, Pippa edged closer to the snowy-haired matron sailing into the room. Maybe now she could get out of here.

Natalie swirled around and glared. "Lillian! I thought you were on my side."

"I have always been on my son's side," Lillian responded regally, settling on an immense silk-covered Victorian sofa. "When I thought he needed a good wife, I found him one, but you disappointed me. You continue to disappoint me. You have no right to slander my son in public or private. He's always done what he thought best for Chad."

"Mother, this really isn't necessary."

Seth raised a weary hand in an attempt to intervene, but Pippa could see it was a losing battle. She was beginning to understand that he was a private man, one who needed solitude like flowers need rain, and that he had no interpersonal skills for dealing with confrontation—unless he could slug them, she admitted with a mental grin. These two strong women would flatten him like steamrollers with their storms and demands while he tried to act the part of gentleman. Apparently, he could only deal with people who could be bought and sold, hired and fired.

"Mr. Wyatt," she interjected formally, "I hear Chad calling for you. Why don't you go up and see what he wants while I have Nana bring in some tea? Lunch should be ready in an hour."

She lied, and Seth knew she lied. They couldn't hear a volley from a firing squad outside this cavern. Pippa ignored his sharp look and maintained her pleasant expression as he accepted this excuse and escaped. Natalie looked as if she would follow, but Pippa stepped in her way.

"Chad shouldn't be overexcited at this point. Mr. Wyatt will pave the way so you may visit him shortly. If you'll excuse me, I'll have refreshments sent in."

She almost escaped, but Natalie's harsh response caught her by surprise.

"You're sleeping with him, aren't you? How much is he paying you? God only knows, it would take a small fortune to keep any sane woman out here, let alone endure his constant demands. How much would it take to get you on my side?"

Pippa literally saw red. She swung around and pinned the other woman with a furious look. "You just nailed your own coffin, Mrs. Wyatt. I would have supported your rights as a mother without a word, but I would never subject that child to the viciousness of a serpent. If I were you, I'd do a full survey of my priorities, right now. You've got them ass backward."

Pippa stalked out, steaming. She'd never lost her temper like that before. Never. She never swore in front of strangers either. She couldn't even tell if she was defending Seth and Chad or herself, or hiding a guilty conscience. She just knew no one had ever gotten under her skin as quickly as that woman had. If she had time to cool off, she might wonder why. Not now.

It took Lillian to pinpoint the crux of the matter.

Finding Pippa typing furiously in her office some while later, she set a glass of iced tea beside her and intruded without invitation. "You're jealous of Natalie."

The amusement in her voice as much as the words jerked

Pippa's head up. She glared at Lillian. "I thought you were my friend."

"I'm Seth's mother before I'm anyone. I'm lousy at it, admittedly. I never had much of an example to follow and never really had the backbone to learn. But a mother's instincts are strong, regardless of how poor her training."

Lillian stood there defiantly, daring Pippa to argue. Garbed in her usual armor of silk and jewels, she could have vanquished presidents with her vitriol. Instead, she chose to let Pippa stand in judgment of her words.

Pippa shook her head. This day was much too long. Seth didn't pay her enough for this. She'd better start looking for another job. But the thought of the little boy in bed upstairs, and Billy waiting outside the fence, held her back. Seth and his needs might terrify her. His mother might scare the hell out of her. But neither was worse than Billy or more compelling than Chad.

All right, so Seth might be equally compelling, but that was only more reason to run. She didn't need this.

"I'm not certain I would call it jealousy," she responded carefully. "It's very hard for me to imagine a woman fortunate enough to have everything Mrs. Wyatt had and who would throw it all away. For what? Out of spite?"

"Her name is Golding now. She married an old high school lover of hers after she divorced Seth. I think she was sleeping with him while she was still married to Seth. I made as rotten a choice of wife for my son as I did of husband for myself."

Turning the conversation away from herself released some of the pressure, but Pippa didn't really want to get involved in family history. She didn't want to get involved at all. Getting involved meant feeling the pain of the people around her.

"No one can foresee the future. I'm pretty rotten at choosing men myself. Maybe we should take up astrology. From what I can tell, it can't work any worse."

"You're avoiding the subject, Pippa," Lillian chided.

"Natalie is having lunch with Chad, and Seth is sulking in his room. Shall we eat by the pool?"

She'd rather emulate Seth and nurse her wounds in her room, but she couldn't turn her back on Lillian's needs any more than she could ignore Chad's or Seth's. She was a glutton for punishment. Where was the backbone her mother had kept telling her to straighten?

Deciding that she had the spine of a jellyfish, Pippa reluctantly rose from her desk, and picking up her glass of tea, followed Lillian through the house. Had she not had her feet knocked out from under her several times lately, she'd have stormed upstairs and dragged Seth from his lair to join them. But an action like that would only confirm the relationship everyone assumed was between them. The nonexistent relationship, she repeated firmly to herself.

"My son is not an easy man to know," Lillian said confidentially as she settled into the poolside chair at the table where Nana had set out linens and silverware.

"And you're not any good at matchmaking," Pippa reminded her pointedly, taking the opposite chair. "Have you had any luck in finding contractors for the gym yet?"

"The gym may be a waste of time if Natalie wins the court suit and takes Chad." Lillian unfolded her napkin and laid it across her lap without looking up.

Well, that was a different direction, Pippa supposed. Glaring down at the selection of silverware and wondering whatever happened to good old-fashioned plastic, she stabbed something on her plate that looked green and slimy and swallowed it rather than answer.

"I hope that man Seth hired will prove Natalie is a bad mother, but the courts really don't look favorably on fathers, you know." Lillian sipped her tea and slyly watched Pippa over the rim of the glass. "It might help if Seth remarried."

"I doubt it," Pippa replied curtly. "It will only complicate matters, unless you want him to remarry Natalie. We'll simply have to continue on the assumption that Seth will win the case again. We can't let plans for the gym stand idle while we wait."

"You're a disappointment, Pippa," Lillian said coldly. "I'm offering you my approval and encouragement, and you're pretending you don't understand. Is my son so objectionable that you couldn't accept him in exchange for all he can do for you? Would you rather go about cleaning up other people's messes than live here in all this wealth and luxury? And what about Chad? Have you given any thought to him?"

Very carefully, Pippa laid down her fork and lifted her gaze to the conniving woman across from her. To survive in this jungle of Seth's, she needed a machete for a tongue.

"Mrs. Wyatt, you are extremely gracious in your generosity, but my life, and your son's, are not yours to give away. Haven't you learned by now that choosing spouses for wealth instead of love is not a stairway to heaven, or even to a good relationship? If you'll excuse me, I'm really not hungry, and I've got a lot of work to catch up on."

Lillian watched Pippa's chin-length hair bounce as she stalked away. Redheads always had a temper, even if they were artificial redheads. Until today, Pippa had done an excellent job of hiding it. Lillian wondered how much to attribute to Natalie's abrasive presence stripping Pippa's polite veneer, and how much was fear of her own emotions. She figured it was a little bit of both.

It probably wouldn't help if Lillian told the poor confused child that she'd married Maxim Wyatt for love and it hadn't made a whit of difference. In retrospect, buying a spouse seemed a much more logical and intelligent way of acquiring one. It hadn't worked in Natalie's case because Natalie already had money. But Pippa didn't. And from what Lillian could tell, Pippa needed the security—financial, emotional, and physical—that Seth could offer her. She couldn't see any reason why Seth couldn't buy what he wanted, and if she knew her son, he wanted Pippa.

Lillian believed in giving her son anything he wanted.

Seth glared at his wine cabinet and wondered if indulging wouldn't help. He took a gulp of his lukewarm coffee and grimaced.

The architect who had designed the balcony overlooking the mountains and valley probably hadn't intentionally designed the acoustic effect of the pool below. Seth doubted if anyone but him knew how well voices carried through his open balcony doors. As a kid, he'd amused himself by eavesdropping on adult conversations, until they'd become so unbearably hostile that he'd quit opening his doors at all. He shouldn't have given in to the impulse to throw them open as Pippa was so fond of doing.

At least his mother hadn't succeeded in buying Pippa as she had bought Natalie. Pippa had acquitted herself quite nobly, if a trifle naively. His mother's motives didn't hold up half so well. She was still at it, building gilded cages for him to beat his wings against. She'd never understood how her suffocating confinement had warped him.

Actually, Seth was rather surprised that his mother would stoop to enticing a glorified secretary into marrying him. Generally, she stuck to her version of wealth and sophistication. He didn't want to analyze Pippa's influence on his mother. He wasn't given to marrying his secretaries.

He wasn't given to sleeping with them either, but he had with this one. And he'd do it again, if she'd give him the chance, even knowing it was a mistake. Pippa was the kind of woman who expected marriage as the next step in a relationship. He had enough women complicating his life without adding a wife. Pippa's middle-class expectations would include a doting husband, a life partner, a man who would bow to her every whim. He didn't have any such stuff in him. He'd been drained dry, then pounded into dust long ago. It was a wonder he could still feel affection for his son. Sex, he could manage. Sex with Pippa might even become habit-forming. But that was all it would ever be. Circuses and sex, he amended. Pippa would teach them about circuses and laughter. For Chad's sake, she would understand.

Besides, as Natalie had so lovingly pointed out, life with him was dangerous. He didn't think he'd caused the accident that crippled his son, but someone or something had. He wasn't so certain about the mail bomb, but the possibility remained that it had been aimed at him. He made enemies. He'd made enemies even before he'd inherited his father's wealth and power. He'd made a career of making enemies. Psychiatrists had accumulated fortunes analyzing his penchant for self-destruction. He could have explained it to them if they'd wanted to listen. They hadn't. No one had. So he'd gone on getting himself beaten up until he'd learned better ways of fighting back.

Now that he could retaliate, he didn't need psychiatrists, parents, or anyone else. Except Chad.

For Chad, he'd do anything. He just hoped it didn't involve marrying Pippa Cochran. He'd hate to see another rose wither and die in his presence.

TWENTY-FIVE

"What this place needs is a good rainstorm," Pippa declared, flinging open the balcony doors of Chad's room on another perfect sun-drenched day.

"Why?" Chad asked with interest. Most of the adults in his life were fairly predictable, but Pippa was more like a character in some book, always saying or doing something unexpected. He'd read the Pippi Longstocking book his father had recommended, but Pippa wasn't poor and didn't do things that she shouldn't. Or at least, Chad didn't think she did. And the Pollyanna book had been really disgusting. Anyone who wandered around looking for the bright side of being crippled had a few knots in her plumbing and needed a good shrink. But Pippa could be like both characters sometimes. Maybe he could write a book about her. It would give him something to do with that word processing stuff on his computer. Writing all those words by hand would take forever.

Chad coughed and Pippa swung around to plump up his pillows.

"Why?" she returned his question. "Don't you like rainstorms? All that ferocious thunder and lightning shaking the sky, the clouds billowing up, the sheets of rain turning everything into a green jungle, and then afterward, when the birds sing and everything kind of sparkles, and the clouds turn blue and pink and light up like a rainbow—you don't like that?"

Chad wrinkled his nose and stared at her. "Clouds don't turn blue and pink. Clouds are black or white." Adults said weird things sometimes. He didn't like thunder and lightning; he wasn't about to admit that. But a blue cloud, that he'd like to see.

She handed him his juice and medicine, and he swallowed them, watching to see how Pippa would wriggle out of that one. His father never lied to him. He knew Chad was too smart to buy the lies other kids believed. But his mother lied all the time. Maybe that was what women did. His mother had said she'd take him home with her. He didn't know if he particularly wanted to go, but it might be interesting to have a mother for a change. He might be able to stay up and watch monster movies then. His dad and Pippa wouldn't let him. But he didn't think Pippa usually lied. He hadn't caught her at it yet, anyway. Still, he knew clouds weren't blue. He had nothing better to do some days but stare out his windows and watch those white puffs change shape.

"Maybe you don't get rainstorms out here like we get back home." Pippa took his cup and set it aside, then handed him the schoolbook he was supposed to be working on. "That would be a shame. Maybe I should take you back to Kentucky with me and show you a real thunderstorm. They're kind of scary sometimes, but afterward, with all those pretty colors lighting up the sky, it's like a movie. I've always thought those blue clouds were like a rainbow, a promise that the next day will be better for having let the rain fall. And it always is. Everything is always greener, and the flowers bloom prettier. Here, every day is the same. It's nice, but not as dramatic."

He sort of liked it that Pippa talked to him as if he were an adult, but sometimes, she wandered a little farther than he could follow. He wrinkled his nose at the book in his hand. "Lightning burns the hills and covers everything with smoke.

It stinks and looks nasty. And the clouds are always gray the next day. Clouds don't have colors."

She finger-combed his hair and Chad thought he shouldn't like it, but he let her do it anyway. That was the kind of thing mothers were supposed to do, but his didn't.

"Clouds do so have colors," she whispered. "Just like circuses have clowns. I'll show you someday."

He lit up at that thought. "Can I see a circus?"

She grinned that Pippa smile he really liked because it meant they were both going to get in trouble with his father. He loved his dad, but he was so stiff sometimes he needed to be shaken up. And Pippa had a way of doing it that almost made his father smile, too. Chad liked it when his father smiled, but he hadn't been smiling much lately.

"I'm working on it, kid. Will a fair do if I can't find a circus?"

"What's a fair?" he asked suspiciously. "Have they got clowns?"

She shrugged. "Out here, who knows? But they've got Ferris wheels that almost touch the clouds. Won't that do?"

"Yeah! I want to ride a Ferris wheel!"

"I kind of thought you might. Now get to work, kid. You're way too far behind."

"Am not."

"Am too."

"You can't say 'am too,' " they responded in unison.

Chad grinned and snuggled into his pillows. So, maybe his father was looking gloomy and his mother was acting strange, but he was going to a fair and Pippa liked him. The world wasn't all bad.

Meeting Chad's tutor on the stairs, Pippa smiled a greeting at this return to normalcy and proceeded toward her office.

Seth sat in her desk chair, scowling at the computer screen as the phone rang incessantly, all the little lights flickering at once. Behind him, in his office, workmen pounded and sawed and shouted obscenities at each other.

If she wanted thunderstorms, Pippa decided, she didn't have to look any farther than Seth's face. Any moment now, lightning would shoot from his fingertips. He'd already combed his black curls into a rat's nest, and toffee wrappers littered the rug. She couldn't imagine how he kept his trim figure and still ate candy like other people drank water. She tried not to notice the little ball of affection bouncing around inside her as she watched him at work.

He glared at her through narrowed eyes, daring her to come between him and whatever he was doing. When she merely shrugged, he pounded the keyboard some more. It didn't look as if he were obtaining any satisfaction from whatever appeared on the screen. The foolish man hadn't figured out that he was rich enough not to have to do what he didn't want to do. He seemed to have this insane urge to carry every responsibility people dropped on his shoulders.

He needed to be needed, just like her.

That was when she knew the bouncing tingle in her stomach was a good deal more than just affection. Damn, spend a night in a man's bed, and it opened a real Pandora's box of chaotic emotions.

She wanted to rumple his hair and kiss his cheek and send him out to soak up some sunshine by the pool. She'd be better off running like hell.

"You must have a hundred and ten rooms in this mansion. Wouldn't it be simpler if you just sent Doug in to buy a new computer and set it up in some other room?" Pippa inquired, with a vague hope of distracting her wayward thoughts.

"He has to go into L.A. to get it and I need these reports now. And the telephone company can't get out here to rewire another room until next week. I need the modem."

"Fine, I'll just sit here and file my nails and watch you

work." She reached over his shoulder, opened a desk drawer, and pulled out her nail kit.

He grabbed her arm, jerked her forward, and kissed her so hard, she had to grab his shoulder to steady herself.

The little bouncing ball of affection flamed into a volcano. Pippa dug her fingers into Seth's shoulders as his tongue fanned the flames. The jelly in her spine turned to pure molten lava.

Pippa would have landed in Seth's lap in another second, but one of the workmen in the other room dropped what must have been a two-hundred-pound cannonball. They shot apart as if they'd been bombed.

Shaking slightly, Pippa pressed her fingertips to her mouth. The permanent ache she'd developed in her lower belly widened with a growling hunger she feared he could hear. He hadn't even touched her breasts, and still they tingled. With sudden insight, she realized she'd worn this V-neck dress with her laciest bra for a reason she hadn't admitted until now. That discovery alone ought to have had her running as fast and hard as she could, but instead, she stood frozen, staring down into the narrow slits of Seth's eyes as he stared back.

"I'm not Chad, Pippa. Don't push me, or I'll take you down with me."

Going down with him sounded real fine. Pippa forced her gaze to focus on his face and not elsewhere.

"Mad, bad, and dangerous to know?" she mocked. She didn't know any other way of responding.

"You're pushing," he warned.

And she was. She knew it. She was playing with fire, and enjoying every damned minute of it. She'd never recognized sexual power before, but she could feel it rushing through her veins now. One word, one look, and he would be on her like a tick on a dog. The image should have cured her of this obsession, but it didn't.

She didn't want to run. She didn't want to back away like a

beaten chicken. But what she wanted was too dangerous to have. Grateful for the racket of the construction just a few feet from where they stood, she sought some middle ground.

"I don't want to push," she said tentatively. That much was the truth. He just drove her to it. "But I can't be Miss MacGregor either. I don't have it in me. Maybe it's time I left."

Seth popped out of the chair like a jack-in-the-box and pressed her back against the desk with his arms propped on either side of her. The position was almost as intimate as if they'd been in bed, and Pippa gasped for breath as she met his gaze. She should be terrified. Seth's greater strength made him more dangerous than Billy had ever been, but she didn't think the heightened pounding of her heart had much to do with fear.

"I haven't taught you all the kicks yet. You can't leave."

Given her current position, that was as absurd a statement as he could utter. But this evidence that Seth's convoluted mind was still at work reassured her. He hadn't turned into a mindless animal. He wouldn't physically attack her. His boundaries were just a little warped.

"I think you'd better let me go before your mother walks in," she warned quietly.

An almost malicious gleam lit his eyes at that reminder. Deliberately, he leaned closer and nibbled at the corner of her lips. Pippa's willpower plummeted to her shoes. He could have taken her right there and then, and she wouldn't have murmured one word of protest. Maybe she was a sucker for dangerous men.

He smiled briefly and stepped back. Seth was almost human when he smiled. She wanted to stroke his mouth and stare at it forever.

"We weren't just drunk the other night, were we?"

Oddly enough, she actually followed his erratic train of thought. Inching along the desk and out of his space, Pippa tried to look calm and worldly. She wasn't used to this kind of talk. She'd only seen it on TV and in movies. Where she came from, people didn't talk about things like this.

"We weren't drunk," she replied with a little more calm than she could have managed while pressed against him.

"Good. And it isn't harassment if we both feel the same way?"

He sounded as if he were asking for the Fielding report. If she hadn't seen the smoke in his eyes, she might have answered in the same manner. As it was, she floundered for a reply.

"I don't think it is," he answered for her. "You can push me as easily as the other way around. And your job doesn't rely on it either way. This is just something that's happened, and we've got to deal with it."

"Deal with it," she answered stupidly. She hadn't come in here expecting to deal with it. She'd had to deal with one too many explosions lately. She'd hoped for normalcy for a change. She should have known normalcy for this household was one explosion after another.

"All right, I'll wait until I've taught you how to throw me over your shoulder, and then we'll deal with it," he announced with the kind of satisfaction reserved for a problem solved.

"Throwing you over my shoulder right now would help." Pippa quit retreating and sought solid ground. She wasn't afraid of this man, no matter how dangerous he looked. It was her damned reactions to him that terrified her.

In response, Seth offered a smoldering look that nearly brought her to her knees. A look that said he knew he'd almost brought her to her knees. A masculine expression of pride and power and something else, something that kept her from kicking him where it hurt, something almost possessive and affectionate and a dozen other things that whirled wildly in her imagination.

"Honesty helps," he said flatly. "You can go ahead and say it, you know. I'm a bastard, this is a mistake, and you'll slap me silly if I come any closer. It won't change anything though." Self-doubt flickered briefly behind his eyes.

"You're so sure of that?" she snapped.

"Actually, no." Seth looked thoughtful for a minute, then searched her face. Apparently finding what he sought there, he shrugged. "Want to try it and find out?"

"No," she answered adamantly, backing away. "We won't try anything ever again. It was a mistake the first time, as you're proving now. We have absolutely nothing in common. Chad is almost well. I think I'd better start looking for a new position."

"Let's stick with the honesty, Pippa," he admonished, crossing his arms and leaning against the desk, giving her space. "Your boyfriend may have just tried to blow you up. Outside of these grounds, you're fair game. You're not going anywhere. You might want to send me to hell, but you're not afraid of me. You know damned well I won't do anything you don't want me to do." He stopped and looked thoughtful again, giving her a considering look. "What you're afraid of is what you want me to do."

"Score one for you," she replied bitterly, then swung on her heel and stalked out.

Seth stared after her in astonishment. He'd been right. For once in his life, he'd actually been right about a woman. It hadn't been his own ego or wishful thinking or any of those other explanations he'd told himself to explain the pull he'd felt from her. Pippa Cochran actually wanted *him*. Not his money, not his reputation, not his power. Him. Physically. In bed. For no good reason at all.

Cynicism should have warped his amazement. She could be playing hard to get or any of a number of games he'd watched women play. Pippa was quite capable of telling him precisely what she thought of him and his behavior in no uncertain terms. But she didn't. Because she couldn't. Because she'd behaved as badly as he had.

It was as if someone had come along and unlocked the door of his cage and thrown away the key. The possibilities were limitless. . . .

No, they weren't.

His shoulders slumped as he slid back into the chair. If he had any conscience at all, he couldn't take her up on what they both wanted. This had to be the meaning of hell, given the opportunity for everything he'd ever wanted, he had to refuse it. For Chad's sake, for Pippa's sake, for his own sanity, he had to let her fly where she would, and sooner or later, it would be out of this house.

She might want him now, but no woman in her right mind could live with him for long. That was a proven fact.

The best he could hope for—all he really wanted—was a brief affair. He could handle that. Could Pippa?

TWENTY-SIX

"Meg, this is nuts. Why do I do this to myself? Am I really that desperate?"

Meg looked worried, but she spoke in her usual reasonable tones, as if Pippa were one of her children. "Well, there's no law against having a fantasy fling. I've never had the opportunity myself, since George is the only man I've ever looked at. You're more adventurous than I am. You deserve a little fun in your life right now, Pippa."

"Fun?" Pippa cried. "Seth isn't *fun*. Seth Wyatt and his insane asylum are a nightmare."

Meg breathed a sigh of relief. "Then you're not nuts. You're seeing things perfectly clearly. Maybe you just need some more normal outlet for your sex drive. Taylor Morgan has a brother who's just recently come through a divorce. . . ."

Pippa shook her head frantically. "No way, José. Find me an acrobat or a longshoreman, but keep me away from your country club friends and the silk tie crowd. They're all vampires. You should have *seen* Natalie Whatever-She-Calls-Herself-Now. I'd like to put her in a sack with Taylor and watch them go at it, fang to fang."

Meg laughed, a real laugh and not one of those forced imitations she'd used so much lately. Pippa relaxed and tried to summon an even more dramatic characterization of Seth's ex-wife. She hated to see Meg worrying, but she was beyond helping her now. She'd already pushed Seth as far as she could without tumbling over with him. Probably into the first available bed. Pushing for the printing plant was out of the question.

"I've seen her in action," Meg admitted. "She's taken up residence in the bed-and-breakfast down the road. Jean quoted her triple the going rate after Miss Bitch demanded silk sheets and coffee served in bed in the mornings. And Jean's rates are ridiculous to start with."

"Natalie is staying in town?" Astounded, Pippa sat back in her chair and took a deep draw on her coffee as she contemplated this new development. "You wouldn't happen to know if she's still a *rich* bitch, would you?"

Meg watched her suspiciously. "What scheme are you dreaming up now, Phillippa Cochran? You can't possibly want that poor man to get back together with a viper like that, can you?"

Pippa grinned. "So Seth's a 'poor man' now, is he? When did that happen?"

Embarrassed, Meg squirmed in her chair. "Well, he sent this insurance adjuster out to examine the damage to Mikey's chair. At least, he said he was from the insurance company. We didn't file any claim. We figured it was the school board's property. But the guy said Seth had liability coverage and they'd replace the chair. The one they sent looks just like Chad's."

The heat in Pippa's belly flamed on full force, and the damned man wasn't even in sight. Seth Wyatt was a heartless, thoughtless monster, right?

Pippa sighed and gave up that particular fight. "He's warped, that's all I can say. He hates this town and everyone in it, for no good reason that I know of. But every once in a while, just occasionally . . ." She drew out her hand expressively. "*Sometimes*, he's almost human. Almost."

"Cracked," Meg agreed. "He doesn't operate in a normal fashion anyway. Maybe he doesn't know how."

"I think that's it," Pippa said gloomily. "Which doesn't help matters any. Anyway, what I started to say was that if Natalie still has money, we could appeal to her poisonous instincts. Maybe she even has maternal ones, who knows? Pull her into your sewing circle or whatever, brag about how Seth's renovating the gym for the kids, wistfully mention his obstinacy about the swimming pool, and see what happens."

Meg giggled. "Think she'll show her checkbook out of spite? Pippa, you're devious. You could be the best thing that's hit this town in years."

Pippa shook her head. "Nah, I'm just new and don't know any better. Sometimes it takes someone with a fresh outlook to see the possibilities."

"Hmpf. I bet Natalie isn't seeing any possibilities right now. But I'll call Lisa and see if she knows Natalie. I like the idea of warring factions doing good instead of evil."

The doorbell rang and Meg started up from her chair to answer it. Pippa pushed her back down. "I can get it. You just sit here and dream up ways of bringing Lisa and Natalie together and into your clutches."

"My clutches," Meg snorted as Pippa headed for the front door. "If I had any clutches at all, I'd use them to wring Seth Wyatt's neck," she muttered to herself. Pippa didn't deserve to be used and tossed away like a toy by a spoiled child. Pippa was a keeper. Any man in his right mind should know that. Of course, that was assuming Seth was in his right mind.

The doorbell continued ringing, more furiously than earlier. Puzzled, Meg glanced up to see what was taking Pippa so long.

Pippa stood in the doorway, her usually rosy cheeks paler than the lowfat cream in the pitcher on the table.

"Billy," she whispered. "It's Billy at the door." She sat down and let the bell chimes echo.

* * *

An hour later, Meg watched in mild astonishment as four large men paced and lounged around her very tiny living room. Or at least, one paced. The others just stayed out of his way.

She'd at least had the sense to send Pippa upstairs to entertain the children for a while. She should have the sense to do the same herself. All this testosterone raging in one confined place would rattle the plaster off the wall. But she couldn't relinquish her fascination with the curly-haired man stalking back and forth across her Berber carpet.

She'd never thought of Seth Wyatt as a particularly tidy man, but he was in a decidedly disheveled state right now. He looked as if he'd just crawled out from under a demolished house. Plaster dust sprinkled his turtleneck, and his worn jeans had a rip in the back pocket. He didn't wear socks, and his mangled docksiders flapped up and down in time to his irritated pacing. Normally, she'd think those the outward signs of a worried man who'd just run out of the house at a frantic cry for help. But Seth Wyatt emanated vibrations of anger and frustration so strong, she was surprised her walls were still standing. She checked the plaster again just to be certain.

"He tracked her clear across the country!" Seth shouted, as if the room's other occupants weren't a mere foot or two away. "If that's not stalking, what is?"

"A man's entitled to patch it up with his girlfriend," the police detective said mildly. "All he did was ring the doorbell. He left peacefully enough after we arrived. It's not enough to warrant an arrest."

"What if Pippa gets a restraining order?"

Meg smiled proudly at her husband's sound suggestion. George might be balding and slightly paunchy, but he displayed more calm intelligence than any other man in the room. She loved him for his practicality, not his volcanic emotions.

The kind Seth Wyatt displayed now.

"Restraining order!" he shouted, clenching his fists and glaring at the circle of men. "Have any of you ever heard of a maniac stopping his depredations because of a *restraining order*?"

"It gives us reason to arrest him if he should try to see Miss Cochran again," the detective replied with a trace of irritation.

"And then what do you do? Throw his ass out of state? Pat him on the back and say, 'No, no, bad boy'?"

The tall black man watching out the window shifted nervously and shot his employer a warning look. "The man's got a point, Wyatt. Listen to it."

"Dammit, Doug . . ."

Meg raised her eyebrows in incredulity as the furious tornado halted his pacing and visibly curbed his temper at his chauffeur's warning. It was akin to watching a storm halting in middownpour. She threw Doug Brown a swift look, but he'd returned to watching out the window. Very strange dynamics.

Seth shoved his hand through his hair. "All right, I assume you questioned him?"

The detective shrugged. "He's a cop. He knows the ropes. He's sticking to his story that he simply wants to make up with his girlfriend. He doesn't know anything about any package from Kentucky. He's pretty convincing."

"Most abusive men are," a weary voice replied from the stairway.

Meg didn't like seeing Pippa pale and defeated. Pippa was a fighter, a street scrapper from way back. She didn't want to see her giving up. Billy had taken something out of her friend that Meg couldn't find a way to replace. She shot a look of hope in Seth's direction.

He looked grim and more frightening than his two-ton chauffeur. Meg couldn't discern anything soft or affectionate in those sharp-planed features. Seth looked as capable of snapping Pippa's head off as of protecting her. So much for that little fantasy.

Both George and the detective started to speak, but Seth ignored them. Eyes widening, Meg watched as all that intensity suddenly shifted to Pippa, and Seth drifted in Pippa's direction as if pulled by a magnet.

This couldn't be happening, she told herself. Men who looked as grim and stony as Seth did not drift toward women. They threw them down on the floor and banged them maybe. They punched men in the face for looking at them. But they did not drift. They did not lower their voices or visibly relax just because a woman walked into the room.

Seth did.

The threatening bunch of his shoulders and biceps eased. His fists unclenched. His tight expression warmed. Meg thought she'd faint if anyone looked at her the way Seth was looking at Pippa. Hunger wasn't even the beginning of it. She threw a hasty glance at George, but he was looking at his watch and not even noticing. Men!

"The car's outside," Seth said softly. "Let's go home."

Home. A definite husbandly word to use. Meg knitted her brow as Pippa nodded without arguing. Pippa always argued, and Seth Wyatt had just opened up a can full of arguments. This was Not Good.

"Miss Cochran, if you're feeling threatened, I recommend you take out a restraining order."

"That and a cup of tea should do the trick, Detective," Pippa replied mockingly, then immediately softened. "I'm sorry, I'll do that. It will at least give you the opportunity to do your job."

The policeman nodded curtly. "Without any other evidence of a threat, that's all we can do."

Pippa cut off Seth's growl simply by touching his arm. "I left no visible trail, Detective. Billy had to use his connections in the department or some other influence to trace me out here. You might want to check with some of my friends back home to see if they're all right."

The detective nodded, snapped his ballpoint closed, and stuck it in his pocket. "I've got their names. I'll have to check with your police department first. It's not my jurisdiction."

Pippa didn't smile. "The police back there are his friends, not mine. You won't get far in that direction."

There wasn't much anyone could say to that, Meg noted. The policeman left. George pressed a worried kiss to his wife's cheek, shook Seth's hand, and hurried back to his store. Doug ambled out to start the car.

"I'll be fine, Meg," Pippa said bracingly, hugging her. "I probably just overreacted."

"She'll be fine, Meg," Seth repeated with much more assurance. "I intend to see to it personally."

Meg heard the threat and wondered how Pippa could not. Smiling for the first time since Billy's appearance, she stood up and held out her hand to Seth. "I'll hold you to that. And you may let it be known that I'll cut the heart out of *any* man who hurts her. Understood?"

Seth winced, but a grin flickered around the corners of his mouth. "Understood. I want you in my corner if it comes to a showdown."

Ignoring this exchange, Pippa sailed for the door. "The two of you can share your caveman tactics some other time. I'm hungry."

Seth did grin then, and Meg practically swooned at the sight. Damn, but insane men shouldn't have smiles with enough voltage to fuel a power plant.

Pippa didn't stand a chance.

"I want you inside the house, Doug. Get extra security for the perimeters, maybe staff that guardhouse."

"For pity's sake, Seth!" Pippa cried, her neck aching from watching him prowling the carpet. "Billy's just a good ol' boy, not a demented criminal mastermind. We don't need Batman and Robin."

"Shut up, Pippa," Doug replied brusquely. "I been tryin' to get him to do this for years. There's warped people out there and no knowin' when one will turn up on the doorstep. Even Stephen King's been stalked."

Pippa shut up. It irritated her knowing Seth wouldn't protect himself but he'd protect her. She didn't like the role of helpless female. But she didn't like the idea of anyone harming Seth either. Confused, she just sat tight-lipped and listened.

"The guard at the gate will report to you. Don't let anyone in you don't know, and don't let Pippa out unless you're with her."

"That's it. That does it. That burns the cake. I'm out of here." Pippa leapt from the couch and aimed for the door.

Seth stepped in front of her. She'd never considered herself particularly small, but when he propped his hands at his waist and flexed all those muscles, he dwarfed her. That wide expanse of black cotton-covered chest was definitely intimidating.

"Don't do this, Seth," she warned.

"I've got a damned book to finish, a sick kid on my hands, and a mother you brought out here just to make me crazy. I'll damned well not let anything happen to you until Miss MacGregor returns."

Anger gave way to amusement at Seth's odd slant on the world. Pippa tilted her head back to look up at him. "You certainly know how to push all the right buttons, don't you? And here I thought you had problems with interpersonal communication."

He tried to look grim. He tightened his formidable jaw and narrowed his eyes to slits. But she recognized the tilt at one corner of his chiseled lips. She crossed her eyes, wrinkled her nose, and stuck out her tongue at him.

He choked on a chuckle. She wiggled her tongue, and he lost restraint. The chuckle emerged as a whoop of laughter.

Unable to see Pippa's face, Doug shook his head. "You two are fit for an institution. I'm the one outta here."

Pippa scarcely noticed his passing. Laughter transformed Seth's face. She could see the child in him, the happy boy, and the dangerously sexy man at the same time. Definitely dangerous. He should have been snatched up and put out of circulation years ago. Only isolation and his defensive attitude had saved him from the clutches of some woman before this.

His laughter turned into a sloppy grin as he watched her. "Careful, Pippa, I haven't taught you all the kicks yet. I want you fully prepared to take me out when I make my next move on you."

"A simple 'no' won't suffice?" she asked dryly.

His grin became positively wicked. "Probably not. Remember, I know how to push all your buttons. You just said it yourself."

"That's all right. Just remember I can push yours back."

The grin slipped away from Seth's face as soon as the door closed behind Pippa. In her presence, he could almost feel as if everything were normal, better than normal, but left alone . . .

The mention of Miss MacGregor had him reaching for the phone to call Dirk. He'd forgotten that Mac knew the workings of his household. He still couldn't believe anyone was trying to harm him. The candy was almost certainly Pippa's imagination, but the bomb was not. Unless he wanted to believe Doug or his mother or Durwood was responsible, he'd have to believe Pippa's ex had sent the bomb. But he'd forgotten Mac. If anyone had the capability to make a bomb, Mac did.

Or if anyone wanted the information on how to get a bomb to his desk, Mac had it.

TWENTY-SEVEN

"I'm afraid Darius handles our financial affairs." Natalie shifted her muscular legs nervously as she addressed the question directed at her by Lisa Morgan. "Although, I'm certain if you have created a charitable trust that he will be happy to contribute."

Lisa appeared triumphant. "And I know Taylor's bank will donate funds for such a good cause. Meg, you are positively brilliant. What we need to do now is start a fund-raising committee."

Pippa groaned mentally and turned her concentration elsewhere. Meg was undoubtedly brilliant in gathering this assortment of unrelated people together and wringing money out of them for the children's gym and pool. But fund-raising and committees were not Pippa's pet projects. She'd much rather be back at Seth's, waiting to see how he'd changed those last chapters he'd torn to shreds a few days ago. Or sitting with Chad playing Monster House. Or any of a dozen other things besides listening to these women chew on one another's pocketbooks.

Her gaze drifted to one of the few men in the room. Ronald Dawson, she remembered, the school board president. He looked as supremely bored as she was. He glanced at his watch again, and she calculated he'd make his excuses and be out of there in a few minutes. But she remembered Seth's comments to him at the school board meeting. Here was a man who had grown up with Seth. She'd really like some answers from him.

Picking up the coffeepot, she wandered over to refill his cup, despite his protests.

"Nonsense, Mr. Dawson. Caffeine is essential to survive these meetings." She settled on the sofa cushion beside his and sipped from a cup she'd poured for herself. "Of course, it also helps if you can watch the action as an audience watches two prima donnas on stage. Will the school board approve the swimming pool if funds are raised?"

She set her voice low so as not to disturb the ongoing discussion about committee chairs.

"The liability insurance will be tremendous," Dawson replied gloomily. "With our declining enrollment, I can't see how we can justify it."

"That could be why Seth wouldn't sponsor the project," Pippa commiserated. "It is a shame that his interest in the town occurs just as the population is declining."

With hidden glee, she watched the board president struggle to hold his tongue. She hadn't been nominated Best Busybody in high school for nothing. Another prod, and she'd have him spilling the beans. "I never have understood his reluctance to talk about Garden Grove. It's such an idyllic setting. I don't see how he could bear it any ill will."

Dawson let out a lungful of air and eyed Pippa warily. "You won't quit until you hear it, will you?"

She beamed in delight. "Probably not. If you're in a hurry to go home, you may as well spill it now."

He ran his hand over his balding head, cleaned his wire-rimmed glasses, and returned them to his nose, all the better to stare her down, she surmised. She didn't relent.

"No one comes out looking pretty from where I stand," he said gloomily. "You'd be better off just leaving it alone."

"Maybe. But from where I stand, it looks like everyone is still hurting. I'm a nurse. I like healing wounds."

He nodded, reluctantly accepting that assessment. "It's all childish nonsense, actually. It happened long ago and there's no reason at all for it to carry on, but people here have long memories, and apparently, so does Wyatt."

"A man who's been knocked down once too often tends to be wary of returning to the ring."

She thought she'd phrased that cleverly considering she knew nothing at all about it. Dawson's snort of disagreement warned she wasn't half so clever as she'd hoped.

"Not Wyatt. Damn . . ." He hastily rubbed his mouth as if he could take back the word. "Excuse me, but even the memory of that summer irritates. I really don't think we should go into it."

Pippa handed him a plate of cookies. Ronald Dawson looked like someone who appreciated food. He was remarkably well padded for a man his age. "If the memory irks you this much, just imagine what it does to Seth. And try imagining what would happen if we could erase it somehow. Maybe he'd even consider rebuilding the printing plant."

He contemplated the possibility but looked dubious. "I don't know what he's like today, but the kid I remember would have chewed nails before forgiving us. Damn, but he was the most obdurate, hardheaded . . ."

Pippa shrugged cheerfully. "He hasn't changed much. But he's twice as smart as the average bear and is capable of learning."

"Now, that I can believe." Giving up the fight, Dawson sipped his coffee and nibbled his cookie. "He used to hitch rides into town from that mansion in the hills. We didn't know it at the time. He just showed up at ball practice one spring in a beat-up old produce truck. He was probably about nine. When the coach insisted that his parents had to sign before he could join the team, he argued until he was blue in the face."

A grin slipped across Dawson's face at the memory. "I'm

telling you all this after the fact. You've got to realize none of us knew it then. But Seth went into town and apparently bought himself a father to come sign him up for the team. I figure it was some drunk from the pool hall who needed a little cash. From that moment on, we all thought he came from the poor side of town, that his daddy was a drunk, and that his name was Bob Hill."

Pippa could almost see it. With all those unruly dark curls, garbed in his usual careless style, Seth would have looked the part he played without even trying. Add the smudges of dirt a nine-year-old collected, especially after walking and hitching for twelve miles . . . The pain and affection she felt at the same time terrified her. She wanted to pick up that lonely child and hug him. But Seth had honed himself into a formidable weapon no intelligent person would consider hugging.

"Anyway, he didn't know beans about baseball. He'd never held a bat, never thrown a ball. He got dumped onto the worst team in the league. Nobody wanted him. He didn't care. He was so damned determined to learn that he fought with the coaches for a place, fought with anyone who tried to push him out, fought with anyone who looked at him crooked. And the boy couldn't fight." Dawson grinned and shook his head. "He knew about as much about fighting as he did baseball. We all creamed him at one time or another. He had a mouth on him that wouldn't stop. You just wanted to punch it."

Pippa held her breath so as not to disturb the story, but the image of that tousle-headed little boy burned in her heart, and she could barely listen to the remainder of the tale.

"He was small, which didn't help. The bigger kids used him for a punching bag. He took a bite out of Taylor Morgan's hide once, broke his nose another time, but Seth always lost the fight. Taylor was bigger and had more friends to jump to his rescue." Dawson refilled his coffee cup. "But things started changing about midsummer. By then, Seth had learned the basics pretty well. He had an eagle eye for that ball. He didn't have a lot of power behind the bat, but he could hit the blamed thing every time. He carried the worst team in the league into a respectable position. He still had a nasty mouth on him, but he didn't get beaten up quite so often."

Pippa could imagine the young Seth insulting every kid crossing his path. She'd seen kids like that, ones who craved attention and found it only by riling others. He still carried a lot of that hostility and anger around with him. He'd learned to vent it in more acceptable ways perhaps, but it constantly simmered beneath the surface. In a child, it must have been explosive. Warily, Pippa eyed Seth's mother sitting placidly on the other side of the room, sipping tea from Meg's best china. What had his parents done to him?

"Anyway, by the end of the summer, everyone pretty much accepted Seth as a wise-mouthed kid from the wrong end of town who could hit any ball thrown at him. Taylor and his crowd despised him, but they were on the best teams and their paths only crossed occasionally. Not until the tournament at the end of the summer when Seth's team actually made the finals did it get really nasty." Dawson grimaced. "I ought to leave it at that. I feel like I'm telling tales out of school."

Pippa shook her head until her hair bounced. "You can't stop now. You're just getting to the place that really matters. I don't think Seth resents the fighting and getting beaten up. He simply took those lessons and learned from them. He took karate in college and picked up who knows how many other strange martial arts along the way. He's taught me a few moves that would bring down King Kong."

"I don't even want to think about Wyatt with actual combat training. He broke enough teeth and bones when he didn't know anything." Dawson glanced wistfully at the door but continued his tale. "There'd been a strike at the printing plant all summer. Seth's father had refused to allow a union and had hired Mexican laborers when his employees walked out. Hostilities were raging. There'd been attempts to sabotage the plant and the trucks going in and out. Maxim Wyatt retaliated by pulling all his business out of the local banks and stores. Maxim Wyatt was one tough old man. He had no conscience at all that I could ever discern, even from a kid's viewpoint. The town despised him. It wasn't any wonder that Seth pretended he was a poor kid from the wrong side of the tracks."

He leaned back against the sofa with a sigh and glanced at Pippa. "Can't you see where this is heading without me telling you?"

"Oh, I can see where it's heading all right. But I want to know the specifics. How many years have gone by since then? Twenty-five? More? And everyone is still suffering for it? No, I've got to know everything."

"I can't see how it will make a difference." He shrugged and continued. "The first game of the finals and Seth's team played Taylor's. Taylor's father actually showed up to watch him play. He never came to the other games. He sat out there in his fancy business suit and tie as if he were still in the bank's boardroom. Most of our fathers worked at the plant or in one of the stores, so with the strike and all, they had plenty of time to attend games. None of them wore suits and ties. But we never thought it strange that Taylor's dad wore suits. Kids have their own odd hierarchies. As far as we were concerned, Taylor's crowd went to the country club and ranked highest. Seth didn't have a crowd. He was on the bottom of the totem pole."

"Okay, I understand that only too well. My dad worked in a factory and I wore hand-me-downs most of my life. I get the picture." Pippa hastened him on, knowing by the way conversation was dying on the other end of the room and gazes were cast their way that the meeting was about to break up, out of curiosity if nothing else.

"So, Taylor's dad watched Seth smash every ball Taylor threw him out of the park. Seth was either having a really good day, or he was so pissed at Taylor that fury alone gave him strength. Or both. Anyway, Mr. Morgan was about to strangle on rage by the end of the game. He kept asking everyone who Seth was, where he'd come from, and so on. I think he was trying to get him disqualified somehow. But then, sometime in the last inning, he got a really good look at Seth, maybe when he slid into home and actually faced the crowd. Seth's isn't the kind of face one easily forgets."

Yeah, tell her about it. She could just see that wicked grin beaming up at the crowd, those light gray eyes shining from a tanned, dirty face, taunting people with his prowess. And the curls were a dead giveaway.

"Morgan recognized him. Seth didn't attend the public schools and no one from town ever got invited out to the Wyatt mansion, but Morgan was the town banker. Somewhere along the way, he'd been out to the house to get papers signed or something, and he'd seen Seth. He probably swallowed his teeth in shock, but he didn't waste time in letting people know who the boy was."

"And that made a difference?" Pippa asked in amazement, even knowing the answer. People were so perversely inexplicable sometimes. He was just a kid. He wasn't responsible for what his father did. But people wouldn't see it that way.

"It made a difference the way Morgan told it. That was the last game Seth played. He showed up for the next, but the coach wouldn't let him play, wouldn't even talk to him. The rest of us shunned him. Maybe we were just a little bit scared of him and all the power he represented. Maybe we were scared about how we'd treated him earlier. I don't know how it all boiled down. I just know none of us spoke to him again, and his name was dropped from the rolls. He sat there all dressed in his uniform—and who knows how he got it washed between games—and watched the game from the same bench as the rest of us, but he wasn't with us, if you know what I mean. We shut him out. Completely."

Pippa sighed. "And he's been shutting you out ever since in retaliation?"

"Well, to be fair, he tried a few more times. It couldn't have been easy. I don't think his parents ever knew about his hitch-hiking. He didn't go to school with the rest of us, but I ran across him in a few places where kids hang out. He was always alone. And then there was a fire at the printing plant, and another at the bank, and people started looking at Seth with more than suspicion. When the police hauled him in for questioning, that was the end of that. His father found out and the next year he got shipped out to boarding school."

Pippa could almost understand Seth's antipathy for Garden Grove. Even she was beginning to think twice about helping these narrow-minded morons. But all she had to do was remember Mikey and the other children, and she knew this stupid war had to end. Seth and Taylor were grown men now. They could put aside their differences for the sake of the children.

"Thank you, Mr. Dawson, I appreciate your insight. I hope I'll have your support when I try to make Seth see reason. I don't think you carry the same hostility for the Wyatts as the rest of the town."

He set his cup down on the tray. "My father had no connection with the Wyatts, so I was pretty much an outsider in all this. My one regret is that I didn't have the gumption to stand up to Taylor and his crowd. I still can't. The school board depends too much on their wealth and support. Don't expect too much from me, Miss Cochran."

"Well, that's certainly honest. I can respect that. Maybe Seth is right and Garden Grove doesn't deserve his help. But I have friends here. I'll try."

She hoped she'd hit him where it hurt, but Ronald Dawson was too experienced at concealing his own opinions behind the bespectacled facade of schoolteacher. His loyalties lay with the school board and keeping his comfortable position. She really couldn't condemn the man. She'd like to, but she wouldn't.

The meeting broke up shortly after that. Pippa waited for

Doug to put in an appearance. He'd refused to be trapped into attending the meeting this time, using the excuse that he had to patrol the "perimeters" for the sake of caution. Though she looked over her shoulder for Billy whenever she left the house, she still despised the idea of being baby-sat every minute of the day. Lillian apparently took it with equanimity. She merely glanced at her diamond-studded watch and looked around for Meg.

"I think the meeting was highly successful, don't you, dear?" she said, addressing Meg as if she were a teenager.

"I think we're making progress, Mrs. Wyatt," Meg answered cautiously. "We've almost got agreement on the renovations so the contractor can give us estimates."

"Yes, I believe once my son sees how well this works out, he'll be more agreeable to lending a hand in other projects. He's terribly stubborn sometimes." She said this in her loftiest tones, as if stubbornness were an attribute to be commended.

Pippa grinned and winked at Meg. "That means he's too busy to bother with anything that doesn't interest him. It'll work out. I'll just push papers in front of him and demand his signature until the thing gets done."

"Phillippa!" Shocked, Lillian glowered at her. "That's no way to conduct business."

"That's how Seth conducts business." Unrepentant, Pippa shrugged.

"Then perhaps I should spend more time in the office. His father would never have done things that way."

"I could just about vouch that Mr. Wyatt never did things the way Seth does," Pippa agreed with enthusiasm. "And I didn't even know Mr. Wyatt."

"Well . . ."

The door popped open and Doug filled the doorway. "Ladies, if you're ready, I apologize for my tardiness."

Lillian didn't even glance in the chauffeur's direction as she gathered her bag and notes. Pippa, however, heard something in Doug's voice she didn't like. She scanned his impassive face, noted a slight puffiness in his jaw, sensed the tension in him, and balked.

"What happened?" she demanded.

Doug sent her a scathing look. "Let's just get in the car, all right?"

"Not until I know what happened."

He wrestled internally with the problem, but he wasn't the complicated man that Seth was. He spat out the answer without hedging it.

"I got your old boyfriend locked up."

TWENTY-EIGHT

Gulping from his coffee cup, Seth stared at the words on his computer screen with disbelief. He couldn't believe he'd written that. He had definitely never intended for the story to take that turn, but the damned characters had grabbed an opening and run with it. The really damnable thing about it was that it made sense. He'd have to go back and rewrite the beginning, add a scene in the middle, shuffle some chapters around. . . .

Shit.

Slapping down the cup, he stood and paced the Oriental in the outer office. Now that he didn't have a computer, he perversely wanted to write on one, and Pippa's was the only one available besides the one he hadn't unpacked upstairs. She must have sprayed hers with her perfume. He could smell the herbal fragrance everywhere.

Pippa. It was all her damned fault the book had done a hundred-eighty-degree about-face. He'd hired her to simplify his life, not complicate it. He should have known better. Hell, even Chad had known better. Or rather, Nana had. A young, attractive female in the house was bound to be an unwanted distraction. A complication he didn't need.

He glanced at his watch and cursed again. Where the hell were they?

How long could a blasted meeting last? He'd sent Doug with them. What could happen between here and town?

Remembering a night when he'd driven from his mother's house toward home and nearly lost everything, Seth battled a moment's terror. The police would have called him if there'd been an accident, wouldn't they?

Maybe he should get out the Jag and hunt them down. But he couldn't leave Chad alone. Nana slept too soundly at the back of the house. He could wake her. But if he did, it would mean he was succumbing to a panic attack.

What the hell was she doing to him?

Phillippa Cochran was just a secretary, an assistant, a nobody who would go away once her job here was done. He'd never worried if Miss MacGregor didn't show up on time.

Miss MacGregor had never been late.

Shit. Double shit. Seth looked at his watch again. Five minutes later than the last time he'd looked. He glared at the glossy cover with the mummy's head on the wall. Pippa had stuck a mustache on it. A mustache.

He grinned. He couldn't help it. She had the sense of humor of a wicked child. Irrepressible, irreverent, hopelessly unsophisticated. He couldn't imagine either Tracey or Natalie even looking at these macabre covers, much less vandalizing them. Miss MacGregor would have heart palpitations.

Pippa Cochran had stuck her tongue out at him and his pretensions.

She'd thrown open the doors and cleared the air with fresh mountain breezes.

She was making him crazy, and not just with lust, although that would do it faster than anything else. His damned hormones had gone into overdrive, and he still hadn't finished the book. The deadline was only a week away.

How could that be? Had Pippa been here over a month already?

The quiet sound of expensive tires cruising up the drive relieved his temporary insanity. They were home. He could go back to work. He had enough adrenaline pumping through his blood right now to rewrite that opening chapter. To hell with women and their complications.

He heard her open the office door a few minutes later, but he had the heroine screaming bloody murder and chasing the gopher. He couldn't look up.

She slipped quietly away without disturbing him.

Which disturbed the hell out of him.

Seth battered the scene into shape, slapped in a few more adjectives for good measure, resisted her pull for as long as humanly possible. He printed the chapter, scanned the page, scribbled some marginal notes for Pippa to fix in the morning. He backed up his work, labeled and filed the disk, sipped his cold coffee, and scanned the office for something else to occupy his mind.

Cartons of debris lined the walls, waiting to be hauled out by the construction workers in the morning. The glass on one of his art prints had shattered and no one had bothered taking down the print for repairs. He let his mind roam back to the package, searching for the label. He couldn't remember one. He'd just assumed it was from his publisher because all unopened packages on his desk were from his publisher. But this time, there'd been one for Pippa. Which one had he opened?

Summoning the image of Pippa's cheerful smile, her upbeat attitude, her lilting laughter, he couldn't see how anyone could want to harm her. But then, he couldn't see how child abusers did what they did either. He'd grown up neglected, thrust out of his parents' life by their war with each other, but he'd never been abused by people he trusted. Of course, he didn't trust many people, and he'd taken a hell of a beating from the rest of the world, but it wasn't the same. Pippa trusted everyone, never hurt a soul. How could anyone even dream of harming her?

But someone had. She'd been bruised and battered the day she arrived. She still wore the scars inside her. She hid them well, but her wariness when he got too close served as warning. She wasn't afraid of him in particular. She was afraid of reaching out to any man. He couldn't blame her.

So the best thing for him to do right now was go on up to bed, where he belonged. They had no place in each other's lives. He didn't need the complications of a woman. She didn't need the pain he would inevitably bring her. He was a mature, sensible man, not a case of raging adolescent lust.

He turned down the hall toward Pippa's wing of the house.

She answered the instant he tapped on her door, as if she'd been waiting up for him. That possibility knocked the breath and any remaining sense out of him.

She'd removed her makeup, revealing dark circles beneath long-lashed eyes. Instead of making her look washed out as it would many women, the lack of cosmetics created the image of a forlorn waif, with translucent skin and huge eyes. She'd been running her fingers through her thick hair, and the auburn layers had fallen haphazardly. With only a circle of lamplight in the background, she looked tousled and sleepy, and Seth had the urge to bury his fingers in the satin strands of her hair and lead her to bed. The wariness in her expression stopped him.

"Is there something wrong with Chad?" she immediately asked, although she must have known he'd be hollering at her through the intercom from Chad's bedside if there were.

"He's sleeping. The doctor says he can get up and take mild exercise tomorrow. May I come in?" He could see Pippa struggling with herself now, and he didn't push. Whatever this frail thing was that had developed between them couldn't take the pressure of his usual carelessness. He was walking on eggshells here. He didn't know why he was trying so hard with this woman, but for some reason, she seemed worth the effort.

"You were late coming home. I wanted to make certain everything was all right."

She didn't even attempt to hide her relief. He figured he should be insulted that she accepted his offer of conversation more willingly than an offer of sex, but oddly enough, he understood. Conversation offered no ties that bound. Sex—with Pippa anyway—offered more strings and knots than either of them could afford.

She opened the door completely and Seth wandered into the room she'd made her own. It had once been bland and obviously professionally decorated. Now a handmade quilt splashed hues of golds and browns across the neutral tones of the couch, a handful of wildflowers spilled from a pottery vase he didn't recall seeing before, and colorful paperback books lay scattered across the tables. Framed color snapshots of family and friends littered the bookshelves. They must have been in those boxes she'd picked up at the bus station. Fascinated, Seth drifted in their direction. The only family photos he possessed were ones taken by professional photographers at his mother's insistence. He'd probably been twelve when the last one was taken.

The first one he picked up showed a cheerful, plump woman with Pippa's rounded cheeks surrounded by three equally smiling children. The youngest child had big round thick-lashed eyes that would have broken the most hardened of hearts. He studied the charming image of a toddler Pippa with a dangerous tug at a place below his rib cage. He could imagine her having children who looked just like this.

"That's my mom," she said matter-of-factly, as if there were no one else of importance in the picture. "I don't have anything in here to offer you to drink. Should I go find something?"

"No, I'm high on coffee right now." He gently set the picture down and swung around. "Liquor and you is too dangerous a combination. What happened tonight?"

She offered a fleeting smile and shrugged. Pushing her hair

behind her ear, she wandered toward the floor-to-ceiling windows. Pippa had a penchant for windows, he'd noticed. She also had the balcony doors open. Good thing they lived on top of a mountain. That would be a dangerous practice in town.

Seth followed her, unable to help himself. He hated clichés, but she drew him like a moth to flame. Or a moth to a spotlight, he thought dryly. She lit the room just as effectively. He wanted to brush his fingers against the soft skin of her cheek. He craved her softness and the shining beacon of her smile. But he didn't deserve it. He, of all people, knew that.

"Doug caught Billy creeping around Meg's house."

Her calm declaration brought him abruptly back to the moment.

"The hell he did!" That was a helpful reaction. "Did the cops catch him?"

"Billy and Doug had a few words first. Billy was probably a little more impressed by Doug's methods of persuasion than by anything the cops are doing with him. But Doug really shouldn't take risks like that. Billy could have had a gun."

A gun. Hell, he hadn't even considered that. Cops carried guns. Billy was a cop. Shit, and he'd thought he could protect her by teaching her a few defensive tricks.

"I'll talk to my lawyer. We'll get him locked away so long he won't remember what women are for by the time he gets out."

"He'll be out before you can reach your lawyer. He'll post bond in the morning. Bond for breaking a restraining order isn't very high. Don't worry. He'll think twice before getting near Doug again. Doug worked him over pretty good."

Seth glanced down and caught a wisp of a smile crossing her lips. He'd wanted to be the one to beat the bum to a bloody pulp and bring that smile to her lips. Rack up one more failure in his behalf. "How's Doug?"

"The way he tells it, Billy got off only one good lick. I took a look at his jaw. He'll be all right. Billy needed stitches."

Pippa turned and slid her arms around his waist, shocking the hell out of him. She rested her head against his shoulder. Out of practice and with no instinct for simple tenderness to call on, Seth slid his hands awkwardly around her, pressing her against him. He'd never been much good at affection. It felt kind of good now, just holding her, smelling the scent of her shampoo, rubbing soft circles against her spine as he once had with Chad.

"I'm glad you weren't there. You would have broken Billy's neck with one of those kicks of yours. I don't think I could have lived with that."

She was probably right. He didn't have much control over his temper in such situations. But that she recognized the strength of his anger and the weapons he wielded without his having said a word ripped him loose from his mooring. No one had ever acknowledged his abilities before, not to his knowledge. Everyone he knew took it for granted that he could juggle his father's business, Chad's illness, his writing career, and everything else that came his way without question. He took it for granted himself. But they were heavy burdens, and he liked knowing that she recognized what he could do, even if he hadn't done anything. Her acceptance made him feel almost human, almost good about himself. It was an unusual sensation.

"I wanted to beat him into a pulp for you," he admitted, stroking her back, feeling her breasts against him, acknowledging the pulse pounding heavily below his belt. He shouldn't be doing this. He'd told himself he wouldn't. He never repeated mistakes. But he couldn't let her go just yet. He brushed a kiss across her hair. She smelled like spring.

"I've had quite enough of men who use their fists, thank you," she answered dryly. "I'll take brains any day. Figure out what it takes to send Billy home, and I'll be eternally grateful."

She meant it, too, he could tell. Pippa's soft heart didn't want her ex-boyfriend beaten into a pulp no matter how much he deserved it. Foolish woman. Daringly, Seth brushed a kiss across her cheek. She didn't flinch. She hugged him tighter, as if she could bury herself inside him.

"How grateful?" he whispered teasingly.

"Eternally, I said. I'll talk to St. Peter at the gate."

He could feel her relaxing, recognizing the easy humor between them. They would always have laughter.

"And if he sent the bomb?" Seth asked, because the devil made him do it.

Pippa sighed and finally turned her face up so their eyes met. The tears glistening against dark lashes seared through him, but the desire he saw there scorched him to his soul.

"Then I want him locked up for the rest of his damned life. He could have killed you."

The bomb could have killed *her*, but she didn't even take note of that fact. Her concern for him wormed another little hole in his shell. He took care of others, not the other way around. He didn't like her worrying about him. But he couldn't resist her concern either.

Cautiously, Seth brushed his mouth across Pippa's. He thought he might die and go to hell if she refused him. Pippa's was the one rejection he didn't think he could live with. He didn't know why her kiss was so important to him, and he didn't want to analyze it. He just held his breath until her hands slid around his shoulders.

She opened for him eagerly, capturing him with the hot moisture of her welcome, and joy shot through him. He sank deeper, drowning in sensations he had only dreamed about, could only summon in his imagination.

He hauled her closer, pushing deeper, seeking taste and touch, absorbing the mint and coffee of her breath with the rough tactile brush of tongue against teeth, striving for something just beyond these physical experiences, something he'd never had and had always wanted, something she could offer and he didn't know if he deserved, but he wanted anyway. Needed. Desperately.

"Not like this again," he murmured in a moment of self-realization, nibbling at her ear because he couldn't let her go, but escaping the whirlpool of her kiss before they both drowned. "Not like this. I didn't come prepared. And I want you all night. I want you in my bed come morning. I don't want any more mistakes or recriminations or guilty morning afters. I want to do it right this time."

She tensed against him, and Seth reached down to brush her breast, to stroke it, to force her to acknowledge what was happening between them. Despite his words, he knew it was a mistake, but she muddied his thinking. He couldn't remember why it was a mistake. He just knew it felt right and that it had to be.

"Just sex," she responded breathlessly, really shocking the hell out of him this time. "Just sex. No commitments. No ties that bind. No tags and labels."

"Yeah, just sex," he said roughly, capturing her mouth and sealing the agreement, even as he realized he'd just been cheated. He didn't know of what or even how, but he could feel it deep inside of him as she circled his neck with her arms and pulled his head down to hers. He could sense the emptiness of the gesture, the despair behind it, but he was too far gone to examine anything more than the soft woman's body molding into his.

He'd think about it in the morning. For right now, she was his. He'd put an end to his terminal case of lust and think more clearly when it was over.

Silently, he swept her up in his arms and carried her out of the room. He needed to be close to Chad in case he cried out in the night.

Pippa curled up against his chest without a protest.

Why did he feel as if he were carrying a wounded child?

TWENTY-NINE

Seth set her on her feet the instant they crossed the threshold to his suite. The long graceful fingers Pippa had admired racing across a keyboard and stroking a child's forehead fastened on the buttons of her dress and opened them without fumbling. She couldn't believe this was real, that she hadn't fallen into a dreamlike state and imagined this was happening. The snap of her bra released that fantasy. Seth's heated palms pushed gently against her, and his lips brushed hers, reawakening sensations he'd aroused earlier.

That first time, he'd taken her roughly, hastily, with the insane lust of relief and alcohol and starvation that had swept them both away. It had been revelatory, magnificent, beyond anything she could have dreamed of, and purely temporary, she was certain.

She wasn't so certain now. The kiss he held her with this time was gentle, seeking, inspiring cravings she'd locked away long ago. Lust, she understood. Men liked sex. In exchange for satiating their hungers, they occasionally gave her the affectionate hugs and kisses she wanted. But this was different. Seth was different. He was turning the whole scenario upside down. He sought *her* kisses, not the other way around. He simply touched and stroked instead of grabbing. In his own complicated way, he was offering her the chance to take what she wanted instead of vice versa. Offering, not demanding.

Shaken, she didn't know how to react. She didn't know how to tell him what she wanted. She'd never talked about it before, had never had the opportunity to explore. She just wanted to cling and let him do as he would. But he wasn't. He was waiting, adding fuel to the flames, but waiting.

Pippa caught Seth's hands and pressed them to her breasts, looking up at him pleadingly. He smiled, that devastating dark smile that swirled around in her insides and drove spikes of need through her middle.

"You have the most beautiful breasts," he whispered. "As soft and touchable as a child's toy. Do I hurt you when I do this?"

He squeezed gently, then brushed his thumbs across the crests, driving her into a frenzy.

"No," she breathed. "It doesn't hurt. Please . . ."

She couldn't express the need in words, but he understood anyway. He bent his head and took one nipple into his mouth.

She was his after that. He could have patted her between his palms and molded her into any shape he liked. Instead, he stripped her of dress and bra and ran his hands up and down her sides, finally catching his fingers in the elastic of her panties and pulling them loose to puddle at her feet. He stood back to admire her nakedness, touched the aroused peak of her breast reverently, then abruptly jerked his shirt over his head.

He had a magnificent chest, but then, she already knew that. Broad, muscled, with a light mat of dark hairs curling into the valley spearing down to his belt buckle. His nipples were as aroused as hers, and thrilled, she stroked them. Empowered by his quick intake of breath, she leaned over and kissed him there.

"Pippa," he said warningly, but she didn't heed him. She licked the tautened crest, then nipped lightly.

He grabbed her waist and crushed her against him, nibbling her neck until she shivered, before claiming her mouth again. She hadn't even known her neck was an erogenous zone, but her body hummed like strummed harp strings.

"The bedroom," he muttered against her mouth. "I bought condoms."

She should have felt hideous shame at such prosaic words. But the knowledge that he'd gone out and sought protection just for her mixed with the terrifying realization that they hadn't considered it before. They must have been very drunk that night.

They weren't drunk tonight. They had no excuses for what they were about to do now. She'd never had sex without considering it part of the commitment process. She knew this was no such thing. This was just a release of tensions, a rush of hormones, a result of the ozone in California air. A fantasy fling, as Meg called it. A fantasy fling to end all flings. She knew she would never experience the like again.

So she threw herself into it wildly.

They fell across his bed, flesh against flesh, Seth's greater weight crushing her into the well-sprung mattress. His trousered hips rode between her bare legs, and she could feel the steel of him even through the twill. She should be terrified. Seth wasn't a small man. He could hurt her easily.

Seth caught her nipple between his teeth again, and Pippa quit thinking about anything at all. She let sensation swamp her and swirl her fears away. He returned his mouth to hers again, thrusting inside, taking and asking at the same time.

She wasn't ready yet. The tide of desire sucked her under, whirling her around faster until she would do almost anything he asked, but some tiny rebellious spark inside wasn't ready to go down for the count. She didn't feel any of the warm soft fuzzies she'd sought with prior encounters. In some unconscious part of her mind, she knew what was happening now had nothing to do with warm soft fuzzies. But she wanted something. . . .

Pippa pushed at Seth's shoulders until he fell back, watching her questioningly. She didn't know how to say it. She didn't have to. Seth's eyes lit with devilment, and he rolled over, pulling her on top of him.

"Your turn," he said roughly. "Get these damned pants off me before they cut off my circulation."

Pippa laughed with the sheer joy of it. It didn't have to be a silent rough-and-tumble. She could have what she wanted without asking, without embarrassment, with the natural companionship that had somehow developed between them. She wouldn't question how. She would think about it later. Instead, she jerked open his belt buckle.

Together, they got his clothing off, then he pulled her up against him again, smothering her with kisses as their bare bodies adjusted to this new flood of sensation.

"All night," he warned, nipping at her lips. "Don't you dare leave this bed until I'm ready."

"Bossy," she sneered, licking his lips until he caught her tongue and drank it in.

His hand slid down between them, parting her, stroking, driving her insane.

"Let me pretend anyway," he agreed. "Just for a little while, let me pretend you're in my thrall."

She laughed and gasped as his fingers dipped inside her. No one had ever . . .

She didn't finish the thought. Seth caught her hips, positioned her where he wanted her, and thrust upward.

She exploded, right there and then, without waiting, without patient stroking, without any of the artifices it had taken in the past. She exploded around him, and still shuddering, took him deeper, faster, demanding even more.

He obliged, flinging her over and driving into her until she screamed his name and his release drove them both over the precipice.

He didn't stop there. He suckled her breast until she caught his hair and dragged him upward. He kissed her senseless. He used her for every fantasy either of them might ever have had. And she let him. Couldn't have stopped him if she'd tried. Didn't want to.

They slept the sleep of the exhausted, then woke and languorously returned to favored places, making certain they had it right before exploring in new directions.

Pippa woke at dawn to the sound of Chad's Nintendo shooting through the infant monitor. Recognizing the noise for what it was, she stretched, and her foot brushed Seth's muscular leg. Naked muscular leg.

My dear lord, she whispered to herself, what had she done this time?

She didn't know, but it felt frighteningly right, like all the dreams she'd ever had of waking up at a man's side, sharing his days and nights, his hopes and dreams, as he would hers. Sheer panic tore through her as she turned her head and observed Seth's harsh features in repose. This man couldn't be that man of her dreams.

In sleep, she saw none of the grim cynicism, the knowing in his eyes or in the lines of his mouth. She just saw a relaxed man, a contented one, as he damned well ought to be after last night. He'd finally gotten everything he'd wanted out of her. Now what?

As if he could feel her stare, Seth opened his eyes cautiously. His wariness did the trick. He was as scared as she was. Pippa giggled at the thought.

A smile tugged briefly at the corner of his mouth. "What? Do I have a feather on my nose?"

"No, you just look as if you'd woken up in bed with Cruella DeVille. Your son is awake. I'd better go prepare myself for the day." Self-conscious of her nudity now that they'd reverted to employer/employee status, she pulled the sheet around her. That didn't disguise the heat of their bodies brushing beneath the covers. Without touching him, she knew he was aroused.

"I'm sure it must be your day off," he said with a straight face. "Let Nana handle him." He wrapped his arm around her waist and eased her back against the pillows. "Maybe we both need a day off."

"This probably isn't a good idea," she whispered as Seth brushed his bristly jaw against her cheek and sought her mouth.

"Probably isn't. I've got a deadline and two tons of work."

He kissed her anyway, a deep, soul-satisfying kiss that reduced her to putty again. No spine at all, she thought resentfully; she had no spine at all.

The sound of a wheelchair rolling across the floor from the monitor jerked them both apart.

"Shit," Seth said mildly, pulling back the covers. "He's not supposed to be out of bed yet."

Pippa grinned. "I don't think parents get days off. But I'm not his parent. Can I stay here?"

He shot her one of his usual dark looks, and she felt right at home again. She scrambled for the edge of the bed. "Okay, you heave him back into bed, I'll go get dressed. You'd just better be glad you didn't have twins."

Seth caught her before she could flee across the room, nuzzling her nape with his bristly beard. Naked, she should feel cold, but flames danced along her skin.

"That's what I have you for. I'll expect you on the job in half an hour." He tweaked her breast for good measure.

"Pig," she muttered, shoving him away. "Greedy, greedy pig. I'll be there when I get there."

He didn't protest. He didn't fire her. He merely grinned and watched her run for her clothes.

Maybe she shouldn't have resisted the doctors all these years if this was what was needed to soothe their savage tempers. But it had been easy to resist doctors. Seth was another story entirely.

She hurriedly pulled on her clothes and escaped Seth's suite before either of them changed their minds.

"They ain't got enough evidence to hold him on the mail bomb," Doug reported. "He's out on bail for violating the protective order. And Golding's in town. Reports are he and your ex-wife had a knock-down-drag-out in their rooms last night. They're doing the peaches-and-cream bit this morning though. You got enough bad guys in town to make it worth your time to hightail it outta here."

Seth didn't look up as he scribbled his name at the bottom of a couple of documents and shoved them in an envelope. "I'm on deadline. I can't leave."

Pippa chewed a fingernail worriedly. "What if I leave? Then Billy would follow, and there'd be one less person to worry about."

Seth shot her an impatient glance. "Over my dead body. Don't you have a fax you're working on?"

Obviously, what they did behind closed doors had no effect on their combative relationship in the office. Or not on Seth's side, anyway. He'd probably never change. Grouchy, egocentric, hardheaded . . . Pippa beamed at him. He blinked, almost smiled, and looked back at what he was doing. Stupid man.

"I sent it. And I've cleaned up those chapters. You'll have to accept that I'm better than you. Couldn't you finish those chapters elsewhere? Alaska, maybe?"

He didn't look up again. "Get her out of here, Doug. Nail her to a chair."

Doug raised a quizzical brow, glanced from Pippa to Seth, and shrugged. "Right, boss, she'll be real useful as a chair." He made a shooing motion at Pippa with his massive hands.

She couldn't help it. Billy was out on bond. Crazies were loose all over. She was sleeping with her boss and falling in love with his son and she ought to shoot herself. But she felt like laughing out loud. She'd gone as mad as the rest of the inhabitants of this insane asylum.

Helping herself to one of Seth's toffees, Pippa strolled out of the office he'd set up in the living room. The furniture company had delivered the desk and credenza this morning, but his regular office wasn't finished yet. He'd wanted the furniture carried up to his bedroom suite. She'd told him it was nuts to have them carried up there for a week and then have them brought down again when the construction was finished. He'd said it was his money. She'd told him it was other men's backs. He'd given in. Not gracefully, but he'd given in.

Maybe she should try the printing plant gambit again. Maybe she should stop while she was ahead. She just wasn't certain if she was ahead. Every time she looked at that head of tousled curls, her stomach did flip-flops. She'd sure as hell never felt that way about Billy, and she'd planned on marrying him. Maybe it was nerves.

She still hadn't seen the new ending to Seth's book. He'd handed her the printed changes of the first chapter, wiped out his work on her computer, and taken his disk back to the computer he'd set up in the living room. Secretiveness did not become him. He'd whetted her curiosity. Why had he changed his habits at this late date?

The public line rang. Knowing Meg was the only person in town daring enough to call, Pippa grabbed it.

"Billy's taken a room at the hotel," were the first words out of Meg's mouth.

Pippa grimaced at the phone. "Doug's already told us he's out. Maybe we could set fire to the hotel?"

"Just to Billy," Meg agreed grimly. She hesitated a moment, then asked almost breathlessly, "Listen, have you heard anything about Seth rebuilding the plant?"

"Not a thing," Pippa answered with a note of regret. "He avoids the subject at every turn."

Silence. Then with puzzled hesitancy, Meg tried again. "Well, Taylor is holding a big meeting in town to protest Seth's new development on that land. He wants the city to buy it and take it out of Seth's hands."

Pippa frowned. "What new development? Seth's got his hands full with mad bombers and deadlines. He hasn't had time to consider getting his toenails clipped, much less new developments. What's Taylor up to?"

"I don't know, but he's asking the city to rezone and annex all that property out there. All the city's bonds are through that bank. They don't usually disagree with Taylor and his family."

Oh, shoot, just when she had some funny idea she could end this stupid war between Seth and the town.

"Could we set fire to Taylor, too?" she asked hopefully.

"Not if you want him to vote for the gym renovations."

Well, no one had ever said life was fair. Sighing, Pippa made herself a note. "Okay, I'll call in the big guns. Seth can't very well build a plant if he doesn't have land to build it on. Remember to shoot Taylor for me."

She hung up the phone and glared at Seth's macabre covers on the wall. How many fires could she put out at once? Maybe she'd go play with Chad first.

THIRTY

"Phillippa Cochran, this is my husband, Darius Golding."

The distinguished-looking man with a Meerschaum clamped between his teeth offered his hand. Reluctantly, Pippa took it. Darius Golding had the look of a caricature of a college professor from the movies. He even wore leather patches on his jacket elbows. She couldn't remember anyone telling her Golding was a professor, but she couldn't think of any other excuse for a man to dress like that.

Natalie clasped her gold-beringed fingers together anxiously. "Darius and I want to take Chad to the ocean. He told me he's never been. Seth keeps him so isolated up there. . . ." As if sensing that was the wrong tack, she shifted gears. "You're a nurse, Phillippa. You're the only person in that institution of Seth's I can talk to. I know we got off on the wrong foot, but you must see I'm desperate. I want my son. I've filed with the court to get him back, but I already have visitation rights. I just can't make Seth see . . ."

Pippa glanced around at the room's other inhabitants. Natalie had successfully walled her off from the crowd, but she could sense the curious glances thrown their way. Meg watched her worriedly but didn't intrude. Doug had stayed outside. The meeting hall hadn't filled up yet, but Pippa recognized several faces turned their way. Small towns were always eager for entertainment. She didn't want to provide it.

She returned her gaze to the tanned, sophisticated woman before her. "Chad is recovering from viral pneumonia. He can't exert himself as yet. A trip to the ocean is out of the question. You'll have to consult his physician about when he'll be ready and what he's capable of doing in the meantime. If you have visitation rights, then I should imagine Seth will comply with the order. There's very little I can do to help you."

Pippa wondered why Natalie hadn't exercised any visitation rights in the weeks since she'd arrived, but she really didn't need to ask. The deep tan spoke of days on the beach. The manicured fingers and polished coiffeur required hours of salon care. Chad would have only interfered with such narcissistic activities. She could only wonder what had inspired Natalie's sudden desperation to see her son.

"You're an intelligent woman, Miss Cochran." Golding's mellifluous voice spilled over with warmth and understanding and the command of a professor over a classroom. "You can persuade Seth it's beneficial to his son's well-being to have regular visits with his mother. If the boy's been ill, we won't take him any farther than Garden Grove. We're entirely in your hands on that matter. You may accompany the boy, if that will ease the way. We just don't think it's healthy for Chad to stay penned up in that house forever."

Pippa agreed wholeheartedly with that sentiment, but she also knew Seth would take Chad anywhere he wanted and that Natalie had never offered before, as far as she was aware. She hadn't been born yesterday. She didn't trust this pair, no matter how sophisticated, literate, and elegant they appeared.

"I'm sure you're right." Pippa smiled pleasantly at them. She'd had years of training at smiling and telling the families of patients that everything would be all right. That training paid off now. "I'll be happy to accompany Chad if that becomes necessary. I'll mention your suggestion to Seth. But I'm afraid the details will have to be worked out with him. Now, if you'll excuse me, I believe Meg is trying to get my attention."

She pushed past the twin toads and strolled unhurriedly in Meg's direction, all the while feeling as if she should run like hell. Poor Chad. As if he didn't have enough to contend with, he had to endure warring parents and a mother with the soul of an amphibian.

"Why were those creatures twisting your arm?" Meg demanded in a whisper as she guided them toward folding chairs at the front of the room.

"Just the usual toadspit," Pippa replied absently, checking the room to see who else had appeared. She'd warned Seth about the meeting. He'd thought it a good joke but had agreed to send his lawyer. She didn't see anyone here who looked like a lawyer.

When she caught his eye, Taylor Morgan nodded coldly in her direction but made no attempt to cross the room and greet her. So much for being seen as Seth's representative in this crowd. In their eyes, she was probably no more than a glorified baby-sitter. Maybe that was all she was and she was kidding herself to think otherwise. She'd just spent too many years running her own show to play the part assigned her. Even the hospital had pretty much let her do her own thing as long as it was in their best interests. She was good at managing people. That sounded better than "manipulating."

The audience settled into a low murmur as the town council filed in and took seats facing them. They called the gathering an "open forum," without all the formalities of an official meeting, but to Pippa, it looked as if they'd primed and loaded all the cannon. She glanced around again for Seth's attorney but couldn't see anyone who fit the description.

Standing up, Taylor shot the opening volley. "As head of the local development agency and as a financial officer aware of the high unemployment rate in this area, I would like to bring before you a proposal to annex five hundred acres on the edge of town as an industrial park for the benefit and welfare of the citizens of our community."

A cheer rang out, and Pippa could see Seth's case slide downhill before it even got started. As speaker after speaker stood up to promote the benefits of the city's action, they almost convinced *her*. If Seth didn't want to be bothered with the printing plant, why shouldn't these people be allowed to develop their own? Only her antipathy for the town bullies who had turned their backs on a lonely boy held her firmly in position. To her knowledge, bullies never did anything for altruistic purposes.

As fervored shouts built toward an excited climax, a mild voice spoke insistently from the rear of the room. Eventually, the mayor pounded his gavel and restored order so the speaker could be heard.

"Ladies, gentlemen."

Pippa turned and caught sight of a short, rotund man in a camel blazer, his hand stuck in his trouser pocket as he regarded the audience with interest. The lawyer? He almost looked like one from back home. She'd expected pinstripes and a leather briefcase.

"A moment of your attention, if I might. I'm Landrum Morris, Mr. Wyatt's attorney. I would like to apprise you of Mr. Wyatt's actions on the matter of the land in question."

A hush fell over the room. Seth Wyatt had never explained his actions before. Pippa caught a few curious glances thrown her way, but she knew no more than anyone else. She might sleep with the damned man, but that didn't mean she read his mind.

"Mr. Wyatt, on three separate occasions of which I'm personally aware, has offered to sell the property to the town for its assessed value. His offers have been ignored. He has inquired into the costs of rebuilding, but presses of the sort previously used are obsolete and he could not purchase new equipment, pay a decent wage, and still make a profit. Mr.

Wyatt is not in the business of charitable manufacturing. He has asked the town to use its abilities to offer state-sponsored tax breaks and deductions so he could offer competitive wages, but again, the town has ignored his requests."

Morris waited for the buzz of conversation to die down before continuing. Pippa admired his quiet style. No dramatics, no lectures, just clear facts. She could read the disbelief on faces around her—not many of them trusted lawyers and no one trusted Seth—but they were listening.

"Mr. Wyatt eventually concluded that the town of Garden Grove had no interest in returning to its industrial roots and began looking elsewhere. At the same time, aware that he possessed property valuable to the town, he has kept his ears open for other opportunities. Coincidentally, he learned of a new computerized printing process looking for a home at the same time as Mr. Morgan did."

He paused, and speculation shot through the room faster than bullets. Heads swiveled to watch Taylor Morgan. He sat stony-faced at the front of the room, acknowledging nothing.

Morris didn't break a smile. "Mr. Morgan has entered into an acquisition agreement with this company, using as collateral five hundred acres of property belonging to Mr. Wyatt. I'm certain that he believed the town would back up his offer once the land was acquired and that there is nothing fraudulent about this agreement. . . ."

Even Pippa knew better than that. The buzz around the room warned that others saw it, too.

"But as it stands now, Mr. Wyatt is in the position to sue Mr. Morgan, and should the town of Garden Grove agree to the annexation and acquisition of the property, he will also be in the position of suing Garden Grove. I'm certain you ladies and gentlemen would not care to do anything illegal enough to bring a judgment from the courts against you."

Morris sat down. The audience erupted into a cacophony. Fascinated, Pippa watched Taylor Morgan, but he had returned to smiling affably, shaking his head to something the mayor said, and scribbling notes he passed around the table as the audience shouted for explanations. She could see why Seth didn't bother coming into town. One way or another, he was the one who would get skewered, even when he was in the right. He simply didn't have the political finesse to lie and manipulate to get what he wanted. She tugged Meg's sleeve. "I'm leaving. That's about all of this I can handle."

Meg grimaced. "I agree. Let's get out of here. Can I go with you? George will want to stay for it all."

They pushed down the aisle and retreated to the back of the room. Morris was waiting by the door by the time they reached it. He bowed and held it open for them.

"Miss Cochran, I believe?" he asked as he followed them out. "I've had the pleasure of speaking with you several times on the phone."

"Mr. Morris, my friend, Meg Kelly. I think you knocked their aspirations flat on their rears." From the corner of her eye, Pippa caught Doug leaning against the Mercedes, waiting. Reassured, she lingered.

Morris smiled. "That is one way of phrasing it. Give my regards to Seth. I'm driving back to L.A. tonight and won't be coming out his way."

"Knowing Seth, I daresay he's already forgotten you were coming and why. Have a safe drive." Pippa offered her hand in farewell.

Morris took it but shook his head at her parting words. "Oh, he'll remember eventually. Mostly, he has different priorities."

They watched him stride confidently toward his low-slung, sporty Mercedes.

"Odd little man," Meg offered.

Pippa laughed. "What did you expect of Seth? Johnny Cochran?"

Meg tagged along behind her as Pippa aimed for the safety of the Mercedes and Doug. Knowing Billy could be anywhere made her nervous. He hadn't used his gun yet, but there was always a first time.

"All right, so I'll have to give the Grim Reaper credit for trying," Meg said grumpily. "But I don't think he tried very hard." She looked up at Doug, standing with arms crossed and listening with a dangerous frown. "Hello, Mr. Brown. You missed an enlightening meeting."

"Name's Doug, and I ain't interested in being enlightened. I just wanna get outta here before that maniac shows up again." He swung open the car door.

"He's not been around, has he?" Pippa asked anxiously as she climbed in.

"Nope, but I ain't too fond of none of these other characters creeping in and out neither. That canker sore of a woman Seth married been out here consorting with the enemy. I don't like the looks of none of it."

"Natalie? Natalie's been consorting with someone?" Meg asked with obvious interest as she climbed in beside Pippa, not any more concerned that Seth's chauffeur didn't behave like a chauffeur than Pippa was.

"With that shiny-haired Morgan fella. Someone ought to push them all off a cliff." Doug roared the engine to life and eased the car from the lot.

Pippa giggled. "I suggested setting them on fire, but Meg disapproves."

"Setting Chad's mother on fire wouldn't be a smart move," Meg agreed. "But I'm beginning to wonder about Taylor. Surely he knew better?"

Pippa knew Doug was listening, but she figured he'd heard most of it at the door. He might act aloof and disinterested, but he had satellite radar for whatever happened around him. "I imagine Taylor knew better but figured if he moved quickly enough, he wouldn't get caught. That's why this all came up so unexpectedly. I'm wondering what Seth will do now, though. Could he buy that company?"

Meg gasped and flopped back in the seat at that possibility. "Taylor would choke, but a new plant . . . Do you think he might?"

"Don't get your hopes up," Pippa warned. "And figure Taylor won't take it lying down. It could get nasty before it gets better."

Doug let Meg out at her house, waited until she was safely inside, then drove the car back through town the way they'd just come.

"Did we forget something?" Pippa didn't like sitting in the backseat alone, but Doug liked having the front to himself. She'd quit arguing with him weeks ago.

"Nah, but I wanted to see if that Chevy behind us is lost and thinks we can lead him home." Doug glanced in the rearview mirror, then swung the Mercedes sharply to the left at a yellow light.

Pippa glanced through the heavily tinted windows, seeing only the headlights stopping at the intersection. "It's a small town. Could just be kids cruising, looking to see who's in the fancy car."

"Yeah, right, like Madonna's gonna come down here on a Tuesday night and have a burger at the drive-in." Doug turned the wrong way down a one-way street.

Pippa held her breath until they turned down an alley. Good thing traffic was light. She glanced over her shoulder again. No headlights. "There isn't much point in following us if they know the car belongs to Seth. Everyone knows where he lives."

"Yeah."

She didn't like the way he said that, but she didn't question it either. They both had watched entirely too many murder movies. Real people didn't get pushed off cliffs by other cars.

Billy liked Chevies.

Doug's silence made Pippa more tense. She glanced over

her shoulder several more times, but she saw no more telltale headlights.

They slowed to turn up the gated drive to the mansion. Just as Pippa decided it must have been kids following, an engine roared behind them, and a car shot past, headlights unlit, leaving a trail of dust in its wake.

"Smartasses," Doug muttered, punching the gate opener.

But it had been more than that. The other car had come close enough to scrape paint. Another inch or two and he could have spun the Mercedes around and off the road.

Instead of dropping Pippa off and taking the car to the garage, Doug parked in front of the house and followed her up the steps. Too shaken to protest, she stepped into the foyer, heard Seth at his computer, and hurried toward her room, leaving Doug to report what he would. She had too much thinking to do and it was better done alone, without the unnerving distraction of Seth.

She kicked off her shoes and threw her purse on the couch. Nervously, she padded through the suite, reaching for the brush in front of her bedroom mirror and jerking it through her hair, wondering if her roots needed touching up, but not really seeing herself.

What if Chad had been with her tonight? Or Seth? Maybe that was what Billy had been hoping, that Seth would be in the car, too. Billy hated it when she saw other men. He didn't even like her talking to the doctors and administrators she'd worked with. He'd wanted her to quit working when they got married. She should have recognized the signs earlier, but she'd just contemplated the joy of staying home, tending the yard and house, and having children. Stupid. The first thing abusive men did was separate their wives or girlfriends from other people, from the help and support they needed.

She hadn't read enough on stalking. Maybe she could check the Internet tomorrow. How many stalkers followed their victims across the country? Didn't they prefer personal confrontation to something so detached as driving a car off the road?

Maybe it had been some kind of warning, a threat. Pippa jerked her head up and stared at her image in the mirror. The car hadn't hit them, just showed them how easily it could be done. Was the warning for her? Or Seth?

Before she could carry the debate further, Seth slammed through her bedroom door. She hadn't even heard him enter the suite. Barefoot and wide-eyed, she stared at him.

He looked ready to commit murder. But he didn't scare her. She gravitated in his direction without hesitation, buried her face against his shoulder as he swept her up, slid her arms around him as if she'd done it every day of her life. He crushed her so tightly, she read his fury and frustration, sensing nothing sexual about this hug. His fear should have frightened her, but it had the opposite effect. She wanted to reassure him.

"Doug's just being dramatic," she murmured against his shirt, running her fingers up and down the comforting jersey.

"Right, and you just saw a ghost. I'm sending you and Chad to Hawaii tomorrow. Then I'm hunting down your demented boyfriend and toasting him in the fires of hell."

That smacked of a little more possessiveness than she was prepared to deal with right now. Pippa struggled to pull away, pounding on his arm when he didn't immediately release her. "For all you know, they could have been checking to see if you were in the car. There were a couple of people at that meeting tonight who probably could have killed you, given the right opportunity." When he still didn't release her, she shouted, "Let me go, Seth Wyatt!"

He dropped his arms. Dark brows pulled down in fury, he glared at her. "Chad needs you. I'll be damned if I let anything happen to you."

Chad needed her, but not the omnipotent Seth Wyatt. He didn't need anybody. Well, neither did she. She was tired of needing. To hell with the lot of them.

"I'm not your toy to stick on a shelf and away from the other kids. I'm a person, dammit, and I'll do what I damned well please. I'm not going to Hawaii or anywhere else unless you come with us."

"I thought all women *wanted* to go to Hawaii," Seth shouted back. "I'm trying to keep you alive and do you a *favor*. You're my employee. I order you to take Chad to Hawaii."

"I quit, then!" she screamed back. "You can take your job and cram it where the sun don't shine. I'm not leaving this house until I'm damned well ready to."

"It's my house," he pointed out, furiously.

"It's my *life*."

Seth glared at her and ran his hand through his thick curls. "What if they were trying to kill me and you got hurt in the process? Do you think I could live with that?"

"It's my choice," she said coldly. "For this past year, I've let Billy 'take care' of me. I let him take over my life. I let him tell me what to do and who to do it with. Because he was 'taking care' of me." She heard herself screaming but couldn't stop. All the words boiled over and hissed, as if they'd been kept in a pressure cooker too long. "Billy always knew what was right, what was best for me. Do you damned well think I'm going to let another man walk right into his shoes? Not on your life, buddy. Never again. I make my own choices from here on out. You just stay out of my way."

She flung the hairbrush at the wall to punctuate the argument, but she was nearer tears than anger now that the pot had boiled over. Seth's stunned expression told her how very thoroughly she had ruined everything. He possessed only one method of dealing with emotional overload, and she'd just triggered it.

"If that's the way you want it," he answered in his frostiest tone. "Wander outside this house at your own risk, just don't take Chad with you when you do."

He swung around and stalked out again.

Pippa watched him go with despair. Deep inside her, she still *wanted* him to take care of her. She just didn't dare trust another man again.

So that was what Billy had stolen, she thought wearily, turning toward the bed. He'd stolen her ability to trust.

THIRTY-ONE

"Have you found a circus yet, Pippa?" Chad asked, sitting on the bed in his Superman pajamas as Pippa threw open the balcony doors.

The sun danced off the auburn highlights of her hair as she swung around. "I'm looking, but I've got the dates for the county fairs if we can't find a circus. It's too early for them yet, but we'll get there."

Seth leaned against the doorjamb and admired the broad, easy smile she bestowed upon his son, a smile she hadn't given Seth in days. This early in the morning, she hadn't applied lipstick, but she didn't need it. Pippa glowed with color, from the flashing green of her eyes, to the pink tint of her cherub cheeks, to the moist red of her mouth. Moist, *luscious* red mouth, he added contemplatively. Pippa had lips that could drive a man crazy.

A truly ambiguous statement if he ever heard one.

Of course, half the problem was that he couldn't keep his own mouth shut when he should. Another ambiguous statement. If he'd kept his mouth off hers, they wouldn't be having these lovers' spats that interrupted routines. If he'd kept his mouth off hers, he wouldn't have had to rewrite those last chapters either, he thought grumpily. And if he'd kept his damned mouth shut, she'd still be in his bed instead of freezing up like a Popsicle.

Right at this moment, watching her cheerfully tease Chad into taking his medicine, Seth couldn't decide which mistake was the one he shouldn't have made.

Heaven only knew, he still wanted her. He wanted her so much he ached with it. But if life had taught him nothing else, it had taught him that the aches of lust were easily assuaged and had never killed anyone yet. He just wasn't certain this ache was entirely lust. Pippa was such a new experience for him, he couldn't be sure he didn't want to be Chad right now.

Which was stupid, he granted. He wanted her as a man wants a woman, not as a boy wants a mother. But Pippa somehow combined the two in a way that was totally hers, and that he craved more with each passing day.

Discovering he liked being fussed over and teased did not pacify Seth's grumpy mood. He certainly didn't need to pay someone to annoy him. He had an entire household like that already. He would've called Mac to see if she had a return date scheduled yet, but Dirk was still checking on her.

It didn't matter. Chad needed Pippa. He couldn't let her go.

She would drive him insane if she stayed here and he had to keep his hands off her.

He didn't have time to waste worrying over it. He'd finished the damned book. He deserved a little celebration. He didn't dare let anyone but his editor see the manuscript the way it stood now. If he'd made a fool of himself, he would limit the number of people who knew. He could always change it back to the original. But dammit, he *liked* the way the thing had turned out. He just wanted to know if his mind had turned to mush or if anyone else thought it was as powerful as he did.

"I'm going into L.A.," he announced as he sauntered into the room.

Pippa's smile froze on her face, but at least she didn't frown.

"Is there a time I can tell people you'll return?" she asked with the brisk efficiency of a proper administrative assistant.

Seth nodded approvingly. "I have a meeting with my lawyer and dinner plans. I may stay overnight. Hold all my calls until I get back to you."

Her eyes widened perceptibly, and Seth's stomach clenched with the impact. She had such damned long lashes, like velvet fringes. But he didn't suffer from the impact of those lashes. He suffered from the impact of the empathy between them, the brain waves shooting back and forth, the questions she didn't ask, the disappointment she didn't voice. Natalie would have shouted and cursed. His mother would have resorted to shrill accusations and tears. Neither woman would have cared enough for his feelings to keep her mouth shut. Pippa did. Or she was being extremely efficient this morning and dismissing him as if he were one of the damned doctors she used to manipulate.

Efficient assistants would not look at him as if he were a major disappointment.

"What about the book?" she asked calmly. "What shall I tell your editor?"

"It's done." Seth knew he sounded curt, but he couldn't seem to help himself. He deserved a night in L.A. And she'd made it plain that she didn't want to have anything to do with him and his "overprotective" nature. Heaven forbid that he should be classed with that Neanderthal ex-fiancé of hers. "I'll have it FedExed when I get to L.A."

The velvet fringe blinked, shuttered closed, and turned away. "I'm glad you're done. Now you can relax a little."

Damn, now he felt guilty as sin. She'd worked as hard as he had these last weeks. She'd walked through hell with him, never wavering once. And he was leaving her in this house full of maniacs.

Well, that was what he paid her for. He'd have to keep remembering that. No strings, they'd said. No commitments. Just what they wanted at the moment. Besides, she was safer here behind locked gates until they caught the crazy cop. He'd see Dirk when he got to L.A. Something had to be done to get the creep behind bars.

"Have you read the report on the town meeting? Meg says Taylor Morgan is telling everyone your lawyer has it all wrong." Pippa stood up and eased toward the door now that Chad was peacefully eating his breakfast, unconcerned by their adult conversation.

Seth followed her, lowering his voice so as not to disturb his son. "I'll sue Taylor Morgan's pants off if he tries to go through with the purchase of that company. You can tell the town gossips that. Beyond that, it's none of their business."

"Of course." She nodded her head, bouncing her hair across her cheeks and not looking at him as she headed for the stairs.

"Pippa." He hated the strained sound of his voice as he spoke her name. He mastered flat and cold before she turned around. "I know what I'm doing. Have a little confidence in me."

She looked at him with an open curiosity and a wariness that pierced the impervious armor around his heart. He didn't want her to be afraid of him. Seth clenched his fingers to keep from touching her cheek. He walked on uncertain ground here. He knew he was sinking deeper, and he didn't know yet whether to struggle against the treacherous quicksand or wait patiently and pray help would arrive before he sank. He had to get out of here just to straighten his head out.

"There are good people out there," she said softly. "Taylor Morgan isn't one of them, but he isn't the whole town. Remember Mikey and the kids before you decide anything. Kids don't deserve the rap for what their parents do."

She hit him square on with that one, and he narrowed his eyes. "Who have you been talking to?"

"Little birdies." She smiled sweetly, then scampered down the rest of the stairs.

Seth watched her dart into the office below. If there were any little "birdies" around here, it was his twitty assistant. She practically flitted from room to room. And like a bird, she brightened every room she descended on.

She would have him writing poetry instead of horror if she kept it up. With bad mixed metaphors.

Growling just to remind himself that he could, Seth stalked down the rest of the stairs and out to the Jag waiting for him in the drive. He'd blow a few cobwebs loose before he reached the city.

"Pippa? Is that you? Meg told me I could reach you here."

The voice from the past jolted Pippa out of her fugue. She stared at the computer screen and tried to remember what she'd been doing before the phone rang. It didn't matter. She smiled joyously at Charlene's voice. "Charley! How you doing? It's good to hear a familiar accent."

The voice on the other end of the line laughed. "Don't drawl out there, do they? When you comin' home, honey?"

Pippa wrinkled her nose. "Don't know if I am, Charley. I kinda like this place. And I keep hoping Billy will get the hint and go back there and leave me alone. He can't live on nothing for long."

"He's out there?" Charlene asked, scandalized. "I'm sorry, honey. I swear I didn't tell anyone anything, but he was over at Mr. Postman when I took that box of your mail over. Do you think he could have got a look at it somehow? He could have flirted with one of those bubbleheaded teenagers, or told them he was acting under the authority of the law or some such. They'll believe most anything."

"Box of mail? You sent me a box of mail?" Pippa held her breath as she waited for the answer.

"Didn't you get it? I sent it weeks ago. I declare, UPS is getting as bad as the post office. I'll have them trace it. It was mostly bank statements and bills, but you had one of those envelopes saying you won a million dollars. I thought about keeping it for myself, but who knows, maybe you really did win. You deserve it more than most."

Pippa didn't know whether to laugh or cry. She shook her head, answered with whatever fell off her tongue, and hung up as soon as she could.

Billy hadn't sent the mail bomb. Someone else had.

She hit the intercom and called Doug.

He lumbered in and glared at her. "You gettin' to be worse than the Man, girl. What you want?"

"You're just peeved because Seth didn't take you into L.A. with him," Pippa reproved him.

"A bodyguard guards bodies," he grumbled, flopping down in the easy chair and sprawling his long legs across the floor. "He thinks he's immortal."

"I'd wager he has no such foolish notion. Sir Galahad thinks he's protecting us. I just got a call from home." Pippa sat back, replaying the conversation in her head, trying to work out all the angles. "Billy didn't send that package from Kentucky. A friend of mine did. Billy probably saw the address on it and flew out here as soon as he could. I don't think he had anything to do with the mail bomb."

Doug's eyes narrowed into slits as he glared at his king-sized shoes. "That means one of them packages for Seth blew. I shoulda opened them all. To hell with his playing at Christmas. It's my job and I fu—" He changed gears. "I messed up." Stamping his feet flat, he started to rise.

"If you head for that beer bottle, I'll crack it over your head," Pippa warned him. "We have to work this out. If that bomb wasn't for me, then it was for Seth. And so was the candy. Someone's trying to kill him, and he's out there on his own right now."

Doug turned his lip up and snarled, then grudgingly lowered himself into the chair again. "You got a nasty mouth on you."

"Yeah, I know it. I steam Seth every time I open it. But I

don't believe in pussyfooting around when something needs doing. Should we call the police?"

Doug grimaced. "They ain't done nothing yet. I vote we call that fella Dirk. I think Seth's told him a hell of a lot more than he told the cops. Call his lawyer, too, and tell him to have Seth call us. I wish the man would carry a cell phone like normal people do."

"That's what he has me for: answering phones. His car is probably the only place he gets any privacy. I can't blame him. Where else is he likely to go?"

"No place you can call," Doug answered grudgingly. "I'll take care of that. You call the lawyer and get that Dirk person on the line."

Well, that told Pippa something she didn't want to know. Seth was heading for L.A. and another woman. Creep. All men were creeps in one way or another. When would she ever learn that?

Probably never. As Doug stomped out of the room to make his own calls, Pippa hit the numbers for Seth's private detective. She'd call the police, too, just in case, although one would have thought they'd have traced the package by now. Maybe they were checking out poor Charlene first. If she could really learn to despise men, she'd just let Seth protect himself and she'd sit here and watch instead of making an idiot of herself.

She wouldn't do that either. "Wimp," she muttered as she reached Dirk's secretary. She couldn't even watch men she despised get hurt.

"Miss Cochran? Mr. Ridgewood is on his way to Garden Grove now. I left a message on Mr. Wyatt's machine."

Pippa looked at the blinking light and sighed. "He didn't pick up his messages before he left. He's on his way into L.A. If Mr. Ridgewood checks in, tell him to call here."

Not good, but not necessarily disastrous. The bomb may not have had anything to do with anyone in Garden Grove. It could have come from New York, or Japan, for all anyone knew. The

Chevy that had followed them the other night had probably been Billy playing tough. He wanted her, not Seth, she thought.

Muttering an uncomplimentary expletive beneath her breath, Pippa dialed the police. The detective wasn't in. She left a message. She called the lawyer and got voice mail. The office wasn't open yet. With all the complex communication equipment in this world, it had become virtually impossible to talk to anyone, Pippa thought, hanging up.

Now what? Maybe she was worrying over nothing. No one knew Seth had gone to L.A. except the people in his household. He should be fine. But someone was trying to kill him.

Okay, who? Natalie, probably. Her husband? Maybe. Pippa shrugged. He didn't seem the emotionally unstable type, but who knew what Seth had said to him over the years. All right, add the professor. And Taylor Morgan. Heck, she'd like to punch Seth a time or two herself. He probably had people waiting in line wanting to wring his neck. Maybe he ought to go sleep with his editors for a while. They were probably the only people in the world who might protect him right now. Unless his next book stank.

This was not productive. Pippa looked up as Lillian entered.

"Has Seth already left? I thought I'd have him stop by the house and pick up a few things for me. I guess I'll have to send my driver. Did he look over those contracts that arrived yesterday?"

Lillian appeared more anxious than usual, driving Pippa's already frayed nerves a little closer to snapping. "He left a little while ago. I don't think he had time to look at the contracts. Are they urgent?"

"Well, they should be mailed by tomorrow. I'll look at them and leave him a few notes. I wish he'd talked to me before he left. I'd already told Stan he could have the day off, and I believe he made plans. He won't be happy."

Pippa didn't think highly of Lillian's lazy, narcissistic driver. He spent more time with the barmaids in town than driving

Lillian anywhere. Maybe upsetting his plans would save some poor girl's virtue for a day.

"Just don't tell anyone where Seth has gone," Pippa warned. "He didn't take Doug with him, and that crowd in town is out for blood."

Lillian wrung her hands. "Surely they wouldn't harm Seth? Maxim used to do dreadful things and no one ever tried to harm him. I thought the police decided that bomb was for you. I didn't mean to say anything, but I thought you should be a little more cautious."

No sense in worrying Lillian any more than she already was. Under Pippa's constant warnings about Chad's lungs, Seth's mother had scarcely touched cigarettes in days, and she'd like to keep it that way. Pippa managed a smile. "I'm just worrying like an old mother hen. Why don't you look at those contracts? I think I'll stop in and check on Chad."

Lillian happily carried off the contracts. Tired of listening to the constant pounding of the workmen in Seth's office, Pippa hit the voice mail button and headed for the stairs. She was halfway across the foyer when Doug opened the door to usher Dirk inside.

The detective appeared even colder and sharper than she remembered. He looked like the kind of man who would carry a knife and know how to use it. His dark eyes scanned the interior as he walked through the door, spotting Pippa instantly.

"Miss Cochran." He halted her with just the command of his voice. "Doug tells me Mr. Wyatt isn't in. Is there any way we can reach him?"

She didn't like the shrewd way he looked at her. If she were guilty of anything, she'd want to confess on the spot. But she didn't have to admit her indiscretions to him. As a matter of fact, as totem poles went, Dirk's position was probably beneath hers.

"There's a room back here away from the workmen where we can talk, Mr. Ridgewood. If you'll follow me?"

Sometimes, she really enjoyed the authority empowered by administration.

"Dirk," he reminded her. "Please call me Dirk. It makes me sound like one of those TV hotshots."

Pippa threw him a grin over her shoulder. "All right, so you're another man I can't hate. Come on, I'll have Nana bring us some tea. Doug, you coming?"

"You think I'm letting you handle this, girl?"

So much for administrative authority. Dirk grimaced at the tea as it was served but sipped it gingerly before he spoke.

"I've traced the UPS packages. As far as I can tell, they appear harmless. It must have been the post office box he opened."

"That discounts Billy," Pippa agreed. "I just had a call this morning from the person who sent my package. Is there any way of tracing the post office package?"

Dirk squirmed in discomfort as he looked from Pippa to Doug. "I'd rather speak with Mr. Wyatt. Do you know when he will return?"

"He didn't leave word," Doug replied stiffly.

"When he's through with his girlfriend," Pippa answered at the same time, defiantly.

Doug threw her a glare and Dirk raised his eyebrows but neither man commented on that particular bombshell, although Pippa noted they exchanged knowing looks over her head. She wanted to smack them both.

"I think we'd better find him," Dirk said slowly, weighing each word. "I think we have strong reason to believe the bomb was meant for him. The candy had enough poison in it to kill any ordinary man."

THIRTY-TWO

Doug shot out of his seat and stormed the room. "I shouldn't have let him have it! It had no damned label! I'm just what everyone says—a worthless piece of shit."

"Shut up, Doug," Pippa snapped. She really snapped. All those frayed nerves wore right through. She'd been terrorized enough for a lifetime, and now she would put an end to it. She blocked his path and pounded his NFL barrel-wide chest. "Sit down and let's see what else the man has to say."

Dirk's thin lips twisted wryly as Pippa shoved a man three times her size into the nearest chair. Doug didn't offer any real fight, but his glare alone should have sent her screaming. Hands on hips, she glared back until, deeming Doug sufficiently cowed, she turned on Dirk.

"Can the poison be traced?"

"Not easily. But toffees like that are handmade. The poison was in the coating. We're looking for manufacturers. The problem, of course, is Seth's international connections. The candy may not have come from L.A."

"It was mailed from L.A.," Doug growled. "It didn't have a return label, but it had a postmark. We just figured it came from his lawyer or something."

"Then we'll know more shortly. Did Seth give you that report I sent him the other day?"

Doug rolled his big shoulders and shot Pippa an uneasy glance. "Yeah."

More secrets no one wanted to tell her. Fine, then. She was just a glorified secretary. Why should she know? Or care? But she cared, damn it. She cared too much. That was half her problem. She couldn't let anything happen to Seth. It would devastate Chad.

"So, don't tell me what was in the report." She threw up her hands and paced. "For all we know, someone tried to bomb that report out of existence. Why should that matter to me? I'll just go wash Chad's hair."

Doug snickered. Less experienced in Pippa's manipulations, Dirk jumped to his feet and halted her escape.

"Not yet, Miss Cochran. It's possible someone intended to destroy Seth's mail along with him. You're quite right. Sit down, please."

"Hook, line, and sinker," Doug murmured in Dirk's direction. "You're as bad as Seth." He grinned at Pippa. "Seth just didn't want you knowin' he's checkin' up on your Billy friend. You already know about the Witch and the Serpent."

Natalie and Darius, the Witch and the Serpent. Doug had been reading too many of Chad's storybooks. Pippa wanted to grin back at him, but she just couldn't manage it. She collapsed in a chair and dug her fingers into her hair. "What about Taylor Morgan and his crowd? Has anyone looked into them? After what the lawyer said the other night, I'd think they'd be prime suspects."

"Morgan is," Dirk acknowledged. "He's leveraged the bank beyond industry standards, and the auditors are circling like buzzards. The company he's wanting to bring in here is cash heavy. If Seth interferes with the acquisition, he could bring the bank tumbling down around Morgan's ears."

Pippa gasped. "What will that do to the town? Will the investors lose their money?"

"Seth ain't gonna let that happen," Doug scoffed. "He's just gonna make Morgan twist in the wind awhile. The man's got a mean streak when it comes to Morgan."

Seth probably had a right to despise Morgan, but that "mean streak" could get him killed. Doug didn't seem overly concerned. Pippa struggled between ragged nerves and common sense. "Maybe we should spread a rumor that Seth's bringing the plant here. Maybe that would keep Morgan away for a while, until we can find out who sent those packages."

"That would take out at least one potential danger," Dirk agreed. "But we'd better check with Mr. Wyatt before spreading rumors. He might have other ideas."

"Like going to L.A. without a bodyguard." Pippa sent Doug a fuming look. "Have you reached his girlfriend yet? Or does she want to kill him, too?"

"I figure you're more likely to do that than she is. She ain't got the guts. And I wouldn't precisely call her a girlfriend neither." Edgy, Doug didn't rise to her bait. He punched his fist repeatedly into his palm but didn't seem to realize he was doing it.

Pippa grabbed the cordless telephone when it rang. At the sound of Seth's voice on the other end, she nearly fell to her knees in thanksgiving. "Seth, you've got to get back here at once. Billy didn't send that bomb."

Seth heard the fear in Pippa's voice and froze. He didn't immediately make the connection between her words and himself. He simply heard her fear and cursed for not being with her. He could protect himself, but Pippa couldn't. She was incapable of hurting anyone or anything. He'd taught her the basic essentials of self-defense, but she didn't have the anger or the fear necessary to bring a man down. And he'd left her two hours away. He would never forgive himself if anything happened to her because of him.

Eventually, her words sank in. As his fear for Pippa subsided, Seth relaxed enough to grin and wink at his lawyer across the desk from him. "All right, Miss Worrywart, I'll check Morris for handguns and bazookas before I leave. I won't see anyone more deadly than the L.A. freeway before I get home, I promise. Tell Dirk to get tails on Natalie and Morgan and maybe Darius, just for fun. If we catch him with one of the high school girls, Nat will be so busy nailing his hide to the wall, she won't have time for me." He hung up before she could argue.

Morris shook his head worriedly. "If Miss Cochran was warning you, you should pay attention. You would be amazed at the number of contract killings coming through the courts these days. A man as prominent as yourself should always take precautions."

"I'm scarcely a notable personage," Seth scoffed, standing. "No one connects Tarant Mott with Seth Wyatt, and Seth Wyatt is a recluse, remember. Only Garden Grove knows I exist anymore. I can't live behind iron doors all the time. Women like to worry. It gives them something to do."

Actually, Seth kind of liked the idea of Pippa fretting over his health and welfare. People worrying over him didn't happen very often. He could remember weeks in that lonely hospital bed without a soul stopping in to visit. His mother had gone on a bender right after the accident, and Natalie had been as friendly as a rattlesnake. Tracey had stopped in a time or two. He supposed he owed her an explanation for breaking their date tonight, but he wasn't in the mood for explanations. He'd only made the date to let her down gently, figuring she was due that much. He could put off that scene without regret.

So, maybe he'd go back home and celebrate with Pippa. If she could worry about him even when she was mad at him, maybe she could be pacified and the evening could end much more pleasurably than he'd planned.

Seth frowned as he started the Jag and eased it into traffic. The brake pedal felt mushy. He'd have to take it back to the dealer if it continued. He couldn't drive the hills with mushy brakes. Maybe they'd just overheated out here on the hot pavement.

Before he left town, he ought to think of some little gift Pippa would like. She didn't wear much jewelry, and she'd probably consider anything expensive a bribe. She had the scruples of a nineteenth-century schoolmarm. Sometimes.

Grinning at the memory of Pippa in his bed, her sassy hair sprawled across his pillows as she reached for him, Seth rejected the schoolmarm image. She was the one who had insisted on no strings, no commitments. She offered him every man's fantasy.

Why was it that when offered what he thought he wanted, he wanted more?

Seth glowered at the heavy traffic on the freeway. With this no strings, no commitment business, Pippa could walk out any day, take up with some other man, go back to that idiot cop if she wanted. He had no way of keeping her with him. He had never realized he had a jealous streak. Pippa's accusations about his possessiveness had enraged him with their unjustness, but maybe she had a point. He'd never really cared when he thought Natalie was cheating on him. He didn't care if Tracey slept with every man in town. But the thought of any other man touching Pippa was making him crazy. She'd already admitted she had terrible taste in men. It wasn't possessiveness on his part, Seth rationalized. What if she hooked up with the wrong kind again? He wanted to be the one who looked after her.

He snorted. If that wasn't possessive, he didn't know what was.

Which was why she'd thrown him out of her bed in the first

place. Damn. He'd spent the years since Natalie avoiding the hooks of women, and now when he found one he'd like to hang on to for a while, she didn't have a hook on her. What was wrong with the damned woman, anyway?

Nothing, probably, he realized gloomily. He was the one lacking. Money wouldn't buy Pippa. She'd hold out for pretty love words, words he didn't have in him, even if he wanted to encourage her. Which he didn't. He just wanted her in his bed every night.

Shit.

He'd buy her a bouquet. Women liked flowers. Maybe she'd even consider the gesture romantic. Maybe she'd forget his idiocy for a while. Damn it, he deserved a celebration and he wanted to celebrate with Pippa. He'd buy champagne, too.

Spotting a hole in the traffic, Seth swerved the Jag across two lanes and aimed for the next exit. A truck changed lanes and lurched in front of him. Seth slammed his brake.

The brake pedal hit the floor without stopping.

Oh, damn, not like this—

He jerked the wheel to the right, grabbed the emergency brake, and pulled.

The Jag sailed off the freeway and toward the ramp below, nose first.

Images of that long-ago night, flying off a cliff and into a tree, swept through Seth's mind before the car smacked the pavement and he thought of nothing more.

An ambulance siren wailed in the distance. Closer, a steady drip, drip annoyed his sleep. Pain shot through his head. Seeking the comfort of the fog of narcotics, he tossed restlessly. His arms wouldn't move with him.

Jolted into near consciousness by the restraint, he lay still. The ambulance wailed closer. The nightmare. He was dreaming. He could sense someone's presence beside the bed. In a moment, Natalie's voice would begin its litany of guilt, cursing him for living. He couldn't bear it. Not now. His head hurt. He needed sleep.

Chad!

No, nightmare. Chad was fine, remember? Chad was with Pippa. In a moment, he would wake, and he'd see for himself. Wait, the car . . .

As if the thought had conjured her, Pippa's voice soothed his ear. Eager to escape the nightmare, Seth quit struggling.

"Wake up, Seth. You're scaring everyone to death. I know you're in there. You won't let a little head banging stop you. I have to call Chad and tell him you're just fine. Don't make me lie."

His pounding head couldn't translate all the words, but they sounded a hell of a lot better than his usual nightmare. Relaxing, concentrating, he sought the patience and soothing honey of Pippa's drawl slipping through what remained of his consciousness.

"I can't sing, Seth, so I can't use a siren song to wake you up. And reading you one of your books would scare me into nightmares, so I'd better not try that. I nag well, though. If you don't wake up soon, I'll stand here and nag until you wake just to get rid of me. Please, Seth, I promise not to tease you anymore. I'll be the world's most efficient assistant. I won't draw mustaches on your covers again. Just squeeze my hand so I know you're in there."

He could hear the pleading in her voice. Pippa never pleaded. She ordered. She laughed. She yelled. She never pleaded.

Something wet and warm hit his bare arm.

Pippa was crying. He didn't like that. He'd seen her cry over Chad and it had scared him half to death. Why was Pippa crying? Was Chad ill?

The murky fog slowed his brain, but fear for Chad cut a channel through it. He sought a light at the end of the tunnel, anything, just let him out of here and back to Pippa, to Chad.

A gentle palm stroked his brow. Fingers clung to his hand,

the hand he couldn't move. A cool, herbal fragrance wafted through his senses. Pippa. Pippa was here. It wasn't a new nightmare. He remembered that nightmare now. Natalie had been in it. Pippa had driven that nightmare away.

"If you don't wake up soon, I'll remove these blasted bars, and climb up there and sit on your chest, Seth Wyatt," the voice said.

He heard the warning, although not the sense of the words. Tentatively, he wiggled his fingers, seeking Pippa's.

Two hands gripped his as her voice poured excitedly over him again.

"Yes! You're awake. You're there. Come on, Seth, you can do it. I can hear the rusty cogs of that brain of yours grinding. You don't want to leave Chad with Natalie and Darius, do you?"

A wheel clicked. Anger spurted straight through him with the icy blast of a fire hose.

He crushed Pippa's hand and jerked her toward him.

But as he tried to speak, his words failed him.

THIRTY-THREE

Tears streamed down Pippa's face. Not tears of relief. She knew too much about head injuries to believe Seth was out of the woods yet, even if he was in the best hospital in L.A. Tears of hope, maybe, just at feeling the life in his hands.

Carefully, she unwrapped the tie holding still the arm with the IV. Then she lowered the bar and sat on the bed beside him, still squeezing his hand. "Don't try too hard," she whispered. "You've got to give your head some rest. Would you like some water?"

He grimaced, and a rusty sound she recognized as "whiskey" grated past his lips.

She laughed with nervous relief. One hurdle cleared. He could still speak. Whiskey. Like Chad demanding Coke. Oh, damn, but she loved this miserable, cantankerous creature.

Which scared the hell out of her.

She leaned over and kissed his suntanned cheek anyway. "If a little wine can make you drunk, I'll not recommend whiskey."

The hand she didn't hold reached up and grabbed a hank of her hair, pulling her toward him. Seth's eyes opened, and the bottom fell out of her stomach as she stared into stormy gray.

"Chad?" he demanded.

Pippa propped one elbow across the hospital gown covering his muscled chest. Releasing his hand, she stroked the tight line beside his mouth. "Chad's fine. He knows nothing about the accident. He's with Doug and Lillian right now." She watched Seth's eyes cloud with confusion, and the pain of love within her ached even greater. She really had no sense whatsoever when it came to men. "You ran your car off the road and rammed your head when it flipped over. The Jag is mincemeat, you've twisted your ankle and bruised your ribs, but otherwise you're only banged up a little. Say prayers of thanksgiving for seat belts and air bags."

He seemed to relax a little. He closed his eyes and tentatively lifted the arm with the IV bandage. "Get it off," he demanded.

"You've been unconscious for nearly twelve hours. Maybe we should wait." She wrapped his hand in hers again. "I don't want you conking out on me again. You scared us silly."

He lay still again, watching her warily from beneath the white bandage covering his forehead. She'd lit only a small light in a far corner of the room so it wouldn't hurt his eyes. Shadows hid his expression, but she thought his mouth softened just a little bit as he looked at her.

"You're crying," he accused.

She hadn't realized she was still at it. Hastily, she rubbed her sleeve across her cheeks. "I always cry when I'm scared," she informed him haughtily.

A hint of a smile quivered at the corner of his mouth. "Then my book didn't scare you."

Oh, damn, she wanted to laugh and cry at the same time. She wanted to throw herself into his arms and pour kisses across his battered face. She wanted to spill all the dizzying love and desire into words and cover the arrogant jerk with her prayers.

She sat up and tapped a warning finger on his chest. "Man-eating gophers don't scare me. Losing my gullible employer does. You need to start drinking liquids. Should I get you some Coke?"

The ghost of a smile disappeared. "Call Dirk. And the police."

Now that she'd reestablished the familiar security of their employer/employee relationship, she should feel less shaky, but if anything, the dizzying emotions inside her swirled faster. Biting her lower lip, Pippa hesitated. "How's your head? The nurses can't give you anything stronger than aspirin until you're conscious for a while."

Wearily, Seth closed his eyes. "My brake lines were cut. Call the police, Pippa."

The flatness of his voice terrified her, but she followed his orders. Pulling the phone into her lap, she dialed the operator, connected with the police, spoke with the detective on duty, and hung up. Recalling Dirk's number from the depths of her memory, she dialed that and left a message. It was nearly midnight. She didn't expect to hear from him anytime soon. Before she could return the phone to the nightstand, Seth's hand closed over hers.

"Call Doug. Tell him not to let anyone in the house."

Starting to get scared, Pippa punched in Doug's private extension. He answered on the first ring.

"Seth's awake. He says it wasn't an accident. Keep everyone out."

She held the receiver away from her head as Doug's expletives exploded in her ear. Even Seth could hear them. He took the phone away.

"Look, I'm remembering some of the night of the first accident. Shut up, Doug, and listen." The voice on the other end quieted. "I remember a phone call, someone I knew telling me to meet them at that bar, but I can't remember the voice. I was annoyed and told them I had to pick up Chad and didn't have time for games. I vaguely remember whoever it was promising it would take only a few minutes. But listen, Doug,

I do remember this—whoever it was never showed. I sat there nursing a beer, and no one ever came."

Pippa couldn't hear Doug's end of the conversation, just the questioning tone. She wasn't certain she followed Seth's reasoning, but she sat quiet. He was awake and alert. She couldn't ask for anything else.

"No, I can't remember if the voice was male or female, but it was someone I knew. Shut up and let me work it out. My brakes were tampered with while I was at my lawyer's. Have the police check the car and look for witnesses. Maybe we can find a clue this time."

Pippa held back a gasp. How many people knew he'd gone to L.A. to see his lawyer? Probably everybody in town if Lillian's driver complained about losing his day off.

"It fits the pattern, Doug," Seth replied to some question on the other end. "Someone set me up at the bar thinking they could have the car tampered with then, but knowing I was picking up Chad and driving back on the coast road served their purpose better. I know it sounds crazy. If you come up with something better, be my guest. I just know I went to a bar where I'd never been before because someone I knew called me. Maybe they hoped I'd get drunk while waiting for them. I don't have a criminal mind, so I can't say. But I figure it gave someone time to find a place out on that road where they knew I'd have to drive after picking up Chad. They knew my routes. I remember the accident now, Doug. A car bumped me from behind, then sideswiped me while I tried to keep control. It was definitely deliberate."

Seth met Pippa's gaze without flinching. Lines of pain etched the corners of his mouth. He looked almost as drawn and haggard as he had the nights of Chad's fever. But certainty had burned off the clouds of fog that had been there earlier. He was definitely alert and operating at full steam. He wasn't delirious. He was saying someone had deliberately run his car off a coastal road five years ago, and that someone had quite possibly attempted murder again since then.

Seth hung up the receiver and wearily leaned back against the pillow. Pippa removed the phone from his hand and set it back on the table.

The whole thing seemed unreal, like a scene from some TV movie. She wanted to check over her shoulder for ghosts, for some invisible danger she couldn't name. Instinct and training told her to calm the patient, get Seth to drink liquids, and keep him warm and comfortable. Instinct and training told her nothing about crazed murderers.

"You may be overreacting," she said, trying to assuage his fears as well as her own. "Maybe you should just rest until morning, when your head will be clearer. You took a nasty blow. No one will bother us at this hour."

"Call security, Pippa," he warned, not opening his eyes. "The only reason I'm not throwing you out right this minute is because I want Doug staying with Chad and I haven't got anyone else to see you home safely."

Under protest, she called security. And then she rang for the night nurse to let her pour water and aspirin down Seth. He wasn't her responsibility. Chad was.

While they waited, she turned out the light so Seth could open his eyes without hurting his head.

"Bring your chair over to the other side, away from the door," he murmured in the dark. "And have them unhook this damned IV. I'm taking liquids on my own. I'll be healthier with my hands free."

Security arrived shortly after the night nurse had disconnected the IV and given Seth aspirin. Succinctly, Pippa gave the guard a rundown of Seth's fears. No hospital she knew of had sufficient security staffing. The man couldn't possibly park outside Seth's door all night. But she didn't tell Seth that.

After everyone left, she took the chair on the far side of his bed and wrapped her hand around Seth's. He didn't protest the gesture. Perhaps, if he were feeling better, he would have told her he could take care of himself and didn't need nursing. But right now, he held her hand as if he needed it as much as she needed to hold his.

A strand of hair tickled Seth's nose and he rubbed impatiently at it before complete awareness set in. As sleep slowly ebbed, he became conscious of soft warm breath on his cheek and a faint scent of herbal soap. Smiling at a memory, he blinked and gingerly turned his head.

Pippa had managed to curl awkwardly in her chair and fall asleep with her head pillowed on her arm on the mattress beside him. He could barely see her face for the fall of thick hair over it. A strange warmth surged through him at the sight, and the protective tendencies she had cursed him for awakened stronger than ever. He hated disturbing her, but he didn't think hospitals had changed that much since his last prolonged stay. The racket of rubber wheels rolling down the hall warned morning had arrived.

He pushed a dark strand of hair from her face and brushed her cheek with his finger. "Up and at 'em, sleepyhead," he murmured. Raising Chad had taught him a thing or two about tenderness, he supposed. Why he should feel it toward this tenacious gnat, he couldn't say. He'd ponder it sometime when he had less important things on his mind.

She stirred sleepily. "Go 'way." She pushed at the hair tickling her chin.

"I think we're about to have visitors. Do you want to get caught sleeping on the job? In your patient's bed?"

That brought her head up. Blinking to clear the sleep from her eyes, she glared at him. "I'm not sleeping in your bed."

"Are too," he answered wickedly, drinking in the sight of a sleepy Pippa, hair mussed and one cheek as creased as the sleeve she'd slept on.

Long lashes flapped dangerously as she studied him,

declining to respond to his foolishness. Suddenly, as if the sun had just risen over the horizon, a sultry smile formed along her lips.

"I take it you're feeling better this morning?"

Oh, damn, he didn't know what that smile had shot him full of, but it burst into a thousand fireworks beneath his skin, and he couldn't drag his gaze away. Seth focused on her mouth, those luscious lips that taunted him with their closeness. "Feeling better than what, is the relevant question," he managed to reply, but he didn't have a single thought in his head beyond the desire to have those lips on his.

"Ummm, I can see that."

She leaned over and touched her mouth to his, and the world glowed with sweetness and light. To hell with headaches. Seth plunged his hand into her hair and dragged her deeper into the kiss, until their tongues entwined and he could feel the pounding of her heart in the back of her throat.

They separated and both gasped for breath at once as the door opened.

"I've brought your medicine, Mr. Wyatt," a voice called cheerfully from the doorway. "Can you sit up this morning and bathe yourself? I've brought fresh towels."

The LPN cast a look of surprise at Pippa. "Oh, I'm sorry. No one told me you'd spent the night, Mrs. Wyatt. Sorry if I woke you. Maybe you could help your husband bathe. The doctor ordered these pills for the headache."

Convulsing with muffled laughter, Seth didn't dare glance in Pippa's direction. Looking as she did right now, with her hair mussed and her lips swollen from his kiss, she didn't dare deny her sudden rise in rank. "Thank you, Nurse. I think I'll have my wife help me to the shower this morning." He barely choked the words out with a straight face. He was certain he could hear Pippa's murderous thoughts without her uttering a word. He cherished every one of them.

After he meekly swallowed his pill and the nurse trundled

out, satisfied, Seth finally lifted a challenging eyebrow in Pippa's direction. She was flushed with embarrassment. At his glance, she quickly covered her confusion.

"I'll get even," she promised. "You're on my turf now. You haven't got a chance."

That was the Pippa he knew. Seth grinned. "What's the matter, Mrs. Wyatt? Afraid the name will stick?"

"Heaven forbid." Rising, she brushed at the wrinkles in her cotton shirt, not looking at him.

She was actually wearing jeans. Seth wondered what she'd been doing when she'd come rushing over here. The memory of how he'd gotten here wiped out his amusement quickly enough. "Where are my clothes? I think we'd better get out of here before the next person through the door is someone we don't want to see."

"You had a concussion, your ankle will hurt like the devil, and you'll soak your bandages if you shower. You're going nowhere until the doctor sees you." Smug satisfaction settled across her lovely features. "And no one's brought you any clothes."

"I've hugged a viper to my breast," Seth muttered, sitting up and gingerly sliding his bandaged foot over the edge of the bed. He glared at the wrapping, held back a moan at the complaint from his ribs, and waited for the rest of the damage to catch up with him. The hospital gown gaped at his back, but Pippa had seen a hell of a lot more of him than his back. "There's got to be some store open at this hour. Call them and have them bring some clothes over."

Without warning, the door swung open and Dirk stalked through, his dark gaze quickly scanning the situation, registering it correctly.

"At least find his shoes, Miss Cochran," he said dryly, without further greeting. "We wouldn't want him breaking any toes if he decides to use those weapons of his."

"I hate early risers," Seth grumbled at the interruption,

grabbing the back of the hospital gown and limping toward the bathroom.

He ached in every muscle, but the one that ached the most had nothing whatsoever to do with the accident. A cold shower would take care of that one. He didn't know what the hell he would do about the woman causing it.

Somehow, he had to get her out of here before she became still another victim in the list of disasters his life had become. It irritated the hell out of him that he couldn't pound his fickle memory into line, but he was determined to remember that voice.

Finally, he accepted the knowledge that someone was out to kill him. Now all he had to do was figure out who.

Who had the best motive?

THIRTY-FOUR

"They'd have hired some young street punk to leach the brake line. That's probably why they picked that bar the first time. The punks there know how to do that sort of thing." Dirk shoved his hands in his pockets as he theorized. "This time, they chose a snazzy end of town where everyone plays 'See no evil.' No one will have noticed the kid or remembered him. Damn, I wish we had fewer people with motives, but I figure we can eliminate most of the women. They wouldn't know that bar."

Wrapped in only a towel, still dripping as he dried his hair, Seth limped out of the shower. "Clothes, Pippa, get me some clothes. I want to get back to Chad." He'd ripped off the wet ankle bandage.

"Yes, sir, Mr. Bossman, sir." Instead of snapping to attention, she blatantly admired the wide masculine chest revealed above the towel. Seth Wyatt had the social skills of an orangutan but the form of a Greek god. She watched a trickle of water seep through the narrow band of dark curls on his chest, dimly aware that she'd shut him up.

At his silence, she glanced up and caught him returning her hungry look. He wanted her, but judging by his clenched jaw, he wasn't too happy about it. Throwing the uncomfortable detective an apologetic look, Pippa relented.

"All right, I'll find your clothes, but you'd better make it clear to the doctor it was against my better judgment." She pushed out of the chair and waited expectantly for Dirk to move.

He didn't. He balled his hands up in his pockets and glanced from Pippa to Seth. "If you really want to catch this guy before he seriously hurts someone, you're better off staying here."

Pippa froze. She knew instantly what Dirk was saying. He wanted Seth to act as bait for a trap. But Seth was in no shape for baiting traps. The man had just suffered a concussion and had been unconscious for twelve hours. He belonged in bed. She'd fully intended to bully him back to bed once they returned home.

"You don't really think the jerk will show up here?" Seth asked incredulously. "Whoever it is believes in keeping his lily-pure hands out of it. He's not likely to make a personal appearance now."

"The way I look at it, the guy's gotta be getting desperate. He'll figure you're helpless here, and hospitals offer tons of opportunities for creative killers."

Pippa slid into the chair as she watched the two men concoct a recipe for disaster. Except for the towel, Seth was naked. She could see the muscles rippling beneath bronzed skin. She could also see the livid bruises along his ribs where the air bag or steering wheel had punched him. Unconsciously, he favored his injured leg. She'd seen how he kicked with that leg. Normally, he could spin a sandbag with blows from that foot. He could barely stand on it now. The man was an idiot.

"Feeling suicidal this morning, are we?" she asked as Seth dropped the towel he'd used on his hair and ran his fingers through the still damp mop as he contemplated Dirk's suggestion.

Both men turned and glared at her. She glared back. "He's

not Superman." She gestured at Seth's bandaged ankle. "He's not made of steel. How in *heck* do you keep a desperate man from killing him?"

Seth turned to Dirk. "You'll get her out of here?"

"Oh, that does it, that really snatches the prize. *I'm* the nurse. *I'm* the one who belongs here. And you want to send *me* away? I'm the only one with any brains in this party. If you think I'll quietly disappear so some maniac can murder you in your sleep, you've got more dust upstairs than my granny's attic."

Seth's irritation defrosted slightly with a quirk at the corner of his mouth. "Your granny's attic?"

"Shut up, Seth," she grumbled, sinking farther into the chair and crossing her arms protectively over her chest. "It's not funny."

"Yeah, well, I haven't got time to referee this argument," Dirk said impatiently. "You want me to send someone up here to keep an eye on things? You'll need an outside witness, if nothing else."

Dirk had already assumed Seth was staying. He assumed right, apparently, Pippa realized as Seth made the arrangements for one of Dirk's toadies to perambulate the halls. Dirk not only assumed Seth would stay, he assumed Seth could handle the situation with no more help than a lookout.

"What do you plan to do, shoot him with a hypodermic?" she asked, interrupting their scheming. "Why don't you just let the police handle it?"

Dirk grunted and reached for the door. "I'll have someone send up clothes. You're so good with women, Wyatt, you handle her."

"You're supposed to take her with you, dammit!" Seth shouted as Dirk headed down the corridor.

The detective apparently had a pithy reply to that. Pippa was glad she couldn't hear it. She remained where she was, plugged into the bedside chair, arms crossed, glaring at Seth in hopes he'd return to his senses. The accident must have addled what remained of his brains.

"Pippa, go home," Seth said wearily, lowering himself to the side of the bed. "I'm not in any danger from someone who hires people to do his dirty work."

"Yeah, you're in more danger from yourself. Get back in bed. I can hear breakfast coming. You wouldn't want the nurses to think you're better and send you home so you'd miss all the fun, would you?" she asked sarcastically. Standing, she snapped his sheets back into place and punched up his pillows.

"Pippa," he said warningly, but breakfast arrived in the company of the cheerful LPN, and he wasn't given the opportunity to finish his sentence.

Figuring him safely occupied for the next half hour, Pippa stood up. She needed time to herself. She'd thought him nearly *dead*, and now here he was, asking to get killed. She didn't know why she should care. It was his damned life. He made it obvious she had no say in it. She had given him that freedom. Stupid.

Grabbing her purse, she nodded at the dresser. "I brought your pajamas and toiletries. They're in the drawer if you want them."

She stalked out over his shout of protest. He'd have nurses in and out taking his temperature, blood pressure, filling water pitchers, and giving medicine for a while yet. If anyone wanted to kill him, they'd have to fight the staff to get at him. She had better things to do than watch other people do her job.

Standing in the corridor just outside Seth's room, watching nurses and interns in white-soled shoes hurrying about their tasks, Pippa wondered what other things she had thought she should be doing. She didn't work in a hospital anymore. She didn't have any charts to complete, any medications to dispense. She didn't belong here. She was an outsider, a visitor the staff must work around.

Even Seth didn't need her. He'd hired her to take care of

Chad. That was what she should be doing now, instead of standing here worrying her stomach into a knot over a man perfectly capable of taking care of himself.

Why couldn't she be sensible and do what other women did—find a nice man at school or church, someone with whom she shared common interests, marry, settle down in the suburbs, and have 2.3 children? But no, she had to fall for abusive police officers and bestselling authors who thought she was a professional nanny. Damn.

All right, so she was a head case. She'd have to learn to deal with that. She sure as hell couldn't deal with it while panting and exchanging drool with her employer. That was a road to nowhere if she ever saw one. She'd already lost enough self-respect over her fall for Billy. She didn't need to lose the remainder as Seth's live-in convenience.

Oh, hell, that would mean leaving Chad, as well as plans for the gym, in Lillian's uncertain hands. She'd have to leave Garden Grove and Meg and the kids. She didn't want to. She didn't have much choice.

She could go down to the personnel office here and put in an application. She didn't know what it cost to live in L.A., but she wasn't ready to return to Kentucky. From here, she could visit Meg occasionally, see how the gym was progressing, hear about Chad occasionally. She didn't want to hear about Seth. That would only be rubbing salt in raw wounds. She had a feeling this wound wouldn't heal easily.

Lost in morose thoughts, she didn't pay attention to where she was going. She had some vague notion of finding something to eat, but she really wasn't hungry. Seth might think the big strong macho male tactics would save him from a murderer, but someone had nearly killed him yesterday. If Seth had been in the hills instead of on the freeway, he could still be lying out there now.

And the murderer had no way of knowing that Seth was awake and had notified the police that someone was trying to kill him. After five years of going scot-free for what he'd done to Chad, he must be feeling pretty confident. The bastard.

Finding herself just outside the nurse's break room, Pippa contemplated running in, grabbing some coffee, and heading back to Seth. The surly, arrogant bastard didn't deserve her company, but he didn't deserve to die either. So, she would let him mess with her mind a little longer. He already had her damned silly heart. She didn't think she'd ever get that back. From experience, she figured she was better off without it.

"Did you see that new doctor? Isn't he a hunk?"

A nurse obviously new to the business, Pippa snorted as she turned away from the break room. Doctors ranked right up there in temperament with Seth Wyatt—steel-armored tankers and nary a hunk among them. But then, what did she know? She'd almost married Billy.

As she started to leave, she heard a second voice respond.

"You want hunks, check out the multimillionaire in 305. Have you ever seen such sexy eyes? I thought I'd melt into butter when he asked me for more coffee."

Sexy eyes. Right. The moron ought to see them when he was angry. Well, all right, so they were sexy then, too, Pippa admitted as she hurried away. The man had a corner on sexy. If he would exert himself to learn a modicum of social skills, he could have a harem.

Deciding she preferred Seth's raw energy and blunt honesty to a movie star's charm, Pippa gave up on herself and hurried back to his room. Dirk wouldn't have had time to install his lookouts yet. The police hadn't offered. Someone had to look after the idiot.

"Mrs. Wyatt? Mrs. Wyatt!"

Gradually recognizing the voice as that of the nurse who had walked in on them earlier, Pippa halted and turned around.

Puffing a little as she hurried up, the nurse caught her hand to her large chest and took a deep breath. "The doctor is examining your husband. He doesn't want to be disturbed. Why don't you go down and have a bite of breakfast until he's finished?"

Pippa supposed there were still some doctors who dragged themselves out of bed at an ungodly hour to make their rounds. She hadn't thought Seth's high society doctor one of them, but she supposed Seth was too valuable a patient to lose, Pippa thought cynically.

"I'm a nurse. I won't disturb them," she promised, continuing down the hallway. She'd like to ask the doctor a few questions. Generously, she decided to refrain from asking that someone examine Seth's hard head.

"Oh, no, Mrs. Wyatt!" The big nurse hastened to cut her off. "They're prepping him for surgery. You really can't—"

"They're what?" Pippa shouted. Or tried not to shout. Panic edged into her veins.

"For the blood clot," the nurse hastily explained as Pippa dodged past her. "There's swelling. Surely the doctor—"

There wasn't any damned swelling. She would have seen the signs. The doctor hadn't mentioned it last night. There hadn't been time to run a scan this morning. She didn't know what the damned doctor had told the nurse, but Pippa wasn't buying it. Blind obedience wasn't her style. She had to see this for herself.

The nurse caught her arm and tried to steer her away. Pippa halted and stared her in the eye. "Dr. Graham is Mr. Wyatt's doctor. Is that Dr. Graham in there?"

A startled expression spread across the nurse's broad face. "No, ma'am, it's the new specialist he's called in. I don't remember his name."

The new "hunk" doctor. Panic threatened to leap full-blown into hysteria. She throttled it. There could be a mistake. She, better than anyone, knew mistakes happened.

The nurse holding her wasn't any taller than she was, but packed twice her weight in fat and muscle. Jerking her arm from the woman's grasp, Pippa placed her hands on her hips and threw on her best authoritative disguise. "That isn't Seth's doctor. If you aren't out of my way in ten seconds, I'll call my lawyer, the hospital administration, and the police. And I can tell you right now, I *never* back down on my word."

The nurse moved. Any mention of hospital administration put the fear of God in staff. Pippa had thrown in the rest for fun.

She didn't enter the room gently. She slammed open the door, letting it be known far and wide that she'd arrived. The nurse behind her ran before she was blamed for the intrusion.

Garbed in the black silk pajamas Pippa had brought from home, Seth sat up against the pillows, the white bandage around his bronzed features appearing almost natural with the spill of rakish curls over it. She could tell that he was furious. He shot her a cursory glance at her abrupt arrival, then returned to arguing with the technician attaching the IV to his arm. Seth looked so damned sexy, Pippa almost lost track of her reason for storming into the room. But then she remembered the intruder had called himself a doctor, not a technician. Doctors did not attach IVs.

There was no good reason for anyone to attach an IV to Seth's arm. She'd read his chart. He was taking fluids. He didn't need more.

Marching in, Pippa grabbed the IV bag and read the contents. Sugar water. But remembering the poisoned candy, she dropped the bag and started to turn and glare at the man behind the surgical mask, prepared to add her arguments to Seth's. Before she could confront him, a strong arm caught her around the throat and jerked her head back.

As she crumpled, Pippa heard Seth's roar of rage.

Rack up one more mistake against her.

THIRTY-FIVE

Fury roared through Seth as Pippa's eyes rolled back in her head and she crumpled to the floor. Red, murderous rage drove his arm out until he'd grabbed the so-called "doctor's" neck.

The surgical mask fell away as Seth tried to throttle him. Even then, Seth didn't immediately recognize Pippa's attacker. The billowy surgical cap covering his hair and the malevolent expression warped any familiar demeanor, and Seth's fury blurred his view of the world.

Only as his assailant spoke did Seth recognize with whom he struggled.

"You're supposed to be dead, you bastard!"

Darius.

Seth tightened his stranglehold, but reaching up from a bed wasn't an ideal position. And Darius had a hypodermic in his free hand. Seth didn't want to contemplate what the needle contained, the needle Darius would undoubtedly have stuck in the IV and let drip while he escaped. Seth damned well wouldn't let Darius off easy this time. Keeping one hand on Golding's jugular, he tried to grab the needle.

Darius jerked free, and the hand with the hypodermic shot out. "We'll do this the hard way, damn you!" he growled, grabbing for Seth's arm.

Caught in the covers, Seth couldn't kick his leg freely. He rolled over, groaning as he hit the bed bar against his cracked ribs, but the covers pulled free with his movement.

Darius dived across the mattress after him. "This is all your own damned fault, you realize," he said as he grabbed Seth's arm again.

"Isn't it always?" Using what leverage he possessed from a prone position, Seth caught Darius's wrist and twisted downward. The hypodermic hovered between them, twisting in their deadly arm-wrestling match.

"You must have nine damned lives. Why didn't you die in that car!"

Seth didn't ask which car and which time. The point was moot if he couldn't get the needle out of Golding's hand. He tried to slide out of the far side of the bed, but the damned railing got in his way. He should have had Pippa lower it.

Pippa! Darius had throttled her. What if he'd killed her?

Not Pippa. Not Pippa of the shining smile, the sunbeam who had converted his son from screaming monster to laughing child. He couldn't let anything happen to her. And Seth knew as certainly as he knew his own name that if Darius killed him, he'd have to kill Pippa, too. No way.

With another roar, Seth twisted his assailant's arm so fast he could feel the bones snap in Darius's wrist. Darius screamed in agony, then screamed again and instead of pulling away, tried desperately to clamber up on the bed.

Holding his antagonist pinned against the bed in hopes of preventing escape, Seth found himself in the awkward position of backing away before Darius landed on top of him. "What in hell?"

"Call her off! She's twisting them off! Aagghhh!" At Darius's high-pitched scream, footsteps pounded down the hall.

"Pippa?" Still holding Darius pinned against the mattress, Seth awkwardly maneuvered into a sitting position so he could see the floor beyond him.

"I've got him by the balls just like you taught me," Pippa replied calmly from the floor. "Should I let him go?"

A grin tugged at the corners of Seth's mouth as he watched Darius struggle and scream. He couldn't help it. For what the bastard had done to Chad, he'd see him nailed to a bed of fire ants. "Twist a little harder, just for good measure."

The door popped open as Darius's scream reached fever pitch.

"What the hell is going on in here?"

Seth looked up at the short, mustached security guard and the portly black nurse behind him and wasn't entirely reassured reinforcements had arrived. He twisted Darius's arm a little harder. "Get the cops. And if you've got handcuffs, use them."

"Demerol, Nurse," Pippa quipped from the floor. "I suspect he's in significant pain."

Seth snickered. "Have you made a eunuch of him yet?"

"I need more wrist strength," she replied reflectively. "You'll have to teach me some exercises."

"I can't dispense medication without a doctor's orders," the nurse replied hesitantly.

"I haven't got cuffs," the guard said at the same time.

"Oh, well." Shrugging, Seth rolled up a fist and plowed it into Darius's chin just as Dirk and one of his cronies burst in. "I've been wanting to do that for a long time."

Seth glanced anxiously at the door through which Pippa had departed earlier. She'd given her statement to the police, then wandered off to find clothes for him. He'd still been talking to police, doctors, and lawyers when she returned. He'd tried to tell her to stay, but she'd only given him an odd look and disappeared again. He wasn't much good at reading body language, but hers didn't appear very welcoming. He couldn't imagine what he'd done wrong this time, but he wanted to rectify it as soon as possible, if only these damned people would get out of his face.

"Look, I don't have any idea if Natalie is involved. I doubt it, but at this point, even I wouldn't rely on my judgment. If I'd died in that first accident while we were still married, she'd have inherited everything. This time around, she's out of the picture. Chad gets it all. But if she had custody of Chad . . ." Shrugging, Seth glanced from the door to the police detective. "Either way, Darius would get control of another fortune to throw away." Impatiently, he turned to his doctor. "Shouldn't I be resting or something? Can't you get them out of here?"

From against the far wall, Dirk spoke up. "You've got reporters downstairs looking for you. My guy steered them wrong, but they'll be back."

Oh, hell, just what he didn't need. The nasty media coverage after his accident and breakup with Natalie had soured him for life on the press.

"Find Pippa and bring your car around. I'm getting out of here." Seth reached for the blue linen polo shirt Pippa had bought for him. Blue. Who did she think he was? Tom Cruise? At least it didn't require a necktie.

Gradually, the room cleared. The doctor signed Seth's release after being persuaded Pippa was a registered nurse and that Seth would get considerably more rest in the privacy of his home than in the fishbowl of a hospital room. Now, if he could only find Pippa.

Where in hell could she have gone? Dirk knew what she looked like, but he couldn't search everywhere at once. Seth had described the car Pippa drove, and Dirk had found it in the lot, parked practically in the emergency lane, where she'd left it yesterday in her haste to get to him. He didn't want to imagine how frightened she'd been to park the car so carelessly. Pippa usually took good care of Mac's car.

He didn't want to imagine Pippa frightened because of him. It was a lot easier dealing with the kind of dispassionate concern someone like Mac displayed. Even his mother hadn't bothered calling, although Seth had heard Pippa talking to her on the phone, reassuring her, and he figured she'd done that throughout the time he'd been unconscious. If he could pretend Pippa was doing her professional duty by driving into L.A.—a city she knew nothing about—locating the hospital, and sitting by his bedside day and night, he could accept her attention a little easier. But Seth knew Pippa better than that.

That scared the hell out of him.

He would be more comfortable complaining about those damned expensive—charcoal gray—trousers she'd bought than realizing Pippa actually cared enough to fly to his side the instant he needed her. And he'd needed her, all right. He wasn't entirely certain he would have bothered regaining consciousness this time if it hadn't been for Pippa's nagging. She'd erased the nightmare he'd lived with all these years, replacing it with a panicky concern that had dragged him right out of wherever he'd been.

Shaking his head over the perversity of his nature, Seth buckled his belt, located the duffel bag Pippa had brought from home, and tossed his stuff into it. He'd been lying in the hospital bed with a cracked head, and he'd been worried about worrying Pippa. Just exactly what did that signify? Insanity?

Where the devil had she gotten to?

Annoyed that she hadn't returned, worrying over why, worrying if he was nuts for worrying, Seth checked the hallway. He didn't want reporters tracking him down, but he didn't want to leave Pippa either. Stupid thought. She had a car. She could find her way home.

But he wouldn't leave without her. In his entire life, he'd never given a damn about anyone but Chad. He'd gone his own solitary way, forged a life requiring no one, and he'd considered himself safe and content compared to the nightmare of his childhood. Now here he was, opening himself up to disaster again, letting someone else in besides Chad. Would he never learn?

Eventually, probably, when Pippa decided it was time to move on, after she tired of his antisocial behavior, got mad enough about his unreasonable attitudes, whatever it took to tick her off. He'd be much better off if he just found Pippa and put her firmly in her place.

Seth considered starting with the cafeteria since she probably hadn't eaten in twenty-four hours. But when he hit the elevator and saw the sign for the pediatric ward, he acted on impulse. Playing with the children would be just like Pippa.

The elevator door opened on a cheery lobby decorated with teddy bear wallpaper and strewn with colorful plastic toys and children's books. The only cloud on the sunshine-filled space appeared to be a bulky young man facing a corner, which Seth found slightly disconcerting. Still, he'd seen odder things in hospitals.

He'd taken a limping step out of the elevator, cursing the pain in his ankle, when the hulking young man slammed his fist against the wall with such force that Seth jumped.

Pippa's voice followed, in brave tones barely disguising panic. "Billy, be reasonable. I'm not going home with you."

"It's that damned fancy man, isn't it? He's been laying you, hasn't he? But I heard what happened to him on TV. I knew you'd be here, holding his hand, but he won't be going anywhere soon. Now that I've found you, you're coming with me."

In two strides, Seth crossed the lobby, grabbed the hulk's upraised arm, jerked it backward and up, and probably dislocated his shoulder if his scream of agony was any indication. At this rate, he'd personally provide the emergency room with its quota of patients for the day.

Pippa managed to look both relieved and angry at the same time as Seth twisted Billy's arm. She also looked more beautiful than she had any right to be.

"My turn," she said coldly, with a challenging glare.

Before Seth could argue the stupidity of that declaration, she balled up her small fist, threw all her weight behind it as he'd taught her, and punched Billy in the stomach.

Seth could have told her she'd only break her knuckles on such a foolish stunt, but she acted too quickly for him to do anything but catch Billy as he staggered backward in surprise. The pull on his dislocated shoulder had Billy howling, and Pippa nursed her bruised fist with a look of satisfaction.

"Why don't you let him loose so I can hit him again?" she demanded.

"I ought to," Seth agreed. "But you'll just blame me when you break your hand on the worthless slug. There should still be a few cops around. Why don't you go call them? I don't think your little friend here is going anywhere soon."

Pippa's sour look at his recommendation cheered Seth immeasurably. She wasn't frightened. She was fighting mad. He intended to keep her fearless. To do that, he had to get her out of the way while he had a little talk with Brother Billy.

"My ribs ache like hell, Pippa," he warned. "I'd appreciate a little speed."

Concern instantly wiped out anger. She dashed for the hall and the nurse's station, out of sight around the corner. Damn, but he was actually learning to push her buttons as well as she pushed his. Seth jerked his captive's arm a little higher.

Billy the Cop yelped and struggled briefly, but Seth had the man's measure. He'd dealt with bullies before. They were all cowards who whimpered as soon as the tables were turned. This brute was twice Pippa's breadth, and though much of the muscle was going soft, he could still kill a woman without much effort.

Seth restrained his anger at the thought. Another thing he'd learned over the years—the winner of any battle was the one who kept his cool.

"Pippa has friends," Seth informed his prisoner coldly.

"You're not getting off this time. You've made it painfully obvious that you're incapable of learning a lesson. My lawyers will see to it that you're locked up for a good long time where you can get some of that counseling you need to curb your temper."

Billy muttered a filthy expletive and tried to jerk away.

Seth jerked back. "I have friends, too," he warned. "I can see you get that counseling in one of two ways: the easy way or the hard way. You won't think you're quite so big and strong after a few of my friends in the prison system get through with you. You're not in Kansas, anymore, Toto."

Billy stepped backward, aiming for Seth's soft shoes. Seth kneed him from behind, jerking down on his arm.

"In another minute, you're going to make me angry. I wouldn't do that, if I were you. I hear Pippa coming back." And he could. Seth recognized the rhythm of her walk, could see the bounce of her hair in his mind's eye. "You're going to apologize to the lady, do you hear me? She loved you, and you returned her affection by destroying everything. I know a choke hold that could snap your neck. Have you got your speech prepared?"

Seth wrapped his other arm around his victim's neck and pressed Billy's head backward, until Billy nodded curtly. Seth relaxed his hold only enough to let Billy speak as Pippa rounded the corner and entered the lobby.

"I'm sorry, Pippa," Billy sputtered.

Pippa halted and stared at them with suspicion.

Seth jerked Billy's arm again.

"I didn't mean to hurt you, Pippa. You know I didn't. I just lose my temper sometimes."

Seth almost believed the man's plea. He could almost feel sorry for a man driven by fury and frustration at a woman's wiles. Almost.

Pippa's eyes narrowed to slits. "I've heard that tale before,

Billy. Save it for the judge. Seth, the cops are on their way upstairs. I think I'll wait on the ward."

She swung on her heel and walked out.

"Sorry, pal, guess you weren't very convincing." Cocking Billy's head back farther with his arm, Seth jerked on the dislocated shoulder until Billy screamed and folded in on himself. Seth staggered beneath the sudden deadweight and cursed his injured foot.

It might take Pippa a hundred years to regain the trust this brute had stolen from her. Seth would have suffered the agonies of hell to make the bastard pay. He righted himself without further complaint.

After the police arrived, Seth shoved his prisoner in their direction and hurried after Pippa.

Pippa nestled a curly-haired toddler in the crook of her arm as she turned the pages of a storybook with her other hand. A ring of rapt children sat around her, listening to the story and eagerly absorbing the pictures she held up for them to see. She thought she could easily spend her life here, if she didn't have to work for a living. Pediatric nurses deserved a special place in heaven, but they didn't have time for the pleasures of this job, like reading storybooks. They spent their time reading charts of progressive lymphomas and escalating temperatures. She couldn't handle it.

She'd have to go back into administration. Then she could spend her evenings up here with the children. Maybe that would fill some of the empty hours and the gaping hole Chad would leave in her heart. She wouldn't think about the hole Seth would leave. She couldn't. Now that everything was back to the way it should be, she had to leave. She wouldn't be another needy burden hanging on to him.

She'd seen Seth's face as he grabbed Billy. He'd defended her just as he would have defended Chad. He wouldn't admit it to anyone, but Seth was a champion of the underdog. She suspected his taciturnity was his only means of protection against a world spilling over with the beaten and downtrodden. She was just one more victim for him to save and protect.

Turning a page, she knew the moment Seth breezed into the room behind her. The energy of the air changed, vibrating with his presence. The children lost their concentration and watched him with fascination. One bald-headed toddler crawled out of her field of vision, and Pippa could almost see Seth bending over to pick her up. Seth didn't relate well to adults, but she knew he had a soft spot for children.

Sure enough, he carried the little girl back to where Pippa could see them. He didn't smile but waited patiently for her to finish the story, his gray eyes curiously light against his dark complexion. The little girl rested contentedly in his arms until a nurse took her away.

Pippa finished the story and closed the book as the nurses ushered their charges back to their beds for visiting hours. Seth held out his hand and pulled her to her feet. Neither of them spoke.

He held her hand as he led her out to the waiting police officer. Billy was nowhere in sight. Pippa figured they'd taken him down to emergency after what Seth had done to him. Her own blow hadn't accomplished much beyond bruising her knuckles, but she'd had to do it. Violence begot violence, perhaps. She shouldn't have behaved as unreasonably as Billy, but she'd stored up a powerful lot of rage that needed venting. She hit him for Clio Kitty's sake, if nothing else.

She answered the officer's questions without thinking. Conscious of Seth's large hand wrapped reassuringly around hers, she recited her lessons by rote. Need rose up in her much as sap rose in trees. She'd almost lost him forever. She would have to give him up soon. But for just this moment, while she was feeling weak and stunned, she'd cling to his strength and pretend he needed her, too.

When the officer was finished, Seth led her toward the elevator. She was aware he'd dismissed Dirk. She sensed his pain as he limped and occasionally adjusted his stance to ease his aching ribs. She thought she should chastise him for being out of bed, but she couldn't. She had no fight left in her. She let Seth take control.

"Have you ever been to the ocean?" he asked idly as he took Pippa's keys from her bag and aimed unerringly for the parked car.

The question startled her from her lethargy. Throwing him a curious glance, she replied without hesitation. "Not yet."

He helped her into the passenger seat of the car, then skirted the car to climb in the driver's side. His long frame overflowed the minuscule sports seat, but he adjusted and turned on the ignition without complaint.

"I know a place where we won't be disturbed."

She understood what he didn't say, and didn't object.

They'd make love one more time before she left.

THIRTY-SIX

Pippa stood on the edge of the road, letting the wind streak through her hair as she followed the flight of a pelican. If she turned her back on the car, she could see nothing but the wildness of nature, the waves crashing against giant boulders and towering cliffs, the seals sunning themselves on a spit of rocky land, the seabirds squawking and diving for fish. She thought the wind chilly for June, but she welcomed it, thriving on the energy battering against her, soaking up the sunshine pouring down like molten honey, drawing the elements inside her to make her strong again. She couldn't remember when she'd slept or eaten last, but it didn't matter. Nature provided what she needed.

And Seth. His arm circled her waist as she stood there, and she drew warmth and solace from his presence. The first time they'd made love, she'd considered him an element of nature. He was more than that now. He provided the backbone she'd always craved. He supplied the emotional sustenance she thrived on. He offered her shelter and security. And she couldn't accept any of it.

She had to learn to stand on her own, without the need of other people for crutches. She had to provide her own shelter and security. All her life, she'd lived for other people, and never for herself. She could see it happening again: staying with Seth because it was easiest, because Chad needed her, because she pretended Seth needed her. She'd never know what it was to stand on her own two feet, and when Seth tired of her, when Chad grew out of his need for companionship, when circumstances changed, she'd be out in the cold world all over again, lost and helpless as before. She had to make the break now, while she still retained some modicum of self.

She loved easily. Her love for Seth would never die, but it would suffer the torments of hell and slowly decay without the emotional nourishment Seth couldn't provide. Better that she keep it as a bright, shining sun within her, always there when she took it out and looked at it, than to let it wither and fade in Seth's careless hands. He couldn't help it, she realized. She couldn't blame him. He'd never known love, didn't know how to give or receive it, except with his son. He thought money and physical strength were all that was needed to survive in this world. She couldn't even begin to persuade him otherwise.

But she wasn't strong enough to make the break right this minute, not in this beautiful place, with Seth confidently guiding her toward the protected beach below. She could almost sense his pain as he hit his injured ankle at the wrong angle, knew his ribs ached, but he was doing this for her, offering her this gift in recompense for all that had happened, and she couldn't reject him.

It wouldn't last. Smiling slightly at that realization, Pippa let the wind blow away her sadness and accepted the moment as it was: beautiful and wild and carefree, no strings attached.

"No wonder the movie business developed out here," she exclaimed in delight as they reached a cove protected on all sides by steep boulders, with a seal barking not yards away. "How could the imagination not soar with all this splendor at hand?"

Arm around her shoulders, Seth idly rubbed her upper arm and gazed over the crashing breakers. "It makes everything else look small, doesn't it? If we're nothing but specks of sand, why worry over past or future? Now is everything. I think that might explain the California state of mind."

Pippa threw him an uncertain glance, then smiled as she realized he was smiling, too. "Not quite a joke, but close enough. You're improving."

The look in his eyes nearly melted her bones. Without the frost in them, those gorgeous gray eyes of his conveyed starry promises she would never be able to resist for long. She tried concentrating on the blunt, thick lashes instead, but she didn't fool him. Long fingers traced the outline of her lips.

"I must be improving if you're not nagging. Does this mean there's some hope for me yet?"

"You have what it takes," she admitted. "You just have to apply it." Her toes curled, but not against the cold. Seth's hand opened and spread against her jaw, caressing lightly with fingertips while holding her firmly. She read the kiss in his eyes before he offered it.

She thought he whispered "Teach me" before his mouth covered hers, but she couldn't be sure. She couldn't be sure of anything while her blood heated to boiling and bubbled madly everywhere except her brain. No man had ever succeeded in separating her head from her shoulders with just his kiss, but Seth could.

The strong fingers that had throttled a murderer and nearly broken Billy's neck now caressed her breast with gentle strokes, asking and not demanding. He didn't need the politeness. She would have thrown herself into his arms without a word or gesture. Pippa slid her hands around his neck and returned his kiss so thoroughly, even Seth couldn't misunderstand. He murmured something appreciative against her mouth, and fingered her aroused nipple through the thin cotton of her blouse. She quaked at just his touch.

"You make this as simple and natural as the sun shining," Seth said wonderingly, lifting his head long enough to locate the buttons of her blouse and unfasten them. He spread the cloth, pulling it from her jeans. He grinned when he discovered she wore nothing beneath.

"It's not me." The sun beat warm against Pippa's bare skin, and Seth's broad hand protected her from any wind that breached the rocks around them. She felt no shame or shyness beneath his admiring gaze. "It's us, together. I never knew it could work this way."

He lifted his head to search her face. She read the uncertainty reflected there, knew Seth wasn't ready to accept what she knew with every cell of her body. She smiled, then tugged upward on the designer golf shirt she'd bought for him. He looked good in colors. He looked better with nothing on at all.

Grimacing at the tug on his ribs, he threw the shirt off, allowing her full access to the bronzed expanse of his chest, but giving her little time to admire it. With a hungry growl, he reached for her, pulled her against him, and devoured her mouth.

So, it wouldn't be a gentle farewell, but an impassioned one. Following on the acts of violence and the adrenaline rush of earlier, this fierce release was what they both needed. Pippa threw herself into it, body and soul, fearing this would be the last time she would ever know this meeting of man and nature, this physical satisfaction merging with emotional desire. Recklessly, she threw caution to the wind and waves and gave herself as freely as the sun gave warmth.

Seth had dropped the blanket he'd brought from the car. Now he lowered her to it, spreading out the folds hastily with stray hands and feet, not releasing her from his grasp, as if afraid she'd escape. That tiny crack in his arrogance only made her love him more. She could explore this man's psyche for a hundred years and never know him, but she would always love him.

"You drive me mad without even trying," he murmured against her ear as he sprawled across her, pinning her to the blanket. "I want to be inside you, and on top of you, and roaming around in your head, all at once. I want all of you, Pippa. Everything. Open for me, Pippa."

Since she didn't even have her jeans off, she knew he meant more than the obvious, but she had no way of promising what he didn't know he asked. She threaded her fingers through his hair and tried to bring his mouth to hers, but he'd already moved on, finding her breast and kissing it until her cries joined those of the gulls overhead.

They shed their remaining clothes hurriedly, not noticing the chill of the air in the steam of their bodies. Seth's tongue claimed territorial rights she relinquished eagerly. His exploring fingers took full liberty, until her body quaked and opened for him, offering further uncharted territories. Pippa gripped his hips as he covered her, lifted herself to his thrust, and urged him to delve as deep as he could.

She gasped as Seth reached deeper than she thought possible, then withdrew and slammed deeper still. She lost track of her hands, his mouth, the position of the sun, and the gravity of the earth. She spun on Seth's axis, entered his orbit, became one with his molecules. She flew with him wherever he took her, spiraling higher into the sky, spreading her wings, and exploding into golden dust motes as they touched the sun's core.

Breathless and barely conscious, she lay beneath the heavy blanket of his body, absorbing the sound of waves mixed with the beat of Seth's heart, the thin film of sweat oiling their joined bodies. She could imagine doing this every hour of her life. This was life as it was meant to be, and Seth had given it to her.

He stirred and gradually lifted his weight off her, propping himself on his elbows as he smiled sleepily down at her. "We may be getting the hang of this. A little more practice, and we could be perfect."

Pippa's heart thumped wildly and enlarged to encompass her throat and stomach at the same time. For one brief moment, she imagined that sexy smile hovering over her for the rest of her nights. She had whirling images of Seth taking her into his arms at dawn, of their racing across the pool in the sunshine, of the three of them laughing together at a fair somewhere.

And then he abruptly rolled away and the images burst into dandelion dust, floating away on the breeze.

"We'd better get back before they send the cops out looking for us." Seth brushed a kiss across her forehead, then covered her with her blouse, but his tone was brusque.

Pippa knew what he was doing. He was building that wall again, shutting her out, cutting off all hope and emotion. She understood. But she could never live with it, not knowing what she did about the man behind that wall, the loving, vulnerable man who craved a human touch as much as she did.

Cursing to herself, she dragged on her shirt while he reached for his trousers. The expensive fabric was wrinkled and coated with sand where they'd rolled over it.

She eyed the crashing waves cautiously. "I don't suppose we could swim in that?"

"Not unless you want to freeze your fanny and risk your immortal soul," he answered carelessly, not looking at her.

She thought she might just do that rather than suffer what lay ahead, but she'd discovered a new determination within her. Maybe she'd already started growing that backbone.

She realized that standing on her own two feet could include fighting with Seth until she tore down his defensive barriers. Of course, with Seth, it couldn't be a normal fight. He would just close himself off and disappear rather than argue. She had to drag him out, expose him before the world, smack him into opening his eyes. And if all that failed, what had she lost? Only what she couldn't have in the first place.

As she pulled her panties on over the stickiness they had made between them, and she recognized that once again they had taken chances they shouldn't have, an odd reassurance flooded through her. Maybe she was mule-headed and blind.

Maybe she was about to make a fool of herself. But what they could have was worth taking that chance. This would be the first challenge she'd face on her own. She had to be strong.

Tucking in her shirt and buttoning her jeans, she watched Seth briskly shake out the blanket and fold it up. She could see him withdrawing before her eyes. She could reach out, pull him back, tease him into lightening up for a little while longer, but she wouldn't. He had to learn to do it by himself.

Without waiting for him, Pippa turned on her heel and began the climb up the rocks on her own.

Seth ground his teeth and snapped his pencil and didn't look at Doug lingering in the doorway. "I tried, dammit, I tried. She won't listen to reason."

"Yeah, women have a habit of that," Doug agreed laconically.

"I offered her more money. I offered her a job overseeing the gym renovation. I told her I'd open a damned clinic in town if she wanted to go back to hospital work. She wouldn't even talk about it." Seth spun his chair around and glared out the newly replaced window behind him. The expanse of lawn revealed the same emptiness as the last time he'd looked. No cavorting nymph in a bathing suit, no twirling dervishes. Miss MacGregor had driven Pippa into L.A. that morning.

"Woman who'd turn all that down ain't got no brains in the first place," Doug said.

Seth detected a note of derision, but he ignored it. "She said she'd be back on the weekends to see how the gym was progressing. She'll want to see Chad again. Maybe I can talk to that friend of hers and see what it is she needs to be persuaded to come back." Seth watched as Durwood ambled toward the damaged oak by the drive. It seemed to have survived the crash with the BMW. He wished he could say the same for himself.

"Why bother?" Doug sneered. "All women are alike. Just hire yourself a new one. There's plenty out there."

Seth recognized sarcasm when he heard it; he just didn't bother acknowledging it. Pippa had treated Doug as her best friend, and Doug had responded to the treatment with absurd eagerness. He was probably hurting right now. He could let the man vent. Seth narrowed his eyes as he tried to discern what kind of gardening tool Durwood was producing from his box. Damned if it didn't look like a saw.

"What is Durwood doing?" he asked with a degree of anxiety.

Doug grudgingly stepped farther into the room to look over Seth's shoulder. "Sawing down a tree, looks like to me."

Two phones rang at once, and Seth cursed. Miss MacGregor was still in town and his mother was manning the outer office. She didn't like answering phones. The last he'd seen, she'd been pulling together some complicated set of numbers involving expansion of the printing plants with the new computerized equipment his new company would build.

Keeping one eye on his maniac gardener, Seth reached for the phone and hit a button. Morris spoke into his ear.

"Natalie is willing to settle for every other weekend and a month in the summer," his lawyer informed him without preamble.

"That's what she had in the first place and she never took advantage of it." Seth glared at the second blinking light on the phone, then returned to the surreal scene outside his window. His gnome of a gardener was applying a rusted old carpenter's saw to the broad rough trunk of the towering oak.

"She swears that was Darius's fault, that he always scheduled activities when he thought she would bring Chad home. Seems he had an aversion to the kid."

"Yeah, I can imagine he did." Not eager to savor that knowledge, Seth glanced up as his office door bounced open. His mother stood there, impatiently waving a stack of papers containing colored graphs. She'd taken to computers like a duck to water.

Deciding when his brain degenerated to using clichés, he'd better shoot himself, Seth agreed to Natalie's terms, providing she accepted any nurse or tutor he sent with Chad. He had Pippa in mind, but that was foolishness. Pippa would have either turned Natalie into her next best friend or taken Natalie's head off. And Pippa wasn't coming back.

The pain of that acknowledgment hit Seth hard. He'd been fighting it, pretending all was well for hours now. But all wasn't well. Pippa had been gone for half a day, and already the place was falling down around his head. And he couldn't deal with it. Wouldn't deal with it. He damned well wanted her back here, where she belonged.

Which was the stupidest thought he'd had in a long time. Employees came and went. They didn't belong here for long.

Pippa did.

Agony that had nothing to do with his bruised ribs ground through him.

He could do this. He'd suffered worse. All he had to do was remember the screaming fights of his parents, their careless disregard of his existence, the beatings he'd taken at the hands of the town bullies, the appalling pain of Natalie's hatred and Chad's injuries, and he would wipe out any piffling wound Pippa might inflict. Time would heal all wounds. He'd had other women before. They all went away eventually. He'd lived.

Pippa hadn't been just sex. The sex was great, better than anything he'd ever known or could hope to know again. But it wasn't the sex.

Groaning, Seth slammed down the phone, pushed past Doug and his mother, and headed for the front lawn and his demented gardener.

Pippa was the welcoming smile he'd never known, the laughter he'd never shared, the window on the world he'd never experienced. Damn her, she was the fountain of his imagination. Images and ideas crowded his brain, demanding attention, screaming for release, and he couldn't focus on any of them without her.

Crossing the lawn in a few strides, Seth grabbed Durwood's collar, jerked him back from the tree, and tore the saw from his hand. With one swift knee jerk, he broke the metal blade in two.

He would have to get Pippa back.

THIRTY-SEVEN

"I miss Pippa," Chad grumbled as Seth pushed him through the new automatic door of the gym.

"We all do. She'll be back to visit soon," Seth replied absently, avoiding the stab of pain brought on by the sound of Pippa's name.

"I just talked to her last night," Meg said brightly. "She has a lovely apartment in L.A., and she visits the children in the hospital every evening after work. She says to tell you hi, and she'll see you as soon as she finds a car and gets some time off work."

Seth ignored Meg's curious look. He checked the construction under way, frowned at a gaping hole in the floor, and wandered off to investigate the locker room. It looked to him as if the doorway needed widening to allow for larger wheelchairs.

He tried to ignore the contractor idling in his direction, but Pippa had taught Seth to see far more than he wanted to see. He'd almost learned to accept Meg's mixed looks of adulation and disparagement. Somehow, Meg had become an extension of Pippa, and he could deal with her. But he wasn't accustomed to dealing with anyone else yet. He still didn't like coming to town. But if he would ever have any chance of getting Pippa back here where she belonged, he'd have to learn to handle things like the gym, at least.

"Mr. Wyatt." The contractor tugged on his billed cap respectfully.

"Oscar Hamble, right?" Seth remembered the scrawny kid who used to play on the same team with him. He'd once envied Oscar because Oscar's father came to every game.

The contractor grinned. "Didn't think you'd remember."

Seth grunted. "I remember every damned last one of you."

That had the guy trembling again. Oscar, like all his teammates, had turned his back on Seth once they'd learned his identity. He'd thought Oscar a friend until then. He hadn't bothered with friends after that.

The contractor straightened his shoulders and glared back at him. "Maybe you don't remember everything so good, then. Maybe you don't remember my daddy used to work for yours. He told me he'd lose his job if your old man ever found out we'd encouraged you to play with us. We didn't have a whole lot, but my dad put food on the table. We wouldn't have had nothing without that job."

Seth twitched his shoulders to ease the tension. He didn't want to hear this. He didn't want to be reminded of any of it. That was half the reason for avoiding the damned town in the first place. He saw no point in reopening old wounds. He'd moved on with his life. Why hadn't they?

Or maybe he hadn't moved on. He could almost hear Pippa taunting him. Maybe he'd harbored that wound so long it had festered. Damn, but he ought to write a book.

Sighing, Seth held his hand out. "How've you been, Oscar?"

Oscar slapped his palm across Seth's and grinned. "Much better now that I've got that contract for building your new plant."

Oh, hell, now he was in for it. He didn't know the contract he'd signed belonged to a local firm. They would probably delay the project until it ran into millions of dollars of overruns, just to get their revenge on him. He really was losing it.

Oscar slapped him on the back. "After we got that contract, I talked my men into donating their time for the gym. Seems like if you can give up the money for these kids, we can't do less. Come over here; I want to show you what Jimmy dreamed up. He's got a kid with a bum leg. . . ."

In utter astonishment, Seth tagged after the contractor. Oscar hadn't grown more than a few inches since those long-ago days. The towering first baseman he'd once thought him now rolled along like a drunken sailor on short legs. He couldn't believe the man had dismissed all the years between now and then and slipped right back into his old commanding ways. He'd forgotten how Oscar used to boss him around because he was a year older and a foot taller. He hadn't changed—an inch, Seth thought with a furtive grin and racked up another one for Pippa.

He wanted to share the joke with Pippa. He wanted to tell her about meeting Oscar. She'd love hearing that the men were donating their labors. She'd laugh and say she'd told him so. He wanted to show her the plans for the new company, the one that would hire half the people in this town once it opened. She'd probably hug his neck, which could lead to all sorts of interesting activities.

Somehow, he had to get Pippa back.

Pippa glanced up in surprise at the knock on her apartment door. It was a very modest apartment. The whole place would fit into one room of the suite Seth had assigned her. But it was hers, she thought defiantly, and she wasn't expecting anyone. She didn't have to answer the door if she didn't want.

Just the freedom of having her own place and doing as she pleased with it gave her the ease to answer her own door. She'd called an auction company back home and told them to sell the house and contents. She didn't have to live with her mother's choice of furniture. She could afford her own. Sort of. Glancing around at the sparse contents of her small room before she opened the door, she straightened her shoulders and stuck her chin out. The apartment and its contents were hers and she was proud of them.

Her haughty chin dropped the instant she threw open the door.

"May I come in?" Seth asked.

He looked wonderful, as if he belonged on a movie screen. He'd had his hair cut and styled. He actually wore shaving lotion—some sexy, outdoorsy scent that crept seductively around her as they stood practically toe-to-toe. His open-collared silk shirt was dark brown instead of black, but even that was a step in the right direction. She'd be drooling in half a minute.

Pippa stepped aside. "Come in. How's Chad?"

Nervously, she showed him to a papa-san chair she'd bought for a song at Goodwill. She'd always loved the womb-shaped chairs, but there had never been room for one in her mother's house. She'd bought a bright white cushion for it, which had cost more than the chair, but it brightened the whole room. She wanted a white rug next.

Seth regarded the round seat dubiously, but lowered himself into it with all the athletic grace Pippa knew he possessed. She didn't know why he was here. He would have called if anything was wrong with Chad.

"Chad's healthy, but he keeps asking after you."

Pippa held her tongue and didn't comment. She wouldn't let him use Chad as a weapon against her. "Would you like something to drink?"

He debated that as if it were the question of the century, then finally shook his head. "I'd better not. I want a clear head for this."

Uh-oh. Pippa curled up on the canvas sling-back chair that was the room's only other seating. She eyed Seth's closed expression warily. He hadn't tracked her down in the depths of L.A.'s suburbs without a fully orchestrated plan of attack. He hadn't touched her or kissed her and he wouldn't accept a drink that might lead to those temptations. Pippa had his number before he even opened his mouth.

"All right, I'll bite. Why do you need a clear head?"

Seth took a deep breath and looked her directly in the eye. "I want you to marry me. It's the best thing for both of us. Chad is crazy about you. You even get along with my mother. Durwood is chopping down trees without you to steer him. You know the sex between us is terrific. You can help me in dealing with the town. I'm building their damned plant, and already they're arguing with how I want to do it."

Pippa fought the irrepressible urge to giggle. She would be rolling on the floor with laughter if she allowed herself a single cheep. Seth Wyatt, her six-foot tower of strength, sat there with his very best glower, demanding that she marry him because it was best for the town. He'd threaten her with something dire in another minute. Intimidation was a method of dealing with people that appealed to him. She wanted to shout with laughter and drag him into it, make the silly fool see what he was doing, but she feared she would hurt him if she tried. Seth didn't take rejection well. He'd probably not like laughter much better. Oh, lord, how she loved this impossible man.

"I'll talk to Meg." Pippa couldn't bite back the smile. She really couldn't. He looked so damned uncomfortable. Maybe she should lean over and pat his hand.

Seth scowled. "What does Meg have to do with anything? You can talk to her all you like when you come home with me. We can get a marriage license here or go over to Vegas and get it done immediately, if that's what you want."

Gently, Pippa shook her head. "No, Seth, I won't marry you so you can have a live-in assistant. Tell Chad I've got a car now, and I'll come out to see him when I get off work Sunday. Now, would you like that drink?"

He looked stunned. He stared at her as if he couldn't comprehend what she'd just said. Pippa almost felt sorry for him, but she felt sorrier for herself. She wanted more than anything to say yes—yes, she'd marry him regardless of how he proposed—but she couldn't. For both their sakes, she couldn't. A woman with a backbone wouldn't accept a business proposal like that. And she was a woman with a backbone these days. Sort of. Kind of. It was a limp thing right now as she watched despair etch Seth's eyes.

"Pippa, I just asked you to *marry* me," he protested. "Isn't that what all women want?"

The urge to giggle returned. This time, she did lean over and pat his hand. "You just *ordered* me to marry you, and no, that isn't what all women want. I may love you, but I can survive without you. Unlike women of your mother's generation, women today can live without men. Calamity, isn't it?"

He looked stunned, bewildered, and just a tiny bit hopeful. "I thought women married the men they loved."

She really shouldn't have said that, but she couldn't hold it back. He'd needed some reassurance, and she'd handed him what he needed. She would probably never overcome that weakness. But she would damned well learn to develop a spine. "Nope," she responded cheerfully. "Love and marriage are a very nice combination when both parties are in agreement, but we're oceans apart, and you know it. Maybe your mother or Miss MacGregor can learn to deal with the town for you."

Seriously disgruntled, Seth wrestled himself out of the pillowed chair. "I'm offering you a fortune, freedom to do whatever you want, and you're too shortsighted to see what I'm asking. You can't believe I'll turn into another Billy."

Pippa leapt up after him. "Of course not. Your methods of bullying are much more effective. How's Doug doing? Has he found a girlfriend yet?" Her heart yammered a protest as Seth walked toward the door, but she kept a cheerful face despite her terror that she might never see him again.

"He's helping shuttle some of the kids out to the pool a few days a week. I can't swim in my own damned backyard half the time." Seth curled his fist around the doorknob and watched her through shuttered eyes.

"You didn't swim in it anyway," Pippa answered carelessly.

"Maybe I should take that drink you offered." He waited, stiff and unbending, his face a mask of indifference.

Caving only slightly, Pippa leaned over and kissed his cheek. "I'm rescinding the offer. If I'm not marrying you, I'm not falling into bed with you either. We're entirely too careless when we get together."

A reluctant smile tugged at his lips. "Yeah, we are that. I don't suppose I can hope you're pregnant?"

She shook her head. "You won't win that easily. Go home, Seth. Hug Chad for me. And maybe try hugging your mother."

Laughter fled, and she fought tears as Seth scowled at her, hesitated, then stalked out without kissing her good-bye. She'd done it now. She'd developed a backbone and lost the only man she would ever love.

Morosely, Seth sat beside the open door to his balcony and reflected on how Pippa had literally and figuratively opened all the doors and windows around here. She'd battered down all their old habits, forcing them to look at themselves from different perspectives, and nothing would ever be the same again. Even his mother was a new woman, taking charge of the office and the construction of the new plant. She had Mac snapping to her orders.

"I traced the toffees to a storefront candy shop in Burbank."

Dirk's voice intruded upon his reverie, and Seth reluctantly turned back to the subject at hand. He hadn't wanted anyone to hear if Natalie was involved in her husband's villainy. She was still Chad's mother. Seth waited for his hired detective to continue.

Dirk sipped from the beer Doug had handed him. Doug didn't drink the stuff anymore.

"One of Golding's former students makes candy and sells it for a living. He's been boffing her off and on for several years. She didn't think anything of it when he asked how toffees are made. Darius isn't talking, but I figure he slipped the poison into the final coating. The girlfriend says he knocked the pot over and spilled it when they had a box done."

"Pin the mail bomb on him, too, and I guess I can assume he's the only murderer around," Seth replied lethargically. He'd like to see Darius fry because of Chad, but his mind had left the past and moved on to contemplate his increasingly bleak future.

"Done that. Tied it to the thugs who tried to beat you up at the bar. Apparently Darius has still another vice—drugs. When the money started running out, he had to deal to cover his debt. We tracked his supplier to the bar. The supplier has some pretty tough connections. He recognized you the night you were there and figured he'd be a wealthy man if he knocked you off for Golding. When that didn't work, he suggested the mail bomb."

Seth raised his eyebrows and silently waited for Dirk to continue. Drugs. Natalie should have known, but she was too self-absorbed to pay attention.

Dirk gave him a cautious look but continued. "Apparently your mother isn't too circumspect about your security precautions. She complained about them to Natalie, who probably told Darius. Natalie admits she has some old boxes of your books in the house with your publisher's labels on them. It wouldn't take much to use a computer to duplicate them. I don't think she's involved any more than that, if that's any help."

Seth grimaced and took a deep sip of his iced tea. Maybe he ought to help himself to one of Doug's beers. "So much for security. I suppose now I'll have to hire you to plug all the holes around here."

Dirk shrugged and took a long haul on his bottle before replying. "The bastard got around my men in the hospital with that stolen ID and doctor getup. No one can guarantee perfect security. You'd do better to cut down on your list of enemies."

Right. He'd wave his magic wand and turn a whole community into happy little elves. That was the kind of thing Pippa did.

Pippa.

The agony where his heart should be had nothing to do with his damaged rib.

Seth stood in front of the open windows in his room where he and Pippa had stood that evening so many weeks ago, the evening that had shattered so many of his self-delusions. He'd thought himself a controlled and unemotional man like his father. Pippa had caused him to lose all control and revel in the passion of the moment. He'd thought happiness some ephemeral quality that people merely talked about. Pippa had taught him to laugh at the smallest things. He'd quit allowing people into his life because they brought only pain. Pippa had brought joy.

How could he go on knowing all those things were out there—joy and happiness and passion—and never know them again? He needed Pippa to open his eyes and keep them open, or he would gradually slink back into the former shell of himself. But she'd refused him.

His old cynical self would say that she'd never really cared, that she'd merely used him as a safety net while her old boyfriend roamed the streets, but the self Pippa had unearthed knew better. Unfortunately, Pippa hadn't uncovered enough of it. He couldn't figure out what he'd done wrong, what he needed to do next. He hadn't learned his lessons well enough.

Pippa cared. Pippa had said she loved him. But she wouldn't marry him. Why?

The quiet sound of rubber wheels rolling across the carpet interrupted Seth's reverie. He'd had all the thick rugs and padding ripped off the floors up here so Chad would have easier going for his chair.

Seth turned and attempted a smile for his son's worried gaze. "Come to get trounced at checkers?"

Chad didn't smile back. "Pippa isn't coming back, is she?"

So, the boy had put two and two together, probably with Nana's help. He ought to retire the old woman. She was a pestilent nuisance. But an efficient one.

"She was here last Sunday, wasn't she?" Seth replied evasively.

"I mean *really* coming back."

From beneath a tumble of black curls, Chad shot him an impatient look that Seth figured mirrored one of his own. The boy was too damned much like him. He needed a softening influence Natalie couldn't supply.

Sighing and running his hand through his hair, Seth settled into a chair beside the fireplace. There was no point in lying to the boy. Chad was too smart to accept lies.

"I asked her to marry me, and she said no. I don't know what else to do. It's me she's mad at, not you," he hastened to add at Chad's crestfallen expression.

Chad wrinkled up his brow in childish thought. "Maybe if you gave her something she really wanted? Kinda like letting me go to school with Mikey, but something Pippa wants?"

Seth bit back a sad smile. "We'll talk about school later, after we see how the gym works out."

Chad clenched his chair arms in frustration. "I don't *care* about the school. That was just an *example*." He threw out the word as if it were one all six-year-olds used. "Couldn't we give Pippa something she really wants so she'll come back and live with us?"

"I don't think money will buy Pippa," Seth said gently. "If the gym and the new company won't do it, nothing will."

With the energy of youth, Chad refused to give up. "She likes blue clouds and circuses and clowns and Ferris wheels," he insisted. "She told me so."

"Blue clouds?" The other suggestions spun wheels in Seth's head, but he asked the obvious in distraction.

"Blue clouds, like after thunderstorms. She says they have them in Kentucky. The sky lights up all blue and pink and yellow, better than a rainbow. She says it's God's promise of a better day. I'd like to see them someday," he added wistfully.

"Well, I'm not certain I can arrange blue clouds," Seth answered haltingly, his mind racing over new scenarios. "But maybe we can arrange clowns and Ferris wheels. Do you think that might help?"

Chad sat up and grinned. "Yeah, that should do it. Pippa loves circuses. She'll love us if we can give her one."

Out of the mouths of children.

She'll love us if we can give her one. Pippa already loved them. Seth believed that with whatever confidence he still retained. Pippa wasn't a Tracey, throwing herself into his arms for what he could offer. Pippa had come into his arms and given herself because she loved him. Love. Foolish word, one he didn't know much about. But Seth wagered Pippa knew a lot about it. And craved it as much as he craved her.

He would have to give Pippa what she wanted. A circus brimming with clowns and Ferris wheels was a cinch compared to what Pippa really wanted. Even blue clouds might be easier.

THIRTY-EIGHT

Sitting curled in her papa-san chair, tears streaming down her cheeks, Pippa stroked the loose pages of the manuscript Lillian had sent her. She couldn't believe Seth had written such a touching story. Not Seth, the inhuman monster.

But the vulnerable Seth, the wary, unprotected creature hiding behind the hard shell of the monster, that Seth could have written this story.

She was amazed at how he'd transformed an entire book with a few simple changes. He'd cracked open the carapace, exposed the tender insides of his protagonists, and let them emerge as whole new creatures. Utterly amazing. The man had talent. Amazing talent.

Of all kinds. Sinking deeper into the cushion, Pippa contemplated that sorry thought. His talent for lovemaking would bar her from ever enjoying another man. She'd thought him incapable of loving. But he wasn't. The book proved that. He simply wasn't capable of expressing love. No one had ever taught him how.

And she'd blown it, utterly. Blown the chance to teach him how to express love. Blown the chance to know his lovemaking every night. Blown the right to tease him and watch him grin every day.

The manuscript had arrived with a note from Lillian. Pippa suspected Seth's mother of matchmaking again. Well, this time she'd hit the right chords. It had just happened too late.

The phone rang and Pippa pried herself out of the chair to answer it. It rang far too seldom for her tastes. L.A. was a huge town, full of people with other lives and interests beyond hers. Maybe she'd been too hasty in selling the house in Kentucky. At least there, people knew her and she had friends. She didn't know how she'd make friends in the immensity of the city.

"Pippa!" Chad's excited voice in the receiver had her smiling. "We're gonna have a carnival! It's Dad's birthday, and the carnival is coming here!"

Pippa's brow furrowed in disbelief, but she didn't let Chad hear her doubt. "That's marvelous, Chad. Are you and Mikey going?"

"Yeah, and Dad and grandmother. And Doug said he'd take Mrs. Deal. She's Holly's mother."

Pippa hadn't the vaguest idea who Holly or her mother were, but she was happy Doug had a friend at last. "That should make a wonderful birthday party," she agreed enthusiastically. "Is it there in Garden Grove?"

"Yeah! That's the best part. Everybody can go. Will you come, Pippa? Please, please, will you come? It's a party. Everybody has to come."

She suspected the fine hand of Seth or Lillian behind this plea, but she was feeling too lost and unhappy not to accept the Wyatt family conniving this time. She wanted to go to a carnival, to see the Ferris wheel, play silly games, and hear the merry-go-round. All right, so she wanted to see Seth again, too. But she wouldn't make any more of it than that.

At least, she'd try not to. She had to remember the emotional vacuum Seth lived in. She'd seen no evidence of the walls crumbling. She didn't think she had. Her irrepressible optimism had fooled her often enough.

"Tell me when and where," she agreed. Chad's delighted reply assured her she was doing the right thing, whatever the consequence.

The rainbow-colored lights of the Ferris wheel illuminated the darkening clouds on the horizon. It seemed only fitting that a rare California summer thunderstorm should form on Seth's birthday. Pippa glanced worriedly at the billowing black clouds, then proceeded to ignore them in favor of the festive flags flying at the entrance to the field Seth owned—the one next to the foundation of the new plant.

She could see people roaming the construction site as freely as they did the fair, pointing out new features, following a map of the blueprints. What genius had persuaded Seth to introduce his new company to its neighbors in such a manner?

Whoever it was, she gave them a mental pat on the back as she climbed out of her little Mazda with her arms full. Maybe she should leave the package behind until she found some help.

But she was in too much of a hurry to see Chad. And Seth. Okay, so she wanted to see Seth. So, shoot her.

A cheerful calliope greeted all arrivals as Pippa hurried across the grassy parking lot, carrying her surprise. She saw no ticket booths. Of course, if this was a party, they wouldn't charge admission for the night. She'd never heard of anyone hiring an entire carnival for a party, but Seth was capable of it. She wondered who he'd invited.

The entire town, she decided a minute later as she waved at Meg-and-family and noticed other familiar faces in the crowd. She didn't hurry to Meg's side as she once might have done. She wanted to find Seth first.

She could scarcely miss him. Hands full of multicolored helium balloons, Seth loped toward her. The tight brackets around his mouth and the nervous desperation in his eyes faded as he approached her. Her heart twisted at the sudden flash of white teeth and the warm smolder of gray eyes. She hadn't known how much she missed him until even her bones ached at the sight of him.

He stopped shy of hugging her, and Pippa gulped a little. She felt like a sixth grader with her first boyfriend. Tentatively, she handed him the immense, gaily wrapped package in her arms. "This isn't really from me, but from a bunch of people."

The tension in his stiff posture eased further, and he grinned like a little boy. "A birthday present? May I open it now?"

He acted as if no one had ever given him a present before. Amused, Pippa nodded. "That's what presents are for."

He handed her the bouquet of balloons so he could tear into the wrappings. She'd had a packager find a box that would contain her gift, and Seth had to tear through that, too, before he could find the contents. Nearly four feet high, and slender, the box made an awkward container. Seth had to set it on the ground to rip off the top.

As he caught a glimpse of the contents, he threw Pippa an uncertain look. Then apparently deciding it was a joke, he grinned again and ripped the thin box down the sides. A cheap, plastic, nearly four-foot statue of a baseball player emerged.

By this time, Chad had wheeled up and a small crowd had gathered. A short man wearing a baseball cap in the back of the crowd shouted, "We kinda forgot to give it to you before!"

Seth glanced around, found Oscar, and scowled slightly, but he lifted the statue to read the inscription. " 'Most Valuable Player'? "

Someone else yelled, "The team lost the final game without you. There wasn't much argument over who deserved the trophy."

"Most valuable player," Seth murmured again in amazement. A slow grin gradually worked its way across his face. He looked up and winked happily at Pippa. "Well, it looks like I've finally got something to sit on that mantel in my room. Thank you all. I don't have to make a speech, do I?"

"You can thank Pippa for reminding them they owed it to you," Meg pointed out.

Pippa started to protest, but Seth engulfed her in a hug, then, picking up his trophy and cradling it in one arm while holding her shoulders with the other, he addressed the crowd. "Maybe the new plant can start a softball league. But I want first base."

The crowd cheered and jeered, a few men approached to slap him on the back, others merely waved and wandered off on their own pursuits, tugged by wives and children. Seth's arm tightened around Pippa's shoulders as Meg planted a kiss on his cheek, stole balloons from Pippa, handed them to Chad and her kids, then herded them all off in the direction of the ice-cream stand.

Wonder still hovered around the edges of Seth's expression as he accepted greetings from a few more of the crowd, but Pippa could tell from the pressure of his arm that he was nervous as hell. He didn't know how to accept accolades of any sort, not even in jest. Bravely, he smiled and shook hands. When one teenager hesitantly mentioned that she adored his books, Pippa thought Seth would literally crumble.

She looked at him questioningly. He nodded stiffly at the girl, and as she wandered off, he shrugged for Pippa's benefit.

"Chad got a little excited when he saw one of my books at Meg's house. Meg may have kept quiet, but unfortunately, there were a number of other people in the room at the time." He shifted his shoulders uncomfortably and stared over the heads of the happy crowd swirling around him.

If she hadn't introduced Chad and Mikey, no one would ever have known his identity, and now the whole town knew Tarant Mott and Seth Wyatt were one and the same. His privacy was lost, and it was all her fault.

Horrified at the realization, she bit her lip and struggled for an appropriate reply. "I'm sorry. They all know who you are now." Stupid statement. Her brains had gone begging.

Seth smiled. "Yeah. I'm getting the impression that's why

they're all here tonight. It's okay if I'm eccentric now. I'm a writer. They aren't afraid of writers."

Pippa knew she should be more serious about the situation, but his reply conjured interesting images, and she bit back a giggle. "So much for the Big Bad Wolf image. Writers are harmless. Everyone knows that."

He growled and bared his teeth at her, and her heart soared. He wasn't furious with her. He almost seemed playful. Hope reeled out the strings of her heart. She tied a balloon to his statue's neck.

Thunder rumbled overhead.

"I don't suppose you've got a big top with lightning rods anywhere around here?" she suggested, glancing at the roiling clouds.

"Where else would we put the clowns?" Catching Pippa's elbow, Seth dragged her down the main sawdust path laid through the field.

He gathered corn dogs and cotton candy and towering soft drinks as he passed the stands, until their hands and arms overflowed. They had to find Chad and tie balloons to his and Mikey's chairs, then lay the trophy across Chad's lap so they could nibble their way through the feast. Pounding his chair in excitement like any normal six-year-old, Chad scarcely noticed their presence. Beneath the protection of the canvas, clowns rolled out on unicycles and miniature fire trucks and every conceivable kind of vehicle until the children screamed with laughter.

Thunder clapped and rain poured outside the tent, but the brilliant lights inside focused all attention on the show. The kids in wheelchairs had front-row seats. The rest of the bleachers filled with an audience escaping the rain. Seth dragged Pippa onto a bleacher behind the chairs, then ignored her after the show started. Pippa smiled and hugged his arm as she watched his intent gaze absorb all the absurd activity in the ring. He'd really never seen clowns. Amazing.

She wondered if the next book would include a clown killer, or more likely, a clown hero.

By the time the show ended, the rain had stopped and they'd consumed enough junk food to make them sick for a week. Chad looked a little green around the gills, but he glared challengingly at his father as they edged toward the entrance. "I want to ride the roller coaster."

"You'll make yourself sick. Try the merry-go-round first." Still holding Pippa protectively with one arm, Seth guided his son's path through the crowd with equal care.

"Merry-go-rounds are for kids," Chad scoffed.

"You're a kid." Seth swatted his son's shoulder affectionately.

Pippa watched this byplay with amazement. Not too many months ago, Chad would have been screaming and turning blue with rage and Seth would have been panicking and caving in to whatever he wanted. The argument now threatened to be no more than a typical childhood struggle.

"I want to ride the unicorn," Chad threatened.

Pippa threw Seth a nervous glance. She wasn't entirely certain Chad had the physical capabilities of sitting on one of those up-and-down horses. Seth didn't appear concerned.

"You'll ride whatever is available. I'm not chasing anyone off the unicorn just for you." Free of the crowded tent at last, they pushed with the rest of the throng onto the midway.

"*Then* I'll ride the roller coaster," Chad announced with satisfaction.

Amused, Pippa pinched his skinny arm until Chad looked up at her, almost hopefully. "Brat," she whispered.

"Am not." He puffed up belligerently, fighting a smile.

"Am too." Pippa tousled his hair until he dodged.

Before they could repeat the refrain of the old argument, Seth's reverent exclamation intruded. "My God, will you look at that?"

They both glanced up where he was pointing.

The setting sun had broken free of the lingering clouds,

casting buttery light across the horizon, illuminating billowing black with tints of indigo, and casting rosy hues over the lower stratus until one whole side of the sky looked as if a mad oil painter had cleaned his brushes across it.

"Blue clouds," Chad whispered in awe.

"Yeah. Maybe God's watching over us after all." Seth kneaded his son's shoulder with affection and assurance. "Wish me luck, kid, and go find Mikey."

Pippa didn't even ask what he was doing as Seth motioned George over to take charge, then led her away. Her heart pounded in her ears now. Awe couldn't describe the emotion swamping her as she glanced up at the magnificent clouds, then back to the determined man dragging her down the midway. Seth's curls tumbled in dark disarray across his forehead, and she had the insensible urge to reach out and brush them from his eyes. One look from those eyes warned her she'd better tread carefully. She wasn't a wimp, she told herself. She had a backbone now. She'd never been afraid of Seth. Just sometimes, it was better to let him have his way.

He pulled her to the front of the line at the Ferris wheel. Pippa had already noticed that even the ride booths were shuttered closed. The rides were free to one and all. Since Seth was paying for it all, she supposed he had the right to bully his way to the front. But when he gestured at the operator and the wheel immediately started unloading its human cargo, she threw Seth a questioning look.

He ignored her.

Completely devoid of all passengers, the wheel halted, and the operator gestured for them to come forward. Walking rapidly, Seth tugged Pippa toward the waiting seat. If she had had any presence of mind at all, she would have dragged her feet and screamed at the top of her lungs. But she didn't. Couldn't. The whole scene—the carnival, the clowns, the crowds, the clouds—all created a little glass ball of a world that

Seth alone controlled. Sort of. Just enough to make her feel helpless and light-headed and outside herself.

The attendant lowered the bar, pulled back the lever, and whirled the wheel into the evening sky.

It didn't stop for more passengers. They soared around once, fast enough for the breeze to sweep through their hair, color their cheeks, and bring them closer together for warmth. All Pippa's senses screamed into alert as Seth circled her shoulders and smiled down at her.

They reached the pinnacle of the arc and halted.

The panorama of the carnival spread out before them. Beneath the early dark of the clouds, colored lights glittered and blinked in garish Christmas displays. The calliope music lilted hauntingly on the wind. Merely cheerful colors from this distance, the crowd milled far below, going about their happy business, while she and Seth swung at the top of the world.

Pippa took a deep breath and finally dared a glance up at Seth.

He stroked her cheek lightly with one finger. "I wanted to give you something in return for everything you've given me."

Those weren't exactly the words she wanted to hear, but right now, right at this wonderful, marvelous moment, she would accept anything he offered. Anything. She couldn't bear another minute away from his presence. She didn't know how she'd thought she could.

"Whatever I gave you must have been pretty spectacular to deserve all this," she answered lightly, not daring to hope for more than a joke at her expense. "I never thought plastic trophies had that much value."

"I love you, even if you are an idiot."

Before Pippa could absorb the impact of his words, Seth caught her chin and held her until she was so thoroughly kissed, she wouldn't be able to walk straight if they returned to the ground now. She wrapped her arms around him as she remembered why she'd left. She'd needed to hear the words, needed him to acknowledge what was between them. She'd had to be positive he wanted her for the right reasons, to know she'd broken through that stony wall.

Gazing at him starry-eyed as they held on to each other and gasped for air, Pippa noted his smug look of satisfaction.

"We can do more than kiss if you'll just say yes," Seth stated with some semblance of calm.

Pippa's lips curled at the corners. "Say yes to what? Sky-diving from this seat?"

"You do this to me on purpose, don't you?" Looking a little more ruffled, Seth patted his pockets until he found what he was looking for. Producing a jeweler's box, he snapped it open and took a deep breath. "I'm perfectly capable of taking you out to movies and restaurants and whatever you deem suitable for a dating couple, but I'd really rather you just said yes right now so I don't have to suffer in uncertainty any longer than necessary."

As a proposal, it had to rate right down there with his man-eating gophers, but for Seth, it was a love poem more beautiful than anything Emily Dickinson ever wrote. Pippa scarcely noticed the glittering diamonds on the gold band inside the box. She couldn't tear her gaze away from Seth.

"I love you," she prompted.

Seth grimaced, ran his free hand through windblown curls, then realizing he'd already discovered the right tactic, he pulled her close and kissed her again, brushing her mouth with his and murmuring, "I love you, too."

Pippa giggled and hugged him back.

"I'll make you say it every day," she warned.

"Every night," he compromised. "I've got to get some work done during the day."

"All right, every night. And any time on the weekends."

Seth groaned and pulled her so tightly into his embrace that she could feel his heart beat next to hers. "You'll be the death of me, won't you?"

"Yeah, but we'll die happy."

She wrapped her arms around him and covered his face with kisses as the wheel jerked to a start and the notes of the calliope pounding out "Love Makes the World Go 'Round" soared above the cheers of the crowd waiting below.

For a recluse, Seth had made a spectacular entrance into the human race. And for a man thoroughly steeped in cynicism, he was making a remarkable plunge into the terror of trust that married life required.

Pippa smiled as the last piece of blue cloud dipped into the horizon—a definite promise for better days ahead.

8. Savor sensual desserts to die for!

9. Surrender to everything chocolate—from buttercreams to mints to sumptuous truffles.

10. Indulge in tea for two with exotic teas and trimmings.

11. Make your garden grow with tools, gloves, bulbs, and a gardening book for inspiration.

12. Arouse your taste buds with rich, mellow coffees from around the world—and beautiful mugs to go with them.

*Each basket will have a retail value of approximately $250.00 and will also contain a copy of Patricia Rice's first wonderful contemporary novel, *Garden of Dreams*.

Mail this entry form, to be received by
September 30, 1998, to:
BLUE CLOUDS SWEEPSTAKES
PMI Station, P. O. Box 3581
Southbury, CT 06488-3581

Name______________________________

Address____________________________

City/State/Zip_______________________

Phone (day)_________________________

Phone (night)_______________________

See next page for official rules.

THE BALLANTINE PUBLISHING GROUP
"A DOZEN GOOD REASONS TO TREAT YOURSELF TO *BLUE CLOUDS*" SWEEPSTAKES

OFFICIAL RULES

1. ELIGIBILITY: NO PURCHASE NECESSARY TO ENTER OR CLAIM PRIZE. Open to legal residents of the United States and Canada (excluding Quebec) who are 18 years of age and older. Employees of Random House, Inc., its subsidiaries, affiliates, advertising and promotion agencies, and members of the immediate families and persons living in the same household of such employees are not eligible. Void in Quebec and where prohibited by law. All federal, provincial, state, and local laws and regulations apply.

2. TO ENTER: Complete an official entry form or hand print your name, complete address, daytime and evening telephone numbers, and the words "BLUE CLOUDS" on a postcard. Mail your entry, to be received by September 30, 1998, to: Blue Clouds Sweepstakes, PMI Station, P.O. Box 3581, Southbury, CT 06488-3581. Limit one entry per person. No mechanical reproductions permitted.

3. PRIZES: On or about October 15, 1998, a random drawing will be conducted from among all eligible entries received by Promotion Mechanics, Inc., an independent judging organization, to award (12) prizes of a romantically themed gift basket. Contents of each basket will be different and will be valued at approximately $250. Winners will be notified by mail. 1,500,000 entry forms will be distributed, but odds of winning depend on the number of eligible entries received. Canadian residents, in order to win, must first correctly answer a mathematical skill testing question administered by mail.

4. GENERAL: All taxes on prizes are the sole responsibility of winners. By participating, entrants agree to (a) these rules and decisions of judges that shall be final in all respects and (b) release sponsor from any liability, loss, or damage of any kind resulting from their participation in the sweepstakes or their acceptance or use of a prize. By accepting a prize, winners agree to the use of their name and/or photograph for advertising, publicity, and promotional purposes without compensation (unless prohibited by law). Sponsor is not responsible for late, lost, misdirected, or illegible entries or mail. All entries become the property of sponsor. No prize transfer. No prize substitution except by sponsor due to unavailability. Return of any prize/prize notification as undeliverable will result in disqualification, and an alternate winner will be selected. Limit one prize per household.

5. WINNERS' LIST: For a list of winners, send a self-addressed stamped envelope, to be received by October 15, 1998, to: Blue Clouds Winners, PMI Station, P. O. Box 750, Southbury, CT 06488-0750. List will be available after January 1, 1999.

Sponsor: The Ballantine Publishing Group, 201 East 50th Street, New York, NY 10022.